KADE'S GAINE

KADE'S GAINE

L M LISSETTE

Dreams In Ink

ISBN: 979-8-9904134-0-5

First Printing, 2024

For my readers.
May you find a love that could only be known as perfection.

Contents

Being known as the butcher of the Blood Pack and carrying the title of Enforcer, no one should have the balls to bang on my front door before sunrise. I've been lying in the dark for hours, staring at the ceiling, but that doesn't make me any less annoyed. My pack knows better than to bother me, but whoever's banging on my front door wakes the woman lying with her head on my chest.

Raising my arms, I push against the wooden headboard and stretch my limbs. "It's Monday," I groan.

"What?" Sunday mumbles, sliding her leg over mine.

I push against her forehead until she rolls off me. "It's not your day anymore," I snap. "Get out."

She jumps when the front door slams open. "What's going on?" she whispers, pulling the sheet around herself.

"I suspect we're about to find out," I say, yawning. A pair of boots clunk heavily across my kitchen floor. "Hm. Sounds like Tynan."

Sunday springs from the bed and frantically runs around my room, pulling clothes from the mirror and bed posts. "Why didn't you tell me Alpha was coming here?" she hisses, pulling her blonde hair into a ponytail before jumping into her shorts.

I slide my hand under my pillow until I reach my blade's handle. "How would I know what his insane ass is doing?" I ask, crossing my ankles. I chuckle as she throws my jeans toward me. "The door's unlocked," I offer, nodding toward my French doors. "See you next week, Sunday."

With a huff, she wrestles a shirt over her head and snatches her boots from the chair. "I have a name," the woman snaps.

Sighing, I run my eyes over her body. Despite her scowl and the deep scar on her left cheek, Sunday is beautiful. Some other man would probably be excited to wake up next to her. I took her in after Tynan cut her. He won't mess with her now, but I'm bored. Soon, she'll be fair game, and he'll set his sights on her again.

"I don't care," I grumble, dismissing her.

I bet Sunday would love to keep going, but the boots begin stomping down the hallway. She darts toward the double doors and pushes one open. I turn away from her as she glances back at me. They all do that, hoping I'll change my mind.

"Kade!" the psychopath himself yells from my hallway.

"What do you want, Tynan?" I snap, closing my eyes.

The unmistakable sound of my bedroom door being kicked in causes my hands to ball into fists.

"Cover that shit up," Tynan barks.

Slipping my free hand behind my head, I look at the intruder and roll my eyes. Tynan is short with a pinched face. I'm pretty sure his hair is naturally black like mine, but it's always greasy. He cuts it to match my length. I shaved my head a few years ago just to prove a point to one of my weekdays. She laughed when I showed her the idiot had copied me.

"You're in my house," I state. "In my bedroom... uninvited." I watch his eyes trail over my body. "Jealous?"

Tynan lifts his upper lip in a sneer. "Get dressed," he snaps. "The kid negotiated a deal with the Lunar Pack. I need you to take care of something for me."

I roll my eyes and scowl. "I told you I was done with that kid," I grumble. "That was **our** deal. I bring you the kid, and you never ask me for help with him again."

"No," Tynan scoffs. "Our deal was that I wouldn't ask for anything regarding him if you burned his house." He grabs my jeans from the edge of the bed and throws them at me, making me shield my face. "He won't be there, which is why I need you to supervise the clean-up of the mess he made."

"That's not what I remember," I say, rolling out of bed. My blue blade catches Tynan's eyes as I flip it in my hand to lie along my forearm. I slowly approach him, watching his eyes flick toward the door he'd kicked open. "I suggest you rethink our terms and make this the last time you mention that kid."

Tynan steps toward the door. "Fine," the tiny Alpha barks. "The team is ready. I need you to watch over them." He catches the handle and tries to pull the door closed between us. "And then you're done."

My foot stops the door from closing. "You won't like the consequences if you forget," I sneer in his face. I lift my arm to his throat, pressing my blade against his skin.

* * *

After two days in the summer sun, the smell of the bodies in the basin reaches us long before we arrive. Deep shades of red and brown stain everything in the militia's mobile base. Something floral mixes with the metallic stench of human blood in the breeze, but I'm not getting my boots dirty to find out why.

Lying back in the wagon, I close my eyes and listen to Tynan's team whine about having to dig such a large grave. It's clear our crazy Alpha's super soldier, Bastian, was here. No one can leave a path of destruction like that kid. We have yet to find survivors within this large regiment.

Fingers slide over my abs and pull at my waistband. "There's someone watching us," Thursday tells me from beside the wagon.

I snatch her wrist. "It's not your day," I snap, turning to glare at her.

"Fine," she replies, frowning. "What about our audience?"

"Sleep with them. I don't care," I respond. Releasing her wrist, I return to relaxing in the sun. "Just don't be claiming their kid is mine."

She claps her hands loudly. "Kade!" she barks. "We don't leave witnesses."

Taking a deep breath, I stretch my neck. "That's the Lunar Pack, Thursday," I grumble. "They're here to babysit you for me."

"My name is Vera," she scoffs.

Irritated, I jump up and latch onto her throat. "Fine," I growl. "When my calendar tells me the day of the week is 'Vera,' you can come back to my bed." A flash of white disappears behind some foliage just inside the tree line, catching my eye. I push against Thursday's throat to shove her out of my way. "Where did you say our audience was?" I ask.

She turns as I drop my hand from her throat and points to where I'd seen the light. "She was right there," she struggles to whisper. "She was on a horse." Thursday coughs a few times, trying to clear her throat. "That really hurt, Kade."

Grabbing my shirt, I jump off the wagon. "Then stop pissing me off," I say, pointing toward the crew currently dragging bodies to the grave. "Watch them. I'll be right back."

"Kade," she calls after me as I walk toward the trees. "Alpha won't be happy if you leave us here."

I've never seen anything like that light. Thursday said the Lunar Pack's spy was on a horse over here, but she and her horse are gone now. I step into the trees and let my eyes adjust to the darkness.

"I know you're there," I say, hoping to create movement. I stop beside a large tree that will conceal me from the prying eyes of my pack. "I don't recommend hiding from me. I kill things I have to hunt."

Looking down, I scan the ground for hoof prints, but the moss is thick in this area. The crew has started to fire the base, causing smoke to mix with human blood and making it impossible to catch the scent of her horse. The faintest clink of a metal bit sounds from deeper in the woods. Closing my eyes, I smile and lick my lips. *She's smart—just the way I like them.*

I slip my shirt on and fasten some of the buttons as I lean against the tree, focusing on the sound of the horse's bit. She won't be able to stop it from working the metal in its mouth. When I finally hear it again, it's directly in front of me, but further away this time.

"Kade!" Thursday hisses from behind me.

My growl rumbles, giving away my position. "What?" I bark, opening my eyes and scanning the trees for the light.

"One of them survived," she says, stepping around the tree. "He says he's their leader—a General or something."

"Cut it into his forehead when you kill him," I sneer. "It starts with G." I push off the tree and begin walking toward the horse's noise. "Get back to work."

My growl stops as I focus my attention back on the cunning girl who is running away from me. I jog through a clearing and weave around some trees, catching a few horseshoe prints on the softer footing. The horse is skirting the basin about 30 yards inside the woods. I cut in closer to the tree line and continue jogging until I'm sure I'm in front of them.

When I cut back into the deeper area of the woods, I'm far enough away from the slaughter site to detect other scents in the air. The ground here is wetter, and I can't be sure which way she'll go to avoid the swamp. I stop and rest against a tree. As my breathing slows and I take in my surroundings, I pick up the faintest scent of horse accompanied by something sweet.

She's deeper in the woods. I look down at the standing water in the swamp. *Great.* Sighing, I step into the water and feel it seep into my boots. *She better be the most beautiful thing I've ever seen.*

I've had a few close calls with the Lunar wolves but never cared to interact with them. There's enough drama with Tynan as our Alpha. I don't need any more. But this woman is glowing for some reason, and she's already displayed more intelligence than anyone in our pack.

There is no way to move silently through this soupy swamp. The water is dark, and I seem to find every stick buried within its depths. If she didn't know I was tracking her before, she sure as hell knows now. I adjust my course to drop behind her, and as soon as I clear the deeper water, I begin to see horse tracks. The sweet smell is goat's milk soap with strawberries.

I push past my hatred for the sloshy feeling of wet boots and follow the tracks her horse is leaving. A twig snaps ahead, making me look up, and I catch her glowing light for just a moment before it disappears into the trees.

Swinging wide, I jog past her again. The terrain is drier now that we've cleared the swamp. I quickly pick my way around the trees and brush to make it back out in front of her. When I cut in toward the basin, the absence of horse tracks confirms I'm in front of my prey again. I lean against a tree and slow my breathing, listening for the horse's bit or footfalls.

I smile when I hear them approaching.

"Why are you following me?" the woman asks.

I open my eyes and shift my gaze in the voice's direction. I had hoped for beauty, but nothing could've prepared me for this moment. Her dark brown hair gently flows in waves halfway down her back. Her soft skin is flawlessly tanned from long hours in the sun. She angrily glares at me through piercing green eyes.

The only thing that could steal my attention from any part of her body would be her glowing white aura. My heart is pounding with such force that it's clear the coloring matches its pulse. I heard stories about wolves finding their mates, but for the Blood Pack, it's rare.

I push off the tree to step toward her. "You were worth the hunt," I whisper, grinning.

"I asked you a question," the woman growls.

I stop as she turns the horse to face me. "You know why I'm here," I say, keeping my eyes on her. "You're mine. You belong to me."

Laughing, she turns the horse around. "You've been misinformed," she says before urging her horse forward. "You should go back to your pack. You aren't protected out here."

"I don't need protection," I snap, following her. "Get off that horse."

She spins the horse around, nearly knocking me in the face with its head. "This is precisely why I didn't seek you out, Kade," she says, sighing. "There's no place for you in my world."

I've never walked into a situation that I couldn't control. I know how anything will end before it even begins. I could never have planned for this beautiful woman. I didn't know she existed. She glares at me as I slide my hand over the horse's neck and step beside its shoulder.

The saddle she sits on is tanned to a slightly lighter shade than her skin, highlighting her leg's glow. I lick my lips, wanting a taste, but inch my fingers toward her calf instead. Warmth travels over my hand and up my arm when I reach her. I'm sure I hear her gasp at my touch, but I can't focus on anything over my own body's reaction to her. I spread my fingers as they pass her knee and dig them into her thigh.

"I'm of the Lunar Pack, Kade," she whispers forcefully, bending her leg to push the horse away from me. "Darya is my Luna. You are our enemy."

I step back to her side and reach for her skin again. "I promise not to hold that against you," I murmur. "How do you know my name?"

The woman lays her forearms over the saddle horn and looks away from me. "I was curious," she whispers. Her body heats under my hand, and her skin reacts with raised bumps, but she refuses to look at me. "For someone so beautiful, you have an ugly heart."

I slip my fingers along her arm to her hand and linger at her pinky. Sighing, I drop my hand when she doesn't acknowledge me. "I have a job," I tell her. "I'm good at it." I slide under the horse's neck to stand within her view. "Isn't your pack all about acceptance?"

She raises her eyebrow. "You kill people," she says. "That's your talent?"

I wince. "We all have skeletons," I respond, stepping closer. "When do I get to see yours?"

She quietly laughs, collecting her reins into one hand. Her free hand reaches down for my cheek. The silky feel of her fingers along my jaw causes my eyes to roll closed. "My world is bright and filled with love and support," she whispers, making me want to feel her breath on my skin. "Something you know nothing about in your dark pit," she growls, pushing my face away. "So, go back to the hell that allows you to thrive. You could never fit into my world."

To hell with this. She's already decided I'm a monster. I lunge at her waist and pull her off the horse as it spooks. "No one speaks to me like that," I snarl into her ear, holding her against me. Now that she's off the horse, her strawberry soap is overwhelming. I open my mouth to exhale as I slide my lower lip over her temple. "What is your name?" I whisper.

She digs her nails into my chest, starting my growl before

ducking and spinning away from my grip. "It doesn't matter," she tells me, backing away. "You'll never have a reason to use it."

"Then give me a reason," I plead, unsure where this need comes from. I advance on the gorgeous woman, taking longer strides than her backward steps. "Why should my life be any different? I'm respected and feared. They leave me alone, and I do whatever I want, whenever I want. Even that half-whit Alpha is scared of me. What makes being good and golden so much better?"

I smile when her back lands against a tree, stopping her retreat. Slowly taking the last three steps, I press my body against her. Our skin connecting creates a magical celebration within my nerves. I slip my fingers through her hair and tug gently at the tips. The beautiful woman remains still as I explore my boundaries but shies away from me when I brush the pack marking that winds down her right arm.

"I'm not asking you to change," she says barely above a whisper, her breath tickling my jaw. "There is no place for you in my life. You can't scrub hard enough to remove the stains on your soul."

"Then I will help you cross into my darkness," I whisper as air rushes from my lungs. Her body's heat seeps through our clothes, and I watch a bead of sweat roll slowly down her temple. My chest swells painfully, pulling enough air to clear my thoughts. "I want you."

I would have already had her a few times if she were any other wolf. The string of broken hearts I've left behind could wrap around the world several times. None of them meant anything to me. They all loved me but left my bed for the last time when I got bored.

"Kade," she snarls as I tuck into her neck, hoping for a taste. "I don't want you."

Sighing, I close my eyes. My lips rest against her skin. I love the meat of a mountain lion but have never craved it in the way I need to put this woman in my mouth. I wouldn't be satisfied with one taste. If I slide my tongue over her skin, I won't be able to stop until I've had my fill. Something about her makes me want to lose control.

I grit my teeth as I lift away from her neck. "I don't think that's how this works," I say, rubbing my cheek over her hair. It's soft and silky. I watch it shine when it drops from my beard scruff. "You're my mate." I slip my hands up her arms and pull away to cup her cheeks. She parts her lips when I lick mine, making my eyes lock on them as my next target.

Something presses against my thigh and slices through my jeans. "I said I don't want you," she whispers forcefully, her growl rumbling to life. Blood slowly trickles down my leg as she stares into my eyes. "Now, back up."

Groaning, I back away to see my stunning prey had stolen the blade I keep on my lower back. She gasps when she sees that she's cut me, clearly not expecting the blade to be that sharp. "It's alright," I say softly, taking another step back and holding my hand out for the knife. "It'll heal."

She lifts the blade to point it at my chest. "I think I should keep this," she says, winking.

I scoff and snatch her wrist, twisting the handle out of her hand. "I don't think so," I say, shaking my head. I flip the blade around and wipe my blood off on my jeans before sliding it back into its sheath. "Wouldn't want you to hurt yourself."

"I didn't mean to cut you," she quietly admits, looking me over. "How did you get that blade so sharp?"

I loosen my belt and push my jeans down to inspect the wound. "That's a master's secret," I mumble, pulling at my skin. "At least you didn't hit anything important." I look up as I pull my jeans to my hips and catch her staring at me. "Enjoying the view?"

The woman narrows her eyes and folds her arms over her chest. "You can't help it, can you?"

"What?" I ask, tightening my belt.

"Being an asshole," she answers.

I move to lean against a tree, facing her. "You told me to back up, and I did," I scoff. "What more do you want from me?"

"I had a blade to your balls, Kade," she says, holding her hands out in wonder. "What else were you going to do?"

I shrug. "I'll admit that was an effective way to motivate me," I say, leaning my head back and closing my eyes against the sun breaking through the canopy above.

"Shouldn't you be leaving?" she asks.

"What kind of mate would I be if I left you alone out here?" I respond, looking back down at her. She's noticeably relaxed and might look more beautiful. Her white top is loose-fitting and thin. It waves in the breeze without sleeves, asking me to slip my hands over the few ribs I can see.

"The unwanted kind," she answers. "You're in my territory. You're the only one in danger here."

"That's not what it looked like in the basin," I remark, lifting my eyebrow. "Seems the lines are a bit blurred around here."

"Leave, Kade," she barks.

"Give me your name," I order.

"You have no need for my name," she snaps.

Pushing off the tree, I reach out to her. "Maybe you'll change your mind while I escort you home."

The woman stares at my hand for a moment before shifting her gaze back to my eyes. "I don't need your help," she says.

"Your horse is gone," I remind her, smiling. "I promise to be a gentleman."

Her head snaps toward the basin as Thursday calls for me from the tree line. This beautiful woman before me is all I will ever need. I'm not interested in anything that idiot has to say. Thursday has perfect hearing, though. It won't be long before she finds us.

I take one step closer, and the woman puts her hand on my chest, stopping me. "We should go," I whisper.

Her arm shakes as she looks from her hand to my eyes. Releasing the pressure, she allows me closer until her heaving breaths tickle my lips. "I can't let you into my world, Kade," the beautiful woman whispers. "You will only break it, and I won't survive that."

She slips from between me and the tree, letting out a shrill whistle. I reach for her as the horse thunders toward us, but she grabs the saddle and flings herself onto its back. I slide my fingers over my lips where her breath landed just a few moments ago as I watch her disappear into the woods.

"Kade, you're bleeding!" Thursday shouts, running to my side. She tries to reach for my thigh, but I shove her off me. "Let me look at it," she demands.

"It's fine," I tell her. "You done out there?"

"Toby took the wagon back a while ago," she answers. "We fired the rest of the tents. There's no blood left." She follows my gaze into the woods where my mate had ridden off. "Who was that, Kade?"

"None of your business," I scoff, turning to shove her back toward the basin. "Let's get out of here."

2

Fixing my doors has been an irritating task for over a decade. Tynan considers them a suggestion that he rarely takes seriously. The scraper's sound is nearly therapeutic as it smooths the wood. Miles taught me how to throw blades at boards, while my father showed me how to fix them. I slide my hand over the smoothed wood and stare into the distance.

"What's eating at you, kid?" Castor asks, holding out a glass of sweet tea. "You haven't been right since you got back from that job."

I sit back and look over the older wolf. Castor was my father's best friend. He lives in the only house close by because I wouldn't let anyone else near me after my mother died. He doesn't judge me but won't be afraid to tell me when I've screwed up, either.

"I was thinking about when I was younger," I tell him. "Do you remember Miles?"

Castor chuckles. "I remember you getting caught stealing cookies for him a few times," he says, smiling. "Your mother and her rolling pin."

"Yeah," I say, wincing. "That thing hurt." I narrow my eyes and rock my chair. "He wasn't a killer, was he? Miles was great with knives, but was he teaching me to do this?"

"Miles didn't get his hands dirty," Castor starts. "He could. He had the skills and would handle business, but if someone needed… fixing, we had the ring for those kinds of issues."

"That's right," I say, nodding. "He had fighters. Whatever happened to them?"

The ring had a bad reputation, but the fights were always fair. Miles had a few wolves that were trained in hand-to-hand combat. If someone stepped too far out of line, they were sentenced to a fight. I watched enough to know I never wanted to go up against those wolves.

Castor frowns, sighing. "Tynan," he answers.

My old friend doesn't need to elaborate. Tynan's mother had a farmhouse near the center of the compound before he killed her. It has a basement where the Alpha lets his inner demons play. He would've drugged the fighters and chained them down there until he'd had enough and killed them.

"Why is he still Alpha?" I scoff.

Castor shrugs. "Everyone's scared of him, Kade."

"So, I'll kill him, and you can take over the pack," I reply, grinning.

"You know that's not how it works," the old wolf says, frowning. "The pack would be yours." He rests his boots on the porch railing with a sigh. "I heard he got one of your girls."

I look down at the bottom step where Friday's blood stained the wood. "He didn't appreciate me leaving his crew in the basin." I should be pissed, but I can't find it in me to care. "Castor, what do good people do?"

The old wolf laughs. "What?"

"I'm being serious," I say, chuckling. "Obviously, I'm not a good person. What would I have to do to be one?"

Sunday quietly walks through the open doorway where my front door will eventually be re-hung and places a plate of turkey sandwiches on the table. Castor eyes her slender frame loosely wrapped in one of my shirts. She's wearing it unbuttoned with nothing underneath for attention. I snag her hand as it trails over my cheek and kiss her fingers before shooing her back into the house.

"We play the hand we're dealt, kid," the old man grumbles. "The skills Miles taught you turned out to be useful. I think they kept you safe when you were younger, and now they keep you busy. If you wanna try something new, maybe stop thinking about yourself and help someone just because you can." Castor's eyes flick back to my doorway. "Keeping her close is a good start."

"Hmm," I hum, rolling my eyes. "You give me too much credit. She was supposed to be a distraction. It's not working. There's more in there if you wanna take them for a spin."

Castor chuckles, grabbing a sandwich. "I just might take you up on that," he says before taking a bite. "You seem distracted without their help, though. You gonna tell me what all this is about?"

I rest my head against the back of the chair and kick my feet up on the door. "It's nothing, old friend," I tell him.

"Kade, you've been home for a month, and you're just getting around to fixing this door," Castor scoffs, shaking his sandwich at me. "Something's got you twisted. Your father would never forgive me if I left you like this without at least trying to help."

I slouch in the chair and close my eyes. "I just need some time," I mumble. "I'm fine."

"Well, you want some help hanging that door?" Castor offers.

Hands slide over my chest and down my abs. I reach up for the cheek of the person rubbing their face over mine and recognize the feel of Sunday's scar. Her teeth graze my jaw before nibbling my ear.

"Nah," I say, sighing. "I think I'm gonna go distract myself for a while. You'll be alright?" I ask, turning to the older wolf.

"Oh, yeah," he replies, smiling. "You know us old dogs. We just keep kicking."

I pull Sunday around the chair and kiss her cheek. "Why don't you round up the rest of the girls?" I suggest. "I'll be right in."

She squeals childishly and runs into the house. I roll my eyes, laying my head back again.

* * *

"I can't remember the last time you closed my bar, Kade," Rooster says, pouring me another drink. "I mean, besides this week."

His moonshine this month is blueberry-flavored, but it has me thinking about strawberries. I finally kicked the weekdays out of my house a few days ago and was happy when Thursday didn't show up last night. I hate Rooster's bar, but I've been coming here all week because he recently received permission to bond with his mate. They are currently the only mated pair in our pack.

"What was it like?" I ask quietly as the last of his customers slinks out the door. "When you bonded..." Cutting myself off, I wince and look down at my hands.

"Kade," Rooster starts, pulling a stool to sit across the bar from me. "Man, we go way back. You've never had trouble with the ladies." He snorts and gulps his drink. "Shit. I spent most of my life jealous of you."

I click my tongue. "They just turned into a convenient way to remember the day of the week," I tell him, frowning. "If Ari wanted you to close this place and be a farmer, would you do it? Would it be worth it?"

"Brother, I'd give up my wolf for her," Rooster announces. "Hell, I'd give up meat for that woman."

"Well, that's dramatic," I scoff, shaking my head.

Rooster pats my hand and takes my empty glass. "No, man," he says, grinning. "That's the bond. I would do anything to feel her touch." Rooster leans on the bar and stares at the wall behind me.

"Ari's smile is my joy. I will spend the rest of my days making sure she's happy."

"But what about your happiness?" I ask, narrowing my eyes. "How could you be happy giving up things that you love?"

Sighing, Rooster turns back to me. "If you find your mate, you'll understand," he says. "I was miserable for years because she was all I could think about. Now that I have her, she's so deep in my heart that I don't need anything else."

"Years?" I mumble, frowning.

"I tried to drown her out of my mind," Rooster says, chuckling. "Trust me, I had enough alcohol. She wouldn't leave. I hated the wait, but Ari was worth it." He looks up as the door behind me opens. "We're closed, Vera."

"I'm not here for you," Thursday scoffs.

I put my finger to my lips for Rooster before turning around. "What do you want?" I snap at the woman.

"I was out of town last night," she answers, lifting her eyebrow. "I thought you might have missed me."

"Hm," I hum, turning back to the bar. "You thought wrong."

She sits beside me and taps the counter, waiting for a drink. "Don't you want to know where I was?"

"I said we're closed, Vera," Rooster growls.

"But the door was not," she points out. "And I want a drink."

I nod to my friend when he looks at me. He blows his lips out before plopping a glass on the bar and pouring a minimal amount of moonshine for her.

"I was running an errand for Alpha," she announces proudly.

"I've warned you to stay away from Tynan a million times, Thursday," I grumble. "When you end up on his wall, you'll only have yourself to blame."

She laughs and sniffs her drink. "I don't have to worry about that," she boasts. "He's got Baby Beta down there. He's pretty pissed, so he'll be busy for a while."

That's her nickname for Bastian. Thursday has aimed a lot of aggression at that kid over the years. I spin around and turn her toward me. "What did you do?"

Thursday raises her eyebrow. "Oh, it wasn't me. That worthless mutt was playing house with the Luna and her boy toy," she says, grinning. "Like Alpha would ever let him go."

Staring at her, I replay her words in my head. "The kid was with the Luna?"

"Mm-hmm. They were swimming out at Cattail Lake," she says, knocking my hands off her shoulders. "Get this! She begged him to stay with her! Can you believe that?" She shakes her head and tips her glass, letting the moonshine slide down her throat.

"What were they doing at Cattail Lake?" I ask. I've been too distracted. I should know everything this pack is doing, but I can't get that woman out of my head. *Rooster might be onto something.*

Thursday scoffs and taps her empty glass. "I just told you," she barks, irritated. "Swimming."

I tip my head toward her glass, asking Rooster to refill it. "Engage your brain, Thursday," I grumble. "Why were they so close to the territory line?"

"There's quite the story behind that," Thursday says before sipping her drink. "Apparently, Baby Beta negotiated a meeting. Alpha's demanding the Luna's head or her daughter as payment for the pack and our forgiveness for killing Miles."

I watch the liquor swirl in my glass as I move it. "She has a daughter," I whisper thoughtfully.

"You know, your eyes look silver in the dark," Thursday says, slurring her words.

I point to her glass so Rooster will fill it again. "They're blue."

"I don't care," she mumbles. "I prefer other parts of your body."

Rooster flinches. "I wasn't jealous of some of your choices, brother."

Chuckling, I hang my head.

"You're no prize either, Rooster," Thursday scoffs, clumsily dropping her empty glass on the bar. She blows her lips out when I point to it and tip my head at Rooster. "Are you trying to get me drunk, lover?"

Looking up, I shake my hair out of my eyes with a smile. "Yes, I am," I tell her. I wink at Rooster. "You still keep that horse out back?"

Rooster's brow furrows as he nods. "Yeah," he answers slowly.

"I'm gonna get rid of her and take off for a little while," I tell him. "Thanks for this." I shift my eyes toward Thursday's glass.

"I've always got your back, Kade," Rooster says, sighing.

I lean my head on my hand and watch Thursday drain another glass of moonshine. Rooster's new supplier is quite skilled, and their booze is strong. Thursday's never been able to hold her liquor, and it doesn't take much to render her useless. She's soon falling off her stool, and we can't understand a word coming out of her mouth.

"Alright, I'm out of here," I announce, standing up. "I'll have your horse back in a week or two."

"Sure, brother," Rooster says, looking at Thursday curiously. "Be safe."

Digging in my pocket, I produce a few silver pieces to drop on the counter before slinging Thursday over my shoulder. I carry her out the back door to the small horse pen Rooster built to hold the animals his customers brought him as payment. He usually takes them down the tracks to sell, but this horse would attract too much attention.

I throw Thursday over the back of the short black and white draft horse. Miles called them "Gypsies," but I'm pretty sure a gypsy was a wandering entertainer. I don't really care. He's calm and won't mind the long ride back to the basin. After slipping the horse's bridle over his head, I jump onto his back behind Thursday's limp body and aim him toward our witch's cottage.

I could travel faster as a wolf but can't talk to the beautiful woman if I shift. My chest is tight in anticipation. The hope that I'll find my mate again burns my soul. Rooster said he felt like this for years. I was content before I met that woman in the basin. I didn't care about anyone, handled business, and actually enjoyed being an asshole.

I look down at my hand latched onto Thursday's waistband to hold her on the horse. My fingers are against her skin, yet I feel nothing. When I touched my mate, something inside my core reached for her. My desire for that woman is clouding my thoughts and unsafely distracting me.

Tynan uses the back trails, so the pack tends to avoid them. However, I know he doesn't venture out in the dark, making them the easiest way to travel undetected. I push the horse to canter over the soft ground. We move quickly to the other side of the compound and pull up behind Jax's cottage.

The witch's humble abode has a weird smell to it. He's always messing with potions and brews. The pink smoke flowing from his windows tonight means he's at it again. The door opens, and the dark-haired, skinny man stumbles onto the porch, coughing. He leans on the railing and waves a hand at me as he tries to catch his breath.

"Well, this is..." I start, trying to find the right word, "pretty." I shake my head and swing from the horse's back. "Help me with her."

Jax laughs through his coughing. "Shut up, Kade," he spouts. He joins me beside the horse and squints as he takes in Thursday's lifeless body. "What did you do to her?"

Clicking my tongue, I grab her arms and twist her around as I pull her down. "I didn't do shit," I scoff. "She's drunk."

"Okay, but why is she here?" the witch asks, grabbing her legs as they slide off the horse.

"I need your help with something," I answer, nodding toward his house. "You still got that potion that makes them forget things?"

We walk through what's left of the pink smoke and toss Thursday on the couch.

"I don't know what you're talking about," Jax says innocently.

I openly stare at him. "Jax, I don't have time for your games," I spout. "Can you wipe her or not?"

"How much?" he asks, scowling.

"Just tonight," I say, flopping into an armchair. "I need another favor."

Studying me, Jax opens his hutch. "What's up?" he asks before disappearing behind its doors.

"I heard Tynan's got the kid locked up again," I say, sighing. "You know anything about that?"

With a small vial in hand, the witch slowly closes the hutch and turns to sit on the floor with his back against it. "He dragged a sledgehammer through the compound this afternoon," he whispers. "I heard that kid screaming from here."

My jaw clenches. "So, brew up your little tea and get him out of there," I order.

"Kade, I can't heal him," Jax grumbles. "Tynan will know it was me, and then I'll be the one on that wall. Besides, he's the only one with the keys."

"Tynan's afraid of the dark," I say, narrowing my eyes. I know Jax is right about the keys, though. "Do you remember around ten years ago when Tynan caught that wolf traveling to join the Lunar Pack? He tried to convince him to stay with us, but the wolf refused?"

"Yeah," Jax says, nodding. "The one that got away."

"Well, that's another story," I say, cringing. Cody was the first wolf I killed, but he did tell me how he escaped before he died.

"He got away by shifting. The front paws form first, but they can be slipped out of the cuff as they do. The back paws are easy after that."

"Kade, that kid is hurt," Jax reminds me, shaking his head.

"I didn't say it was gonna be easy, Jax," I scoff. "If you won't heal him, he'll have to shift injured. I can't fix that." I frown at the witch. "The Luna wants him. Try to get him close to her pack."

"What does Darya want with him?" Jax asks, confused.

Studying the witch, I slowly sit up. "You know the Luna?"

Jax shrugs. "When we were kids," he answers. "It was a long time ago."

"What's she like?" I ask, intrigued.

Sighing, Jax looks over at Thursday. "An angry little terrier mutt."

I sit back and laugh. I don't believe my mate would be loyal to an angry terrier. She would demand greatness from her leader. She'd follow someone who would do anything for her wolves and always be there for them. Her Luna would want to take in a wolf that had been wronged for his entire life and beaten to the point of total submission.

"You'll get that kid to her, right?" I ask more urgently. "Wait until dusk tonight," I add, looking at the brightening sky through the window. "And get him the hell out of here."

"Listen, Kade," Jax starts, standing up. "You are asking me to put my life on the line for a kid who would kill me if given the chance."

"What's your price?" I ask, rolling my eyes.

Jax raises his gaze to the ceiling and skews his face in thought. "The weekdays," he answers, lifting his eyebrows.

"Fine," I agree, digging in my pocket. It should've taken more thought, but I don't want them anymore. "Not here." I throw my keys at him. "And take a bath."

He flips me off before grabbing my keys from the floor. "Asshole," Jax grumbles. "Come on. Help me with her. Where are you going, anyway?"

I open Thursday's mouth so Jax can feed her the potion while considering how I should respond. "Hunting," I decide.

* * *

It's faster traveling without a wagon, but I've still been circling this damn basin for two days. With miles of barren wasteland, my only choice to remain hidden is to stick to the edge. A few storms came through over the past month, erasing any sign of my prey. The ground lacks horse or wolf tracks, so no one has traveled through here since the last rain.

As the second day closes, I spot a trail carved into the side of a cliff. It's well-traveled but still lacks any tracks that would tell me I'm going in the right direction. It takes all night to lead the exhausted horse up the trail, but the view that greets us proves worth the struggle.

We round the edge of a rock wall to find ourselves among the vivid colors of a flower field. The sunrise touches the petals, making their dew coating shimmer. Their fragrance is powerful, and the way the colors sway in the breeze captivates all my attention. There's no way that woman doesn't come here. This is the kind of beauty she would demand in her life.

I step forward, sliding my hands over the top of the flowers so they tickle my palms. I close my eyes and feel my beautiful mate's skin under my fingers. The breeze reminds me of her breath kissing my lips. I slide my tongue over them, wishing I'd taken that taste for the millionth time.

The horse bumps its nose into my arm, reminding me these sensations are all in my head. *How did Rooster do this for years?* I scan the field, finding evidence of a few farms in the distance. Based on the dots moving on a far plain, the closest one looks to have cows. Since wolves would raise beef, that one would be my best bet.

Just as I step toward the cattle ranch, a voice travels up the cliff.

I stop to listen but can't make out their words. One thing is clear, though—they are climbing the trail. There's a lone cluster of trees in a gully to the north.

Sighing, I pat the horse's neck. "I'm sorry, old boy," I whisper to him, looking back at the cliff wall that blocks the trail. "We're not supposed to be here." I jump onto his back and swing the reins to smack his hindquarters, sending him galloping toward the trees.

I jump from the short, fat horse when we reach the small grove, and he's nearly caught his breath by the time the owners of the voices enter the flower fields. They dismount and walk with three wolves. The breeze blows in my direction, carrying a floral scent more potent than the field's. I step toward the edge of the trees and lean against a thicker oak.

The two women are on the shorter side, but the man I recognize. I had a few run-ins with Anthony back in his militia days. Miles always saved my ass. I doubt he'd remember me. One of the wolves in their group is enormous, with thicker shoulders than I'll ever have. I've heard enough stories to know who he is. He's traveling beside the dark-haired woman and lovingly rubs his head over her hip.

I had no idea where I was going or how I would find my mate, but I somehow stumbled into the Luna and her Alpha. *They don't look like evil Alpha killers.* I might have been a kid when Miles died, but I remember the pack's uproar. There were numerous attempts on the Luna's life throughout the first few years.

I was trained to kill so that I could protect our pack from these people who look peaceful, maybe even kind. I look down at my hands. *Have I ever actually killed an enemy? Perhaps my mate was right. Maybe I don't belong.*

I slip around the tree and sink back into the cover of the foliage. The horse is sleeping in the center of the grove. I sit beside him and watch the flies attempt to land on him, only to be swatted or flinched away. I haven't slept in three days, so when my eyes droop, I don't stand a chance.

* * *

The next day, the horse wakes me by nudging my boot. "Hey, buddy," I whisper, scratching his cheek. "Thanks for standing watch." The horse sniffs my hair a few times before deciding I'm not edible and moving away. "Maybe she'd like you, big guy," I think out loud. "Rooster would understand why I gave you away."

While I stare at the unique gelding, a horse sneezes. I jump to my feet when I realize it wasn't him. Staying low, I move around the trees until I can see into the field. It's a foggy sunrise, but I can see Anthony riding with the gray-haired woman who was with the Luna yesterday. Beyond an older man with them is my prey. She's riding a horse beside a younger girl.

My mate's laughter hits my ears like a beautiful song. I don't need to hear my heart pounding because her aura is flashing so fast it's nearly blinding me in the dim light. She throws a chunk of beef into the air and points as a hawk swoops to grab it. She laughs when a few more join in, hoping to snag some meat she's brought them.

I move closer to the field and step on a branch lying near the base of a tree. Cringing, I drop back behind the thick trunk. When my breathing settles, I realize I haven't heard any sounds from the field.

"You can't be here," the beautiful woman hisses from the other side of my tree, making me jump.

Her voice causes a sigh of relief, and I reach around the tree to grab her, pulling her into my hiding spot. She lands against me, looking as perfect as the first time I saw her. My hand slides up her neck to hold her cheek. I rub my thumb over her lower lip, noting that her breathing is just as labored as mine.

Her hands brace against my chest, but her fingers rest on my skin above my shirt's collar. She has to know how exciting that feels to me. Her skin reacts to my touch in the same way.

"Just give me your name," I beg. "You live in my dreams. I smell your soap everywhere I go. Your voice is the sweetest song I've ever heard." I stop and search her eyes. "I can't go one more day without knowing who haunts me."

The woman closes her eyes and leans forward until she's lying against my chest. "Go home, Kade," she whispers.

When she sniffles, my arms instinctively wrap around her. I grit my teeth, trying to make sense of this. I have never cared about anyone. Women have come and gone for most of my adult life. I don't even know this woman, but I will do anything to make her smile. I want to hear her laughter again more than any other sound.

Her fingers curl, pulling my shirt into her closed fists. I relax into her body and put my cheek on her head with a sigh. My beautiful mate fits perfectly against me. I slide my fingers over her back and shoulders, trying to memorize her while providing some comfort.

Inhaling deeply, I pull in her strawberry soap. "I don't want to see you sad," I whisper. "I just can't get you out of my head."

She leans back and lets me wipe the tears from her face. "That is the Luna's guard with us, Kade," she hisses. "You can't be here."

"Gaine?" the little girl calls from the field, making the woman glance in her direction.

"Your name is Gaine?" I ask, trying to capture her eyes again.

She turns back to me and cups my cheek. Nerves that I've never felt before come alive at her touch. Air rushes from my lungs, and my eyes roll closed as I hold her hand to avoid losing this sensation. "Go home," she whispers against my lips. "We don't belong in the same world."

3

I don't normally wait until the weather turns cool to start chopping wood, but I'm glad I did this year. It's been over a month since I felt Gaine's touch, and every minute has passed at an excruciatingly slow pace. I don't even have a clear enough head to invent a reason to go back to her. A run would do me some good, but I can't stand the thought of Tynan's voice in my head right now.

I place another log on the stump and swing the ax at it, sending the halves flying. It's not even aggression I'm taking out on these poor trees. It just feels like insanity. *That woman is making me crazy.*

Rooster slowly moves into my line of sight with his hands out. "Hey, bud," he says soothingly. "Castor said you were struggling a bit." He grabs one of the halves and puts it on my stump. "You wanna talk about it?"

"No," I snap, swinging my ax, barely giving him the chance to move out of the way.

"Alright, then," Rooster responds. "I'll just keep you company for a while." He retrieves more of the halves, which I'd been ignoring, and places them on the stump for me to split.

I've been at this for days. I have enough wood for the next five winters. I could keep the entire compound warm for at least a few years. I know he's waiting for me to wear myself out, but that won't happen.

"Castor tells me you sent the weekdays away," Rooster remarks, ducking as a log nearly hits him. "I'm not sure I've ever seen you do that. How will you know what day it is?"

I ignore him and keep swinging the ax, hoping one of these cuts will sever my need for that woman. For Gaine. *Who am I kidding?*

"Ari's cooking up some venison stew," Rooster tries after a few more logs. "How long has it been since you've eaten?"

I hurl the ax toward the standing trees in the distance, and Rooster whistles as it lodges into the side of a tall pine. Sitting on the stump, I wipe the sweat from my forehead. My eyes fix on my back porch, where Castor has been watching over me.

"I found my mate," I whisper, turning to Rooster. "She's perfect and beautiful and amazing. She haunts me even when I'm awake."

Sighing, Rooster puts his hand on my shoulder. "Yeah," he murmurs. "They do that."

"She sent me away—said she doesn't want me." I sigh, wishing none of it were true. "She's Lunar Pack," I add.

Rooster sucks air between his teeth. "And the hits just keep on coming." He grabs a larger log and pulls it beside me, waving Castor off when the older man moves to join us. "When did this happen?"

I rub my face and sit up. "A couple of months ago," I tell him. "When I went down with the scrub crew."

"That's why you took Chester?"

"That horse has a name?" I ask, laughing.

"I've had him for two years," Rooster scoffs. "I had to call him something besides 'horse.'"

Grinning, I nod. "I suppose," I say. "How did you do this for years, Rooster? What's your secret?"

My friend laughs heartily. "Brother, I have no idea," he replies. "I gotta head back to the bar. Why don't you come with me? I think you've got more than enough wood for now."

"I'm not in the mood to deal with anyone, Rooster," I grumble.

He puts his hand out to me. "It's still closed," he says, smiling. "I'm just trying to feed you, Kade."

"Sure," I say, shrugging. I stand and snatch my shirt from the ground. "You'll be alright, Castor?" I yell.

"Go on, kid," Castor shouts. "You know us old guys."

Rooster throws his arm around my shoulders, and we wander through the woods, taking it slow so we can talk. Like me, Rooster was groomed to be the muscle of the pack. He's skilled with long blades and bows. But he met Ari when we were 17, and everything changed for him.

"I always wondered why you left the blades for the booze," I say, chuckling. "I never did see what was so great about pouring drinks for drunks."

"Ari's always made me want to be better than what the pack wanted for us," Rooster says, releasing my shoulders. "I couldn't follow that path, you know?"

I breathe out a laugh. "So you decided to get them drunk instead?"

"Eh, it pays the bills," he says, grinning.

"But how do you know what she wants?" I ask. "If you knew she wouldn't want you to be like me, what made you pick the path you followed?"

Rooster narrows his eyes as he studies the trail before us. "You take the road that makes her happy," he says.

"Well, that's helpful," I growl.

"What is it that she doesn't like?" Rooster asks. "The pack? The killing? The hair?"

I scoff at my friend's shaved head when he flips his hand as if fluffing his own hair. "In general, I'd say she just doesn't like me," I grumble, rolling my eyes.

Rooster groans. "I don't think that's possible, brother. I'm not sure there's a single wolf on the planet that doesn't like you."

"I am arguably the greatest person alive," I agree. "But she's somehow slightly better than me."

"Now we just gotta get you in her good graces," Rooster says, twisting his face in thought. "Any idea what she likes?" He steps onto the bar's deck and turns to me while digging around for his keys. "I mean, besides disapproving of you."

I click my tongue. "This is not helping." I lean my back against the wall beside the door and fix my eyes on the trail we'd just taken. "She's smart, brother," I murmur before sighing and turning toward him. "Whatever she likes must be perfect, just like her."

Rooster pushes the key into the door and pauses. "Kade, you need more help than I can give," he says, shaking his head. "You need a woman's guidance."

With a wink, Rooster pushes open the door to reveal his mate, who is setting out a meal at the bar. She loses her broad smile when I step through the doorway behind him. Ari is a strong, independent wolf who has a difficult past. Frowning, I realize Rooster's right. As the only woman in this pack who doesn't desire me, I need her help. But I doubt she'd be willing after I caused her years of misery.

"Kade," she sneers as a welcome.

"Ari, please be nice to our guest," Rooster groans. "He's hungry and brokenhearted."

"Good," his mate barks, dropping a second plate onto the bar.

I close the door behind us and lean against it. "Ari," I start with a sigh, unsure how I could ever apologize for the damage I've done.

"No," she snaps back. "You're in my territory now. You don't get to wag your tongue and smooth anything over." Her growl starts low as she crosses the room toward me. "You killed everyone that meant anything to me and forced me to play house with that kid. I had to watch my mate pine for me while everything in me wanted nothing but him, and my heart broke.

"My father won't dance with me at my wedding. My mother won't fix my hair. I have nothing left except my mate. And the only reason I have him is because that kid screwed up so badly that Alpha tried to get him killed. So, you, Kade, are not welcome in my life. Turn your ass around and walk out that door. Never come back!"

She stops with her finger jammed in my chest. She's always had a loud growl, but today, it hits me harder. Every word she speaks is true, and I own my role in her struggles. The asshole in me wants to match her glare and put her in her place, but there's something else present inside me that appeared the moment I met Gaine and has only grown stronger with time.

I reach for Ari and pull her to me. She fights, slamming her fists into my ribs a few times before limply falling against my chest. I wrap her tightly in my arms as she quietly sobs into my shirt. Rooster only shrugs when I look up at him before he ducks behind the bar to grab a third plate. He didn't like my methods but understood I was doing what was needed to protect his mate when he asked for my help.

After a while, Ari's sobs dry up, but she stays against me. Her hands slide to my waistband, and she slips her fingers through the belt loops. "I hate you," she whispers through more sniffles.

Sighing, I lean my cheek on her head. "I know," I murmur. "I'm sorry."

Ari was 12 when Tynan convinced her parents to join our pack. I think they only agreed because she told them about Rooster. We watched over her for the first few years while Rooster chose his new path, but when Ari turned 15, Tynan set his sights on her, and everything changed.

I had no choice but to solidify my position as Tynan's enforcer and convince him to use her as a tool to placate his "super soldier."

Ari was directed to bed Bastian and convince him she was his mate. Her family fought the order, and Tynan threatened Rooster. I did what I had to, and she has every right to hate me.

The fact that Ari's still against me and hasn't jammed my knife into my neck means Rooster has told her what he knows of the past few years. She doesn't need to be told the rest. I can't take back what I did, and knowing why I did it won't make anything better.

Rooster produces a pot from the kitchen and nods toward the bar. I lean over and scoop the back of Ari's legs to lift her to my chest. I try placing her in Rooster's lap, but she's latched back onto my shirt, her face buried against my shoulder.

Her mate shrugs. "When she's ready," he says, grinning. "We should eat, though. I'll have to open up soon."

I haven't felt hungry in days, but we spend the rest of the daylight hours devouring the venison stew. Rooster tells me what I've missed with my head stuck in the fog Gaine is creating, and I tell him what I saw when I encountered the Luna's party. Once I've had enough stew, I lean back and heat my body, letting Ari sleep against me.

"My new brewer is Lunar Pack," Rooster whispers, watching his mate nuzzle into me. "Ari's delivered my order the past few times. I don't like her going alone." He slides his finger over her cheek. "Why don't you go with her this time? Maybe you could visit your friend while you're there."

I sigh and look down at Ari. "The kid was good to her," I whisper. "I made sure of that."

"I know, brother," Rooster says quietly, reaching out to me. "There's not a mark on her." He squeezes and shakes my hand. "I think we'll do anything for the love of a good woman. You'll figure this out."

Chuckling, I tightly wrap my arms around his sleeping mate. "Is this what it's like?"

"Better," Rooster whispers, smiling.

I relax into Ari as Rooster collects our dishes. Her forehead is warm against my cheek, but my skin yearns for Gaine's touch. My nerves' celebration pulled so much of my attention that my mate slipped right out of my arms. She was within my lips' reach, and I could've taken the taste I was dying for, but when I opened my eyes, Gaine was gone.

A loud chirp erupts between Ari and me. Instantly recognizing it, I reach into her shirt to find the pendant I had Jax make for her. Ari fights me as I yank it from its chain and throw it as hard as possible against the wall. It shatters and falls silently to the floor.

"Easy, Ari," I hiss, cupping her cheek. "Go on. Get in the back room and stay there until he's gone." I kiss her cheek and push her off my lap. Rooster grabs Ari's arm and pulls her toward the back room, knowing what that pendant signaled.

The front door crashes open as Rooster reappears. "Where the hell have you been?" Tynan bellows, obviously already hitting his private stock.

"Anywhere you weren't, Tynan," I grumble, reaching over the bar for a glass and the nearest bottle. "What do you want?"

"Alpha," he snaps, snatching my glass.

Flexing my jaw, I grab another one. "You can call yourself whatever you want," I say, raising my eyebrow. "But that doesn't answer my question."

"I got an errand for you," Tynan spouts, slurring and spitting as he talks. "Then I need you to fetch my soldier. I seem to have misplaced him." He watches Rooster cautiously move our plates out of view. "What do you want?"

Shaking my head, I fill my glass with blueberry moonshine. "It's his bar, Tynan," I scoff. "Or did you want that too?"

Tynan leers at me. "If you weren't so damn useful, I'd skin your wolf and use it as a rug," he snaps before gulping his drink. "I'd put them eyes in a jar on my mantle."

"Then I would always be there to silently judge you," I respond, glaring at him with the eyes he hates so much.

Tynan blows out his lips. "I dropped a body at your house," he says casually. "I need you to get rid of it. Maybe you could leave it on Lunar land. They might want it back."

Rooster stiffens on the other side of the bar. His eyes nervously flick toward me, but I've learned not to react to Tynan's taunting. Breathing deeply, I look at the wall behind the bar. The door Rooster shoved Ari through is still cracked open, and I know she's listening. This is the version of me she's used to.

"Whatever, Tynan," I grumble. "I'll take care of it."

"And my soldier?" he asks, growing more irritated.

I turn to look in his direction. "I'll see what I can do."

Tynan switches gears, realizing he won't get the reaction he wants from me. "Where's that pretty pet of yours, Chicken?" He leans over the bar to see if Ari is hiding behind it.

Barely shaking my head at Rooster, I reach for the blade on my belt. "She's bonded, Tynan," I growl.

"Why would that stop me?" he scoffs.

Tynan backs away from the counter and moves to walk around me, gaining access to the area behind the bar. Spinning on my stool, I pull my blade and catch him just under his jaw as he tries to pass me. The short man stops with wild eyes and a sharp breath.

"I would think very carefully about your next move, Tynan," I sneer, my growl building beyond my control.

"ALPHA!" he screams, red-faced.

"Then act like it," I snap, pulling my knife from his skin. Stretching my neck to quiet my growl, I slip the blade back into my belt and turn to the bar. "I'll let you know when I find your soldier," I add, dismissing Tynan.

The short, greasy man huffs as he throws his glass across the room. I'm familiar with the glare he's wearing. Tynan is sick and twisted but weak in general. His power comes from the fear he's created with his sadistic ways. Very few wolves have left his wall, but those that have will never disobey him. I don't return his glares, so he believes they hold power over me.

We watch him stomp across the room and breathe a sigh of relief when he slams the door shut behind him. Rooster peeks in the back room before turning to me. "A body?"

I down my drink and drop the glass. "Yeah, I gotta go check that," I tell him. "He said they were Lunar Pack."

"He doesn't know about... you know? Right?" Rooster stammers.

My eyes widen. "Shit. I don't know," I answer, jumping up. I point to the door behind him. "Keep her close," I tell Rooster. "I'll have another pendant made." Stopping at the door, I hold the curtain aside to be sure Tynan is gone before pulling it open. I glance back at my friend to see his mate sliding into his arms. "I'll go with her. Just give me a minute to deal with this."

I slip between the trees in the growing darkness, moving through the woods instead of taking the trail home. There's no way Tynan knows about Gaine, but I have to see for myself. Running on a full stomach is never great, but the tightness in my chest has nothing to do with that meal. The thought of never feeling her touch again has me panicked, sprinting at a blinding speed.

I burst through the edge of the trees and fall to my knees next to a dark-skinned, middle-aged man. I dig my fingers into my forehead, releasing a noisy sigh of relief. Closing my eyes, I see Gaine's face in my hands. I watch my fingers wipe away her tears and search her eyes as she begs me to leave her. *Why did I let her go?*

* * *

"So, that pendant was an alarm?" Ari asks the next day.

"Jax made it for me," I answer, slowing to jog beside her. *"I didn't think you'd take it from me, so I had Rooster give it to you."*

"I don't understand," she admits.

We're heading to Rooster's drop-off spot for his brewers. Ari wasn't excited that I would be going with her, but she was intrigued by the amulets I had Jax make for this trip. Since we had to move fast, I knew we'd need to shift. I figured the witch had something that could stop Tynan from being able to reach us. I'm glad they're working.

"Our honor forbids us to touch a bonded wolf," I tell her. *"I assumed Tynan lacked any desire to follow our code. I'm having another one made for you."*

"And these?" She tucks to poke the pendant hanging from her neck.

"That's a ward Tynan himself wanted," I answer, chuckling. *"Now we get to use it against him. It's a proximity ward. We can only communicate within close range."* I bump my shoulder into hers. *"So don't get pissed and take off on me."*

It's nice to hear her giggle. I made sure she was safe over the years and knew Bastian was sweet to her, but I'm not sure she had much reason to laugh before now.

"Ari, how did it feel for you before you bonded?" I ask, hoping we're at the point where this conversation won't be incredibly awkward.

She trips a bit as she looks in my direction. *"What do you mean?"* she asks, confused. *"Like, with Bass?"*

"No," I say, sighing. *"Did you ever think about leaving? To get away from all this, could you leave Rooster?"*

"Not for a minute," Ari answers, giggling. *"He's always been in my heart, Kade."* She slows, and we walk a bit while she responds. *"When we were kids, you two meant so much to me. But Rooster has been my path since the moment we met."* Tilting her head, Ari looks at me. *"What's this about?"*

"Hm," I hum, cringing. *"I found my mate."*

"And you don't want her?" she asks.

"I feel her in my soul," I gush, unable to hold it in anymore. *"I want

that woman in every way. Her voice is my damn theme song. I want to jog to its beat for the rest of my life."

I don't know when she started laughing, but I can't help joining in when I notice it.

"This is a whole new side of you," Ari says, nearing hysterics.

Sighing, I lead her off the path to a small stream and lay down after a quick drink. *"Rooster thinks you might be able to help me win her over."*

"Oh," she gushes in realization. *"She's denying you?"* She flops in the grass beside me. *"I want to meet the wolf strong enough to send you packing."*

"Well, she's Lunar Pack," I grumble. *"So, that's not gonna happen. Rooster would kill me."* I rest my chin on my paws. *"What would sweep you off your feet, Ari?"*

"As beautiful as they are, Kade, bonds are pretty simple," she tells me, poking my nose with her paw. *"All Rooster needs to do is say my name, and I'm there wholeheartedly and in love. I'm sure if she's able to deny you, she has a powerful reason."*

I roll my eyes in her direction. *"She said I'd break her world."*

Ari lifts her head to tilt it from one side to the other. *"Well, you probably will."*

I close my eyes to see Gaine uninterrupted and sigh. I rub my cheek over the ground, wishing it would feel at least a little like her touch. When I roll to my side with a groan, Ari places her paw on my shoulder.

"Tell me about her," she says. *"Maybe there's something you can use."*

"I've replayed every moment with her a million times, Ari," I grumble. *"She's all I can think about. You better hope we're not attacked because I'm bloody useless with how distracted I am!"*

"Precisely," Ari says soothingly. *"I'm not distracted. Maybe I'll find something you missed."*

I don't deserve her help or kindness, but I appreciate Ari as she rests her jaw over my eyes and lets me recall every moment I spent with my mate. She giggles as I describe every little detail of her body and hair. I spend too long focusing on her eyes, but when I talk about her laughter, Ari stops me.

"*She laughed at you?*" she asks, confused.

"No," I say slowly, recalling the moments in the field. I hadn't given them much thought since she wasn't in my arms until later. "*She was in the field with the Luna's guard. She threw meat up to some hawks and laughed when they caught it.*"

"*Besides laughing, what else was she doing?*"

"*There was a little girl with her,*" I recall, looking past her laughter. "*They were pointing at the hawks as they approached.*" I focus on the memory of the birds as they wait for the next cut of meat to be launched. "*They were gliding... almost at a standstill in the breeze.*" I lift my head from under Ari's jaw. "*Why would that be funny?*"

"*It's not the birds,*" Ari announces excitedly. "*I bet she likes the idea of flying!*" She pushes my shoulder, laughing. "*I've heard the older wolves talk about a kite festival that the immortal Alpha, Miles, used to take them to every year. You need to ask one of them. Take her to see the kites, Kade.*"

I roll back to my side, pouting. "*Ari, how do I get her to go?*"

Her giggle is so fun and playful that I despise myself for every hardship I caused in her life. "*Kade, I hate you,*" she starts, still laughing. "*But I'm here with you.*" She waits for me to open my eyes before continuing. "*I don't know what it is about you, but you have us all wrapped around your finger. I equally hate and adore you.*"

"*Everybody loves me, baby,*" I boast, knowing it's true but not fully understanding it.

"*Something tells me that when you finally make a plan, she's not gonna be able to say no,*" Ari assures me. "*So far, you've just crashed into each other.*"

I lift upright and consider her words. She's right. Both times I've encountered my mate, I hadn't planned on it. I didn't know who she was the first time, and the second... I don't know what I was thinking. But this time, I'll have a plan. I'll have a destination picked out and sweep her off her feet. She'll have no choice but to accept me.

"She's Lunar Pack," I whisper, remembering the line that cannot be crossed.

"So?"

"I asked Miles once why our mates couldn't be human," I tell her thoughtfully. "He said, 'To quote Cinderella, a bird may love a fish, but where would they live?'"

"Who's Cinderella?" Ari asks, tilting her head.

"I don't know. That's not the point," I grumble. "Even if I did manage to win her heart, the Lunar Pack would never accept me, and I won't have her within Tynan's reach."

Ari studies me as I rest my chin on my paws, defeated. "Do you want her, Kade?"

I lift my head to rub my whiskers over hers. "At the risk of making myself sound as weak as a puppy, more than I want air in my lungs," I admit. "There is a hole in my soul that I was unaware of before I met her, but now it is slowly killing me, and I need her to feel complete." I close my eyes and see Gaine's smile in the field. "I want to make her smile like the birds did."

"Then go get her," Ari whispers gently. "She might be denying you, but she has that same emptiness. Find a way to feel that joy together, and your heart will shine through. The rest doesn't matter right now, Kade. I think it's kinda cute, hearing you be all mushy and stuff, though."

I fluff my lips in a scowl. "Shut up."

4

It took over a week to gather enough information about the event Ari suggested. While on a hunting trip a few years ago, one of the older families snuck off to attend this kite-flying festival. They seem confident that it's still held annually. Castor helped me narrow down the dates, and now I am in a rush because the Fall Flier Festival should be happening very soon.

"He's the fastest horse I've got," Castor says, handing me his young gray gelding's reins. "I sort of want him back, Kade. I had to trade my cart and eight cows for him."

Laughing, I put my hand out for his. "I'll do my best, old friend."

"You gonna tell Alpha you're leaving?" Rooster asks.

"I hadn't really planned on it," I say, irritated that I'd forgotten Tynan's habit of losing his mind when I disappear. "This damn woman. She's all I can think about."

"Last time you took off without telling him was a bit messy," Rooster reminds me, leaning on my porch's railing.

Wincing, I recall the bodies Tynan had accumulated in the week after I killed Ari's father. I couldn't stand the thought of watching her mourn the last of her family when he attacked me and forced my hand. I needed time away, but Tynan went wild with rage when he couldn't find the wolf he depended on to foster the fear that created his power.

"I'll track him down before I leave," I promise them. Digging in the saddlebags, I find my leather jacket and pull a small blue pendant from its pocket. "Jax finished this a few days ago," I say, handing it to Rooster. "I meant to test it, but you know how it goes. I've been distracted."

"I haven't stopped thinking about Ari for the hour I've been here, brother," Rooster says, laughing. "I get it."

After throwing my keys to Castor, I swing into the young horse's saddle and leave them to track down our demented leader. Although no one lives in the cabins near Tynan's mother's farmhouse, most dwellings are in clusters around the compound. I'm sure that was for safety reasons, but it's never helped anyone.

When I was a kid, the compound was burned to the ground by the Luna's people. Miles didn't seem to mind and told us we weren't to touch the Luna, but his rule ended with his death. Suddenly, anger and hatred spread faster than that fire, which was how Tynan easily slipped into the role of Alpha. Who better to torture the Alpha killer than that sick, twisted fool?

As I ride through the house clusters, a few of the women nod in the direction of Tynan's area. He takes half of Rooster's booze shipments for himself and keeps the jugs in his sheds, so he spends a lot of time there. I dismount as I approach them and listen for his insane ramblings. When I turn toward the largest building, the horse jerks back on his reins. It's not unusual to smell fresh blood in the compound, but this horse lives on the outskirts and isn't used to it.

Stepping up to the door, I tie him to a post and slide my hand over his neck. When the horse settles, voices filter through the silence he leaves behind. I relax against his shoulder and focus on Tynan and Jax as they have what seems to be a heated discussion.

"That other one was useless," Tynan scoffs. "Did you test these two?"

"I did what you asked, Alpha," Jax answers. "They are full-blooded and universal donors. You just have to give it time."

"I always wondered why my mother didn't shift," Tynan grumbles. "That stupid bitch told me I'd grow into it!" Something crashes inside, and someone else groans. "Then I found out she slept with that worthless human and gave me even less wolf than she had!"

"Tynan, he raped her," Jax grumbles.

"They all want it," Tynan snaps. "They just think they don't until they get it."

My hands ball into fists as my jaw clenches. The desire to protect women usually costs the men of this pack their lives. Tynan's never had a willing partner in his bed. They are actually safest when he has someone on his wall. Maybe whatever this is will provide enough distraction to keep him off them while his wall is empty.

"Tynan!" I call out before banging on the door.

He flings it open and glares at me. "What do you want?"

Grinning, I lift my eyebrow. "You seem testy," I say, looking over his head. "What are you tinkering with?"

Tynan moves the door to block my view, but not before I see the man and woman he has strapped down to beds. They are hooked up to tubes, and the woman wears the Lunar Pack marking.

"Stuff," Tynan spouts. "Now answer me."

I step back and pull the horse's reins free. "I'm heading out for a while," I tell him. Jax moves to where I can see him and nods, understanding my response is also for him. "I need my head space. I'll be back."

"Whatever," Tynan grumbles. "Go clear your head. You better find my soldier while you're gone." He slams the door as a way to excuse me.

I chuckle and turn the horse away from the shed. "Come on, bud," I whisper to the gelding. "Let's get out of here."

* * *

I hate that Castor gave me his fastest horse. Each long stride of its gallop quickly brings me closer to rejection. I had confidently packed the saddlebags, memorized the maps a few older wolves had drawn, and set out on this mission to claim my mate. I'm unsure where that confidence went, but the pit in my stomach threatens to eject the eggs I made for breakfast when I slow the gelding near the ranch's fence line.

Knowing exactly where I was going and having this fast horse under me, it took less than a day to find myself at the edge of the first terrifying adventure of my life. I'm relieved that it's at least sunset. Although wolves can see in the dark, I'm generally alone in embracing the night. This will allow me to slip around the fields unnoticed and get some rest before I face my beautiful mate again.

I slide from the saddle and loosen the cinch, letting the horse relax as we follow the fence. The ranch looked small from a distance, but these expansive fields tell a different story and seem to be leading us away from the main buildings.

When I try to turn back, the horse tugs his reins and pulls me further up the fence line. I dig my heels into the dirt and push his shoulder to force him to turn. The horse just sidesteps and continues pulling me forward. I grab his left rein and wrench his head around as a fresh fire's scent hits my nose.

Once I can finally stop him, I crouch to look through the trees. The fire light blinds me slightly, but as my heartbeat speeds up, the pulsing of Gaine's white light becomes more pronounced. The younger girl sits on one side, and Gaine's aura blocks someone else. A few horses are tied nearby, which would explain why the gelding was fighting me.

I tie my horse and slowly move closer to the campsite, attempting to stay behind them. Once I'm near enough to hear Gaine's voice, I sit behind a thicker tree and close my eyes, listening to its sweet sound. I can't understand her words, but I doubt I'd enjoy the experience more if I could. I can feel my grin as my body relaxes, ready to sleep for the first time in months as if she were telling me a bedtime story.

I don't travel as a human often, so I hadn't thought to plan for the horse. His sneeze causes me to jump and stops the conversation by the fire. I stand and press my back against the tree. Keeping my breathing slow, I try to listen for the trio but only detect the young girl and a man talking.

After another minute, I peek around the tree and come face to face with Gaine. "Shit, woman," I hiss, yanking her around the tree to land against me. My body instantly celebrates her existence by somehow being excited and relaxing at once. I latch onto her belt loop and the back of her neck, determined not to let her go this time.

Gaine pushes her elbows into my chest while her clenched fists rub over her lips. She moves stiffly as I take a few deep breaths, then stretches her fingers to rub them along my jaw. I lean into her touch as she wakes those nerves.

"I had to see you," I whisper when she pulls her fingers away.

"I told you to go home," Gaine murmurs, her eyes darting between mine.

Sighing, I dare to release her neck and hold one of her hands. "I did," I breathe out. She fights me, but I slowly move her hand to my cheek to excite those nerves again. My eyes roll closed as I relish how my body reacts to her. "It didn't stick."

Gaine slides her fingers over my skin, and I release my pressure on her hand. She pushes my hair away from my eyes, making me open them to see her studying me. "You can't be here," she pleads. "It's my sister's birthday. That's my father with us. He'll kill you, Kade."

"Nah," I whisper, smiling. "Everyone loves me. I should wish her a happy birthday."

Sighing, Gaine leans forward to put her face in her hands. I slide my arms around her, and when she leans against me, her forehead rests on my lips. This is the comfort I felt when I held Ari, but there is a beautiful perfection mixed in that could only result from my mate being the woman in my arms.

I kiss her forehead before tucking her under my chin and licking my lips. The fire's flavor is strong, but I still detect a hint of her strawberry soap. Although I would love another taste, I don't want Gaine to leave my protective embrace. Nothing will harm her when she's this close to me. I will die to keep her safe.

"You alright, Gaine?" the man by the fire yells.

My arms tighten around her, not wanting her to leave me. Gaine leans back to look into my eyes. Her gaze is different this time, and I never want to see it again. "What's wrong?" I ask, cupping her cheeks.

"Not here, please, Kade," she says, shaking her head. "He's not bound by the same laws. He's been exiled. Please go."

I wipe her tears with my thumbs. "I won't leave you again," I whisper. "I can't stand how it feels when you're gone."

"Gaine?" the man calls again, closer this time.

My growl builds quickly as I pull her back to me and peek around the tree.

"Kade," Gaine whispers, staying within my grip but reaching for my face. Her finger slides over my lower lip and gently pulls at it, demanding my attention. "Will you meet me at my house?"

Instantly forgetting about our intruder, I look down and open my mouth. My growl settles into a hum when she gives me the tip of her finger to taste. I catch her hand and slowly slide my tongue over her knuckle. "You did that on purpose," I murmur, sliding a second finger into my mouth.

"I'm just having trouble with my buckle, Dad," Gaine yells. "I'll be right out." She pulls her fingers away from me, making me frown. "Follow the fence to the woods behind our cottage," she whispers. "There's a creek that crosses the meadow. I'll meet you where it enters the forest."

"I'll go help her, Dad," the younger girl calls out.

"Please, Kade," Gaine pleads. "Don't go near the house. There's a ward."

No matter how determined I am to hold onto her, Gaine keeps slipping from my grip. She sidesteps and is gone before I have a chance to react. My arms miss her, and my taste buds still tingle with joy, having finally enjoyed her flavor. I push off the tree and walk toward the gelding, rubbing my fingers over my lower lip where she'd pulled it.

"Who's that?" the young girl asks, returning me to reality.

Cringing, I drop behind a thinner tree. It takes a few deep breaths to stop my hum. I've never heard it before. I assume I did it as a baby or a very young child, but I've had no reason to hum as an adult. It's something outside of our control that our bodies usually do when we are happy or experience an incredibly pleasurable feeling. *I should've known Gaine could trigger it.*

"No one," Gaine responds, making me scowl.

"It looked like a boy," the younger girl chimes playfully.

Gaine scoffs. "What would I be doing with a boy?"

Smiling, I restart my journey back to my horse. I'm walking away from her, but my core still feels like I'm going in the right direction.

* * *

Two days later, when I crouch to pull my jacket from his saddlebags, the horse stares angrily at me. He hasn't appreciated being tied to a tree while we wait for Gaine. I tested the ward as soon as I arrived. I don't know what it's a ward against, but I can't cross it. My face is probably bruised from how hard I hit it.

The small family arrived home last night. My heart thumped a blinding beat through Gaine's aura as she walked from the barn to their cottage. I had stayed away from the edge of the woods, but she must have seen me since she stopped to look in my direction before the younger girl asked what she was staring at. I spent the night wanting to hold her while she slept.

As the sun rises on this new day, I can only hope my wait is over. I throw the horse's gear over his back and pull the cinch tight. He snorts at me as his saddlebags follow. Moving to the gelding's far side, I secure those leathers and hear a stick snap nearby.

"It's just me," Gaine murmurs when I reach back for my knife.

I breathe a small laugh. "Just you?" I whisper, turning to face her. "You will never be a 'just me.'"

"Were you leaving?" she asks, looking over the horse before fixing her eyes on me.

"We are," I tell her, smiling as I step forward.

Gaine backs away, putting her hand up to stop me. "Kade, I'm not going anywhere with you," she states firmly.

Surprised, I stop and narrow my eyes. "What happened?" I ask, reaching for her. "I'm only here because you asked me to meet you."

"Kade, you've seen my world," Gaine says quietly. "You've seen my pack. We have love and laughter. There's a kindness to the support we give each other." She rolls her eyes upward and blinks a few times. "I can't let you destroy that."

"How do you know I'll break it?" I ask, wishing I'd chosen Rooster's path. "Maybe I would make it stronger or protect it."

Gaine crouches against a tree and puts her head in her hands. "And who would you kill to make that happen?"

"I've never hidden who I am, but I am more than my reputation,

Gaine," I scoff, searching my life for anything I could use as an example since helping the weekdays would probably be inappropriate. "I protected a girl until she was allowed to bond with her mate."

When Gaine looks up, her face shines from tears, making my chest ache. "Who died for that?"

Torn, I can't decide whether to hold her or run away. I would never answer that with any form of honesty. Admitting that I killed Ari's entire family doesn't exactly provide proof that I'd fit into Gaine's beautiful world.

"I won't hurt you," I whisper, kneeling before her. "You will always be safe with me."

"I would be exiled for being with you, Kade," Gaine says, leaning away from me. "I could never be safe with you. You're the butcher of the Blood Pack!" Her voice rises from emotions as she speaks. Her chin trembles, and I hate myself for causing these fresh tears.

Sighing, I stand and return to the horse. "Why am I here, Gaine?"

"I don't know," she sobs.

I swing up into the saddle. "Then come with me," I say, reaching down to her. "Let's forget about the Lunar and Blood Packs and just be Gaine and Kade for a minute."

Gaine stares at me as she recovers from her crying. Her breath hitches a few times, but her eyes remain locked on my hand. The horse dances and tosses his head when I lean onto his neck to get closer to Gaine. She rubs her hand over her jeans, looking like she might reach out to me.

"Gaine? Is that you?" the young girl who always seems to interrupt us calls out. "Did you find a new horse?"

Startled, Gaine jumps to her feet and freezes with wide eyes. The horse continues his dance, but I smile and reach out to my mate again. "Am I meeting the family, or will you take this chance with me?"

After throwing a desperate glance at the young girl, Gaine

lunges at my waist and flings herself onto the horse's back behind me. I doubt this young gelding has ever had two people on his back because he takes off like a bullet through the trees. It's not long before we've cleared the open meadow and slipped beside more cattle fields, turning the cottage into a distant memory.

When I slow the horse to walk along the barbed-wire fence, Gaine settles her legs over my saddlebags and presses her body against me. I lean back slightly as she sets her chin on my shoulder and brushes her cheek against mine. I've never paid much attention to such simple actions, but Gaine's touch is beyond anything I've ever experienced.

"You better not make me regret this," she whispers, slipping her hands into my coat.

Groaning through my teeth, I rub my lips over her cheek. "No promises," I growl before kicking the horse and sending him galloping south.

* * *

We spend a day creating distance between the packs and us. Although the silence was painful, I gave Gaine the second day to get used to my company. As the sun sets on our quiet day, I stop the exhausted horse and turn to watch Gaine slide from his back.

"We should stop for the night," I say, swinging from the saddle. "He could use a break." I pat the horse's neck before sliding my fingers under Gaine's arm. I frown when she shies away before I can hook her fingers.

Gaine shivers, pulling her plaid button-up shirt snugly against her chest. "Are you gonna tell me where we're going?" she asks, looking around the small clearing.

"And ruin the surprise?" I reply, grinning. "Not a chance." I rub my hands over her arms before pulling my jacket off to throw it over her shoulders. "I smell a buck. Why don't you see to a fire, and I'll go grab us some dinner?"

"A buck?" she scoffs quizzically. "You can tell the difference?"

I lift my eyebrow. "Can't you?"

Gaine has studied me curiously every time we stopped for the past few days. I don't know what she's looking for, but I assume she's not finding it since it's a continued behavior. When I pull my shirt over my head, her eyes cut through my skin as they slide over my body.

"What are you doing?" Gaine asks, turning away as her cheeks flush.

"Shifting," I answer, tying the rope holding the proximity ward around my neck. "You wanna come with me?"

Gaine cautiously shakes her head. "I can't," she whispers.

Sighing, I reach for her and smile when she lets me pull her into my arms. "I'd like to feed you, Gaine," I say, tucking close to her neck. "If you feel compelled to take off, take my jacket. I wouldn't want you to get cold."

Gaine's soft giggle is a beautiful song that hits my heart like a punch to the chest. I am glad she didn't respond because I might have missed her stomach rumbling if I had been distracted by her words.

"I'll be right back," I whisper, kissing her forehead.

I can't remember anyone ever watching me change into my wolf. It's not generally something we share with others. But I step back from Gaine and pull my pants and boots off to shift before her.

Some older wolves don't shift often and say it's painful. I'd call it "uncomfortable." For me, the hardest part would be my muzzle, but that is only because I'm blinded as it extends or retracts. I can handle anything if I can see what is happening around me. I don't like that I lost sight of my beautiful mate's eyes this time.

Once I've completed my shift, I shake my fur out and step toward

Gaine. She lowers to one knee and reaches for my chin. I have never let anyone put their hands on my wolf. Her touch is foreign, yet pure. She slips her fingers through my fur and allows me to rub my muzzle over her cheek. I pull away and tuck my chin, embarrassed when my hum starts.

Gaine continues to study me, reaching for my jaw. "Kade," she whispers, tucking her other leg. "You're beautiful."

"You're not so bad yourself," I say, wishing she could hear me.

"We have a few black wolves in our pack, but I have never seen their coats shine like this," Gaine tells me, running her hands down my legs.

While she's distracted, I slide my nose over her jaw and bury it in her hair on my way to her neck. She's still focused on my fur when I roll my head to nip at her earlobe. It's not until I taste her skin that she remembers who she's admiring.

"Stop, Kade," Gaine says, clicking her tongue. "We might be away from the packs, but that doesn't change who we are." She reaches up the sleeve of my coat to rub her pack marking.

"I would wear that mark if I could," I profess to deaf ears. I bump my nose against hers and rub my whiskers over her cheek before backing away.

Gaine sits back on her heels and tilts her head. "Can you even see out those eyes?"

I pull back, confused. *"What?"*

"They're silver," Gaine says, squinting as she stares at my eyes.

"They're blue," I huff, shoving her over with my paw and leaving to track down the meal I'd promised her.

5

When I return with the buck, I find Gaine has built a cozy fire for us. She quietly sings while looking over the collection of knives I keep in my jacket. I watch her through a bush for a moment, but when she rubs my coat's collar over her lips, my hum starts, giving away my position.

I want to feel Gaine's touch over my skin, ride with her, and hold her while she sleeps, but I decide not to shift back after seeing that. In many ways, she's right about me. I'm an asshole. I've killed more people than I've been kind to, and I never say the right thing around her. We come from two different worlds. But Gaine seems more willing to talk to me when I can't respond.

My plan is still working when we end the fifth day beside a large lake that I use to mark the Tenns Territory. We're further west than we need to be, but I like fishing in this lake and hope to convince Gaine to join me. We haven't stopped for long enough to clean up, and if I were being honest, I really want to watch her bathe.

Having been to this lake often, I know the shallow area is short, and there's considerable depth at the drop-off. I wait for Gaine to dismount before stepping into the water. She follows me but hesitates on the bank. I turn back and gently tug on Gaine's hand, asking her to join me.

"I can't go swimming, Kade," Gaine says, shaking her head. "It's cold, and I don't want to be stuck with wet clothes."

I lift my paw to put it in her hand and push her shirt up with my nose.

"I can't," she whispers. "If I shift..." She winces and looks away, frowning.

"It's alright," I say, wanting to will my voice into her head. *"I understand."* I poke the pendant hanging from my neck with my nose.

Gaine drops my paw and turns back to the horse. Sighing, I walk into the water and step off the edge, letting the lake pull me into its depths. The fish swim past me like I was meant to be in their world. Although my pendant is solid, it has an air pocket in the center where a small cluster of herbs is held. It floats casually into my eyeline, reminding me I have the other Jax made for Ari.

Arms latch onto my chest, startling the air from my lungs and hauling me back toward the surface. My air bubbles make it impossible to see, but this has to be Gaine. No one else would even think about jumping into the lake after me. I pull at the water with my paws to help her.

Gaine coughs and chokes when we reach the surface. She keeps her arms around me while I pull her to dry land. I allow Gaine to use my fur as handles to pull herself onto the ledge of the drop-off. I nudge her, trying to keep her moving toward the bank, but she stops to catch her breath.

"Come on, baby," I murmur, rubbing my muzzle over her cheek. *"You gotta get out of the water."*

As wolves, our muscles are thick, and the friction they create helps to keep us warm and can quickly dry us off. As humans, our muscles are thinner and can't handle the work without fuel. She could dry herself and her clothes, but she'll need to get out of the water, and I'll have to feed her very soon. I nudge her again, but she remains on her hands and knees, coughing and gasping.

"Oh, you're not gonna like this," I grumble, triggering my shift back to my human form. I watched Tynan's super soldier, Bastian, shift a few times. That kid just thinks about it, and suddenly, he changes form. For the rest of us, it's a process. I've never wished I were someone else until this moment. Every reformed bone drains my soul and fills me with a foreign feeling that could only be fear.

Gaine doesn't even notice until I scoop her into my arms and carry her to shore against my chest. She tries to fight me, but her muscles tremble from the exertion of hauling me to the surface and the dropping temperature. She melts into me when I sit with my back against a tree and begin heating my body to help her dry off.

"I won't hurt you," I murmur against her forehead. "Save your energy."

It feels natural when Gaine lets me tuck her under my chin. She settles into my body and wraps her arms around me, absorbing my heat and creating her own to dry her clothes faster. I startle her when I lift my head to look around. The saddle is lying over a fallen tree, and my leather jacket was thrown on the ground, having not been involved in Gaine's act of heroism.

"Beautiful woman?" I start slowly, noticing a member of our party is missing. "Where is the horse?"

Gaine lifts her head to glance around. She groans and lays back against my chest. "I may have forgotten to tie him," she mumbles. "You were drowning."

I click my tongue. "Woman, I was not drowning," I scoff. "But we'll come back to that." I smile and shift her around so I can see her eyes. "You were trying to save me? That's so sweet. Does this mean you don't hate me anymore?"

Gaine takes a deep breath and narrows her eyes in thought. My noisy sigh is involuntary as she slides her finger over my jaw. "I could never hate you, Kade," she finally tells me. "I should. You deserve it. But my heart desires you, and that scares me."

Gaine's taken my breath away several times in the past few days, but this admission will never have an equal. In her vulnerable state, it would be easy to claim her. She would never enjoy another's touch again because of our bond. If she were any of the weekdays, I wouldn't care, but I want so much more from Gaine.

I tuck her back under my chin and hold her fingers to my lips. After nipping at her knuckles, I kiss her fingertips with a sigh. "I don't need to drown," I murmur, slouching to cradle more of her body against mine. "You'll break my heart with your words."

"You're too strong for that," Gaine whispers, tracing her fingers over my chest.

We lie together for longer than necessary to dry her clothes. I don't know if I'd give up my wolf for her because I'll need it shortly to feed her, but I would definitely give up mountain lion. Even though the thought of its delectable meat makes my mouth water, I would never taste it again if I could earn this woman's trust.

Gaine's stomach growls, pulling me away from my thoughts. "Let's build a fire, and then I'll grab us some catfish," I tell her, puffing my chest out to lift her away from me. Her drowsy gaze makes me smile. "You make exhausted look beautiful."

I enjoy the playful ease of her touch as she grins and smacks my shoulder. Gaine lifts off my lap and digs through the saddlebags while she shakes her head. She turns to face me once she finds my jeans.

Standing, I lean against the tree and fold my arms over my chest. I've never lacked confidence and couldn't care less about covering up, but Gaine looks incredibly uncomfortable when she holds out the clothing. Hoping to return her to the easygoing woman she was just moments ago, I accept the clothes offered while she pulls on my coat.

We silently work together to collect wood and start a fire. While Gaine makes a flameless base of embers, I find her some thin, flat rocks to cook the fish on. Once she is set with the fire's warmth and the proper tools for the fish, I shift and head back into the water.

* * *

I wake to low flames in the morning. My body began to shut down as I listened to Gaine's story about when her family moved to the lake to live with the Lunar Pack. While talking about her mother, she rolled to put her head on my shoulder, and I don't remember much after that.

I rub my hand over her back and roll to wrap around her. Gaine moans quietly and snuggles into my chest but doesn't wake. Her body has heated as we normally do when we sleep. Miles used to tell me never to trust a woman who wouldn't eat. He'd like Gaine. She knows how to fuel her body, and it quickly recuperated from her moment of weakness.

Gaine slipped from my jacket during the night but threw it over us as a blanket. I slide my hand up her arm and study the pack marking. It starts at her pinky knuckle and winds lazily up her arm. I push her shirt's collar to see if it loops over her shoulder. She wakes when I shift slightly, trying to find the end.

"What are you doing?" Gaine murmurs, licking her lips and capturing my full attention.

Lying back down to study her face, I smile at her peacefulness. "Trying to find a flaw in your perfection," I answer.

"Hm," she hums. "You are my greatest flaw."

I scowl. "Now you're just being mean."

Her drowsy giggle tells me she only said that to get a rise out of me. I let her snuggle back into my chest and look at the horizon. The sun is rising, but thick clouds stop it from reaching us.

"There's rain coming," I whisper, watching the clouds roll toward us. "Gaine, you're gonna have to shift."

She pushes herself upright and wipes her brown hair out of her face. "I can't," Gaine says, shaking her head. "Kade, I'm an elder. I can't let them find me."

I sit up with her and hold her cheek, stopping her from leaving my side. "An elder?" I ask, confused. "Aren't elders supposed to be old and, I don't know, grumpy?"

Gaine lifts her eyebrow. "Well, you have the grumpy part right."

"Can I kiss you before you turn old?" I ask, chuckling.

"Kade, this is serious," Gaine replies, rolling her eyes. "I'll never hear the end of it if they find me. And what about you?"

I roll onto my back and slip my hands under my head with a groan. "I don't care as long as I get my kiss," I say, winking. "You're all that matters."

"Kade?" she grumbles.

I sit up quickly and pull her to me by the back of her neck. I had only moved Gaine here as a playful act, but now that she's this close, I can't breathe. Tipping my chin, I touch my lower lip to hers, and the air trapped in my lungs rushes out. Gaine's eyes roll closed, her lips dragging over mine as she gets lost in the moment.

A strong breeze kicks up, brushing my hair across Gaine's face. She pushes her forehead against mine before I can capture her lips. I whine, but she just frowns at me.

"I'm the Seer, Kade," Gaine tells me. "Even if the Luna doesn't hear me, the rest of the pack would. The bachelors are always after me to help them find their mate." She sits back to rub her hands over her forehead.

"I can't say I blame them," I say thoughtfully. "Hang on. Is that how you knew who I was?"

"Kade," she starts, smiling as she peers through her fingers. "Can you focus for just a moment?"

"I am focused," I say, grinning. I pull her back to me and rub my lips over her face, intentionally staying away from her mouth. "Do you trust me?"

Gaine's breathing becomes labored as she moves to keep my lips against her skin. I've never been more aware of someone's hands on my body. Although she leaves one on my chest, Gaine has slipped the other up my arm, and her nails are threatening to rip the skin on my neck as she holds me to her.

"No," she whispers hoarsely through raspy breaths.

Chuckling, I kiss her cheek. "Well, you should." I stand up, pulling out of her grip and digging through my saddlebags. "I have a little present." I produce the second proximity ward. "We won't be able to hear each other, but your pack won't hear you either."

Gaine cups the pendant in her hand curiously. "How does it work?"

"I suppose it's a lot like the ward at your house," I answer, shrugging. "Jax says the distance is roughly a quarter of a mile, so as long as we don't get near any Lunar Pack, you should be alright."

"Most of the distant wolves only know of me, not who I am," Gaine says, adjusting the rope necklace.

Taking a deep breath, I stand to slide my belt out of its loops. "I need to shift first so you can put this on me," I tell her, adjusting my blade's position.

Gaine slips the pendant's rope over her head and takes my belt. She narrows her eyes and then smiles. "Now I understand the black leather and blue blade," she says, laughing. "It blends in with your fur."

"It was Miles' idea," I say, smiling. "He gave me that blade when I turned nine." I stop and chew my lip as I study Gaine. "That was the spring before he died."

"He comes back every full moon," Gaine tells me, sitting on her heels.

"I miss him sometimes," I admit, untying the saddlebags from the saddle. Another gust blows through, and thunder rumbles in the distance. "We don't have time for memory lane. Come on, let's get going. I have a place where we can weather the storm."

We drop the saddlebags in a hollowed-out log, and Gaine watches me shift first so she can strap my blade to me. Her hands slide over my body, and her fingers dig into my fur. The belt is designed to fit in front of my left shoulder, go between my front legs, and loop behind my right elbow. The blade sits nearly between my legs but on my chest.

Gaine's hands inspect everywhere within reach, not just where the belt lies. She smiles when I tilt my head. "Our junior guards' caretaker is very particular about muscle build and diets," she explains. "You have an impeccable build on your wolf, Kade."

"It matches the rest of me," I say, licking her cheek.

Brushing her fingers over her face, Gaine shakes her head. "At least I can pretend you're taking me seriously when I can't hear you," she remarks, stepping back. "Turn around, Kade. I might be your mate, but this is not yours to see."

I pout as I move closer but turn away from her. Once lying down, I reach my back legs out, and Gaine does her best to touch them as much as possible as she undresses. Her intelligence settles me somehow as she makes sure to let me know she is there and safe even though I'm not allowed to see her.

When she completes her shift, Gaine moves before me. I'm unsure why she bothered to compliment my wolf. Gaine is stunning. Her brown fur fades to a mix of blonde and red at the tips, with some black at the neck. It's longer than most, and the pendant is hidden in her coat. Her ears are slightly rounded at the tip, reminding me of teddy bears.

I stand faster than I intend and accidentally scare Gaine into stepping back. Tucking my chin, I step forward slowly until I can easily touch her. My hum instantly starts as I slide my muzzle over her cheek and along her head. I continue down her neck and bury my nose in the fur over her shoulder blades. Gaine's hum is the sweetest sound I have ever heard when it starts as I playfully nip at her shoulders.

Mother Nature doesn't seem interested in letting me appreciate my mate's beauty. The wind hasn't let up much, and a close lightning strike urges us to move out toward the small farm across the lake. Gaine stays close to my shoulder while I'm horribly distracted, watching her soft fur roll with her skin as she jogs along, not paying me a bit of attention.

I lean over to try pulling her lip with my tongue, and she lifts her head out of my reach. Gaine stops suddenly, leaving me to trip over the limb she was avoiding and fall on my face. The string of obscenities running through my head would probably offend her, but when I look back, it's clear that Gaine is having a good laugh. I don't have to hear her. The joy in her expression is unmistakable.

Gaine pokes my muzzle a few times with her nose and shoves my shoulder with her paw as I stare at her. She's much more relaxed than she was in her human form. I sneak a lick of her jaw when she pokes my muzzle and chuckle at her attempt to nip me.

After that, I do my best to pay attention to the trail. It's raining hard when we make it to the farmhouse. The old woman who owns it doesn't like people much but has an affinity for animals. I'm unsure if she knows what I am, but she's always welcomed me to stay in her barn and will typically have a stew or roast that she's willing to share.

"Well, hello, Midnight," she calls excitedly in her raspy voice as I round the house to find her sitting on her porch swing. Gaine stops and slinks back behind the corner. "I haven't seen you in a spell."

I've always hated the name, but the old woman provides a safe place where I've been able to rest comfortably. She even doctored my paw when I cut it crossing a washed-out creek bed a few years ago. I probably could've prepared Gaine better about where we were headed, but she's distracting.

I circle back to nuzzle her cheek. *"It's okay, Gaine,"* I say, rubbing my whiskers over hers. *"No one will ever harm you."*

The old lady stands and shuffles across her porch to see around the corner. "Oh," she exclaims. "You brought a friend. Well, come on out here, sweetheart. Let me see you."

I swing my hips to allow the old lady to see Gaine better. I don't know the woman's name, but her soft spot for wolves has always made me chuckle. Gaine remains frozen until I lick her lip, pulling it up with my tongue. She nips at me for taking the kiss but then redirects her attention to the human.

"Aren't you a beauty?" the woman says, reaching her knuckles for Gaine to sniff. "It's okay. Any friend of Midnight's is a friend of mine. We'll have to come up with a name for you."

Chuckling, I nudge Gaine after the old lady as she leads us to the front door. *"I hope she picks something cute,"* I say, mouthing her ear. *"Like Buttons or Precious."*

The woman disappears into her house and returns with an umbrella and a delicious-smelling bag. My stomach growls, making her laugh as she leads us to her barn. It's a large building that had once been used to store hay. The air is musty, and the wind easily howls through, but the remaining hay offers natural insulation against the chill.

I wish I could hear Gaine when the old lady stiffly kneels to gush about my mate's beauty while emptying her bag. I wholeheartedly agree with everything she says. The woman talks about her fur and its shine. A few colors are mentioned, and she even comments on how clean Gaine appears while eyeing my muddy paws.

Plates and containers begin to line a low table on the dirt floor. The old lady's food includes different cooked and raw meat options. I can't help licking my lips when she produces a few strawberries.

"Beauty," the old woman whispers. "That's what we'll call you." She opens the final container to show us a few slices of pumpkin pie. "No cream for you," she adds, wagging her finger at me. "We wouldn't want you to get fat."

Gaine's face instantly switches from apprehensive to the joyful expression of a wolf laughing at my expense. Our host picked the perfect "pet" name for her. I step closer to my mate, not caring that I've put my body within the old woman's reach. Twisting my head, I rub the top of my muzzle over her whiskers and along her cheek. My hum starts when she gently mouths my ear.

"Huh?" the old woman says, surprised. "What's that sound?" She rubs her hand over my shoulder and nearly bumps into my belt.

I jump away from her and shove Gaine back, putting myself between the women.

"Easy, Midnight," she says soothingly. "I didn't mean any harm."

The old lady has never made me think she was a threat, but I still lift my lips instinctively when she stands. A wolf wouldn't carry a blade, and she was only inches away from discovering mine. I back and curl my body protectively around Gaine.

"Alright, then," the woman says, sighing. "I'll leave you to it. That should be enough for both of you." She lifts her umbrella and retreats to the doorway before turning back. "I'd like to meet the kids one day, so don't be strangers." She slides the door nearly closed, leaving it cracked for us to slip through when we leave.

In the dark, Gaine's tips look like white fire. *She just keeps getting more beautiful.* She quickly turns her attention to the short table. It's been a while since I've had duck, so the de-feathered, raw carcass catches my attention. I pull a few strips of meat before nudging it toward Gaine to share. She shakes her head when she sees me licking and taking tiny tastes of the strawberries.

I love to watch this woman do everything. I'm unsure if it's because she's my mate or if she is as beautiful as I think, but she does everything perfectly. She cups a chicken breast in her paws to pull at the thickest meat, and I close my eyes to picture her fingers tangling in my hair as she tastes my lips.

Gaine hums as she rubs her whiskers over mine, but my eyes don't open until she licks my lip. I had women in my bed for years— every night, someone new. *Who cares what their names were?* But gone are the days that anyone else will excite me anywhere near the level of this woman kissing me. Now, my fantasies about her will be filled with feeling her lips on mine for the first time.

Stuck in a childish euphoria from her kiss, I hum the rest of the way through our meal. I really want some of the pie, but I can't stop watching her slowly lick the filling before eating the crust. She tries to push the second piece before me, but I shake my head and nudge it back with my nose.

Once the plates and bowls are emptied, I take her to a back corner of the barn where the old lady had laid out blankets for me to use when I visit. We climb over the hay and pull the blanket around to create a bowl shape. Gaine tucks her hips and curls into a ball. She pats the bottom of the bowl, urging me to lie with her.

I carefully move my paws around her legs and gently lay on her feet when she extends them. I'm fixed on her beautiful face when she sweetly cleans my muzzle, freeing it of bits of meat and juices from our meal. My chest swells as I take deep breaths, not wanting to forget a single detail of this moment. Her scent, the sound of her hum, the gentleness of her touch, and the way she's looking at me.

I roll slightly to my side and place my front leg over her shoulder, inviting her to lie down. With one final pull at my lip, Gaine tucks her nose under my chest beside the blade. Her deep, comfortable sigh is a thing of beauty. I lay my chin over her neck, scanning the area around us.

"I will keep you safe," I profess, wanting her to hear me more than anything. *"You are mine."*

6

⟨❦⟩

At the risk of missing the festival, I slow down for the last two days of our trip. It's easy to enjoy Gaine's company, and figuring out each other's signals has been fun. When traveling alone, I only stop once every two or three days. With Gaine, my desire to cuddle up is much stronger than the need to keep moving. I tuck into my chest and wake my beautiful mate at sunrise the last morning of our trip by licking her ear.

The more time we spend together, the more I understand what Rooster said. It doesn't matter what I have planned for today when Gaine yawns and gently licks my jaw. She sleepily rubs her whiskers over mine before tucking back into my chest. I'll force them to have a second festival if we miss it. I lay my chin back on her shoulder and try to recall the last time my hum was silent.

I suppose we could've laid there all day, but we're not far from Humble, and my timing could not have been more perfect. Music begins filtering in our direction a few hours after sunrise. Gaine is startled awake but quickly calms when she sees I'm not concerned.

As my beautiful mate settles into our morning routine of stretches and shaking the dirt and leaves out of our coats, I note the chimneys sending smoke into the air. We'll need clothes, and since it's a sunny day, we should find clothing hanging on lines

64

somewhere. It's the first time Gaine's looked nervous since the old lady's barn, but she seems to trust me enough to follow me toward the closest chimney.

Finding a line with acceptable clothing and a blanket to steal takes a while. After shifting, I stand guard over Gaine while she picks her clothes. She looks stunning in the long, flowy dress she chose. I don't do her justice in my jeans and flannel shirt.

"What is this, Kade," Gaine asks, draping the blanket over her shoulders to hide her pack marking.

"This is where I was taking you," I say, winking. "I can't take credit for our impeccable timing, though. That was sheer luck."

Gaine giggles as I put my arm around her, leading the way along the edge of town. "I smell popping corn," she remarks, smiling. "It's been a long time since I've had that."

"Then I shall be sure you get some," I announce.

We weave around some cottages before coming to the edge of the field, where the humans are readying their kites. I slip my hand into the blanket and link our arms to aim Gaine toward a small fire pit where an older man is popping corn. Her eyes stay fixed on the children tying strings to their kites as I dig a small piece of silver from the side of my knife's sheath.

"Kade," Gaine quietly gushes. Her smile was worth the trip. "What are they doing?"

I usher her away from the people and point to a cluster of trees in a secluded area. "It's a kite-flying festival," I tell her. "They gather in this field every fall to fly their colorful kites. With this breeze, I suspect we'll have a good show."

It's warm in the sun at the edge of the trees where we lay out the blanket. I give Gaine the flannel shirt to keep her mark covered and lie with my head in her lap. She happily describes the kites to me as I stare at her. Gaine's smile could brighten the darkest night, and there is no sound sweeter than her hum as she excitedly watches the children play with their flying contraptions.

For as long as I can remember, the older wolves have told me everything happens for a reason. We've had horrible weather and lost our horse, which I'll have to find a way to pay for. We spent more time as wolves than I would have liked, but that time helped Gaine become comfortable with me.

"Do I have something on my face?" Gaine asks, pulling me from my thoughts. She wipes her mouth a few times as I smile at her. "What?"

"They really undersold this whole mate thing," I say, laughing.

"Well, the bachelors don't pester me for nothing," Gaine grumbles. She grins, holding a piece of popped corn just out of my mouth's reach. "You're not what I expected."

I latch onto her wrist and pull her hand to me. When I take the popped corn, she lets me draw a few of her fingers into my mouth. There is a trace of butter on them.

"What were you expecting?" I ask, raising my eyebrow.

Gaine pulls her fingers from my grip and leans back on her hand, thoughtfully studying the kids' kites. "I've known about you for a while," she starts, sighing. "When we would meet new wolves, I listened to the tales of their travels. We just lived by the river, so I found other regions interesting."

Groaning, I close my eyes. "I probably don't want to hear this, do I?"

"The women all said you were beautiful," Gaine reports, giggling. "It was the rest of their claims that scared me." She tickles my forehead with a leaf, making me open my eyes. "The wolf they told me about would've killed that old lady."

I have enjoyed all of Gaine's attention during this trip. However, her gaze as she studies me, looking for any sign of those stories, would have to be my favorite. I realize that all the women I've been with have only wanted to share my power. The idea that others would be too afraid to argue with them must have been appealing.

Gaine fears the power my reputation creates. Her curious expression means she doesn't see any hint of why she was afraid of me. I would ruin this moment with my words, so I quietly smile as I trace her jaw with my finger.

A shotgun blast reminds us we're not alone. Startled, we quickly turn to see the children dart across the field with their kites in tow. I sit up as they take flight. The spectators clap and cheer for the children until they stop, and everyone turns their attention to the kites soaring above us.

I focus back on Gaine. She smiles brightly and points to the vibrantly decorated paper and cloth kites. The popped corn spills in her excitement as she reaches for my arm, wanting me to look at one of them.

"Kade, you're missing it," Gaine says when she catches me staring at her. "Look at the big balloon!"

She points to the colorful balloon filling up with hot air. I read that they used to ride in hot air balloons in the old days, but this one is tethered to the ground and just for show. It's designed as a patchwork quilt shaped like a teddy bear and looks like it took a long time to make. It also reminds me of Gaine's wolf.

I move behind my mate and pull her to my chest. Her joy is contagious as the people in the field move from the kids' kites to the adult-made fliers. Their designs are more extravagant, and I enjoy the long, colorful tails that they've given them. Gaine explains why some are easier to fly while others can make loops and swirling tricks.

I'm not paying her words the proper amount of attention. I hadn't known what I asked of Gaine when I suggested we just be Kade and Gaine for a while. If I could erase our lives and carve a small space in this world for us to start over, I would do it in a heartbeat. I like that I can glare at someone to convince them to leave me alone, but she makes me want to abandon that life.

Gaine cups my cheek, pulling my attention away from everything else. I look down into her eyes and smile. My gaze travels to her lips as she licks them. The pressure in my chest takes over, and I hold her chin with my fingers to guide her lips to mine. Our hums harmonize as our tongues meet. My fantasy couldn't even compare to the perfection that is Gaine's kiss.

Before I'm ready to stop enjoying her taste, someone begins singing along with a guitar, and Gaine pulls away from me, blushing. She tries to create distance between us, but I'm not ready to end this experience.

The music is loud but slow, and a few couples are dancing to it across the field. One of the strangest things Miles taught me was how to dance. He said any kid he trained would know how to handle a woman just as well as a blade. My mother practiced with me when I was younger, and as she got older, it was just something we did together. I've never been more thankful.

Standing, I reach my hand out to Gaine. "Join me," I say, smiling.

"Kade, we can't dance," she responds, shaking her head and glancing toward the field.

"Do you trust me?" I ask, desperately hoping the answer has changed.

Gaine cringes slightly, still watching the field. "No."

"Well, I'll just stop asking since there's a strong possibility of you continuing to reject me," I say, pulling her off the ground and into my arms.

Smiling, I softly guide her deeper into the trees to hide us from the humans. Once out of their view, Gaine allows me to extend her left arm and gently spin her. When she lands against me, she's more relaxed. The music speeds up, but I hum a slower rhythm for us to dance to and lead her between the trees.

We sway to my humming, staying within the shelter of the trees for hours. I slow our tempo when Gaine rests her head on my chest. She lines her legs with mine to easily follow along. My hum rumbles quietly the entire time, and I smile when Gaine's restarts as she nuzzles her face into my neck.

I'm unsure when the music ended, but it's dark and quiet when we stop dancing. Grabbing the blanket, I lead Gaine just inside the barrier of the grove and sit, leaning against a tree. She settles between my legs and rests her head on my chest, letting me drape my arms around her. A large bonfire is lit in the middle of the field, and the adults are readying white kites to dance against the night sky.

The festival will end at the close of the day, and I'll need to bring Gaine home. I can't keep her out here forever, and my pack won't be safe from Tynan if I stay away too long. I look down at Gaine as she studies the events in the field. I hate the thought of leaving her side again.

"Why was your father exiled?" I ask, wondering what it would take to get thrown out of the Lunar Pack.

Sighing deeply, Gaine rubs my arms. When she reaches my hands, I lift my fingers and experience a childish excitement when she threads hers with mine. There's a quiet moan that escapes my throat as I tighten my grip on her. Simple touches have never excited me, but Gaine is an experience that could only be labeled as perfection.

"My father received his gift when I was about ten," she starts. "The current Historian had died, and the abilities were passed to my father and aunt as the only related elders. The gifts work together and are passed to an elder's children—siblings. One is a historian, while the other is a seer. That was when we moved to the lake."

"Do you have to live at the lake as the Seer?"

"No," Gaine answers. "We have to be near the Luna. We are her aids."

"Wait," I say, squinting in thought. "You said it has to be siblings."

"I did," she responds, sighing. "My mother was not an elder and didn't like that she had to follow the elders' rules. She wanted status, and what better way to elevate your standing than by bringing forth the next Alpha? My mother manipulated my father into thinking she would be above the elder restrictions, so he commissioned a potion for her.

"She quickly became pregnant, and the Luna was furious. Everyone waited to see what would happen. At the end of her term, we thought they had defied the odds and beaten the rule imposed on all elders. But my mother died giving birth to my dead brother. As she exhaled for the last time, my eleven-year-old sister and I were flooded with our gifts and later learned that our aunt had suddenly passed at the same moment as my mother."

"That's a steep price," I whisper, remembering the death of my parents. "I'm sorry."

"At the age of eleven, all of the history and violence scared my sister so much that she had to be drugged by our witch to stop her from hurting herself," Gaine continues. "The Luna depended on her Historian to provide information on the past so that she could use it to make better decisions for our future."

I rest my chin on Gaine's head. "She exiled him for inconveniencing her?"

"It's more than that, Kade," Gaine says, turning her head to rub her cheek over my chest. "He knowingly broke a magical law for personal gain. He put the pack at risk to elevate his position." She pauses and squeezes my fingers. "He also took an action that caused the death of two wolves. Because of my sister's age, he is allowed to live near the pack. Once she's old enough, he will be forced to leave pack land forever."

Now I understand why she hesitated. Gaine avoided the part that would mention why I'd never be welcomed into the pack. The

Luna would look into my past, and I would be denied or removed, stripped of my mate since she must remain with her leader. But even that couldn't convince me to ask her to be a part of my pack. Tynan would never stand for his enforcer being preoccupied.

There are no words for this moment. I tighten my arms around Gaine and lay my cheek on her head. We sigh, melting into each other. Gaine curls her legs and rolls to her side. I can't bring myself to loosen my grip on her even when she wraps her arms around my waist.

We quietly watch the white kites floating in the warm air of the bonfire. With their long flowing ribbons and tails, they resemble angels and ghosts. A man talks loudly and seems to be telling a story as the kites dance. If we hadn't just introduced the thought of never being able to be together, we might have moved closer to hear his tale.

* * *

I don't remember falling asleep, but Gaine is gone when I wake. It takes a moment to remember where I am. The field is empty, with only a charred pile of wood in the center remaining as a reminder of yesterday's event. Gaine's scent is still overwhelming. Her dress lays on my lap while the shirt covers my chest.

Staying awake each night to watch over her has done this to me. Gaine should've never been able to slip from my arms. I hold the shirt to my face and take a deep breath before I look around, hoping for any sign of the direction she took. The pendant isn't here, so she still has it. She won't be able to ask for help if she finds danger.

I stand and shove the pants over my hips. My belt won't fit right, but I need to find my beautiful mate. I trigger my shift, watching my surroundings as best as possible until my muzzle forms. Once completed, I shake my fur out and chew at the belt, trying to adjust it so it won't cut into my skin.

Gaine's scent trail is easier to detect as a wolf. I follow it back in the direction we'd come from. She cut in closer to town, probably trying to throw me off, but she picked up speed once she cleared the last house. The tracks I find are spread out in a longer stride than I've seen her do during our travels.

It's been a few days since I've eaten anything besides the pieces of popped corn Gaine fed me, so my muscles complain as I dart through the brush. Charging forward as fast as I can, I continuously gain ground on her but still haven't reached her by midday.

I slow my pace when I notice the sounds of civilization. Angry men's voices filter in, and I hear a few mention officers' ranks. I growl and shake my head, hoping Gaine is still far ahead of me.

"It's one of them!" a man shouts, making me slide to a stop.

I look around but don't see anyone.

"Get it!" another yells. "There it goes!"

A whip cracks, and horses begin thundering through the woods. Harness chains and a heavy wagon rattle over firm ground ahead of me. *I was that close.*

Sighing, I race forward until I'm parallel to the wagon. It's traveling on a road that Gaine must be using either as a clear straightaway to build speed or because she doesn't know where she is. Either way, they've spotted her and won't let her leave their sight.

I move closer to the humans for a head count. There are four in the wagon with the driver and three more on horseback, all heavily armed with pistols and shotguns. My belt digs into my shoulder as I launch over a fallen tree, trying to keep up. They have the advantage of a clear road, so I'm falling behind.

The scream that follows a rifle's shot knocks the wind from my lungs. I try to stop to get my bearings but end up falling on my face in my panic. The men whoop excitedly, and another horse charges around the wagon to catch up with the rest. The hooves stop not far up the trail, and the men happily congratulate each other.

I had hoped to pull their attention away from Gaine so she'd have the chance to escape. That doesn't seem possible now. Forcing my paws under me, I move closer to check on Gaine. The men on horseback stand guard while the wagon's men move around my downed mate. I know the shot hit her somehow, and she's in pain, but the sight of her ribs rapidly rising brings forth a wave of relief.

When they lift her by her legs, Gaine screams once more, but this time, I'm better prepared for it. Blood drips from her back leg, and it looks as though the shot went straight through. There are too many men and guns for me to try to take them on directly, so while they are preoccupied, I move to a clear area and look up the road.

"There's a base in Union City," a man says. "Let's take her up there. They'll pay for her."

Union City is just inside the Tenns Territory, further east than the lake where we stopped. This road is headed in that direction, so with this knowledge, I turn north and dart through the woods. Once I've cleared them, I use the road to travel faster. It's free of debris and smooth without ruts or holes. If I had a wagon, I'd be happy.

I slow to take in my surroundings again. Gaine's scream is clouding my thoughts, but once I look beyond the edge of the woods, I notice the limbs and downed trees that have previously been pulled off the road. I step into the bushes and trigger my shift.

The moment I'm able, I begin pulling the limbs aside to find the thickest tree I can drag. The horses could easily jump it, but they'll need to remove it to get the wagon past. Against nine armed men, I'd never survive a fight in the open, but I'm betting they've never experienced anything like me.

Once the tree is set, I loop my belt around my waist and sink back into the woods to wait. I note each log and rock in the area, which I can use as perches, allowing easier access to the riders. With my plan set, I fix my gaze on the road, turning every movement into a horse in my mind.

Each passing second is excruciating. My emotional breakdown bottoms out when I begin fearing that I've set this up in the wrong direction or on a road that they aren't using. My stomach growls, and I want to punch it for interrupting my panic attack. As I near the end of my patience, hoofbeats finally reach my ears.

I sigh in relief before moving into position, hiding where the lead horses should end up when the wagon stops. A long stump lines a thicker tree, giving me perfect cover for the first strike. I'm unsure how I'll take the rest of them out, but the first will be silent and unnoticed. The clopping hooves come closer until someone yells about my log, quickly followed by the idea that they should scout ahead and check the trees along the road.

Perfect.

The single soldier comes toward me and pauses once he rounds the slight bend that hides us from the rest of his group. The moment the horse is close enough, I jump onto its back, slicing the man's throat and pulling him from the saddle. The horse kicks at us and shoots forward, away from the rest of their group.

I drag the body from the road and crouch as I slink back toward the men, looking for the other riders who were scouting the woods for anyone who might be attacking them. The second man had dismounted and died while relieving himself. *Two more.*

Moving closer to the road, I see a few wagon riders working together to move the log. One is still sitting with Gaine, and the last is holding the fussy harness horses. I dart across the road unnoticed while the men are busy and silently search for the remaining two riders.

My prey doesn't surprise me often, but I'm unsure how to proceed when I find them. Admittedly, I've always liked watching the girls together when I had a few at once. Castor had told me that sometimes human men prefer the company of other men, but I thought he was pulling my leg. I see he wasn't as I stand watching these two men passionately kiss how I only dream of doing with Gaine.

Shrugging, I step forward and twist my arm around one neck while stabbing the other to slice the artery. The man I grabbed tries to yell for help while clawing at my arm but barely gets a gasp out before I wrench his neck, severing his head's connection to his body. I quietly lay him down and remove his boots while glancing toward the road. I pull his jeans free before I hear the tree moving out of the wagon's way.

Jumping into the pants, I move toward the wagon to see which side the tree is being dragged. They are moving it to the opposite side from where I'm standing, but the man in the wagon with Gaine is right before me. I reach up and slice his throat, pulling him back with me and laying him just inside the woods.

"Where the hell is everyone?" one of the men working with the fallen tree asks.

"Y'all get out here!" the driver yells.

But no one comes. They remain silent, taking in their surroundings. I slip toward the front, finding a small rock along the way. I toss it at the wagon, and its muted thump catches everyone's attention. Both tree movers walk back along the horses' sides, and the driver turns to discover that the man he left with Gaine is gone.

I step out and slit the throat of the man holding the horses. This could have gone better, and I instantly regret taking out the holder as the horses rear up at me. The driver flails around, trying to regain control of the horses, but I've just sprayed them with human blood. That will not be happening.

I jump out of the way as they dash forward, nearly running me over. I resign to allow the remaining two men on the ground to survive this day and latch onto the wagon's side as it goes by. The driver stands and lifts a rifle, getting off one shot before I pull myself up to stab his midsection a few times. I quickly finish him off when he doubles over to give me easy access to his neck.

He falls into the back of the wagon with Gaine as I climb over the driver's seat to gather the reins. The leathers crack against the horses' backs as I yell to urge them on. It will be a long ride to the one person in this area that I can think of to help.

The sun rises as I push the stumbling horses to gallop into the old lady's front yard. I'd stopped only to throw the driver's body out and saw Gaine's ribs moving. I attempted to check her wound but abandoned my effort when she screamed, trying to move away from me. The road I finally found that would take us in the right direction was narrow and had horrible footing. I'm relieved the horses remained upright for the trip.

I pull them up in front of the large barn the old woman had let me use for years and jump off the wagon. Gaine doesn't open her eyes as I scoop her into my arms. I shove the barn door with my back and carry her to the bowl we'd created in the hay. Since she's unconscious, I finally get to take a look at her injury.

"What are you doing here?" the old woman growls behind me, cocking her rifle.

I put my hands out before me. "Please, old lady," I say quietly, turning to face her. "I brought her to you for help."

The woman's eyes travel over me, taking in my blood-soaked clothing. She looks down as I move to show her my mate. "What did you do to Beauty?" she shouts. "Get away from her!"

"Her name is Gaine, and she's my mate," I whisper. "She was shot. Can you help her?"

The old woman squints, studying my face. "Midnight?"

Sighing, I roll my eyes. "At the risk of offending you, I've never liked that name," I admit. "My name is Kade, but yes, I am the black wolf you have assisted in the past." I crouch beside Gaine's head and rub her ear. "Please. She's bleeding."

The old lady studies us before lowering her rifle. She crawls over the edge of the hay bowl and looks over Gaine's body. "Agatha is my name, young man," she mumbles. "Was it just the one shot?" She points to Gaine's back leg, which is coated in blood.

"Yeah," I answer, moving Gaine around so she can see the wound. "It looks like it went straight through."

"Alright," Agatha says, sitting back on her heels. "We'll need to clean it to see how much damage it did. She's lucky it was a hunting rifle and not a shotgun. This looks to be a clean wound." She stands to leave but turns back to me. "You weren't followed, were you?"

"I took care of most of them," I tell her before laying Gaine's head across my lap. "She has somehow become everything in my life. Please help her."

* * *

Agatha continuously tries to feed me, but I turn everything away for the next two days while I lay with Gaine. The old woman had cleaned her wound but left it open, saying it was better to let it drain and heal from the inside out. I'm not sure I believed her until Gaine started producing her own heat this morning, easing my fears.

I remove one of the blankets covering us as the barn door slides open. Agatha steps through, holding a few bags and an umbrella. The old woman has been patient with me as I've anxiously watched over Gaine.

"Whew," Agatha gushes, stamping out her muddy boots. "It's raining cats and dogs out there." She pulls the door closed behind her. "I know you prefer to leave it open, but it's really coming down."

I eye the old woman's bags as she approaches us. "Is that more medicine?"

"No, my black wolf," she answers, smiling sweetly. "This is a meal I made for your beautiful mate." Agatha produces a few jars of broth and some chicken breast sliced from the bone. She holds out a bowl with a crushing stone in it. "We'll make a paste with the chicken and broth. You both need to eat."

"I'm not hungry," I object, taking the bowl from her. "I'll do whatever we need to for Gaine, though."

"I came to check on you last night, Kade," Agatha says, lifting her eyebrow. "You didn't wake, but your body was emitting an incredible amount of heat." She places her hand on my arm, making me flinch. "I bet it takes a lot of energy to do that, which was why you were too tired to notice I was here. That can't be safe."

I narrow my eyes at her and tilt my head quizzically. "Why aren't you afraid of us?"

Agatha smiles and places a few pieces of chicken into the medicine bowl. "Some years ago, I was fishing on the big river with my husband," she explains. "It was the last trip we took before he passed. A rebel band came through and stole our fish—beat us both pretty good for not wanting to give them up."

"Hm," I huff. "I thought they only bothered us."

"Oh no," the old woman grumbles. "They take what they want, even from each other. Anyway, a family close by saw what happened and helped." She smiles, chuckling at the memory. "A little wolf came running into their house, quite proud of the fawn in his mouth. Oh, they tried to say he was their dog, but we never saw it again."

"So, you just guessed they were werewolves?" I ask, confused as to how someone would assume something like that.

"Ah, I would love to claim that much intelligence, but no," Agatha says, adding some broth to the chicken I'm pulverizing. "I was confused about why a wolf would bring meat and disappear.

Their son finally admitted a few days before we left that it was him and asked me to keep their secret." Smiling, she sighs noisily. "And I have until just now."

"We're not all good," I mumble, looking away.

Agatha brushes her fingers over my cheek before sliding her hand along Gaine's face. "Maybe not yet," she says. "But you did what was needed for your mate, and that's a step in the right direction."

"I'm not sure she'll see it that way," I reply, frowning. "I do appreciate your help, though." I pull the grinding stone from the bowl. "What are we doing with this?"

"Well, we're going to put a thin layer on her tongue and try to convince her to swallow it," Agatha answers. "If you'll help with her jaw, I'll paint her tongue, and we'll hope for the best."

We work together for a few hours "painting" Gaine's tongue until she has eaten an entire chicken breast. It is nowhere near the amount of food she needs, but it's a good start. I scowl at the turkey leg Agatha forces into my hand, but I can't argue with her logic. The woman would've made a great den mother for our orphaned wolves.

Having fed me as a wolf, Agatha knows the spices I like and combined them to convince me to eat the turkey leg. She laughs when she notices I'm chewing on the bone and produces a final container with a piece of her pumpkin pie. I sigh and look down at Gaine, wanting to share it with her.

"Did she like the pie?" the old woman asks quietly.

I smile and nod. "She did," I tell her. "I may have enjoyed watching her eat it more, though."

Agatha giggles, collecting the empty dishes. "She'll be well enough to enjoy some again soon."

"Why hasn't she woken?" I ask, returning to my overbearing, nervous ways.

"She lost a lot of blood," Agatha answers, pulling Gaine's lip to expose her light pink gums. "But she also had a bit of infection in there. The tar has drawn that out." She winces, wrinkling her nose. "I'm sorry to say that it'll affect her sense of taste for a while, though. Things will probably taste a little 'tar-ish' until it leaves her bloodstream."

Frowning, I slide my hand over Gaine's shoulder. "She licked the pie filling out before eating the crust," I say for some reason, but then smile crookedly at Agatha. "I've never wanted to be food so badly in my life."

The old woman laughs heartily as she places a fork in the pie container. "I don't think you two are on the same page yet, but you're reading the same book," she says thoughtfully. "Maybe you should ask her what chapter she's on. That might help you catch up."

Agatha scoops a small amount of pie with her finger and works it into my mate's mouth. We smile broadly when Gaine slides her tongue out to lap up the rest of the filling on her finger. Although her eyes don't open, my beautiful mate's sigh as she works her jaw is enough to ease my heart of its desire to see improvement.

"Why don't you two get some rest?" Agatha suggests. "Let your bodies enjoy that food. I'll wake you in a few hours for another meal." She smiles and helps me tuck around Gaine before covering us with the blankets.

I've never had a reason to lie with a wolf, but everything with my mate seems natural. I bury my face into Gaine's fur and breathe in her scent. I didn't think this could ever happen to me. I was happy being alone. Now, I'm a broken shell of what I was and desperate to be a wolf worthy of this woman's heart.

I wrap my arms tightly around Gaine, wishing for a way to never let her go.

* * *

After a few more days, I pet the wagon horses while I wait for Gaine to shift. The weather has turned, and winter has set in. Their coats are thick, and the steam from their nostrils is warm on my cheek. I've always gotten on well with horses. I wish Gaine would come to me this easily.

"She can't hate me after I saved her life, can she?" I ask the gray one. He sneezes in my face, making me frown. "Yeah, I'm gonna pay for that, aren't I?"

Gaine had appreciated Agatha's assistance once she woke up but only tolerated me. Her cold stares made me thankful that I couldn't hear her. Although I am desperate to feel her in my arms again, I'm quite sure Gaine will not allow me to hold her. Nothing of the woman I kissed remains in her gaze.

The barn door slides open, and Agatha steps out, quickly closing it behind her. "She needs a minute, Kade," the old woman says. "Just let her dress, and then you can go in." She places her hand on my arm as my body tenses, wanting to simply shove her out of the way so I can get to Gaine. "Be gentle, my Midnight. She won't tell me why she's crying."

I sigh and look down at the older woman. There are so many possibilities, all involving me. "How's her wound?"

"It's healing well now," Agatha says, smiling gently. "She'll still struggle to run on it for a while."

"Alright," I say, rubbing my forehead. "Let me see just how mad she is at me." I grip the door handle but turn back to the old lady. "Maybe you could bring her some pie," I add with a wink.

I slide the door open while Agatha laughs. I find Gaine sitting in the middle of our hay bowl with a blanket tightly wrapped around her shoulders. Her eyes are red, and her skin glistens from tears.

I grab a few more blankets and sit beside her, engulfing us in a blanket cocoon. With only a gentle tug, Gaine falls against me and releases exhausting sobs onto my chest. I can't deny my confusion. As I rock and shush her, I'm unsure of what has my mate all twisted up.

Within a few hours, Gaine cries herself to sleep, and I can only give Agatha a confused look when she appears with the pie I'd suggested. She slips her fingers through Gaine's hair and gives me the same gentle smile I've received for years. Agatha helps me tuck the blankets around Gaine before sneaking away, leaving the pie for when we're ready.

I imagine the worst as I hold this woman for whom I would probably do anything. My mind replays every moment since I first met her, and I find more reason to cringe than to smile. I only hope that I can make right whatever is wrong this time.

"You have to let me go, Kade," Gaine whispers, scaring me.

I look down at her, still against my chest. "Honey, I'm not holding you here," I say quietly, rubbing my hands over her. One is on her hip while the other gently cups her elbow. "Do you need help sitting up?"

Instead of pulling away, Gaine slides her arms tightly around my waist. "Kade, a mouse may love a cat, but their worlds will never combine," Gaine says through her sniffles. "Our bond would have catastrophic repercussions that I wouldn't survive."

"Gaine," I start, sighing.

"Kade," she says forcefully, stopping me before I can even try to defend us. "Being with you would cost me my family, my pack, and maybe even you. I would be left with nothing but an empty pit of regret."

"I can keep you safe," I profess. "Look what happened when you left me. I can protect you."

"You're the reason I was in danger, Kade," she argues, shaking her head without lifting off me. "I wouldn't be here if it weren't for you. Being with you put me in danger. I shouldn't have come here with you."

"Gaine, you don't mean that," I say, embarrassed that my desperation is clear in my voice. "You were enjoying yourself. We had fun."

Gaine sits up and grabs my cheeks. "We did, Kade," she whispers. "I loved the festival. Dancing with you was..." Her voice trails off as she sighs. "My father was exiled for performing magic that killed two wolves. How many have you killed with your own hands? How many wolves have felt your blade that you so easily plunged into those humans?"

"They shot you," I spout. "They were taking you to the militia base. Was I supposed to just let them?"

"You're missing the point, Kade," Gaine whispers, leaning her forehead against my chin. "Your past will tear apart two lives. The Luna would never let you stay, and that psychopath Alpha of yours would never allow you to live if you went back to your pack."

I latch onto Gaine, pulling her to me. I can't let her go. I search the hay around us for any type of valid argument.

"I can't let myself love you," Gaine says, crying again. "I won't survive losing you."

There's no arguing with that. I thought about this a million times before returning to find her the first time. The more time I spend with Gaine, the more seated in my soul she becomes. Losing her would rip me apart. Perhaps she is less attached or has more freedom as an elder.

"I'll take you home when you're ready," I whisper, knowing nothing I say will convince her that we have a chance.

It's not long before Gaine's crying wears her out, and she begins to fall asleep. I roll down into the hay with her and experience my beautiful mate sleeping in my arms differently than before. I hold onto her tightly because if I give her any room, she'll disappear again. She's already told me that I have to say goodbye, but my soul won't handle that today.

* * *

Too soon, Gaine prepares one of the wagon horses and declares it is time to go home. I scowl and try to convince her to allow a few more days to heal, but I know she's ready. As hard as it is for me to think about leaving her, she must also find it difficult to send me away. The longer we spend together, the more painful this will be.

"Thank you for everything," Gaine tells Agatha as we leave the barn. "We will not forget your kindness."

Agatha smiles, touching Gaine's cheek. "You will always be the beauty to his beast," she says, reaching for me. "I hope you two find your way. Hearts often get lost when we guard the maps."

I have no idea how she knew what was happening between me and Gaine, but I appreciated her every attempt to gently mend us. "I'm sure we will meet again," I say, squeezing the old woman's shoulders. "I'll stop in for pie, if nothing else."

Gaine steps onto the wagon and gingerly slides her leg over the mare's bare back. Agatha hands me a small bag as I climb onto the wagon and nods toward Gaine before touching her finger to her nose. Once on the mare, I find a few small tins of pie slices in the bag.

"Always a pleasure, Midnight," the old woman says. She nods one more time and turns toward her house. Agatha never was one for goodbyes.

Gaine remains quiet as she guides the horse out of the woman's fields and into the woods. Once we are within the protection of the forest, she nearly bursts as if under pressure. "How did you know you could trust her?" she asks. "You snarled at her when she simply touched your wolf, and you trusted her to doctor me?"

I wrap my arm around her waist, latching onto her hip. "Gaine, you'd been shot," I say as if that would explain any of my reasoning.

"Yes, I remember," Gaine hisses.

"The old lady has always been kind," I tell her. "Sure, initially, when we were there, I was nervous that she would discover my blade and ask questions. But I only know how to hurt, not heal. You needed help, and she was the only person I could think of."

"And you just figured you'd smile at her, and she'd ignore the blood all over your stolen clothes?" Gaine hadn't told me how much she'd witnessed of her rescue. I'm beginning to realize that she was awake for most of it.

"At some point, you will need to accept that I will do anything for you," I state, lifting my eyebrow even though she can't see it. "If I have to admit what I am to the world just to save you from harm, I will do it. Gaine, you're worth it."

"I'm not," she grumbles, dropping the subject.

It doesn't take long for the silence to get to me. In just a few very short days, I will miss this woman more than I could ever miss air, so I want to hear her voice as much as possible. She shared some of her family's stories and told me about her father's punishment. I'd only heard her mention the Luna when she spoke about her anger and the exile.

The version I saw of her was very different, though. She was gentle and quiet, but how her travel companions looked at her spoke volumes. When I recall the scene, they all had a tenderness in their eyes as they looked upon their Luna. They clearly loved her— even Anthony, who I'd only known as militia.

"What's the Luna like?" I ask Gaine softly, hoping she'll engage.

"She's kind," Gaine responds, leaning against my chest. She sniffles and rolls her eyes up in an attempt to hide her crying. "The Luna protects us from those who would cause us harm. She's brought peace to our lands."

"That sounds nice," I whisper. "I saw her once. She was in the field of flowers before I saw you there."

"She was coming to talk to my father but got called away," Gaine responds.

"So, how does it work?" I start, trying to clear my confusion. "She doesn't shift, right? So how does she hear you?"

"The Luna can hear all of her wolves," Gaine says calmly. Her tears have dried as we've turned the conversation away from our issues. "She can hear us when we talk to her or each other. Dad said she has the ability to filter us into the background like... a guitar played in the corner of a field. She can choose whether to listen to us or not."

"And she can talk to you?"

"Mm-hmm," Gaine answers. "Only as wolves, though."

I think I would be driven mad if I had to hear all those voices all the time. Jax's pendant was a lifesaver, allowing me to run without having to hear Tynan's bullshit. "She can't hear wolves that aren't in her pack?"

"No," Gaine answers. "Otherwise, she'd know what that Alpha of yours was up to before he could do it."

I lift my eyebrow. "Ah," I start thoughtfully, recalling the conversation I'd overheard before leaving. "Tynan can't shift. So, it wouldn't help if she could hear him."

"What?"

"It's just something I never noticed until I stumbled across a conversation he was having," I tell her. "What does a wolf have to do to join the Luna's pack? Is there a vow or something?"

Gaine laughs heartily at me. I'm sure to her it's funny, but we've only experienced pain in the Blood Pack. I was born into it, and although we have had wolves join us, I don't know how. The Luna's pack started with the Lunar Pack, so all her wolves have the mark on their arm. When I saw her in the field, I noticed that she had one on each arm. The Blood Pack only has scars.

"Well, it's all quite civil, Kade," she finally settles enough to tell me. "The Luna can lay her hands on a wolf and calm even the most distraught of us. If a wolf accepts her as their Luna, they are welcomed into the pack with her touch. If in wolf form, the mark appears instantly. If not, it will when they shift."

"But you don't hear everyone?" I'm failing to see what is so special about the Luna's Pack. One woman can't make life all that great for thousands of wolves.

"As a wolf, any of my pack members can talk to me," Gaine says quietly. "Either directly or as a group. For example, if they need to speak to the elders, they could talk to all of us at once." She pulls my hand from her hip and places the horse's reins in it. "If someone were to attack my cottage, I could shift and broadcast a message to the entire pack, and they would all race to assist us."

Her voice fades toward the end, and she turns her head to lay her cheek against my chest. I look down to see her eyes close. No one but Tynan would ever think of storming my house. They wouldn't dare. I suppose that would be comforting if it wasn't fear that makes my house secure.

Gaine and her family feel safe due to the protection of her entire pack. If I needed help, I doubt the weekdays would even bother to provide aid. Tynan would just get pissed that I was too busy to do his bidding. Admittedly, it calms me to know that my mate has the protection of so many. Although I would do anything to keep her safe, she is surrounded by hundreds of wolves that would do the same.

Sighing, I cradle her against me. I have never wanted anyone as badly as I crave Gaine. I can't stand the idea that I will need to leave her behind and go back to that nightmare we call a pack. But if I bond with her, she will lose the protection of the Lunar Pack. The Luna would throw her out on her ass, and I will be all she has.

I've never questioned my abilities before. *But what if I'm not enough to keep Gaine safe?*

8

The winter wind howls outside my room when I finally acknowledge my surroundings. I closed every curtain when I got home a few days ago to ensure the sun wouldn't disturb me. It's probably cold, but this blanket cocoon traps my body's heat. *Only one thing is missing.*

"Kade?" Castor whispers over my door's creak as it opens. "Hey, kid. I brought booze and breakfast. I wasn't sure which would be appropriate."

Castor's footsteps are always silent, but I feel him sit on the edge of the bed. The liquor's scent is strong and hits my nose through the layers of blankets. I've never been much of a drinker, but after my stomach's retch at the smell, I might just swear off the stuff altogether. I pull the blankets off my head and glare at the glass in Castor's hand.

"Get that shit out of here," I order, watching my breath steam as I talk. "Bring back some wood." I throw the blankets back over my head.

The old wolf kicks the mattress, causing me to jump. "You can't wear this bed forever," Castor shouts. "Get up. It can't have gone that bad."

"It was worse than that bad," I admit from under my cocoon.

Castor pulls the blankets off me and raises his eyebrow, smirking. If he were any other wolf, I'd probably kill him. I'm not vulnerable, and nothing affects me—not until Gaine. *She might actually be the death of me.*

"She didn't like the festival?" he asks, sitting with a plate of toasted bread.

I roll onto my back and jam a pillow under my head. "No, she loved it," I mumble, yawning.

"Did you have performance issues?" Castor hisses, looking around as if someone might hear him. "It happens to the best of us, kid. You couldn't keep that track record going forever."

I reach under the pile of pillows for my blade before remembering I'd given it to Gaine. "Damn that woman," I growl, grabbing a pillow to throw at Castor.

My old friend digs through the pile of linens on my bed, not finding my knife. "Kade," he starts slowly, furrowing his brow. "I think you were ten the last time you slept without a blade under your pillow." He continues to study me as I roll my eyes closed and turn away from him. "What did she do to you?"

"She broke me," I grumble. I turn to Castor and twist my face in thought. "She was perfect, beautiful, and irresistible. Her kiss could only compare to fairy tales. I slept with her in my arms, and every one of my nerves celebrated her existence."

"I fail to see the issue, Kade," Castor says, shaking his head with his eyebrows raised.

Sighing, I rub my forehead. "She won't have me," I groan. "And may every wolf of the past forgive me... I agree with her."

"What?" my old friend spouts.

"My mate wouldn't be safe in this pack," I start, grabbing a piece of toast. "Tynan wouldn't stand for me being distracted. And do you think the Luna would jump at the chance to welcome me into her fold? You don't let a snake into the hen house, Castor." I sigh, turning my eyes to him. "I could never keep her safe like her pack will."

Castor rests his hand on my chest. I nod to him, understanding why he would remain silent. There are no words for my situation. He's never known a mate, so he has no idea how I feel.

I fought with myself for the entire ride back to her cottage. My decision to leave Gaine and agree that we shouldn't be together felt right as I looked into her eyes, imagining how it would feel to watch her lose everything. I rode back to Castor's and dropped the mare in his field with my head in a fog. It wasn't until I fell into my bed alone that the reality of my decision hit.

"What would it take to undo everything I've done?" I ask.

Castor laughs until he notices I haven't joined him. "Like, take back all the shit you've pulled?" He moves to sit in the armchair by the doors. "Kade..." Castor stammers through random noises before falling forward with his elbows on his knees. "Kid, I don't think your mother would forgive you."

"Helpful," I grumble, scratching my forehead. "Thanks."

"I think we can agree that I'm the wrong wolf for this conversation," Castor says, sighing.

Chuckling, I stretch and pull the blankets back over my lower half. "True," I say. "However, you can help me talk through this without emotion, and that's what I need right now."

"Sure, kid. What's on your mind?"

"She could be happy with someone else, right?" I ask for some reason.

I actually want to know how to vindicate myself in the eyes of the Luna and Gaine. I'm willing to put my inner asshole to good use. Maybe the Luna needs a wolf for hire to kill her enemies. *That's why I asked that question... because I'm losing my mind.*

Castor stares at me until I sigh and pull the blankets over my head. "I'm just gonna go get Ari, kid," he mumbles. "My only suggestion is to give the Luna our pack, but you've always refused to take us from Tynan. I don't want to fight with you."

He throws more logs on the fire, making the wood crackle.

"The Belgian mare in my field doesn't look like my Thoroughbred colt," Castor says as my bedroom door squeaks open. "We're going to discuss that when you pull your head out of your ass."

I breathe out a laugh as the door closes. I'll sort that out later. Right now, my brain is overflowing with thoughts of Gaine, and no matter how hard I try, I can't push her to the side.

There was a pain in my chest when I helped my mate from the mare along the creek behind her cottage. Her face was shining from tears, and they wouldn't stop. I pulled Gaine to me and held her in an embrace that might have broken a weaker woman. I only released her to cup her cheeks. I needed to feel her lips. In a last-ditch effort, I pleaded for her to leave with me forever.

Gaine whispered that she loved me before twisting out of my hands and running across the ward barrier. I could hear her crying until she closed herself into the house. It was dark when she left me, but I stared at her door until the sun had traveled halfway across the sky. I don't know where the time went. There's nothing like a good woman to make you regret every choice you've ever made.

I want to be angry at Gaine for turning my world upside down, but this isn't her fault. During one of our talks, while she was heal- ing, she told me about the kids in the schoolhouse calling her the "mate maker." It finally affected her so much that she left school, and her father became her teacher. Gaine doesn't make mates. She only sees them. She didn't do this to us, and we share this pain.

When I close my eyes, I see her. If I remain still, I can feel her body against mine. I hate that her sobs fill the silence. I should've listened and stayed away. Now, I have no choice but to find a way to win her. My soul will rip from my body if I don't.

"Kade?" Ari's whisper startles me. No one has ever been able to sneak into my house, but now I live in an unsafe, free-for-all club-house. *Great.*

I pull the blankets off my head. "I'm here," I declare, sighing. "Thanks for the tip. She loved the festival." Swallowing hard, I close my eyes to hide my emotions. "I just wasn't strong enough to over-power the past."

"You need to get out of your head, Kade," Ari barks.

"Maybe you should even get out of your bed," Rooster adds, marching through my bedroom door with more wood and a large bowl of stew. "We brought you real food because you need to be functional."

"I am functional," I grumble with a scowl, sitting up to reach for the bowl. "I'll still take the stew, though. Thanks, Ari."

"You're welcome," she responds, giggling. "You are the king of doing the wrong thing for the right reasons. I hated you—I kinda still do. But you were trying to keep Tynan away from me and made sure that Bastian was kind to me even with everything he went through. However, our story may have been different had you been honest about why you did it."

"I have an image to uphold," I mumble, dropping the spoon into the bowl. "Had. I had an image."

"You still do, Kade," Rooster says.

"What is the issue?" Ari asks. "What's holding you back?"

I sigh, blowing out my lips. "She's an elder," I answer.

"She's an old woman?" Ari spouts, confused.

For the first time in a while, I burst out laughing. I'm thankful that Ari had the same thought as me, but I also find it funny that she's now picturing my mate as a wrinkled old lady.

"She's an elder, Ari, not an old woman," I choke out as I get my laughter under control. "She's the Seer. It allows her to help wolves find their mates but also ties her to the Luna."

"Aren't there other elders?" Rooster asks. "Let someone else take her place so she can come live with you."

I shake my head. "From what I gather, it's only siblings, and she and her sister are the only ones," I tell him, frowning. "Her father was exiled for causing the death of a few wolves."

"So, they'd never take you," Ari points out.

I don't mean to, but I growl at her.

"Kade," she spouts, flinging her hands out. "You're an asshole. The fact that she is refusing you doesn't really surprise me."

"Look," I bark. "Thanks for the food, but you're welcome to leave. I don't need a list of reasons she should run as far away from me as possible." I flop back onto the bed in a huff. "I already know all of them."

"We have all been telling you for years to take the pack, brother," Rooster mumbles. "You want to prove yourself to your mate and her Luna? Bring them the Blood Pack."

Any time they suggested I fight Tynan, I instantly refused. Being an asshole doesn't make you a good leader. I don't care enough about these wolves to provide for them. I don't want to lead them. But I wouldn't have to if I gave them to the Luna. She would be responsible for keeping them safe, fed, and housed. Maybe she'd even let me have Gaine.

"Are you actually considering it now?" Ari asks, lifting her eyebrow. "Kade, you don't want Tynan to get his hands on her, but if he were gone, she'd be safe here. You could bring her home and live here if the Luna won't accept you."

I don't like the idea of taking Gaine away from her family, but in the worst-case scenario, she would be safe here if I took the pack. *Sure, I'd be killing another wolf, but how much wolf is he really? Does it count if he's not even enough wolf to shift? And maybe he still has those Lunar wolves. I bet the Luna would appreciate getting them back.*

This has been discussed for nearly ten years, but this is my first time considering it a viable option. "Where's Tynan?" I ask, making the pair smile broadly.

"Last we heard, he was over by the sheds," Ari tells me. "We're having trouble getting fresh stock in, so he's nursing the old reserves."

I click my tongue, pulling a breath through my teeth. "Yeah, I don't think that's why he's hanging around there." I jump out of bed and dig in the drawers for some clothes. "You two better find somewhere to hunker down. Tynan won't be a problem, but he's always got backup nearby."

I pull a knife from between the mattresses and test its sharpness. The pair watches as I move around the room, collecting my hidden blades. I pull on my jacket and slip most into its pockets while the longest tucks into my belt's sheath.

"What happened to the knife Miles got you?" Rooster asks.

I hadn't planned on needing it. I gave it to Gaine when I pulled her from the mare at her house. She attempted to object, but I told her I wanted to know she had a way to defend herself if anyone found out who she was to me. It was within her tight grip when she ran to the cottage.

"It's where it needs to be," I growl, narrowing my eyes. "Don't stay here. Tynan won't honor tradition. If this goes wrong, he'll come straight here to claim this place."

"I don't think he has a single wolf who'd go up against you, brother," Rooster remarks. "But still, you be careful." He reaches his hand out to me.

His mate jumps into my arms, nearly making me laugh. "Never mind the past, Kade," Ari says, sniffling. "Just come back to us, alright?"

"You know me," I say, winking at Rooster. "I'll always be here to make you miserable."

Rooster laughs as he pulls his mate off me so we can leave. We stop to pull Rooster's long blades out of my safe. "I can't believe you kept these," he says, testing their edges. "And you kept them sharp?"

"You never know when you'll need a good blade," I tell him, shaking his shoulder as we step off the porch. "Or a good friend."

* * *

The walk across the compound is quiet. Blood Pack wolves have never been interested in my company, so they tend to avoid me whenever possible. My mind is preoccupied with Gaine, but I still see them peering out their windows as I pass.

I approach the large shed where I found Tynan just before I left, but someone grabs me, hauling me between two smaller buildings. Pulling my longest knife, I spin to find Jax with his hands up. The blade slips across the front of his coat and slices it open to release the feathers encased.

"Shit, Jax," I hiss.

The witch puts his finger to his lips, cringing. He motions for me to follow him away from the sheds. "You gotta help the Luna," he whispers, still moving through the woods.

"Why?" I scoff.

"Tynan sent Kerst after her," Jax hisses. "He has power. He pulled a whole unit and took a train."

"A train?" I ask, shaking my head. "Who the fuck is Kerst? What are you talking about?"

Jax urges me to continue following him. "Come on," he whispers insistently. "We need distance. I'm not supposed to know."

The witch has always been a good spy. No one ever suspected that he'd be in my good graces or that he would go against Tynan. Jax had warned me that the psychopath had set his aim on Ari. He helped me convince Tynan that Bastian would be of better use to him if he weren't locked in the basement, which opened the door for Ari's role in the super soldier's life.

We're near Rooster's bar when he finally stops. "Kerst is the General that Toby brought back from the clean-up you did," Jax says, still whispering. "You know, the one with that deep gash across his face."

I roll my eyes. "He's probably the guy I told Thursday to kill. That damn woman was always too thick to listen to me." I try to recall my conversation with her but jump forward to meeting Gaine for the first time. Shaking my head to clear it, I focus back on Jax. "I don't have time for this. Where's Tynan?"

"Listen, Kade, I know you've never cared about anyone but your-self, but this is important," Jax pleads, releasing an exhausted sigh. "Tynan is trying to have himself declared the Alpha of all wolves."

"Can he even do that?" I ask, confused. "You know what? Never mind. I don't care. I'll kill him, and his little quest for power is over." I wave my finger around. "Point the way."

Jax grabs my arm as I start walking away. "Kade, you can't just kill him," Jax hisses. "The order has already been set in motion. If you kill him, you take on the pack. How will you hunt Kerst down with an entire pack in tow? Tynan is the only one who knows how to contact him."

"Clearly, I've missed some things," I grumble, rubbing the scruff on my jaw. "Let's start from the beginning. Are those Lunar Pack wolves still alive?"

"Yeah," Jax answers. "I convinced him that they're helping."

"With what?"

"Tynan is trying to be more wolf," Jax scoffs.

Sighing, I lean my back against a tree. "And what is the deal with that?"

"Kade, we don't really have time for this."

"Jax, I came here to kill Tynan," I snap. "So, you'll give me answers, or I'll move on with my plan. Which would you prefer?"

"Fine," Jax grumbles, scowling. "His mother was half-wolf. A human raped her, and since she didn't have enough wolf in her genes to control her hormones, she got pregnant. Enter Tynan as a quarter wolf. I think he wants to be more so he can shift. I don't know."

"Is that possible?" I ask. Every new bit of information Jax gives confuses me more than the last. Nothing about Tynan has screamed intelligent or emotionally balanced, but these are brand new levels that I'm struggling to comprehend.

"I don't think so," Jax says, wrinkling his nose.

I throw my hands out in front of me. "Then what are you doing?"

"Trying to keep those wolves alive," Jax says in a way that indicates I should have known the answer. "He killed the first one. The two he has now are Rooster's booze makers."

"Alright," I say slowly. "Now, the Luna."

"He's ordered Kerst to bring her back," Jax tells me. "He specifically said he wanted her alive. Kerst told him she was heading south. That demented General had a unit get an old steam engine running again. They left a week ago."

"A train?" I whisper, narrowing my eyes as I stare into the distance. "I don't know that I could catch a train." I assume it would make noise, and locals would be talking about it if I crossed its path, but what are the odds that would happen? "What about the two Lunar wolves you have? Can't they warn her?"

Jax clicks his tongue, scowling. "The wards," he grumbles. "There's one stopping communication and another holding them in the shed. I'd have to break them, and Tynan would know. He barely sleeps or leaves that damn shed."

"Any suggestions?" I ask.

"Kerst is a different kind of crazy," Jax starts thoughtfully. "He lives to cause pain. I'm pretty sure he dreams of eating children while they sleep."

I stand before Jax with a dumbfounded yet expectant expression. "How is this helpful?"

"Uh, yeah," the witch stammers, shaking his head. "Tynan might tell you where they are. He would trust you to watch over that psycho and make sure he brings her back alive. I don't know how else we could help her. Any of the Lunar Pack would kill us on sight."

Jax keeps talking, but I'm not listening anymore. I'd been lying in darkness, wrapped in blankets for days, wishing for a reason to go back to Gaine—something besides just needing her. She could warn the Luna or pass on the message of the danger heading her way. *Not everyone would kill me.*

"Where is he?" I spout, interrupting whatever the witch is saying.

Jax rolls his eyes. "He's in that shed, staring at his donors," he says. "As if their wolf would jump out of them and into him. How the hell did we ever let him rise to power?"

"I was nine," I state. "I had nothing to do with it."

"I suppose," Jax mumbles. "What made you decide to make a play for Alpha now?"

"Nothing," I snap. "Keep those wolves alive until I get back."

Jax doesn't even try to follow me. He knows from our past that I have an easier time manipulating Tynan when he's not trying to impress others. The tiny Alpha nearly answers my questions without thinking. I bang on the shed's door as soon as I reach it, not wanting to give Tynan the ability to figure out I'm here before I can surprise him.

"What?!" he growls, yanking the door open. "Where have you been? I see you're alone. Where the hell is that kid?"

"Hey, Tynan," I say casually, ignoring his anger. "You still playing in your shed? What's going on in there?"

"I'm the Alpha. I ask the questions." Tynan pushes me back and closes the door behind him. "What do you want?"

"My, my, you seem tense," I say, raising my eyebrow. "You should try yoga or maybe some deep breathing exercises."

Tynan's eyes narrow as he sneers at me. Beyond him, two wolves step from around the trees. They crouch and snarl. I'm used to them but aware that they will attack me. Our pack is not loyal to our Alpha. They are afraid of him. The wolves that guard him have been on his wall and will do anything to ensure it doesn't happen again.

"I heard you had an officer here," I say, returning my eyes to the little greasy man. "The one I told Thursday to kill."

"Her name is Vera," Tynan grumbles. "You should've kept her around. She's pretty good." This is about to get incredibly awkward, but I just threw up a little in my mouth and can't stop him. "Women are so much better when you don't have to hold them down or listen to them scream."

I rub my forehead and swallow my stew for the second time. "That's... nice," I choke out. "Tynan, I heard that officer was un- hinged."

"Eh," he grunts, shrugging. "He's not so bad."

"Do you trust him to bring the Luna back here?"

"I let him live," he scoffs. "He owes me."

Sighing, I click my tongue. "How loyal would that make you?" I stare at Tynan until it becomes clear that he has no answer to prove his point. "That woman's pack just annihilated hundreds of his soldiers. Why in the hell would you think he would let her live long enough to make it back here?"

Tynan narrows his eyes and turns to lean against the shed's door. "That's why I was looking for you," he finally says, taking the bait. "I need you to track him down and supervise."

"Do you even know where he is?" I scoff, pushing him to question the General's loyalty a little more.

"No," Tynan grumbles. "He's following the Luna. She's on a boat headed south." He swallows hard, kicking the railing. "Follow the river south. That bastard better be telling me the truth."

"What do you want with the Luna, Tynan?" I ask, still not clear what he thinks he can accomplish.

Tynan wipes his nose and shakes his greasy hair from his eyes. "I need to marry the Luna in a ceremony that will bind her to me and make me Alpha of all wolves," he announces, trying to stand taller.

"Doesn't she already have an Alpha?" I ask, shaking my head.

"I don't pay you to think," Tynan barks.

I scoff, narrowing my eyes. "You don't pay me."

"Whatever," Tynan snaps. "Go get me my Luna. Do your fucking job and quit disappearing!" He slips into the shed and slams the door in my face.

9

The Belgian mare's slow pace gave me two days to consider what to say to Gaine. I've never been a man of many words, and our situation isn't improving my vocabulary. So far, the only thing I'm sure I should say is "Hello." My extreme desire to get this right has me so distracted that I've allowed the mare to wander miles off course a few times.

It's mid-afternoon when we reach the first fence at the edge of their ranch. Although the Thoroughbred had quickly skirted this field, the Belgian would take another day to go around its many acres. I dismount at a gate, and a line of swaying grass catches my attention when I slip the wire over the post.

Frozen in place, I scan the tall yellow grass, looking for whatever created that motion. After a few minutes, the mare shoves me with her nose, wanting access to the field. I lift the post from its lower loop and pull the barbed wire gate out of our way. She drops her head without bothering to step through and greedily pulls at the dried stalks.

Shoving her aside, I pull the fence back into place. I'm just setting the top loop of wire when a low growl rumbles behind me. The Belgian jumps away, yanking her reins from my hand and darting across the field faster than she's ever run at my urging. I scowl at her as I look again for the disturbance in the field.

The stunning brown coat with red and blonde tips my mate wears will never have an equal. She holds her head low, showing off the black edges over her shoulders, and snarls at me as she approaches. Her teddy bear ears try to stay back but continue to prick forward whenever I move.

My breath catches, and I swallow hard. "Gaine," I whisper, lowering to my knee. "You are so beautiful."

She spreads her front legs to brace for an attack, but I don't flinch. Gaine's been on a hunt. There's blood on her muzzle from a fresh kill. Her green eyes are locked on mine, ignoring my outstretched hand. Her head bobs as she snaps her teeth, making the proximity pendant show through her fur for a second.

"You can bite me if you want," I whisper. "But if you do, I'm taking that pendant back."

Gaine stops growling and sits before me.

I relax back on my heel, resting my elbow on my knee. "I spent two days trying to figure out what to say when I found you," I tell her. "I decided I would just respond to whatever you shouted when you realized I came back. I hadn't anticipated you not being able to talk to me."

Adjusting her front legs, Gaine nudges her muzzle forward to urge me to continue.

"I agreed with you when I left, but now I'm conflicted," I whisper, still holding my hand out to her. "I don't like to see you frown, and your tears hurt my heart. I believe you are safest with your pack." I mash my lips together and pull them tight across my teeth. "I've never needed anyone, but I can't stay away from you, Gaine."

My mate stands and steps forward. Her jaw slides slowly over my fingers, and she twists her neck to rub her whiskers across my palm. I smile when her hum starts, but her tongue claims my full attention as it slips inside my sleeve. Gaine stares into my eyes as my chest swells, pulling as much air as possible. Her second lap over my wrist causes the air to rush from my lungs with a groan.

"You are the devil, woman," I growl.

I can almost hear her laughter as she turns away from me. My mate's coat is beautiful from every angle, but her raised tail and bouncing stride make me shake my head. She jogs away from me and disappears in the tall stalks.

I stand and easily pick her out now that I'm looking for her white aura among the dried grass. "I'm not chasing you," I shout. *That's a lie. I'd follow her to the end of the earth.* "Alright," I grumble when she doesn't turn around. "I'm coming."

Although I lose sight of her, I continue across the field in the direction Gaine had gone. I'm still rubbing my wrist when I step into the trees that line a ditch running across the field. Just the hope that Gaine's torture was some form of affection causes me to smile.

I step across the ditch and pull myself up the other side with the low limb of a thick tree. Once I reach the top, I look around for Gaine's white light. Just when I think I've lost her, fingers tangle into my hair and yank my head back. My blue blade catches the sunlight breaking through the branches as it slips around me to rest against my neck.

"I told you not to come back," Gaine whispers so close to my ear that her breath tickles my skin.

Groaning, I snatch her wrist and pull it away from my neck while I spin around. My hands nearly move on their own across her exposed back. "You make it impossible to stay away," I whisper against her lips.

Gaine slides my knife over my shoulder to rest it back against my neck. "Step back, Kade," she says with enunciated clarity.

"You can cut me," I respond with a grin. "Just come closer." I lick her top lip as my hands slide over her hips. Gaine opens her mouth to moan when my fingers dig into her thighs. I lift her to wrap her legs around my waist and push her against the large tree she was hiding behind. Gaine's arms latch onto my neck, and I lose track of the blade when our tongues meet.

I want to feel her hands on my skin, but allowing her to experience me without distractions is exciting. I spread my fingers, touching as much of Gaine as possible. My hips hold her in place while my hands slide along her legs to her crossed ankles behind my back. I smile into her soft moans as I caress the sensitive skin covering the joints.

Urged on by Gaine's enjoyment, I lightly trail my fingertips back up the inside of her legs. Her body heats from her nerves' reaction to me, and she leans her head back, giving me access to her neck. Licking my lips, I abandon Gaine's leg and push her jaw out of my way with my thumb.

When we first met, I could think of nothing but getting my first taste. Although I love Gaine's flavor, my enjoyment comes more from her reaction to me. My lips and teeth stay gentle over her skin while my tongue pushes against it, calling to her deeper nerves and pulling moans from the back of her throat.

Gaine tangles her fingers in my hair and shifts her legs to slide them up my side. She gasps when I dig my fingers into her hip, rocking it to put her in the perfect position if I could just lose these pants. I lift her leg to find my waistband.

"Shit, Kade," Gaine hisses, pulling me away by my hair. "What the hell was that?"

Glancing around, I desperately try to find what she's talking about so we can get back to bonding. This perfect, beautiful, naked woman is in my arms, and I have far too many clothes on. I want to feel her skin against mine. Her legs should be warming my hips, and my nerves crave her attention.

I look down at Gaine's legs, wanting to feel them against my skin. I slide my hand down her thigh before I see the bleeding cut just above her knee. Shaking my head, I gather my senses. "Here, let me look at that," I whisper, lifting her legs away from me so she doesn't touch another blade.

I pull the knife from the sheath along my back. It's longer than the blue blade and sticks out the bottom. One leg probably pushed it into the other when I moved her. Using the rag I keep to clean blood from my blades, I gently wipe Gaine's wound and assess the damage.

"It's not deep," I say, looking up from kneeling before her.

My eyes' journey to her face was a slow one. I swallow hard as I drink in her sun-kissed skin and beautiful curves. Gaine is still heated from my touch, but the air is cold against her skin, causing raised bumps to cover her body. I want to rub my lips over her tight chest until my eyes wander further down and stop between her legs.

I've never tasted a woman's parts before. It wouldn't do anything for me, so I've never cared to. But I lick my lower lip, wanting it to contain Gaine's flavor. I slide the top of my fingers up the inside of her leg, hoping she'll let me in. Although her muscles tremble from my touch, she doesn't lift her leg out of my way. I try the other one but rub my lips over her thigh as an added incentive.

Gaine jumps away from me when a howl sounds in the distance. "You have to go," she hisses. "That's the guard they posted at the cottage when I got home."

Springing after her, I cover her body and pin her against a neighboring tree. My growl rumbles too loudly to hear what Gaine is saying. I slide my hands down her arms, and she spreads her fingers to thread them with mine. My eyes flick toward my hand as she lifts it to her mouth.

Gaine's eyes calmly stare into mine, and her breath moves over my fingers as she whispers. I try to focus on her voice, but my chest is heaving air, causing my growl's volume to fluctuate. I lift her hand to my mouth, and my eyes roll closed when she rubs her fingers over my lips.

"They will kill you, Kade," Gaine's voice finally filters through my growl, settling my breathing. "We can't be together, but I wouldn't survive in a world that doesn't have you in it. Please, Kade. I need you to hear me."

I lick her fingertip, triggering my growl again, but shake my head and release a deep, shaky breath to cut it off. "We need to talk," I tell her before I lose myself to her body again. "You need to get dressed so I can concentrate."

Gaine breathes a quiet laugh as she slips from my grip. "Come on," she says. "You can talk while I dress. It doesn't take them long to find me when I sneak out."

My eyes stay glued to her body while she leads me back across the ditch to where she'd dropped her clothes. I hook my arm around a branch to ground myself to a spot where she remains out of my reach. Although her pulsing aura blocks some of my view when there's distance between us, plenty of my beautiful mate is still visible.

"Kade?" Gaine has stopped dressing and is staring at me expectantly.

"Hm?" I hum, slowly trailing my eyes back down her body before she covers any more of it up. "What?"

"What did you want to talk about?" she asks.

A smile spreads across my face as I lick my teeth.

Gaine rolls her eyes and shakes her head at me before laughing. "Kade, you said we needed to talk," she spouts.

Releasing the branch, I step up to her and grab her by the hip. The noisy sigh I release is involuntary as her body relaxes against mine. I rub my cheek over hers and softly exhale onto her forehead as I cross it to do the same on the other side. Gaine steps onto my boots to put us at the same height, giving me access to her ear. I mouth the lobe with my lips and slide my teeth along its edge.

A howl sounds as Gaine lifts her leg to hook it over my hip. It's closer this time, making my mate retreat and push against my chest. She hasn't buttoned her pants and is still missing a shirt, leaving plenty of exposed skin. I slip my hand between us to unzip my jacket. The nerves across my body may not have felt her touch yet, but they want to, and I'm inclined to agree with them.

Gaine gasps, pulling my jacket open. "Kade," she hisses loudly. "Why do you have so many blades?" She steps back, causing me to advance. "Stop, Kade," she says more forcefully. "What are you doing here with all of this?"

I'm unsure if I was genuinely focusing on her words, but her tone snaps me out of my attack. "Woman," I growl, yanking my coat from her grip. "You need to bond with me so I can concentrate."

"It doesn't make this any easier, Kade," she responds, sighing.

I step back into her. "That's a chance I'm willing to take," I whisper, trying to pull her against me. "You're mine, Gaine. Screw the packs. We don't need them."

When the howl sounds again, it's not far.

"Do you love me?" Gaine whispers, letting me come closer but tucking under my chin so I can't kiss her.

My jaw clenches as I suck my teeth. "So help me, woman, I do," I grumble. I don't even have to think about my feelings. This pull is stronger than my instincts as a wolf.

Gaine's hand slides over my cheek, somehow settling me. "I love you too, Kade," she whispers. "I hope that one day you will find a way to deserve my heart. But right now, I need you to go away so the Luna's guards don't kill you."

And with that, my brain suddenly takes over, stopping the rest of me from forcefully demanding my mate. "Wait," I spout, pushing her out to hold her at arm's length. "You need to warn your Luna. Tynan sent some militia guy after her."

"What?!" Gaine shouts before covering her mouth and looking around.

I can't stop my eyes from wandering down to her bare chest. "Gaine, put clothes on," I growl through my teeth.

She giggles but steps behind a tree and doesn't emerge until she's only missing her shoes. "The Luna's safe, Kade," Gaine says, sitting to pull on her boots. "She's not here."

"I know," I say, kneeling to pull her laces. "She went south on the river."

Gaine's eyes widen as she freezes. "How do you know that?"

"I told you," I snap. "Tynan. You need to warn her."

Gaine only stares at me while I grab her other foot to slip it into her boot. She sighs a few times but then sniffles. I look up to catch the first tear sliding down her cheek.

"What is it?" I ask.

"We're right back where we started," she mumbles, wiping her eyes. "What should I tell her? That I've been talking to a Blood Pack wolf? Or that I trust him because he saved my life when I spent a few weeks with him and lied about it?" Gaine cups my cheek. Her eyes are gentler than I've ever seen them. "Perhaps I should tell her that he is my mate, and I love him with all my heart."

I move between her legs and pull her into my lap. "That would work for me," I whisper, rubbing my lips over her cheeks to catch the tears still escaping.

"Kade, I would be banished from my pack," Gaine says.

"I'll take care of you, Gaine," I promise. "I will take my pack. You'll be safe with me as Alpha of the Blood Pack."

She pulls away to look me in the eye. "The Luna would lose her Seer and Historian until another elder gives birth to two children. I would never be allowed near my sister." Gaine's volume lowers to a whisper as she talks. "She needs me, Kade. My sister's troubled."

"So, you'd rather just hope she doesn't die?" I ask, shaking my head. "Gaine, Tynan's making a play for power. If he gets her, he plans to be named Alpha of all wolves."

Gaine slouches, furrowing her brow. "Well, then, he wouldn't need her," she says, confused. "He would want her daughter."

"Why would he want a kid?"

"Gaine?!" someone shouts from a distance. "I found your horse. You alright?"

"Shit," I hiss, knowing the guard must be talking about the Belgian. "She wasn't fast, but she was my only horse."

Gaine sits up to scan the top of the grass. "I'll bring you a faster horse," she tells me. "Meet me behind the cottage. I'll try to find out where they went. You need to stop them from finding her."

"What? Why?" I spout. "You can just warn them."

"Kade, I can't," she says, lifting off my lap. "If I warn her, I will be banished. If anything happens to them, we will fall into the old ways. Elders were hunted, captured, or killed so that other packs couldn't use our knowledge."

My head hasn't been clear since I met Gaine, but I remember Miles telling me about some of this. He said the need to kill the elders never sat well with him, so he didn't bother. However, many other Alphas put bounties on them over the years. It made them afraid to have children, and most elder lines ended over the centuries.

I don't care about her gifts. I just need her close so I know she's safe. "But if you bonded with me—"

"Not now, Kade," Gaine cuts me off. She jumps to her feet. "I'm fine," she shouts to the man in the field. Lowering her voice, she whispers to me, "Meet me behind my house."

* * *

I don't know how I keep finding myself in this position, but hours later, I'm watching the sunset from behind this damn woman's house again. Every time I'm near her, I find something new and more exciting to fantasize about. I close my eyes to replay my gaze traveling down Gaine's body and resting where her legs meet. Her skin folded over anything that would exhilarate my senses. My tongue slips over my lips, wanting to taste what she had hidden from sight.

My eyes roll when a cold blade rests against my neck. "Just slit my throat, woman," I grumble. I'm frustrated with our situation, but her giggle makes me smile. Opening my eyes, I pull her before me by her wrist. "I want to make you laugh every day for the rest of your life."

"First, you need to save my Luna," Gaine whispers as I steal her breath by rubbing her lips with mine. "Once I can talk to her..." Her voice trails off as I lick her lower lip.

"We don't need her," I murmur, trying to catch her lip in my teeth. "You're all I need."

Gaine turns her head, pulling her mouth away from mine. "Kade, stop it," she hisses. "You know this is bigger than us."

Groaning, I release her and let her pull me deeper into the trees, where she's tied a tall bay mare. "Alright," I grumble. "What did you find out?"

"They are supposed to be going down to the bayou," she tells me, peeking back toward her house. "Her head guard said she wanted to bring her family to the ocean."

"Any idea how far they made it?" I ask, leaning against a tree.

"Neala told me they left the river, but I don't know how far south they went." Gaine innocently slips under my arm to lay her head on my shoulder. I lift my coat so she can wrap her arm around my waist within its warmth. "They started asking why I wanted to know, so that's all I got."

I pull her closer to me, resting my chin on her head. "That's not much," I whisper. "There's a lot of territory down there, and the militia units have many eyes."

Gaine reaches around my back to pull the horse's reins from a branch. "This mare is our fastest horse. We train them to follow wolves so you can shift and lead her to travel even faster. All you have to do is keep them busy looking where the Luna wouldn't be," Gaine states. "We know she wanted to go to the ocean. That's the furthest point south, right?"

"Technically, it's not the ocean," I say. "But I guess it's close enough for someone who's never seen it before."

Gaine releases a shaky sigh. "Kade," she whispers, nuzzling closer to my neck. "I don't want to go back to a world without the Luna. I don't want to be afraid again."

Most packs struggled, needing to keep the fact that they were wolves secret for fear that the militia would discover them. Elder families faced danger from both sides and were forced to hide from wolves and humans. I twist to fit Gaine perfectly against me, sighing when her comfort triggers my hum.

"Will you stay near your guard while I'm gone?" I ask, rubbing my fingers over the rope holding the proximity pendant. "I would feel better knowing there would be no chance of you getting caught alone away from your pack if I fail."

"I didn't think the great Kade could ever fail at anything," Gaine replies, giggling.

"Hm," I hum. "I failed to convince you to bond with me." When she only buries herself deeper inside my coat, I continue. "There's a lot of ground to cover down there, Gaine. First, I have to find these men, and then I'll need to point them in a random direction and hope like hell that your Luna is nowhere near it."

"You can't fail," Gaine says, softer than a whisper.

"I'm distracted, Gaine," I mumble. "I've never been distracted. You are clouding my head and making it difficult to concentrate. I'm so busy thinking about where I want to put my mouth on your body that even you can sneak up on me."

Before I met her, if anyone had giggled at me the way Gaine is now, they wouldn't have survived the day. But this gorgeous woman has me smiling and laughing with her.

"If I survive this and keep your Luna safe, you better bond with me," I grumble, trying to find the gruff wolf I used to be.

Gaine pulls away to look into my eyes. "Kade, you need to succeed," she says, rubbing her fingers over my jaw. "If you don't, my family and I will need to flee the area before the pack turns on itself." She gently kisses my lips before placing the mare's reins in my hand. "If you ever want to see me again, stop them from finding my Luna."

10

The problem with traveling as a wolf over the years was that I'd have to steal clothes anytime I wanted to shift. I also hated only carrying one blade. Although uncommon, you never know when a knife will break, and finding a good one can be difficult.

Having a horse with well-made saddlebags to carry my gear while she follows me across the rugged terrain is a tremendous benefit. We work together to move south through a never-ending cycle of winter storms. She doesn't even complain when we cross the tributaries. The mare's skills are undeniable, and she's been good company.

Luckily, the General and I have been battling the same winter storms. Between the snow drifts and the junk blocking his way, he's still along the river when I finally find him a month later. I watch them from high atop a ridge as the General hollers about the wagon I pushed onto the tracks last night before the snow started. I smiled as I knocked its wheels off, knowing it would grind his nerves.

I pull at the last of my groundhog's muscle. For an herbivore, they're pretty fatty, and he will hold me over for a few days while they clear my mess. I emptied a trash wagon a half mile up the tracks to ensure I could relax after my hunt.

As I push the groundhog carcass aside to rest my chin over my paws, I let my mind wander to Gaine. I know she's worried about her Luna, but I wonder if she's thinking about me. She's the driving force keeping me going, so I don't mind how focused I am on her. Without my beautiful mate, I'd probably have given up on this venture and curled up in front of a fire during the first snowstorm.

Tynan would've sent word that I was coming, so I know I'll have to show my face to the General eventually. The unhinged Alpha has become so irritating that I've resorted to always wearing my proximity pendant. His favorite phrase is, "Bring me that bitch!" I asked him who he was talking about just to piss him off once and had to shift to shut him up.

As the light fades, the General stands staring at the same train car I catch him watching every night. They still haven't figured out how to move the broken wagon, so he's pretty mad, screaming obscenities at any man who comes near him.

Gaine's horse has fallen asleep in a dense grove of pines. It's dry under them, and they seem to be blocking most of the wind. Casting one last glance in the soldiers' direction, I decide they're probably just about done for the night and turn to join her.

* * *

The steam whistle blows loudly, waking me just before sunrise. Its sound helped me follow the General's trail but could easily be the most annoying thing I've ever heard. I quickly inspected the train when I found it a week ago. The headlight will need to go soon so they can't see at night, but I haven't found a way to get close to the whistle.

After stretching my legs and back, I trigger my shift to check the mare's gear. She's been sleeping standing up, only rolling or laying down when I remove her saddle. But last night, she decided to stretch out with her gear on so it's riddled with pine needles and tiny sap balls.

Sighing, I pull my clothes from her saddlebags. "You couldn't have waited?" I ask her, rolling my eyes when she shakes and coughs loudly. "Great. That'll attract some attention." I quickly slip into my jeans as limbs and pine cones crunch under heavy boots. "Keep quiet and let me do the talking," I tell the horse, patting her shoulder.

"What are you doing here?" a gruff voice booms as a rifle cocks behind me.

"Following you," I answer, turning around. I've never cared much for humans. Militia, especially, are a hard bunch to swallow. This man is the poster child why with his greasy hair and unwashed smell. "I prefer to do it at more of a distance if you wouldn't mind."

"You must be the tracker that asshole sent to keep an eye on me," another man snaps from behind him.

The second man steps out to where I can see him. There's been a growing trend lately where the militia officers have begun only wearing parts of their uniform at the most. I have seen a few entirely dressed in regular clothes, but most will wear something signaling that they are at least militia, if not higher ranking than the rest. This man is well-dressed in clothes I'd probably wear myself. The deep gash across his face tells me exactly who he is, though.

"And you must be Kerst," I sneer in return. I pull my shirt over my head before producing my boots and coat. If this guy is as bad as Jax says, I prefer access to my knives or teeth whenever he's around.

"That's General Kerst," the scarred man growls, pushing the soldier with the rifle out of his way. "And you are?" he leads.

I narrow my eyes and study the General for a minute. The deep scar on his face trails across his left eye, over the bridge of his nose, and the claw that caused it had hooked onto the corner of his mouth. My pack isn't the best group of doctors, so he had no hope of looking pretty once they got ahold of him. His eye is clouded and probably useless to him now.

"Kade," I announce.

"And what makes you so special?" the General snaps. "I mean, besides the silver eyes."

Sighing as I lick my teeth, I pull the thin blade closest to my coat's zipper. "They're blue," I growl and sidestep to throw the knife at the other man.

The General flings his arms angrily as the soldier crumbles into him with the handle sticking out of his eye. I don't have many perfectly balanced knives, but that blade was the longest and easily found its mark. The General's hateful one-eyed glare is strangely satisfying.

A sly grin creeps across my face. "There is that," I say, shrugging. "Too bad, really. You could've been twins." Chuckling, I return my attention to the mare and her gear.

"You're gonna pay for that," the General growls slowly.

Hearing his clumsy footfalls, I pull the longer blade from my belt as I turn to stop his advance. I press the edge to his neck just as his grip reaches my throat. I hate the smell of human blood, so I use my forearm against his chest to push him back.

"Send the bill to Tynan," I snarl.

The General scoffs as I shove him aside and crouch beside the soldier. I nudge him to be sure he's dead before removing my blade from his eye. *One down.*

"Why don't you show me around?" I suggest, ignoring the General's furious glare. "I'm especially interested in that container you stare at every night."

The General snatches the soldier's rifle and storms back down the ridge to the train below. The horse joins me as I watch the man's journey. He has to descend at an angle and leaves the woods by the end of the train. When he reaches the rusted-out red container I catch him staring at, he slows and looks in my direction.

"That's right, little man," I mumble. "Get mad. Angry men make mistakes." The horse shoves me with her nose. "Did Gaine train you?" I ask, turning back to her. "You women are all alike."

Swinging into her saddle, I urge her toward the activity in front of the train. It would appear the General had his men working through the night on the wagon, which was dismantled to be removed. Now, they are shoveling the snow drift that built up around it.

I nod to the gawking soldiers as I pass. "How's it going, boys?" I ask, quickly inspecting their light source while riding past it. The headlight is an oil wick with mirrors to amplify its beam. There seems to be a piece of glass in front of it to block the wind and slits in the back to provide air. I'm unsure how, but I need to make its demise look natural or accidental.

The engine rumbles loudly, but the mare doesn't seem to mind as we pass. It's followed by a flatbed with tall metal brackets lined by wooden slats. Split wood is stacked to the top toward the back, and it's clear that they've been using a lot of it to keep this thing going.

As we progress down the train, we encounter more gawking stares from younger soldiers until we reach the General. He screams at his men to return to work before acknowledging me. The angry officer leads me further down the train, stopping beside his favorite red container.

"It's just a bunch of boxes," the General snaps, sliding the large door back. He reveals a reinforced space designed to carry some-thing other than the shipping boxes within its walls.

I dismount and pull the mare's bridle. Hanging it over the saddle horn, I pat her neck with my eyes still focused on the train's container. She steps aside and snatches at the taller shoots of dried grass showing above the snow. I smile when she jumps away from the General as he tries to approach her. I didn't appreciate hitting the ground when I discovered her dislike of humans just a few days into our trip.

There's a small ladder with three rungs hanging from the

container. I climb up and see a matching door on the other side, but the space is pretty dark with it closed. Some small boxes are along the front and back walls, and thick chains hang from the ceiling.

I slip my hand over one set and give it a good yank. "You planning to contain some bears in here?" I ask, eyeing the thick metal links.

"Maybe," the General remarks, wagging his eyebrow.

"Tynan sent you after the Luna," I say, turning toward the closed door. "You do realize she's a woman, right?" Beside the other door, I find a few hefty metal collars bolted down with the same thick chains. I snatch one off the floor and hide my surprise at its weight. "What is this for?" I growl.

The General steps onto the ladder and hangs off the side of the container. "Bears," he snaps, smiling.

When I drop the collar, it clangs loudly and causes the floor to vibrate. A marking by my feet catches my eye, and I shove a large box aside to expose a symbol like what Tynan had on his shed's wall.

"What's this?" I ask just before the train's whistle blows.

The General leans away from the train to look toward the engine. He stares for a moment and then nods. "Time to go," he announces without answering me. Kerst jumps from the ladder and waits for me to exit the container.

Moving slowly, I recall what Jax had told me. *The Lunar wolves are contained in the room, yet Tynan can come and go. They can't call to their pack from in there.* Tynan wouldn't need to shift to communicate with Blood Pack wolves. Not being part of the Luna's pack, we still fall under the era of the Alphas' rule. *But could he talk to any of us from within that room?*

I shake my head and jump from the train. The General rolls the door closed and fastens the latch. I watch as he marches away, clearly not interested in telling me what I need to know. Sliding my hand under my collar, I rub the rope holding my proximity ward. The silence has been wonderful, but it's time to get some answers.

* * *

After a few days of riding beside the train, I realized I needed to stop it from traveling further south. There were plenty of obstacles and natural debris on the tracks already, and with what I was adding, they were moving slowly, but the snow was their most significant obstacle. Once we reached clear tracks, they moved too fast for me to influence their speed further.

With all the racket the train makes, I'm relieved to wake up a week later to only the birds chirping. I finally found some usable tracks to steer the General's train east. A few well-placed comments to the locals saw the demise of the southbound tracks, and my sigh of relief is well deserved.

I slip my arm under my head and glance at the mare. "I believe this is where we part ways, girl," I murmur as she turns to me. "I hope you know your way home. I need you to deliver a message."

Gaine had told me to let the horse loose when I was through with her. I doubt she expected me to ride her this far south when she said the mare would always return home. The horse has been a great ear to bend and tolerated my rambling when I needed to talk, but her part in this adventure is over.

Digging through the saddlebags, I pull some small scraps of paper and a pencil from the bottom. I stare at the horse and rub the soft hairs on my chin, trying to decide what to write. Gaine has plagued my dreams. At first, I could only dream of what I wanted to do to her or how she would taste when I finally got to put my mouth wherever I wanted. But last night, Kerst collared and stabbed her until she bled out in my arms.

I would probably be able to figure out the General's game if I weren't so clouded with thoughts of my mate. Pressing the pencil to the paper, I consider some ways to make my information vague in case someone else finds it but pointed enough that Gaine will understand. The pencil remains still as my brain only considers three words: I love you.

"Damn it," I shout, shoving the papers away.

The horse snorts at me before releasing a giant, eye-rolling yawn. I click my tongue and scowl at her.

"Trust me, my life used to be fun. Women begged for the chance to experience my body. Everyone else feared me." I sigh and flop onto my back. "Now I'm all good and shit like I'm tryna earn my wings." I look at the horse. "You understand, right?"

The horse sneezes and turns away from me.

"Yeah," I grumble. "I hate myself too."

I roll back to the papers and jot down a few small sentences. I piece together some of what I've learned that she would need to know. Gaine is smart, so broad messages should be easy for her. It's clear from what the General has in his favorite container that he's following his own agenda. *I can't even be sure the Luna is still his target.*

I finally write:

> There are more players in this game. Remain guarded until Midnight returns for Beauty.

Sighing, I squint at the horse's long black mane. The small leather pouch that holds my pendant is the perfect color to hide in her hair. While Miles was enjoying the spoils of my kitchen raids, he would teach us to tie different types of knots. He never said why we needed to learn them, but the skill has come in handy many times.

I pull the saddle and loop some of the mare's mane about halfway down her neck. Luckily, her hair is thick enough to hide the knots. I tie the leather pouch's drawstrings to two sections in case one breaks. Lastly, I tuck the pendant inside with the note. If the horse reaches Gaine, she will know without any doubt that the message is from me.

I smooth the mare's mane to make it lie on one side, concealing the knots and pouch. "I've never traveled with a horse," I say, patting her shoulder. "You've been a worthy companion, but I need you to go home to Gaine now. Maybe you could tell her I love her for me." I pull her bridle and rub her cheek. "Just don't tell her I'm losing my mind and talking to horses, okay?"

I push the mare, urging her to walk away. She nods and weaves through the trees before stopping to turn back. We regard each other for a moment.

"Go on," I say quietly. "I don't need any witnesses." I stomp my foot, and she tosses her head before spinning and darting away.

After watching the horse disappear through the trees, I kneel beside her saddle and remove the sections that might be useful. Several pieces of her saddle and bridle would be handy in a pinch. I strip them all and jam them into the saddlebags.

I bury the remaining gear under a mound of leaves and pine needles before heaving the saddlebags onto my shoulder. We'd camped just off the southbound tracks, near the eastbound connection. I step out onto the ledge that hangs over the railway. I had moved a lot of debris onto the tracks to the north to give the townsfolk time to destroy the southern section, but this area is clear. I'll need everyone on board when we pass by this ledge.

* * *

I lay on the side of an overturned wagon, staring at the cloudy sky and dreaming of my mate for most of the day. It's nearly dark when I hear the train puffing toward me. Soon, I'll have to shift to relay reports to Tynan. Without the pendant, I can't escape his insane ramblings and irrational demands. I won't be able to retreat into my mind and experience Gaine's touch from my memories.

Closing my eyes, I feel her arms tightly hold my waist. Her hair tickles my face as I tuck her under my chin. I breathe deeply, wanting her scent to overwhelm me. My fingers stretch as they recall the soft, silky feel of her skin when I held her naked body. My lips burn from her kisses.

There will never be the option to return to who I used to be. I couldn't find satisfaction with different women each night and empty beds in the morning. Even the memory of those other women touching me has my stomach feeling queasy.

Ari said she wanted to meet the woman strong enough to deny me, but Rooster's mate is the wolf who will never have an equal. She slept with Bastian and convincingly pretended to love him while her core burned for Rooster. Holding Ari was easy and comforting. Her touch was innocent, as she wanted nothing from me.

I recall when I tried to distract myself enough to forget about Gaine. Four of my weekdays moved into my house and waited on me hand and foot. They knew better than to be in bed when I woke up, but I fell asleep each night surrounded by them. I cringe, feeling their hands on me, but when Wednesday smiles and puts me in her mouth, my stomach's had enough.

Rolling to my side, I eject last night's meal and scowl at the mushed pile of meat. I had to wait hours for the rabbit to come out of its burrow, and that should've held me for a few days. Now, I'll have to go hunting again soon.

While spitting out the last of it, I hear boots on the gravel up the tracks. I narrow my eyes on two soldiers approaching from the north. "Bout time y'all showed up," I grumble, rolling back onto the wagon. "Been stranded here all day."

"What happened to your horse?" one soldier asks.

I turn and lick my teeth. "I got hungry."

Both soldiers wrinkle their noses and eye the pile of rabbit meat at their feet. I've always found it entertaining how humans seem to find eating anything they call a pet disgusting, but dining on a wild animal is perfectly acceptable.

"Where's Kerst?" I ask them.

"The General is with the train," the second soldier answers. "He's dying to talk to you."

"Hm," I hum, smiling. "Everybody wants something from me." I lift onto my elbow to look down at the soldiers. "But what is it that you want?"

The train is still blocked by debris, and these kids should be helping to clear the track, not scouting ahead. The General doesn't let his men leave the train or travel up the tracks without him, so these young soldiers probably snuck away unnoticed.

Although they both look uncomfortable, the one who asked about my horse steps forward. "You've seen inside that container," he starts. "The size of the chains... What is he hunting?"

They step back as I jump from the side of the wagon. "Kerst didn't tell you why you're here?" I ask, lifting my eyebrows. When they nervously shake their heads, I step closer. "And what makes you think I know?"

They can't back up faster than my advance, so it's not long before I'm in their faces. The soldiers are young but only an inch or two shorter than me. It's enough to seem imposing, and they swallow hard before speaking.

"You're one of them, aren't you?" the second soldier asks quietly.

I shake my head. "One of who?"

He looks away from my stare. "You know," he mumbles. "A wolf."

"Why would you think that?" I ask, looking from one kid to the other.

The first soldier winces. "You killed the Commander, and the General didn't do anything," he says, looking at me quickly before gazing back at the ground. "And your eyes..." His voice trails off.

"What's wrong with my eyes?" I scoff.

"They're silver," he answers.

"Are all humans color-blind?" I bark. "They're blue." I grab my saddlebags and start walking up the tracks. "Let's go. We need to turn east. The track's busted, and your mysterious prey has headed inland."

It took the General another two days to get through all the crap I'd piled over the rails. When they got to the area a rockslide had covered, he walked ahead to verify my story about the tracks near the town. He took one of the kids with him, but the one left behind seems especially curious about wolves.

"Does it hurt when you change?" he asks, looking up at me while hanging off the side of the engine.

I roll my eyes and look down at him from my perch over the engineer's cab. "Kid, what do you want from me?"

The young soldier climbs the side of the cab to sit beside me. "My mother said my father was a wolf," he says softly so no one else will hear him over the engine's steady rumble.

"I'm not your father," I growl, returning my attention to the men clearing the tracks.

The kid chuckles. "I never accused you," he says. "She said they were mates—destined to be together."

Sighing, I lift my eyebrow. "What's your name, kid?"

"Thomas," he answers, extending his hand.

I lean back on my elbows, ignoring the gesture. "Your mother lied to you, Thomas," I grumble. "There's not a drop of wolf in you."

I have a million ways to prove that he's a human if he wants to argue, but the kid's silence means he already knows the truth. Although we face a lot of hate wherever we go, wolves have many closet admirers. Some are men, but most are women. They were easy prey on cold nights. Some poor sap probably wanted to land himself a pretty girl and found out she liked wolves.

"Look, kid," I start, squinting at his frown. "Maybe your father lied to your mom, and she didn't know." I sit up and shake Thomas by the arm. "Being a wolf ain't all that great. Nobody likes us."

Thomas shrugs. "I do," he admits. "You're not so bad."

"You don't know me, kid," I grumble. "I'm not here because I'm a good person."

We both turn to look at the soldiers ahead of the train.

"They're not good people," Thomas says, casually pointing toward the men. "Maybe you're just somewhere in between."

Smiling, I shake my head. I don't understand humans. They are an all-or-nothing type of species. They either like us or hate us. Wolves have a bond with each other besides what a mate feels. Ari both loves and hates me. She grumbles about my existence and tells me how to win over my mate in the same breath.

Then there's Gaine, who claims to love me but steadily rejects every advance I make. I almost had her this last time. She was naked, wrapped around my waist. My touch urged her on, and her legs moved to give me access to my pants. She left her hips in the perfect position. Gaine could've been mine, and I wouldn't be out here with this crazy asshole.

"That's cool," the kid says, pulling me out of my memory. "Can I see it?"

I look around, confused. "Huh?"

Thomas points to the knife in my hand. "It's a bit rusty," he comments.

I study the knife I'd replaced my blue blade with. I hadn't even realized I pulled it out. The tip is still stained with Gaine's blood, making it appear rusty.

"My mate caught herself on it a while back," I tell him, grinning. "I guess I didn't want to clean it off."

"Is that all you have of her?" Thomas asks, looking over the blade in my hand.

"Memories, kid," I tell him. "We always have our memories." I look up the tracks to see the General storming toward us alone. "Looks like your young friend didn't make it back," I murmur. "Perhaps we should keep this little talk to ourselves."

Thomas quickly slips from the cab's roof. "What's your name?" he asks.

"Kade," I tell him.

"Thanks, Kade," he says. "It was nice to meet you."

I shake my head as he jumps to the ground and jogs toward the train's rear. *I'll never understand humans.*

The General makes a point to scream at each of the men he has clearing the tracks as he walks past them. "And what the fuck are you doing?" he yells up at me.

Narrowing my eyes, I work my jaw a few times, trying not to smile at his little display. "Supervising," I answer.

"I don't need a supervisor, asshole," he screams. The General's face is so red I'm surprised it doesn't explode. If this man ever rocked on a rocker, he'd have fallen off long ago.

"Why are you so mad, Kerst," I ask, standing to stretch. "Were you not held enough as a baby?"

"Shut up before you end up like the rest of the dogs," he snaps before continuing toward the back of the train.

* * *

I thought it would take the men a few days to clear the rockslide, but after all the practice I've provided, they've become efficient at cleaning off the tracks. I stand beside the General as the last of the boulders is broken apart. The sun is setting to our right, and he's given the order to turn the train east, heading into the winter weather he was trying to avoid.

"My guy said she was on a houseboat," the General mutters, turning toward me. "I didn't find her there. Where'd she go?"

"I'm a wolf, not a psychic," I grumble. "How the hell would I know?"

The General might just be the angriest person I've ever encountered. His emotions dictate his behavior, which seems useful when he bullies his soldiers but makes him highly predictable. I duck as the General swings at my face and quickly knock him back with a punch to the gut.

Doubled over, the General coughs and sputters before diving toward me. I sidestep to avoid his arms, causing him to stumble forward and fall on his face. His men stop working to stare at their clumsy leader. Knowing they'll be his next target, I nod toward the back of the train when I see the kid among them. He's a quick learner and slinks away unnoticed.

As predicted, the General climbs to his feet and aims his anger at his soldiers first. "What are you staring at?" he screams, glaring at them. When their attention returns to the last boulder, his aggression swings back in my direction. "Get out of my face!"

"Listen, Kerst," I start calmly, eyeing the unbalanced man. "Perhaps you should get these little emotional outbursts under control. I don't think they're healthy." The General's red hue deepens. "The mothers in our pack would put their kids to bed when they got cranky. Do you need a nap?"

"Shut up!" he screams, taking another swing at me.

Deflecting his fist by pushing his arm while sidestepping, I send him tumbling back to his knees. "So, look, I'm hungry," I announce. "I'm gonna go shift while you get your little choo choo of death going. Did you want me to bring you back something to eat? A snack might improve your mood."

The glare I receive signals that I've pissed the General off enough to keep him busy for a while. Nodding, I point at him before walking down the train's length. He'll take that aggression out on the soldiers working in front of the train while I look around inside his special container.

"What are you doing?" Thomas hisses behind me as I climb the short ladder and lift the container's slide lock. "He'll kill you if he catches you in there."

I glance toward the front of the train before jumping down beside the kid. "Why don't you stand guard then?" I suggest. "Knock on the side that Kerst is on so I can sneak out the other." I sigh as Thomas shakes his head worriedly. "Kid, he's got his own little plan, and I need to figure out what that is before he gets us all killed."

"Kade," the kid mumbles, still shaking his head. "Why would I just be standing here?"

Apparently, this kid lacks imagination. Sighing, I squint and shift my gaze back toward the container. "Tell him you saw me poking about and wanted to make sure I stayed out."

"Oh," Thomas spouts, raising his eyebrows. "That's good."

I remember feeling excited when Miles took me under his wing. I imagine the Alpha felt much like I do right now. If I don't teach this kid how to survive, this world will eat him alive.

I clap my hand on his shoulder with a smile. "Remember, a sentry would watch both doors," I whisper. "Ducking under the container would be the quickest way, but mind the engine. I doubt Kerst would bother to tell anyone when he's ready to start moving."

Thomas nods and watches me climb back up the ladder. I lift the handle and slip the slide lock back.

"I'll get the other one," Thomas offers.

"Be quick," I hiss, slipping through the door and pushing it closed.

The ability to see in the dark doesn't help much with what I'm trying to study. Digging in my pockets, I find the flashlight Miles gave me. I pull it out and click the switch, but nothing happens. "Come on, you stupid thing. One more time," I growl at the old flashlight, banging it against my other hand.

I get to work scanning the container as soon as the light turns on. The painted symbols match the design etched into my proximity ward. Following them across the reinforced wood, I see each design has one or two marks near it. There is a line on each side of the symbols on the walls. The ones on the ceiling have a line on top, while those on the floor have it on the bottom. They appear to have only one function—to stop the Luna from calling for help.

I kneel beside a set of chains and tug at them, finding no give from the large metal plate holding them to the floor. The flashlight's beam flickers along the wall to shine on a leather belt. I narrow my eyes and lower them to the small crate.

Turning around, I lift myself just enough to sit on the box and lean to rest my neck right where the belt is bolted. *A noose.* I glance around the container, finding only one other belt fastened to the opposite wall. *Two nooses. What are the odds Kerst knows about the little Luna?*

A light tapping on the container pulls me out of my thoughts. I quickly scan the floor to find two heavy collar setups. *Two Lunas and two Alphas?*

The slide lock beside me moves into place. I jump for the other door and quickly slip through, sliding the latch before climbing to the top of the container. Rolling onto my back, I lay my head on my stashed saddlebags and listen to the heavy boots approaching.

"What are you doing?" the General barks.

"I saw that guy sneaking about," Thomas answers. "I figured you wouldn't want him in there."

"He's not a guy. He's a dog. Stay away from him, or you'll get fleas." The lock screeches, and the door slides open. "Everything's fine," the General announces. "Get back to work." Once he resets the lock, their boots stomp through the gravel in opposite directions.

That man's hate for wolves is as common as it is annoying. Anytime he speaks, I want to put a blade in his other eye. He could make a conversation about the fluffiness of clouds sound like a discussion about how much he hates wolves. We have no connection to dogs or the regular wolves they descend from, and the reference is only meant to be disrespectful.

Regardless of my hate for this man, I have no idea how deep this mission goes. If I kill Kerst, I wouldn't know who they'd get to replace him and may not be able to stop them from capturing the Luna. And, of course, this all comes back to Gaine. I need to keep her safe. For that to happen, there must be a Luna.

I roll my eyes. *Women.*

The train jolts, and the whistle blows loudly, signaling the end of the rockslide cleanup. I relax and smile at the starry sky as the train puffs along, getting lost in my memories of Gaine. I could spend all night inside my head, but I know my ledge is close when we turn the first bend. Jumping up, I pull my clothes off and jam them into my saddlebags before triggering my shift.

It's too dark to be seen up here, but I still watch my surroundings closely until the formation of my muzzle blinds me. When my vision clears, the ledge is just ahead. I quickly pull my belt from where I'd jammed it and leap onto the rocks. The woods provide cover just beyond the thin ledge so I can remain hidden until the train has passed.

I drop the belt and step into it. Lifting it with my nose, I shimmy it over my ears and jam my leg through until it slips behind my elbow. The blade isn't sitting right, but maybe I can get the kid to fix it for me.

Since the train is picking up speed, I head straight toward their next obstacle. I wasted a day clearing part of the eastbound tracks to ensure they looked inviting. Everything I collected is piled on the railway a few miles from the junction.

Judging by the loud squeal of metal wheels, I made the eastbound tracks look too inviting. Since only half the brakes work, the following crash is pretty expected. I dart in the noise's direction until I reach the edge of the trees and find the two rear containers lying on their sides.

It's easy for a black wolf to hide from humans at night, so I stay hidden in the woods as I jog along the train. Although these soldiers know what I am, I'd prefer to control the first time they see me like this. Most humans get a bit trigger-happy when they first see our size.

I slip behind a tree and watch the General scream at his men, angrily flinging fencing debris and barbed wire everywhere. He mainly lists all the items in the rear containers, which seem to be holding food and water. I roll my eyes as he tells the men they'll be going hungry for causing the wreck.

When he aims his aggression at Thomas, I decide it's time to introduce them to who I really am. Without bothering to get up, I let out a soft howl, making them all freeze.

A few soldiers move slowly after a moment to grab their rifles, but Thomas steps toward where my howl had come from. "Kade?"

"Kid, get back here," one of the soldiers snaps. "What the hell are you doing?"

"It's probably that guy that's been traveling with us," Thomas says quietly, taking another step toward me.

I emerge from the woods, lowering my head. Although my coat matches my hair, people usually recognize my eyes first, which are easiest to see at this angle. He holds up his lantern and tilts his head. As a wolf, my back is the same height as their hips, so Thomas kneels to put us at the same level.

The closest soldier attempts to pull the kid back, but I lift my lips, scaring him away.

"Is that you?" the kid whispers, holding his hand out.

I sit before him, out of reach, and adjust my front legs. This would be a sign of comfort or even affirmation to another wolf.

"Can I touch you?" Thomas says lower than a whisper.

Rolling my eyes, I shake my head.

The kid laughs. "I knew that was you," he says.

"Great," the General spouts. "Now we're all acquainted with the mutt. Get back to work!"

* * *

Over the next month, I pass the time by sending the General on wild goose chases. Luckily, we run into a few wolf families that have left behind tracks to keep him busy. Since the General was true to his word about his men going hungry, I sneak Thomas some meat from my kills. He shares it with a few other soldiers, attempting to convince them I'm not so bad.

After three weeks, I finally caught a lucky break with the headlight. I shift every few days to provide the General with new misinformation regarding the Luna's whereabouts. This particular morning, the entire crew was working on a doe one of them shot. With their hunger distracting them, I jumped onto the front walkway and jabbed my knife through the air slits in the back, breaking the mirrors.

I curl up underneath a thick pine tree and listen to the engine puff as the train stops for the night a week later. Now that the headlight is nothing more than a dim lantern, they can't see well enough to keep going once the sun sets. The long winter nights allow plenty of time to sleep and create blockades to keep the General occupied.

It's harder to ignore Tynan's insanity during the quieter moments. Thomas has helped me sneak into the General's cage container a few times so I can enjoy the silence. Jax's wards may be designed to stop the Luna from calling out to her pack, but I appreciate their ability to block my Alpha from talking to me.

Luckily, Tynan is too busy to annoy me tonight, so I easily hear the boots crunching in the light dusting of snow as they approach. I lift my head to find Thomas kneeling to crawl under the low branches. He drags a bag and catches his wool hat when it snags on the tree.

"Hey, Kade," the kid whispers through chattering teeth. "I brought you some bread. I wasn't sure if you ate today."

I tap my paw on the ground beside me. I had a few squirrels this afternoon, but his bag smells delicious.

"One of the messengers brought this in today," Thomas tells me, producing a few biscuits. "These have cheese baked in." He holds a piece out to me. "Wait. My mother always said not to give the dog dairy. Can you eat that?"

I roll my eyes and snatch the cheesy roll from his hand. It's been warmed, so the cheese is melted and gooey. He laughs as I work my jaw and tongue to pull it from my teeth.

Thomas rubs his hands together and blows on them. "The good news is that we're turning south at the next junction," he says. "The messenger said the person we're looking for was at the southern beaches. I can't wait to be warm again."

I whip my head around as he leans to look in his sack and smack him in the face with my muzzle. Thomas snorts and rubs his cheek but jumps away as I trigger my shift. He stares as my wolf transforms back into my human form.

"Jesus, that looks like it hurts," Thomas remarks, wide-eyed. "Why would you do that on purpose?"

Chuckling, I shake my hair out of my eyes. "Nah, kid," I say, grinning. "The more we do it, the easier it is. Besides, I like being a wolf," I add, shrugging. "What's this about the beach?"

Thomas unzips his coat. "Listen, Kade," he says, trying to offer me his jacket. "The belt and knife are cool and all, but they don't really cover much up." He cringes as he looks at me from the corner of his eye. "I wish I had your confidence."

I laugh heartily before covering my mouth, remembering how close we are to the train. "It's just part of our culture, kid," I tell him. "We don't shift into clothes, so we just get used to being naked and seeing each other like this. It doesn't hold the same meaning for us." I lean against the tree between two branches. "The beach, though..."

"Yeah, he said it took him a few weeks to find us," Thomas says, digging through his bag. He pulls a few more rolls from its depths. "He said we're pretty far east, but if we head due south, we should run right into them." Thomas narrows his eyes thoughtfully and hands me some bread. "Who are we chasing, Kade?"

"The Luna," I tell him, sighing. "My Alpha wants the Luna and thinks Kerst will bring her back alive."

"Isn't she important to you?" Thomas asks, confused.

"She's important to my mate," I admit. "And my mate is everything to me. I gave her my word that I would keep her Luna safe."

"You've been putting things on the tracks to slow him down, haven't you?" Thomas sputters through quiet laughter. "I thought I saw a bare footprint in the mud a few days ago."

"I'll have to start paying attention," I say, cringing. "That woman's got my head in a fog."

"Is what they say about mates true?" he asks.

I blow out my lips. "If you asked me six months ago, I'd have told you it was bullshit," I say, chuckling. "But today, my answer would be that it is so much more." I close my eyes and lean my head against the tree. "She is in my every thought. I can't stop dreaming about her. Her tears break my heart. Her laughter soothes my soul. I will do anything for my mate, and she asked me to save her Luna."

Thomas remains quiet until I open my eyes to find him studying me. He bites his lower lip and lays his hand on my shoulder. "How can I help?"

12

Although it's easier to gather information with Thomas's assistance, I don't have time to figure out how to use it. Kerst turns us south at the first junction we come across, and I spend every moment attempting to slow them down so I can formulate some sort of plan. Since he received the new information from his messenger, the General hasn't been interested in anything I have to say and has denied all of my requests for a meeting.

Thomas does his best to stick close to Kerst without him noticing the change. He listens in on discussions and meetings while serving meals and drinks to the hateful man and his messengers. Sometimes, he sports bruises when meeting with me but insists the information he obtains is too important to worry about the General's misplaced aggression.

With a destination in mind, the train's progress speeds up until I have no choice but to abandon my nightly sabotage trips in order to rest and collect information from Thomas. After running hard throughout most of the day, I find it challenging to stay awake long enough to hear what the kid comes to report each night.

We typically meet once everyone else has gone to sleep, and he tells me what he's heard, but tonight, Thomas holds out some jeans and a sweater. "We're running out of time, Kade," he says, frowning. "If we're going to do something, it needs to be soon."

Once I've completed my shift, I take the pants from him. "What did you get today?" I ask, slipping the jeans over my hips.

"When I brought the General his lunch this afternoon, he was meeting with a different messenger," Thomas starts, sitting on a log. "I don't think they are getting their information from your Alpha. He said their informant told him it would be too dangerous to pass on any more information. They whispered after that, but from what I gathered, the group they are tracking began traveling north a few days ago."

"Any idea where we're headed?" I ask, taking the sweater from the kid.

"We're in Sippi," he says. "The General is trying to avoid towns because he says this whole area is infested with wolves."

"He's wrong, but it's good that he's scared," I say, pulling the sweater over my head. "Maybe we can use that against him." Sighing, I sit beside him. "I don't know where the Luna and her group would be, but they won't be in a town. We heard something from that guy with the horses about a market in a town called Stark yesterday."

Thomas takes a sharp breath. "Yeah, the farmer," he says, recalling the same conversation.

The tracks brought us close to a large farmhouse that the General ordered his men to inspect. The farmer had several large horses in his barn. While the rest of the soldiers raided his kitchen, Thomas kept him calm outside by talking about the horses. When they were done, one of the men asked why he had so many. He stated that they belonged to several local farmers and were headed to an annual market in Stark.

"The Luna was riding a big Percheron when I saw her," I murmur, recalling all the information I had disregarded while hunting Gaine. "My mate had several larger horses out in the fields but didn't farm, so there wasn't really a need for them." I narrow my eyes. "I wonder just how much homework he's done on the Luna. She can't shift, so she'll need a horse. She likes the big horses..."

"So, a large market of heavy horses might be a good place to pick one up," Thomas finishes with a smile.

Grinning, I tap my temple. "Exactly," I whisper. "He said it was in three days. That gives us two days to convince Kerst that he'll find her there."

"And how are we going to do that?" the kid asks, leaning to place his elbows on his knees.

"Maybe a wolf sighting will persuade him," I suggest. "If one guy was willing to travel that far with a bunch of horses, there has to be more. So, you convince the General it would be worth taking a look around the horse sale, and I'll make sure some of the locals see some big wolves."

Thomas rubs his forehead and turns to me. "How long do we have to keep doing this?"

"What?"

"This," the kid spouts, waving his hand toward the train. "They're not good people, Kade. They took all that farmer's food but threw half off the train today. The Luna is a woman. What does he need all those chains for?"

Frowning, I put my arm around his shoulders. "Have you ever been to the base in Union City?"

"That's where we were all stationed before getting recruited to work on the train," Thomas answers.

"When this is over, northwest of that base is a good-sized lake full of catfish," I tell him. "It's right at the Tenns line. On the south bank is a pretty sad-looking farm with a wraparound porch and a big, run-down red barn. There's a lady named Agatha who owns it. Tell her Midnight sent you."

"What would I do there?" he asks, shaking his head.

"Start over," I answer. "Live. Find a better path."

"No," Thomas says defiantly. "You're the first decent person I've met in months. I'd rather go with you. I can help."

Sighing, I rub my eyes. "Kid, I'm not decent or a person. I'm a wolf, and my only skills are being an asshole and killing people. Shit. My mate won't even have me. If you stay with me, you'll end up dead just like everyone else. If I don't kill you myself, I'll get you killed."

"You know, I'm not much younger than you," Thomas grumbles.

"When you're as old as I am, I'll quit calling you kid," I promise him, laughing.

"Nice," he scoffs. "So, your mate doesn't want you, but you're still out here trying to protect her Luna? Why?"

I click my tongue and take a deep breath. "When you meet a girl, you think she's pretty and maybe enjoy her company," I say, thinking about the old days. "You spend some time together and have feelings. We don't have choices when it comes to our mate."

"But I thought it was better than just loving someone," Thomas says, furrowing his brow.

"Oh, it is," I say thoughtfully. "It's like when the air is dry, and you shock someone by touching them. Her touch excites me in ways I could've never imagined. She is somehow the most beautiful thing I have ever seen. No one will ever compare."

"That doesn't sound so bad."

I twist my face in thought. "Until you consider the other side of it," I say, frowning. "My mate won't have me, but the thought of having another makes me want to vomit. I've slept with hundreds of women, and now, all I want is her. I will spend the rest of my life proving I'm worthy of my mate's heart."

"Yeah, that doesn't sound so great," Thomas mumbles, wincing.

"It sucks," I grumble.

* * *

Stark is a bustling little town with tall buildings and well-worn roads. A few smaller fishing ponds reside along the outskirts, offering a catfish breakfast before I roll around in the mud. Luckily, it's the perfect shade to transform me into a tan and brown wolf.

The sale barn is full of horses, most having seen better days. The sun is just beginning to rise as I jog to the furthest pen. After working closely for over a month with Gaine's mare, I wasn't anticipating the horses' fear. They pull away from the fence, breaking their ropes and crashing into the panels.

"Knock it off back there!" a man shouts from within the pens. "Damn horses... always fighting about something." A horse squeals in the group, trying to get away from me. "Shut up! What is your problem?"

I stand still, waiting for him to move close enough to see me. The metal fencing provides enough cover that he shouldn't be able to tell my brown coloring is actually mud. When the man opens the gate to catch the loose horses, I slink along the metal panels toward some others.

As they jump away, a shotgun blasts behind me. The fence between us clangs loudly, taking the hit and successfully sending the rest of the horses into a terrified panic. I dart forward to escape the gun that had evaded my detection and round the corner to run straight through the holding yard.

Since the sale is arranged to be a week-long event with festivities, demonstrations, and multiple auction times, the more sightings I can create, the better. This should keep Kerst busy for a while. With Thomas keeping an eye on the lunatic General, I hope to be able to locate the whereabouts of the elusive Luna within the week and steer the unit in the opposite direction.

I jog through the chutes and spook a few horses in each pen to keep the humans' attention in my direction. Each group will spread tales of their brush with death. My appearance will change, altering at will depending on just how close I came to killing them. These little variances will take on a life of their own, and suddenly, one single, mud-covered wolf becomes an entire pack of violent beasts.

The smell of popped corn pulls my attention, causing me to lick my lips as I remember how wonderful the butter tasted on Gaine's fingers. We enjoyed our first kiss as humans shortly after that. My lips will never want to feel another's. The sound of our hums singing together while my tongue tasted hers made the festival more magical than I ever dreamed it could be. Gaine's kiss was everything I wanted and more.

Another shotgun blast booms over the memory of our hums, and the solid hit on the wall nearby pulls me out of my fantasy. *I'm so screwed.* I dart out of the sales pens and pass through the main road before slipping into the trees west of town.

After running for nearly two days straight, I'm exhausted and distracted. I drop onto a wide trail and follow it until I reach a run-down house. The front door is missing, and the furniture is covered in years of dirt and dust, but the walls stop the cool winter breeze. It's not the finest of hotels, but it'll do for now.

The furthest room yields a bed still sporting its linens. I pull the blankets and pile them into the corner under a window that's missing its glass. The train shouldn't be far behind me, so this nap will have to be a quick one.

* * *

It feels like I've only just shut my eyes when a rifle's shot wakes me. I jump to my feet and peek out the window. Not seeing anyone, I stretch my back and legs before leaving the room. The dwelling is brighter than when I arrived, so some time has passed, but I can't tell how much.

As I step out the front door, a horse darts by with a girl hanging off it. "Mom!" she screams. A monstrous wolf nearly blurs as it pulls at the ground behind her. I freeze as the next horse and rider appear. Of all people, the Luna smacks her reins against a black horse's shoulders and kicks his sides as he tears down the trail.

Groaning, I spin around and bolt after them. There's an entire war-torn country, and this stupid woman had to run straight into the town where I led her hunters to distract them. My anger takes over, pushing my legs faster. I hear her yell that she will not leave the other rider and dive into the woods, knowing we're about to enter the town.

I race forward, trying to cut off the Luna, but she's gaining on the other horse, and I don't know how I'll stop both of them. The trees pass by so quickly that they nearly make zooming noises. Hooves begin clopping on the firmer ground while people in the street yell at each other, trying to get out of the way.

"Grab onto me!" the Luna shouts just before more guns are fired, and the massive wolf screams, rolling into a heap. The Luna's horse falls as his legs buckle, and both women are thrown to the ground. Their heads hit the street hard enough to make a thud that has me sliding to a stop.

I duck behind a building as Kerst pulls the Luna's head up by her hair. A distant thundering of paws distracts me as he yells something at her, but I feel the punch that connects with her temple in my chest. I turn and dart in the direction of whoever is tearing up the trail toward us. Whatever I have to do, no more wolves will die today.

With her Alpha's massive stride, it only takes a few minutes for us to collide. Diving onto the road, I knock his front legs out from under him, and he rolls into the dirt. He slides straight as the trail bends and slams the back of his head into a tree.

A gun goes off close by, and someone yells, "Get off me, kid. We got the trader!"

Jumping up, I dig my claws into the trail, pulling myself toward the voice as fast as possible. My eyes land on Thomas as he falls to the ground. The man beside him is one of Kerst's messengers. I leap onto his chest, knocking him over. Glancing in Thomas's direction, I see his panicked expression and blood pouring from his mouth.

The messenger raises his arms, trying to push me off him. I bite down on his forearm and twist until it creates the satisfying sound of bones breaking. The messenger screams and holds his arm as I step on his chest. Giving him one more snarl, I close my teeth over his throat and pull up, letting my fangs tear his trachea. His silent panic isn't enough for what he has done. I step on his throat and let him feel his once-functional windpipe easily collapse under my weight.

After life has left his eyes, I jump off him and inspect Thomas. He only has a few wounds, but the handle of my long knife protrudes from between his ribs. I had given it to him to hold. I suspect Thomas tried to use it on the messenger. His breaths are fast and shallow as he drowns in his own blood.

"I told you you were one of the good guys," he whispers, reaching for my face. "Don't," Thomas coughs out, trying to talk as I let him slide his hand over my cheek. "Don't trust them. They know... Kill you..." He coughs again before his hand drops to the ground near my paws.

"I told you I'd get you killed," I say to the lifeless kid, rubbing my whiskers over his cheek. *"You were one of the good ones, too."* I push his eyelids down with my chin before looking around to get my bearings. Running around in a rage can easily knock a wolf off course. I leave Thomas once I spot the Luna's Alpha. *Alright, here we go. Mister Good Guy.*

I approach the large wolf slowly with my head lowered. I don't smell any blood, but he's not moving. Once I reach him, I push on his shoulder, but there's no response. *Great.* Although his ribs are moving, it would appear the dumbass knocked himself out with the tree. Sighing, I look around for help.

The noise filtering in around me doesn't fill me with hope. Heavy breathing, growls, and snarls are all I hear from the wolves closing in on us. They would smell the human blood, discover their Luna's disappearance, and find their downed Alpha. Not liking my odds against the Lunar wolves, I leave to take my chances with the soldiers.

I didn't realize how far I had run while trying to intercept the Luna's Alpha. Everything happened so fast. Even the old me could never have planned for this. *What a shit show.*

The General has a good head start, and I have to run for hours to catch him and his men. Now that they have their prize, there are no detours or unplanned visits to towns. The General will point his train north and aim it straight at the compound.

13

The General stopped the train for three nights before ordering his men to walk out front to keep it moving after dark. I ran ahead to shift and climbed onto the jail container while they moved slowly, gaining access to my saddlebags.

The Luna hasn't woken up since I found the train. One of Kerst's guys goes in there several times a day to throw around some clove powder and hit her a few times. It didn't affect me much until I was lying on the container. Having to hear it so clearly doesn't sit well in my gut. Gaine would probably be angry with me for not helping, but there are too many soldiers to take on alone.

Two nights later, I'm staring at the moon when someone whispers from within the container. Sighing, I smile. *It's about time.* I climb down to the door after checking that the coast is clear. The slide lock squeaks as I push the door open enough to slip into the mobile prison.

Both women from the attack are collared and chained to the walls—one at each end of the container. The clove scent is so strong that it burns my eyes. When the wolf tethered to the floor snarls at me, the woman on the back wall turns her head. I step in her direction, figuring she must be the one I heard.

"Don't you touch her," the other woman growls at me. I recognize her voice as the one that yelled at the wolf and called to the girl... the woman on the black horse... the Luna.

"Shh, Luna," I whisper. "I'm here to help." I cross the container, eyeing the snarling wolf. He's much larger, but I'm pretty sure he's Tynan's missing super soldier. Narrowing my eyes at him, I reach for the Luna's arms to steady the chains.

"Get your hands off me," she snaps.

"Is that Bastian?" I ask, turning my attention to the short, angry woman. "Shit, he's huge." I look over the chains, seeing they've been wrapped around ropes.

"Forgive me, Kade," the Luna says. "I'm not interested in exchanging pleasantries with you. Now get your hands off me."

Clicking my tongue, I let her go. The General put plenty of seats in here, probably expecting more captives. I choose one and relax against the wall. "I'll just sit here and wait for you to untie yourself," I tell her, working my tongue in my mouth. "You don't happen to have anything to drink, do you? I'm parched."

Sighing, the Luna leans her head back against the wall. The train jerks a few times as the brakes are applied.

"They're gonna come check on you," I whisper, jumping toward the door. "You need to act unconscious. I'll be back." I quickly slip out the door and lock it before climbing back up to my perch.

Once we stop, it's only a few minutes before the soldier who checks on them appears. He tromps through the container and hits one of them before the snarls from the floor catch his attention. The young wolf yelps when the soldier grunts and slams his boot down loudly, cracking a bone. His clumsy footfalls are a relief as he leaves without hitting the second woman.

I climb down the container when the train begins moving again. It's always so loud when it starts up. I slip the door nearly closed and cross the container back to the Luna amidst the banging and squealing of the wheels.

"Luna?" I whisper once I'm beside her.

She turns her head. "Kade, if you're really here to help, untie me."

I reach for her arms again but stop as I inhale her scent. It's a powerful blend of flowers strong enough to erase the smell of the clove powder. I step closer and slide my hands over her skin, scaring her. "Easy, Luna," I whisper against her ear, seeing the fresh blood trickle down her arm. "You're bleeding. Let me take this blindfold off."

I remove the strap over the Luna's eyes and step back, letting her view the container.

"Who are you?" she finally asks, eyeing me.

"You know who I am. You've been calling me by my name," I say, confused. "Which means this must be Bastian." I kneel beside the wolf, looking over his injuries. His back is bleeding, and his jaw is broken. "That looks bad, Luna. There's no bouncing back from that. You want me to put him out of his misery?"

The other woman heaves a few deep breaths. "Please don't hurt him," she begs.

I blow out my lips. "I didn't hurt him, sweetheart," I scoff, reaching for Bastian's head. "I'm just offering to end his suffering."

"Don't you dare," the Luna sneers. "I will break every pack law to protect those I love."

Sighing, I look over Bastian again. I need this woman to let me have Gaine. *It's time for a little honesty.* "I think we should start over, Luna." I stand and approach her with my hands out before me. "My name is Kade," I start, working on the leather strap holding her neck to the wall. "I'm the Blood Pack's enforcer. I was sent to help the militia capture you.

"I broke their light so they could only travel during the day. I kept them off the river. I even sent them to an event in a town." Pulling the leather through the buckle, I release the catch and slip it from her neck. "I didn't expect you to run right at them. What was that about?"

Genuinely wanting to know her answer, I reach up to work on the ropes. The Luna's blood takes on a scent so strong that I can taste it when I step forward. My entire body locks up except my mouth, which begins to water. I have no idea why anyone would want to cover up this perfect scent with those horrible cloves.

"Shit, Luna," I hiss, swallowing my Luna-flavored saliva. "What is that smell?"

"Easy, Kade," she nearly sings to me. "You don't want to do that."

I watch the blood trickling down her arm and lick my lips. "No, Luna, I'm pretty sure I do."

"You're not bonded, are you?"

"You wouldn't be my first if that's what you're asking," I whisper, undeterred. "Just a little taste, Luna. You smell delicious."

"I'm the Luna, Kade," she says more forcefully. "My scent is enticing by design." She keeps droning on, but I just need to satisfy this craving. "You won't be able to return to your pack," I hear through my hunger.

I take a moment to consider her words. My pack doesn't have Gaine, so I don't care. "I'm okay with that," I tell her, turning my head to wrap my lips around her arm.

"You'll belong to me," the Luna spouts quickly. "You'll never be able to bond with your mate."

Chewing my lip, I picture Gaine. "You're sure about that?"

"Yes, Kade, I'm sure," she answers, sighing. "I'd even let you if you were bonded."

I click my tongue. "Damn Gaine," I grumble. "Alright, let's get you down from here." I untie the ropes and wince as I slowly peel them from her wounds. The Luna talks to the other woman as I work on the chains around her ankles. One of my thin knives quickly picks the lock.

I try to help her to her feet, but she falls to the floor before I can stop her. "I'll check on him while Kade unties you," the Luna tells the other woman. She snatches my wrist and pulls me down to her. "If you hurt her, you will beg for death," she growls in my ear.

I put my hands up as I stand. "I get it. Precious cargo."

I turn my attention to the other woman, finding that she's just a girl. She smells nearly as delicious as the Luna but holds a fruit scent. *Maybe all Lunar Pack women are this irresistible.*

"Where's my pack, Kade?" the Luna asks as I pull the last chain off the kid.

"I have no idea," I answer, watching the girl dive toward Bastian and wrap her arms around his neck. "That Alpha of yours just about got himself killed trying to get to you." I kneel beside the Luna and cut myself off before telling her about stopping him.

"I can't hear them," she states.

"Ah, yeah, there is that," I murmur, digging in my pockets. I find the old flashlight and bang it a few times until it turns on. Shining it around the container, I show her the symbols surrounding us. "Nothing gets in or out. I used to sneak in here for some peace. Now I have to shift to take a break from that moron continuously screaming, 'Bring me that bitch.'"

"I thought trains were fast," the Luna says, pulling me from the memory of Thomas helping me.

I follow her eyes to the door I'd left slightly open. "They are. I told you I broke their light," I remind her. "They were stopping at night, but now that they have the Luna, they've got men walking out front. There's crap all over these tracks." I laugh at all the work I did to slow them down. "I might have added some shit."

"Why are you helping me?" she snaps.

Sighing, I jam the flashlight back into my pocket. "Gaine," I grumble. "That damn woman. I was happy. I was an asshole, and no one fucked with me. Then Gaine showed up in the basin." I narrow my eyes at the kids and see the girl pulling at Bastian's collar. Yank-ing its pin, I let the metal fall to the floor. "You women make us soft. She's got me out here doing good shit like I actually want to."

"Do you have a knife?" the Luna whispers.

I dig in my coat and pull out as many as I can quickly grab, shoving them in her direction. I'm probably handing her the weapon she'll kill me with, but at this point, who cares? I'll never be good enough for Gaine, and her Luna wouldn't accept a wolf who just told her he despised women. *What in the hell is wrong with me?*

The Luna narrows her eyes quizzically. "Can we use your light?"

I pull it back out and bang on it until it turns on. The Luna taps the kids before tucking Bastian's limp back legs into his gut and rolling him onto his stomach. I cringe as she starts digging into his back with my knife.

"You're who Gaine was with?" the Luna asks.

Rolling my eyes, I sit back on my heels. "She's refusing me," I grumble. "I didn't even know that was a thing. Can you order her to bond with me?" I ask hopefully.

She turns away from her task to stare at me. "Kade," the Luna says slowly. "I don't even know where to start." She shakes her head.

"How about, 'Gaine, go bond with Kade?'" I suggest, smiling.

The Luna slides her arm across her forehead. "That's not how it works, sweetheart," she says, wrinkling her nose. "It's her choice."

"Well, fuck," I pout, groaning. "I'm never gonna be good enough for the virgin queen."

I regret my words as she laughs at me. I shouldn't have said that. Gaine has cried over her desire for me. I know she wants us, and I'm just being an asshole.

"Not if you call her that," the Luna says, making light of my stupidity. She turns her attention back to Bastian's wound. "Gaine asked you to help us?" she asks, moving to dig at a different angle.

"She said if I ever wanted to see her again, I'd better stop them from catching you," I admit. "I hope she'll forgive me if I get you out of this situation." I can't help reacting when I hear my knife scrape against Bastian's spine. "Why are you even bothering with that? We need to leave. The Bass I knew would've left you long ago."

The bullet she'd been looking for falls onto the floor before us. "Can you please look for something to cover him?" the Luna requests.

Shrugging, I stand to look through a larger crate. The connection the three of them have reminds me a little of Rooster and Ari. We developed an easy friendship in the last few months while I was at the compound. I would've never gotten so close to Gaine without Rooster calming me down and Ari's advice.

I move to another crate, remembering Rooster having no issues with his mate sleeping in my arms. We went on that run to their moonshiners, and Ari calmly relaxed with me by the creek when we stopped. She even climbed onto my bed while they told me how to protect my mate. I find a canvas tarp just as I realize this is how living within a pack should feel.

I turn to watch the three of them again for a moment before bringing the Luna the tarp. The girl cries into Bastian's fur while the Luna whispers to them. Her grip on him is tender yet firm. She's clearly his mate. After what that kid has been through, he deserves her.

"Why don't I tell you the story about the first time my Alpha lost track of me?" the Luna says, smiling gently at Bastian. "I had to visit some wolves who lived far away. We were gone almost two weeks when my companion fell asleep on watch."

I narrow my eyes, remembering something about her companion. Jax had mentioned what a companion was a few times over the years. I also remember his name. "Wasn't your companion a Blood wolf too?" I ask, flicking my eyes toward Bastian. "You seem to have a type." *Maybe getting into her pack will be much easier than I thought.*

The Luna shakes her head. "The point is, Kade, that when my companion fell asleep, my Alpha couldn't reach either of us," she says, smiling at Bastian before lifting her eyebrow at me. "You've heard about my Alpha, haven't you? How strong he is? Well, that intensifies when he believes his Luna is in danger."

I shift away slightly as my mind replays her Alpha's enormous stride and massive body barreling down the trail. My only hope of stopping him was to take his legs out. I'm under no delusion that I would have survived our encounter had he not knocked himself out with that tree.

"Someone we both love very much wanted to keep ducks as pets, so we had a flock at the lake," the Luna continues, turning back to the kids. "My Alpha's story goes like this: the ducks jumped into his mouth, begging to be eaten." She rubs her hand over Bastian's face and grabs his paw. "In his panic, he could only think about killing anything in his way. He shredded the ducks. He didn't eat them." She turns to me. "That was six hours. How long have we been here?"

I swallow hard, lifting my eyes to hers. "Five days," I answer, frowning. *Back to square one. I'm never getting in when she finds out what I did to her Alpha.*

Bastian seamlessly shifts into his human form, and the Luna jumps to her knees, pulling a vial from her pocket. She jams it into Bastian's mouth before whispering to the kids. When she sits up, the kids capture my attention. The girl's arms tightly wrap around Bastian as if he might leave her at any moment. When their fingers lace, I feel Gaine's against mine.

"Kade, what day is it?"

I shake my head. "How should I know?" My eyes narrow as Bastian's jaw realigns. "Is that stuff healing him?"

"Kade!" the Luna snaps, clapping her hands in my face. "When is the full moon?"

Turning away from Bastian, I lift my eyebrow at her. "Well, that's a little more specific, isn't it?" I ask, smiling at her irritation. My entertainment only continues as she presses her fists to her forehead and bites her lip. "My, my, Luna, you do have quite the temper. You should do something about that."

She pulls something from her pocket, and I duck as she moves her hand back to throw it. The object lands on the floor near the far wall. When I look in its direction, a wolf materializes and steps toward me. Although he's snarling and moving to protect the Luna, there is something familiar about him.

"Do you remember Miles, Kade?" the Luna asks, smiling as she slides her hand over the wolf's hips.

I laugh as the wolf stops snarling. "Nice!" I hold my fist out for him to bump. "The original grumpy wolf got his shift back. Good for you!" Gaine had told me Miles visits on the full moon, but I hadn't thought much of it.

"Miles, can you please focus?" the Luna says to the wolf.

Frowning, I turn away from them. Obviously, she can hear him, so I'm going to get cut out of this conversation. I focus back on Bastian when his leg twitches. They were dead weight when the Luna moved them. His jaw is nearly back to its perfect formation.

"Kade, where are we going?" the Luna asks, reminding me she's there.

"That Kerst guy is taking you to Tynan," I tell her, looking closely at Bastian. "That stuff is healing him, isn't it?"

Bastian's eyes snap open to glare at me. "Give me a few more minutes, Kade," he snarls. "No tea could bring you back from where I'll send you."

Leaning back, I lift my hand. "Look, man, I'm here to help," I scoff. "Bygones."

"What's this about?" the Luna snaps behind me.

I cringe, taking a sharp breath and sliding my fingers through my hair. "I may have taken the kid to Tynan when his parents died."

"May have?" Bastian growls.

"And burned down their house," I add quickly, wincing. I frown as Bastian growls so loudly that he vibrates the walls. "Listen, we don't have time for this. They'll be back to check on you at dawn, and then we'll be going too fast to jump."

The Luna whispers to Bastian, and his growl quiets just before he says, "I will accept your decision, Luna."

Standing, the short woman turns to me. "Kade, you will be marked for everything I do not have time to name right now and for causing this boy years of pain and torment."

"Marked?" I spout, backing away. "Look, Luna. I said I was sorry." Suddenly aware that I'm the center of attention, I study each face staring at me. When I end on Bastian, I'm surprised to find his gaze just as calm as the others. "You know, I'm the one that paid the witch to get you out of there."

"Remove your shirt," the Luna orders.

I slowly shrug my coat off and pull my shirt over my head. I look down at the short woman as she moves closer. My breaths deepen as the Luna holds her hand up and lifts her eyes to mine. She's about to punish me for every horrible thing I have ever done, and her gaze is close to how a mother might look upon her child.

"From this day forward, you will wear the mark of shame for all to see," she says, still looking into my eyes. "You have brought dishonor to the name Wolf. Your heart will be covered and your wolf altered. Do you accept this punishment for your crimes?"

Covered? Altered? A mark of shame? I don't need to be forgiven that badly! But when I look down at Miles, he nods. My old Alpha always knew what was going on with me before I could tell him. I need this if I want the Luna to accept me and let me have Gaine.

"I do," I whisper.

The Luna presses her hand to my chest, but the pain she causes travels much deeper. My jaw clenches with a tightness that may crack my teeth, and the air in my lungs seems to solidify. I want to scream as my heart burns from within, but nothing will come out. Although my eyes stay locked on the Luna's caring gaze, all I can see is Gaine. My mate is worth my forced silence as this pint-sized demon kills my will to live.

After a sudden flash of blistering cold pulses through me, we both look down at her retreating hand. It left behind a silver print over my heart. As I lift my fingers to the scar, the air releases from my lungs. Although it looks like metal, the silver flesh still feels like skin under my fingertips. It doesn't hurt as a burn would, but something about me has changed somehow.

A deep, shaky breath leaves my lungs when the Luna's hand slides along my jaw to cup my cheek. "You have paid for your past," she whispers with a gentle smile. "I hope your future will be honorable because the price will be far worse next time." She slips her thumb over my cheekbone before turning away and focusing on the kids.

I pull my shirt back on in a daze. I have done some horrible things. I sat and had coffee with a man, asking him questions about how he escaped from Tynan before slitting his throat. Even Gaine said my soul's stains could never be washed away. Yet I feel new or at least cleansed of my past, even with this mark of dishonor. I'm lighter without the weight of the lives I've taken pulling me into their darkness. *How is any of this possible?*

I'm ripped from my thoughts as I slide my arms into my coat's sleeves. The Luna hauls me to the door and shivers when she stops to look back at the kids. I step closer and open my jacket to her. The Luna folds her arms between us and leans into my warmth.

"Show that mark to Gaine," she hisses. "Tell her that her sister will know what it means." She looks up to find my eyes. "Now, you owe me for that forgiveness. She will fight you, but you get her out of here." Her eyes pool as they dart between mine. "You protect my little girl with everything you have because you owe us."

I narrow my eyes and slowly shake my head. "That wasn't the deal," I whisper, ducking closer to her ear. "She told me to save you, not some kid."

"Kade, that kid is the future Luna," she snaps. "And that boy you helped break is her Alpha. You will get them out of here."

Gaine told me that Tynan would need the kid to be declared the Alpha of all wolves. He'd never survive the Luna, though. Her mark would kill him. "Yeah, alright," I grumble, hoping she knows what she's doing.

The Luna steps away from me and kneels to Miles. I watch her silently interact with him. Her touch is gentle and caring. She slides her hand along his jaw just as Gaine has handled my wolf. The Luna is nothing like what we were led to believe. The Blood Pack was taught to hate her for killing the wolf she obviously loves, and he seems to genuinely return her affection.

Miles nods to her and moves closer to me as she grabs her daughter from Bastian. He shoves me toward the door when the Luna picks up the object she'd thrown earlier. The grumpy Alpha bumps his shoulder into my hip, but I stop in the doorway to watch the Luna fasten a rope holding a medallion around her kid's neck. *They are nothing like I thought. This is why they all love their Luna.*

I jump from the container and turn to walk beside it. When Miles joins me, I smile at him. "I have so many questions, old man," I say quietly.

Miles taught me everything I know about handling knives. We spent a lot of time together while he taught us how to defend ourselves and the rest of our pack as kids. I can't remember a moment when I didn't idolize him. But beside this train with the Luna looming over us, he couldn't care less about me. The peppered wolf hasn't taken his eyes off that woman.

When the kid jumps from the train, our attention shifts to her. The Luna said she'd fight me. I can only assume she has no idea she's about to leave her mother behind. The kid glares at me before turning to walk beside Miles. I quietly move behind her as Bastian shifts in the train.

The Luna steps to the doorway with Bastian and slides her hand over his head before he jumps. He nods to me as he slides in beside the girl. She smiles and hooks her fingers around his jaw before looking up at her mother.

"Mom, come on," she says. "We need to go."

"I love you, little girl," the Luna calls out. "Take good care of our pack. Tell Daddy I love him very much." She nods, signaling for me to grab her daughter as she begins to scream for her mother.

I4

After hours of fighting me, the girl finally collapses into a heap at my feet. We're far enough away from Kerst that he'd never find us, so I just throw my hands in the air and slump to the ground against a tree. My palms are covered in blood from her teeth, and my legs ache from all her kicking, but her harsh words continue to cause the most pain.

I've listened to people hate me for years. Ari would probably be the worst, but she never attacked me the way this kid went after Bastian. I don't understand how he could protectively stand over her now after the hours of anger and hate she lashed at him.

"It should've been you," she sobs from under him. "You left her there. You should be there instead of her."

Bastian stays over the little Luna, keeping her safe and warm while she continues to ramble about the death he should experience for abandoning her mother. Miles sits beside me to watch over them. He seems deep in thought, and his blank stare says more than any words could.

I've lost track of how long I've been away from Gaine. Admittedly, I only had one thought when I came south: to find a way to claim her. I told the Luna I was there because Gaine asked me to save her, but that wasn't really true. Deep down in my black heart, I

160

only wanted to make it impossible for my mate to deny me. But this is so much bigger than us.

I've never met a wolf stronger than Miles. His glare could just about melt your soul. The little girl crying in a heap under Bastian is the next Luna—the woman who will somehow rule over all wolves and help them live peacefully with each other. Gaine will love and honor her just as she does her mother.

And then there's Bastian. That kid has more scars inside and out than I have ever seen on anyone. After walking through brimstone and fire, he stands over and protects this girl who will not stop wishing for his demise.

All three have the same look in their eyes—the same passion Gaine displayed while begging me to help. They love the woman we left behind, and I know where she's being taken. The Luna won't survive the wall. If she doesn't take Tynan out, he'll end her. *I need to finish this.*

"We're wasting time," I bark, pushing off the ground. "Let's go."

I scoop the girl out of the dirt as Bastian steps aside. She's nearly asleep from exhaustion, so she curls against my chest and latches onto my coat. Bastian taps his nose to my hand, making me lift it away from her leg. It's still bleeding from where his mate bit me when I covered her mouth to mute her screams.

I scowl at the mess it's made on my jacket. "It'll heal," I grumble. "Do you know where their Alpha is?" My face skews a bit in thought. "Well, I guess he's your Alpha now too, huh? Is he mine? How does this mark work?"

Miles nods to Bastian and jogs ahead to lead our group while the young wolf shifts beside me.

"She's asleep, right?" he hisses.

"Yeah," I answer, peeking at her to be sure. "Man, that is one thing I will always be jealous about. How do you do that so fast?"

"It's an Alpha thing, Kade," Bastian grumbles. "Look, I can't stay like this for long. I don't know anything about that mark, but Luna told me not to tell Tarq where they're taking her. You need to honor her request."

"Who the hell is Tarq?"

"Her Alpha," Bastian spouts.

I cringe at the thought of lying to that wolf. "So, she's planning to kill Tynan?"

"She can't," the kid replies, sighing. "It's against pack law to kill wolves. Tynan wanted her head or her daughter's hand. That's what he said. She's planning to let him kill her."

"Oh, that's not good." I stop and stare at Bastian. "Gaine told me to keep her safe, and I just walked away from her death plan? That woman is never gonna forgive me."

"You were there," Bastian says, resuming our walk. "You can't tell Luna anything. She does what she wants and sometimes lets us stand by her side." He brushes his fingers over the girl's forehead. "Mostly, it's our job to support the pack while they accept her decisions."

The girl stirs in my arms, but when I heat my body, she nuzzles back into my coat with a sigh. Now that we've left the container's cloud of clove powder, the fruit I smelled on her has become a powerful peach scent. It's clear that Kerst was using the cloves to mask the beautiful aroma of these Lunas. "What's her name?"

"Annalisa," Bastian whispers. "And she's mine." He rubs his hand firmly over his chest. "Is Ari alright?"

"Yeah," I whisper, nodding. "Rooster keeps her close. Says she was cared for." I look up to study the kid. "Thanks for that."

"Listen, I agreed to accept Luna's judgment, but no one else did," Bastian warns me. "I have no idea what will happen when we reach the rest of our group, but they are traveling up the river looking for the boat. I haven't talked to them. I'm only listening. I just want to make sure you will honor the Luna's wishes."

"I promised her I'd get this girl to safety, so I'll see this through,"

I respond. "If that Alpha kills me, watch over Gaine. She might have broken me, but I still love her."

Bastian chuckles. "Yeah. They do that." He grins down at the girl before shaking his head. "Alright. Miles only has until dawn, so we need to cover as much ground as possible while he's here." I flinch as he reaches to squeeze my arm. "I hate you, but thank you for this. We wouldn't have gotten out of there if it weren't for you."

Taking a deep breath, I narrow my eyes. "I think you could've figured something out," I whisper, shifting the girl around so I can run with her. "But if you want to thank someone, thank Gaine. She sent me down here."

"It's surprising what they can talk us into," Bastian grumbles.

I laugh as he shifts and shakes out his fur. "Man, you are huge," I remark, lifting my eyebrow. "I gotta get me some of whatever they're feeding you."

Bastian bumps his shoulder into my leg and nods forward, urging me to jog beside him. Although our wolf is stronger than our human form, they share the same stamina. The girl's weight might slow me down, but I'm still easily jogging beside Bastian when Miles disappears at sunrise.

Waking when I slow down, the girl yawns and rubs her face. Her eyes are red when she looks up at me, but she's much calmer than last night. Without her spoiled brat-type qualities, she looks more like her mother.

"You doing better?" I ask, squeezing her.

"Bastian says we're about half a day from the river," she says instead of answering me. "She made you promise to get me out of there, didn't she?"

Frowning, I look up at the trail before us. "Has anyone ever said no to your mother?" When she doesn't answer me, I look down to find her studying her fingers as they trail over my shirt. Her mother's handprint left an indent in my skin that I'm sure she can feel. "Will that ever go away?"

Annalisa lifts her leg from my arm and forces me to put her down. "Your past won't change, Kade," she tells me. "So, the mark of dishonor will stay with you for the rest of your life as a reminder not to repeat it." She places her hand over the print. "With this, you carry a piece of my mother. She has granted you a fresh start. She gave you a piece of her love to help guide you toward better choices and an honorable life."

I study Annalisa's face as she frowns at my chest. She rubs her fingers over the mark's edges but pulls away when I try to place my hand over hers.

Kneeling to Bastian, Annalisa wipes her eyes. "I'm sorry for what I said," she whispers. "I didn't mean any of it. I know you love my mother very much."

I move away to let them talk. While they are distracted, I slip my arms from my coat and pull my shirt over my head. Sometimes, our eyes play tricks on us in the dark. I couldn't be positive until now that the handprint is shining silver as if it's been polished. It feels just like normal skin.

"Does it hurt?" Annalisa asks, stepping toward me.

She lines her fingers up with the print and closes her eyes. As I look over this gentle little Luna, her pack marking catches my attention, reminding me of her mother's second mark. I lift her left arm and slide my hand until I hook her fingers, studying the design.

"As Lunas, we have two marks," she whispers, following my gaze. "My father taught me how to be a Luna, and my mother showed me how to love my wolves."

I wipe a tear from her cheek with my thumb. "I'm not her wolf, but I felt her love," I murmur. "I feel yours. You carry her with you too."

Annalisa opens her arms to me, and without telling my body, I step into them and envelop her in a protective hug. I close my eyes and bury my face into her hair until all I can smell is her peach scent. Something about these two women is pure magic. They have introduced a sense of peace I'm not sure I deserve.

I look down at Bastian. He has every right to hate me, but his eyes are calm as he watches me hold his mate. "We've really missed out, haven't we?" I ask him and smile when he nods. "Well, let's get you guys back to your family. I have some groveling to do." I lean away from Annalisa and kiss her forehead. "Maybe you can teach me how to get in Gaine's good graces."

Annalisa shakes her head, watching me pull my shirt on. "Kade, I'm not my mother," she says. "I'm just learning how to be me. Gaine is very special to us, though. She's highly regarded within the pack. You'll need to find a place within the wolves that protect her."

"Why couldn't my mate just be a farmer," I grumble, pulling my coat on. "I could watch her sweat in the dirt all day."

Bastian slides his jaw into the little Luna's hand and tugs her forward. "Bastian says we need to go," Annalisa tells me. "He also wants to know what happened to you."

Smiling, I look down at her wolf and wink. "Ari," I answer. "I went to Rooster for advice after meeting Gaine, and he turned Ari loose on me. I'm pretty sure it was all downhill from there."

"Women make you soft," the little Luna says, smiling. "My grandfather says that all a wolf needs is the love of a good woman." She looks at me as she links our arms. "It would appear you already have a lot of love, Kade. Perhaps you didn't know how to accept it until you met Gaine."

I look ahead and narrow my eyes. "I just want to watch her eat pumpkin pie again," I say.

Annalisa laughs. "I probably don't want to hear about that, Kade."

* * *

The following day, we're still waiting beside the river. The little Luna lies curled against Bastian's underside with her face buried in his chest's fur. He stayed awake for a while last night before falling asleep. Although they weren't talking to me, I appreciated their company. I've spent a lot of time alone and find myself thinking of Gaine in all the silence.

This morning is no different as I think about the mare I sent north and wonder if she made it. My note told Gaine I would return to her, but that was before I left that massive Alpha's mate to travel to her death. Little Luna said I would need to find my place among the wolves that protect Gaine. That includes the Alpha of her pack. *I am so screwed.*

"The boat will be here soon," little Luna whispers.

I turn to find her peering at me over Bastian's neck. "And your father?"

"He's on it," she admits.

"I've never been scared to encounter anyone," I say, shaking my head. "Your father has every right to want to kill me."

Annalisa kicks her legs over Bastian's hips, and he slides his front leg off her arm so she can move more freely. "You weren't alone in that decision," she assures me. "Bastian told me you didn't know her plan. If anyone knows how hard it is to stop my mother, it's my father. He's never liked her plans."

Breathing a small laugh, I stand and step closer to the river. "Our pack is about survival," I tell her quietly, looking over the water. "We don't know much about being part of something." I pull a knife from my coat and slide my fingers over the side of the cold blade. "I don't know how to fit into your world, but I can't go back to mine."

I throw the blade over the river and watch it cut silently into the water. When I turn, Annalisa is lying with her back against Bastian's stomach, and they are both watching me. They remind me of the first days of my secret trip with Gaine. Smiling, I remove the blade I'd jammed into my belt's sheath and toss it into the river with the first.

"What are you doing?" the little Luna asks.

"Removing temptation," I answer, producing the blade her mother had used to assist Bastian. "I suppose your father wouldn't appreciate me carrying around a blade with your Alpha's blood on it." I shake my head and toss it after the others. "How's your pop holding up?"

When I look at Bastian, he only sighs and lays his head on the ground. Frowning, I shift my eyes to Annalisa.

"I'm not sure there's a love in this world stronger than what my father feels for my mother," she tells me. "Their companion sedated him."

"He was a Blood wolf, wasn't he?" I ask. "His name is Chase, right?"

"He's Bastian's uncle," Annalisa responds, making me cringe. "This isn't going to be easy for you."

I hurl another knife into the water.

"You sure you don't want to keep a few of those?" she asks as I take another out.

"Would you want me to kill your father?" I grumble. "Bastian says it's against pack law to kill a wolf. By removing this easy temptation," I start, holding up the blade I'd pulled out, "I'll better my ability to follow the rules."

The little Luna watches me throw the last of my knives into the water and smiles when I sit beside her. "You should rest, Kade," she says, reaching for my hand. "Bastian says that when he went up against Daddy, my mother refused to help him. She told him he needed to learn to communicate with my father."

Letting her take my hand, I lie in the grass beside her. "Any suggestions?"

"When you're near Gaine, how does she make you feel?" Annalisa asks.

I shake my head, chuckling. "She's overwhelming," I start. "I want to protect and hurt her at the same time. I feel the need to taste her entire body. Something inside me pushes against my skin with such intensity that I want to force myself on her." Sighing, I roll my eyes and frown. "I'm sorry. I shouldn't be telling you this."

Annalisa smiles, cupping my cheek. "I'm a Luna, Kade. I've known about bonds my whole life." She pauses when I close my eyes. "You're a wolf and have two sides at war within you. The mind will want to worship your mate, while your body only wants to conquer her. What settles you when you're near her?"

Smiling, I open my eyes. "Her words," I answer. "You're pretty smart for a kid."

"I had a good teacher," the little Luna whispers. "Get some rest. I have a feeling you're gonna need it."

* * *

I wake to Annalisa pulling her fingers through my hair. If it were anyone else, I'd have snatched their wrist and broken their arm. But the little Luna's touch leaves behind more than it takes away.

"I don't feel anything when I touch you, Kade," she whispers. "I know you must be missing Gaine, but I can't feel it."

Yawning, I roll toward her and glimpse a large fishing barge approaching the bank. "She is worth every minute I need to spend away from her," I tell the little Luna. "She has a heart so pure it can only be won by honor." I focus on the boat. "I haven't earned it yet."

Bastian rolls upright and rests his chin on Annalisa's shoulder. He stares at me for a moment before rubbing his whiskers on her cheek and leaving to greet the boat.

"My Alpha says you don't fail," the little Luna says. "We will just have to make sure that streak continues." Standing, she reaches for my hand. "Come on, Kade. It's time to resume our journey."

I let her help me up and link our arms for the walk to where the barge had tied to the bank. It's right against the land but appears to have a flat bottom, allowing it into the shallow area. I help Annalisa onto the deck and pull myself after her.

Humans move around us, pushing off the trees at the bank and shoving the boat back into the deeper water. Bastian grabs some ropes and runs them down the deck to pull weights off the river-bed. I'm guided to a door that reveals a room filled with compartments and traveling bags. Clothes hang from nearly every hook in the room.

"I need to see my father," Annalisa tells me as I close the door. "He has been told that you are a Blood wolf and helped us escape. Bastian was careful not to tell them where my mother was being taken but was forced to admit we left her behind. You don't have to come with me if you'd rather stay here."

Sighing, I shake my head. "Let's get this over with," I say. "I miss Gaine with every fiber of my being and fear I may never see her again. I know exactly how he feels."

"Alright," she says with a deep sigh. "Here we go." She leads me across the compartment and down a hall lined with stacked barrels. When we reach the end of the stack, she turns into a dead end and pauses with her hand on a board. "You should probably stay behind me."

I lift my eyebrow as she tugs the piece of wood and pulls out a sizable hidden door. I've never met anyone like these Lunas. Their unmatched strength stems from their desire to protect their wolves. It's clear why they are so loved.

We step through the secret doorway into a large room with mattresses nearly covering the floor. I recognize all of the faces that look up as we enter. Anthony sits beside the gray-haired woman as she slides her hands over the Alpha's shoulders. His snarl starts before he even lifts his head.

"Ayls, sweetheart," I whisper, guiding her by her shoulders. "I'm gonna need you to move aside."

"Easy, Daddy," she murmurs soothingly to her father. "He didn't do this. He's trying to help."

"Let him have me, Little Luna," I say softly, leaning forward with my arms out. "I think we both need this." I use one arm to push her aside while the other points at her father. He rolls to his feet and steps forward with his head low. "Come on, old man. I know the pain you're in."

The Alpha lunges at me, shifting with Bastian's ease. I had planned to catch the wolf, so he easily slips past my arms and knocks me back. "Where is she?!" he screams, slamming his fist into my face.

"Daddy! Stop!" the little Luna shouts.

She steps toward him but stops when I spit a mouthful of blood at her feet.

"Leave him," I spout.

The Alpha holds me down by my throat, swinging his other fist at my ribs. He might not be aiming these blows, but they explode against my muscles with a blinding force. I grit my teeth and let him swing a few more times before catching his wrist and stopping his attack. The Alpha's face is red and pinched with rage, but his calm eyes capture my attention.

"Easy, mate," I choke out against the fingers he still has around my throat. "I'm trying to help."

He pulls free of my grip to crash his fist into my cheek. "Where is my wife?!" he growls.

"She sent me away," I whisper hoarsely, wincing from the bruise he left on my cheek.

The Alpha stops mid-swing and glares at me. His pause gives me ample time to assess him. My nearly silver eyes are unique, but

I've never seen anyone with tan eyes. As he moves them, I catch the black specks in the coloring. His sandy hair is a bit longer than mine and messy, but his confidence is notable as he straddles my hips in his completely naked state of dress.

I could easily overpower the distracted Alpha, but my dominance would be short-lived with how smoothly he shifts. I find it odd that he chose to attack me as a human when his wolf could've ended me in mere moments. Laws be damned. I'd kill the wolf that left my mate to die.

"Why should I trust you?" he snarls through his teeth.

"He's been marked, Daddy," the little Luna whispers, placing her hand on his shoulder. "Mom held court. Judgment was passed." She brushes his hair away from his face. "She sent us all away. He was not alone."

"Tarq?" the gray-haired woman says, rubbing his back.

"Edith, so help me," the Alpha growls. "Get away from us." His glare is fierce as he reaches for my shirt and tears it away from my chest.

I sigh in relief when his eyes leave mine, and his face softens. Being raised under Miles' rule, I know how to honor an Alpha. It's just been a while since I've had to bother with such things. With each blow from Tarq's fists, I could only see Gaine and how I needed this wolf's permission to enter his pack. Challenging him would've ended my chance to stay with Gaine.

The Alpha releases my neck and slides his fingers over the handprint on my chest. I imagine Tarq can feel the piece his mate left behind too. When his growl settles, I look down to see his hand trembling as he traces her print.

"She made me promise to save your daughter," I whisper, recalling the little Luna's lesson. "She seems to love you very much."

The anger he flashes at me is unexpected. "Don't you talk about her!" the Alpha shouts, reaching back to swing his fist again.

Grabbing his throat with my left hand, I quickly swing the right, slamming my knuckles into his jaw and knocking him back. He lunges at me, but I catch his ribs with my boot and send him flying over my head. Although his growl builds, he doesn't shift as I roll over to face him.

I recognize his pain. The same feeling has been deeply seated within my core since I met Gaine and is present whenever I leave her. It's the need for our mates and the fear that we may never see them again. There's nothing we can do about the internal pain we feel, but bringing it to the surface somehow makes it better.

I sidestep, setting Tarq off. He jumps forward, hooking my neck and landing a punch to my gut. Before he can pull away, I swing at his chest to distract him from the uppercut that knocks him against the wall.

The little Luna and a man I recognize as an older Chase rush at us, trying to stop our fight, but we both push them away. I wouldn't even call this fighting. This Alpha is in an amount of pain I will never understand. He needs someone who won't back down from him.

It's hours before we're out of breath, slumped against the wall, watching the others sleep. They gave up on getting us to stop and left us to our demons long ago. Tarq's face is beginning to show the bruises I'd left behind. We were careful not to break anything and just stuck to a rough form of sparring.

"You're gonna help me get her back, right?" the exhausted Alpha asks.

"Yeah," I respond, sighing as I lean my head back.

15

Many days pass on the boat while this close-knit family mourns a woman who's still alive. I can't be sure I want to be a part of this, but I understand why my mate fears its loss. Their love for the Luna seems to create a fierce bond between them. The more I reflect on my interactions with Gaine, the easier it is to see the same passion.

The little Luna suffers from motion sickness, and Bastian spends most of his time comforting her. The gray-haired woman is a witch and, from the rings on their fingers, seems to be married to Anthony. They have matching glares any time they look in my direction.

The Alpha, Tarq, stays close to me, though. I've caught him staring at me a few times, but he mainly lies still with his chin on his paws, quietly sighing. The little Luna says he can only hear her mother as a wolf, so he won't shift in hopes of hearing her voice. She isn't sure why he's staying near me, but I appreciate his company.

I look up as the hidden door opens, and Chase slips into our compartment with several bags of food. He crouches beside Tarq. "We'll reach the dock tomorrow," he whispers. "You need to eat. You'll need your strength when we find Dar."

When the Alpha doesn't respond, I reach for the container Chase is holding. "Let me try," I request. Chase traveled a lot with Miles and proudly stood beside our Alpha as he presented me with my blue blade. He's still as laid back as he was in those days but has kept a watchful eye over the royal family throughout the trip. "He just needs to talk, brother. He's got some things to say."

"He won't shift," Chase scoffs. "How's he gonna talk to you?"

Smiling, I take the food container. "It's not me he needs to talk to." Once Chase leaves us, I lean back on the pile of blankets behind me and lift the container's lid to find raw duck fillets. "You're a duck man, huh? I prefer the feistier prey myself."

The large, tan Alpha only sighs, rolling his head to the side to wipe a tear. I release the three buttons at the top of my shirt and trace part of the Luna's handprint. It wasn't that long ago, but I can't remember the pain she caused while making it. I'm comforted by its presence, even though it still carries its original warning.

The Alpha is peering up at me when I turn back to him. "This mark makes me want to do the right thing," I whisper, lowering the meat with a sigh. "Try to contain your need to kill me, but I was who stopped you from reaching the town."

Tarq rolls upright and jams his nose in my face. His lips lift to show me his teeth.

"Look," I start, unsure what to follow that confession with. "There were too many soldiers. I'm pretty sure they all put a bullet in that horse your Luna was riding. They'd have done the same to you." I pause as he backs up. "You didn't fail," I tell him. "You hit that tree going faster than I can run. I see how they all look at you. They need you."

The Alpha follows my eyes when I look toward the group across the room. Although they're talking amongst themselves, their focus is on Tarq. I suspect they are wondering if we'll try to kill each other again, but there is still a clear sense of caring in their gaze. I smile when he turns back to rest his cheek on the floor.

"Come on," I urge, opening the duck meat container again. "Why don't you have a bite for them? Maybe we could boost morale a bit around here." I place the meat on the mattress and lean back with my eyes closed. "The little Luna said her mother left behind a part of herself. You should try talking to her."

After relaxing in silence, I check to find the meat gone. Tarq is lying with his eyes closed, and his peaceful expression tells me he's following my suggestion. I spent plenty of time talking to Gaine's mare and Thomas when neither could hear me. I should probably credit them for my sanity on this trip.

Pulling out another fillet, I slowly place it beside Tarq's muzzle. His nose wiggles, and his eyes open. He taps his paw on my hand before taking the meat.

"I'm sure the Luna has a stronger pull than Gaine, but I really miss my mate," I whisper, setting out more meat. "I'm not a good wolf, Tarq. I'd like to be someone who deserves Gaine's heart, though. I think your Luna saw something in me and sent me to you. Maybe we'll get there together if we lean on each other."

* * *

Things changed between us after that, but I still felt like Tarq was silently judging me. We jump from the barge together the next day. The number of new wolves that greet us makes me nervous, but none seem to care much about me. They flank Tarq and peel away from him one at a time as if responding to his orders.

Annalisa takes my arm while Bastian sticks close to her hip. "My Alpha tells me they are setting up a perimeter," she whispers, indicating the fleeing wolves. "I can't hear all of them, so my mother is still alive."

"I promised Tarq I would try to save her," I admit. "I wouldn't give up if it were Gaine. I would tear this world apart until I saved her... or die trying."

"They grossed me out all the time," the little Luna says, giggling.

"But I have always wanted a love like theirs. It knew no equal." She looks down at Bastian. "Yes, Love. Until I met you."

I wink when she turns back to me. "Bass was a good kid," I tell her. "Brave and honest. His parents loved him very much but didn't know how to help him. I'm sorry for my role in his life."

"Kade, my mother taught me not to judge a person by their past as long as they were willing to learn from it," Annalisa tells me. "I don't know if you'd have found another path if you hadn't met Gaine, but regret triggers personal growth. We learn from the things we regret. The new path isn't always better, but it can be a step in the right direction."

I mull over her words as we follow her father. Once the last of his subordinates leave, I pat her hand. "How did you get to be so smart, kid?" I ask.

She smiles down at her father as he stops. Tarq sits when she kneels before him. "I had some really great teachers," Annalisa answers, holding her hand out for the Alpha's chin.

The little Luna curls her fingers and urges him to step forward. Tarq rubs his whiskers over each cheek before sliding his jaw down her back. Father and daughter pause as they hug, and Bastian bumps into my leg, urging me to let them be alone.

"You had to shift to get out of there, right?" I ask once we're far enough away.

Bastian ducks his head and quickly glances to our right. I spot a wolf jogging just inside the trees beside us.

"They don't know?" I whisper, scowling when he shakes his head. "Okay, well, how do I get her out of there?"

Bastian tilts his head for a few strides before dropping it in defeat.

"Why did I promise them I'd do this?" I mumble, looking back at his little Luna. She's walking beside her father, running her fingers through his fur. Her eyes are locked on Bastian, but the far-off expression on her face tells me she's not really seeing him. "I need to go to Gaine. Does anyone around here have a horse?"

Bastian nudges me off the trail. The brown wolf from the group in the flower field near Gaine's ranch emerges from within the trees. He's darker, yet still familiar. After bowing to Bastian, the dark wolf darts away.

"What was that about?" I ask.

Bastian shakes his head before raising it and lifting his paws in a prance.

I accidentally spit all over him as my laughter bursts out of me. "Bass," I choke out, trying not to fall. "What the fuck was that?" I don't know that I've ever seen a wolf "prance," but watching Bastian's massive wolf dance around was beyond comical.

The kid stops and lowers his head, glaring at me as I continue laughing. I'm sure I'm attracting the attention of others hidden among the trees, but I can't help myself. Straightening my back, I try to contain my laughter with little success. Bastian rolls his eyes and slings his head toward the trail before us.

When I turn to follow his gaze, Gaine's mare emerges from the woods. "Holy shit," I breathe out. "She made it home."

I dig through her thick mane, quickly finding my little pouch. The straps have been braided into her hair. Smiling, I pull a small piece of brown paper from inside and exhale deeply as I read Gaine's words:

There is no Beauty within a day without Midnight.
White hearts cry out for their darkness.

Without a word, I sling myself into the horse's saddle and turn her back toward the ranch. I don't remember urging her on, but the mare pulls at the ground, sending the world into a blur of color. I know these woods well, having to sneak through undetected often, but I lay against her neck to avoid the tree branches and let her find her way home.

All I can see is Gaine when I close my eyes, causing my chest to tighten. The old Kade would have a good laugh at my obsession with this woman. But the new Kade just wants her in his arms. I've been away from my mate too long, and the ache in my heart is more than I can bear.

I sit up and slow the mare when the pressure becomes too much. Reaching into my jacket, I rub and stretch my chest. My fingertips slide against the Luna's handprint. I narrow my eyes, wondering if that damn woman had planned this. The closer I get to Gaine, the greater this pain becomes.

"It's panic," Bastian says, making me jump.

I turn the horse to find him standing behind us.

Bastian leans against a tree and rubs his chest. "That pain," he continues. "Tarq's mother told me that mark blocks your emotions. It's part of the punishment. It'll hold them in you until you can't handle them anymore."

Slipping from the saddle, I shove the note into his hand. "I'm not panicking. That's from Gaine," I spout. "She is calling me back to her. Don't tell me you wouldn't drop everything and run to the little Luna if she asked for you."

"I never said I wouldn't," Bastian replies, sighing. "But you need to get the Luna, and I want to help."

"No," I answer. "I did what she asked. I rescued you kids. My job here is done, and I'm free to do what I want. Right now, I want to do my mate."

Bastian cringes. "Kade," he says, rubbing his face. "I thought Gaine told you to save the Luna."

"She should get used to disappointment," I retort. "She is my mate, after all."

"You don't mean that," Bastian grumbles. "I know you felt how special the Luna is."

"Kid, haven't you ever wanted to be selfish?" I ask, taking the horse's reins and turning her toward Gaine's ranch. "Just look inside and tell everyone else to fuck off? I don't want what you have. I want what's mine."

"Look at me, Kade," the kid shouts.

I turn back to glare at him as he stomps toward me.

"Take a good look!" Bastian matches my glare as he stretches his arms out to his sides. He waits for my eyes to wander down his body before turning to show me the rest. "I thought only of myself for six years. When I finally gave up and was ready to die, that woman put my pieces back together and held them in place until I was whole again."

Letting my eyes run over his body, I scowl. Bastian was just a boy when Tynan first put him on his wall. When he resurfaced after a few years, everyone could tell he'd been through hell. I'd never taken the time to look him over. Now that I see the amount of scarring, I have no idea how he survived.

"She taught me there is a better way," Bastian whispers. "If you give them a chance, they can help you too."

"Kid, I don't want to learn shit," I shout. "Fuck it all. I just want my damn mate!"

"Alright," the kid mumbles. "I'll help you find her."

Scoffing, I step into the mare's stirrup and sling myself onto her back. "I don't need your help. Why are you even here?"

"Because I thought you were doing the right thing, Kade," Bastian spouts. "After all this time with Annalisa and Tarq, I thought you became something better."

"You were wrong," I snap, kicking the mare to send her galloping up the trail.

* * *

At our grueling pace, we quickly reach the first cattle field. Bastian had stayed behind, but his words still haunt me. I jump from the mare and lead her to the gate, replaying the conversation.

"Can you believe he thought I was going to save the Luna?" I ask the horse. "Why would I do that? I followed her orders. Gaine said I had to accept her as my Luna and let her touch me. Now all I have to do is shift, and that woman is mine."

I lick my lips. I haven't eaten in days, but I'm only hungry for Gaine. She's not been in my mouth for so long that I can't remember how she tastes. Every flavor that touches my tongue is suddenly hers, and I need more.

Once I've closed the gate, the mare and I continue our wander through the field. I haven't seen much of the western side of their ranch. My travels generally took me south from the compound, but I gave the Lunar Pack a wide berth when I needed to go toward the river.

The silence of the empty field gives me a chance to consider what I should tell Gaine. She had sent me to stop the militia from finding her Luna, and I accidentally led them straight to her. Then, when I went to save her, I let that crazy woman convince me to leave her behind and take two kids away with the help of a dead Alpha.

I narrow my eyes as they lose focus. *I'm going to sound insane. Gaine's never going to believe any of this.* But the Luna made a point to tell me Gaine's sister would know what my mark meant. *Surely, she would understand that this was all the Luna's fault.*

"I'm so fucked," I grumble. The mare sneezes in reply, making me scowl. "Maybe she'll be so happy to see me that we'll bond, and she'll have to accept all I've done." I look at the horse as she gives her head a hard shake. "Well, if you have a better plan, I'm all ears." When she doesn't react, I follow up with, "Yeah, that's what I thought."

I stare at the ground before us as we walk. Kicking at the thin layer of snow, I cause it to plume in bursts. It's giving me something to concentrate on instead of thinking about the disastrous reunion I'm about to have with Gaine. The sparkling spray seems to scream "silver linings." She's still safe. There will still be a Luna.

The mare lifts her head and snorts when we're nearly halfway through the third field. My breath catches as I follow her gaze. I can't see Gaine, but the rapidly pulsing white glow running toward me is enough.

I accept that Gaine is my weakness and couldn't stop my body from racing to her if I tried. My arms ache for her, making it impossible to care about anything else. I can't see through her light until moments before we collide and fall to our knees in the snow.

Gaine buries her tear-soaked face in my neck as I hold her firmly against me. She trembles in the winter air, and her sunken cheeks make me frown. Cold air blows up my back as her hands reach under my coat to glide across my skin. Gaine's fingers are freezing, and I can't feel any warmth coming from her body.

Slipping my hand between us, I pull my zipper down and lift my coat out of her embrace to wrap it around her. Gaine's body relaxes against mine as I use the remainder of my energy to warm her. When her sobs settle to sniffles, I sit back on my heels. Instead of looking into my eyes, Gaine clings to me and wraps her legs around my waist.

"It's alright," I whisper, letting her hang onto me. "I've got you."

Gaine is a strong wolf. She was a skilled hunting partner and pretty good at fishing as well. She kept pace with me on the trail. I admired her long, smooth muscles whenever she gave me time to study them.

Gaine is not vulnerable or soft, but something has her twisted so much that she hasn't eaten. Once we stop eating, it takes around a week for our muscles to noticeably deteriorate. It's been a while since Gaine's last meal.

Locking my arms around her, I lift her with me and begin walking toward her cottage. "Let's get you home, baby," I whisper. "You need to eat."

When I reach the next gate, Gaine clings to me so tightly that I can open and close it without holding her. The road I step onto will lead us straight to her cottage. According to the boot prints in the snow, this is the path Gaine took to find me. It won't be long before we reach the barrier around her home.

"You should ride the mare," I whisper, ducking into Gaine's hair. "I'll take you as far as I can, but the mare will carry you to the house."

Gaine's grip on me tightens, and she rubs her face against my neck. I look around for a place to set her down when I feel fresh tears running over my skin. Not finding a viable option, I slowly carry her into the trees on the other side of the road and brace her against one.

"Come here and talk to me," I murmur, using my chest to push her away. I lift Gaine's jaw with my thumb and catch her with my other hand to hold her before me. My mate's face is flushed with red blotches. Her eyes are swollen, and her lips chapped. "What happened, Beauty? Why are you putting yourself through this?"

"We can't find her," she mumbles. "We've lost the Luna, Kade." Gaine slides her hands along my face. "I can't lose you, too. I need you."

I lean further away and stare at her, more confused than ever. "I'm right here, Gaine," I say, stopping her. "You have me. I came back, just as you asked. You'll always have me."

Shaking her head, Gaine pushes me back and untangles her legs. I watch as she tears clothes from her body with a blend of confusion and excitement. When she stops, she stands naked before me. Gaine's skin ripples with bumps from the cold in her state of hunger, and her bottom lip pulls nervously between her teeth.

I've always been the needy one in our relationship. Gaine's bravery seems to have run out as her eyes cast down when my gaze slides over her body. I lick my lips, remembering how much I wanted to taste her. I'm not sure I told my hand to reach out, but my chest heaves air as my fingers trace Gaine's breast and slide down to her belly button.

I step into her and push her chin to make her look up at me. Gaine's green eyes burn into mine while I search for permission. My mate's body might be calling out to me, but I need to know her mind is on the same page. Months ago, I was ready to take what was mine, but today, I need her to want me. I rub my lips over hers, and she opens her mouth to release a soft moan.

"I will always be yours," Gaine whispers against my lips.

She raises her leg into my hand, allowing me to lift her back to my hips. My fingers dig into her thighs before leaving them to twist in her hair. Gaine licks my top lip, causing me to come unhinged. I claim her mouth as my own and slide my tongue over hers. She tastes better than I remember.

Gaine pushes my jacket off my shoulders, and I lower my arms to let it fall to the ground. She pulls at my shirt and tries to lift it off me, but I'm not ready to leave her lips. I rock my hips, causing her to gasp and abandon my shirt.

I groan into her mouth at the sensation of her fingers slipping along my waistband. When Gaine pulls at my button, I lick her top lip, making her head lean back. Her hands slip inside my shirt and stop on my chest. Reaching back for her knee, I use it to rock her hip away from me and gain access to the front of my jeans.

After yanking the rest of the buttons free, I push my pants out of the way and roll my hips. The warmth awaiting me is a welcomed sensation. My body shakes in its need for more. I pull Gaine's leg to twist her into position.

Reaching for her cheek, I roll my hips one last time for her final permission. I slide myself over her wet folds, balancing on the edge of losing control. Gaine's fingers spread over my chest and touch the edges of the Luna's print. I nudge her face to push her back so I can see her eyes.

Even while exhausted and hungry, Gaine is perfect and beautiful. Her breath steams in hot waves as she stares at me, giving me the permission I've wanted for so long. Every twitch from either of our muscles causes me to move against her, and she would be mine forever with one thrust.

But Gaine's fingers brushing over the mark cause me to think about the Luna. I may have done as she asked, but I failed Gaine. My mate asked me to save her Luna, and I brought her a child instead. I've never been a failure.

Sighing, I roll my eyes. "I can't do this," I whisper apologetically. "There's something I have to do."

Gaine's jaw drops. "What?" she spouts. "You don't need to do anything else, Kade. I'm yours. I want our bond."

I peel her legs from my hips and set her down. "You don't want me," I tell her. "You only want to fill a void with the next best thing—a void I created."

I pull at my collar, tearing my shirt and showing her my mark. Gaine's eyes widen as she reaches for it, but I step away and pull my pants up.

"The Luna said your sister would know what this means, but you don't need to ask her. I'm not a good wolf. I'm hateful, I'm deadly, and I lie. I tell people what they want to hear to get what I want." I snatch my jacket from the ground. "I told you I'd save your Luna. I promised your Alpha I'd help him get her back. I told little Luna about that promise as if I were declaring my next move. Bass even thought that's where I was headed."

Gaine wraps her arms around herself and leans against the tree. "I don't understand."

"I haven't done anything I said I would!" I shout at her as if this were her fault. "This mark of shame was supposed to absolve me of my past and give me a chance at a fresh start, but all I'm doing is fucking repeating it!"

"So, you want to try to save the Luna?" Gaine whispers. "The old Kade wouldn't care." She approaches me and places her hand over the Luna's mark. "This is meant to be a mark of shame, but I see it as a chance for a brighter future. Do you love me?"

I pull her against me and slide my hand down her body, slowly drinking in her curves until I tickle her thigh. "I love you enough to keep my promise," I whisper against her cheek.

"Will you come back to me?"

"I will always return to you, my Beauty," I answer, rubbing my lips over hers.

16

There's an eerie silence as I skirt the compound at sundown. The mare gave me all she had, but it still took us hours to get here. I let her walk the last mile since I didn't think she could run another step. My eyes stay on Castor's dark house as I remove the horse's bridle before she leaves me for his hay shed.

I move toward the back corner of the house, letting out a low whistle. Castor isn't one to wander, so my heart thumps at the lack of response. I glance around his wood pile, looking for his ax. Not finding it, I slip along the side of the building toward the front door.

Other than the porch chairs rocking in the breeze, the house is still and silent. Climbing the steps, I pat my jacket pockets and wish I'd asked Gaine for my blade. Castor's door hangs off its hinges and sits ajar as I approach it cautiously.

My back presses against the door's frame as I slowly push it open. The table just inside the entrance lies on its side, and one of its legs is broken. Castor's armchair appears with a gash in its leather, but once the door reaches halfway, the smell of fresh blood hits me. It only moves another inch before stopping.

I step through the entrance, sliding my back along the door. The room is in complete disarray, having clearly hosted a struggle. Carefully moving into the room, I look down at the floor and see a boot blocking the door. I peek around the broken wood and find where the ax had wandered.

I jump around the door and swing it out of the way. "Castor?" I hiss, kneeling beside his body. His ax is planted firmly into his side. It was a lucky strike, landing between his ribs and slicing into his lung. Someone else has been here. They folded his arms across his chest and closed his eyes.

Squeezing my old friend's hand, I view the room again with this new information. Castor's house is small. His bedroom and bathroom are off the living room, and the bedroom door is open. I quietly move across the room, peeking at his perfectly made bed and tidy dressers.

When I step toward the bathroom door, a floorboard squeaks. The handle rattles, and there's a shuffling as someone leans against the door from inside. I pause with my hands on the trim, listening for a sign of who could be hiding from me. Reaching for the handle and leaning my shoulder against the door, I take a deep breath. My eyes snap open as I recognize the scent.

"Ari," I whisper. "It's alright. It's just me."

The door flings open as soon as its lock is released. I barely see the flash that is Ari as she jumps into my arms. Her body rocks against me as she sobs. When I notice Rooster isn't with her, I look around the room to be sure I haven't missed anything. With the scene missing any hint of Rooster's demise, I slowly coax her into Castor's bedroom and close the door.

"Easy, love," I whisper, pulling my fingers through her hair. "Where's Rooster? What happened?" I lean against the door and unzip my jacket to let her tuck inside. My time with Gaine taught me that heating these women seems to soothe them.

Castor looked in on me when I was younger. When I grew up, he was a level head and voice of reason when I needed one. He never openly judged me but nudged me in the right direction when I blew off course. It made sense to ask Castor to help keep an eye on Ari. To do so, he stopped in to chat with her and often stayed for dinner when Bass was gone.

"He was kind to me," Ari finally whispers through shaky breaths. "He used to say everything happens for a reason." She pulls away enough to look up at me. "How could his death have a reason?"

Cupping her cheeks, I wipe her tears with my thumbs. "I fear this might be my fault, sweetheart," I admit. "This would've been Tynan's doing."

Ari leans her forehead against my chest and slips her fingers over my skin. She snaps back when she swipes over the Luna's mark. "What is this?" she nearly shouts, pulling aside my torn shirt for a better look. "Kade, what the hell is this?"

I shrug my jacket out of the way and let her inspect the handprint. "I met the Luna," I whisper when she looks up. "She was a force beyond what I had reckoned."

"She fought you?" Ari asks, frowning. "My parents always said she was kind."

I shake my head thoughtfully. "No," I respond. "This is a mark of shame. She passed judgment on my past and marked me."

Ari narrows her eyes as her fingers trace my mark. "I don't understand, Kade."

"From what I've been told, I'm in a state of limbo," I say, scooping her into my arms and carrying her to an old rocking chair. "With the Luna's acceptance, I've been welcomed into the Lunar Pack. I want my mate, and that's where she is, so I'm going to go. All I have to do is shift, and I will sever any ties I have to the Blood Pack."

"She's here, Kade," Ari whispers. "Alpha has her tied in the field."

Grabbing her out in the open isn't ideal, but it's still easier than in the basement. "Where's Rooster?" I ask again.

"We can't get out," Ari continues whispering, ignoring my question. "When Alpha brought the Luna out, we tried to leave. Rooster said it wouldn't be safe once her Alpha showed up." She sleepily nuzzles into my chest. "There's some kind of barrier keeping us in the compound. We came here to hide."

I rub my fingers over her cheek before pushing her jaw so she'll look into my eyes. "Sweetheart, where is Rooster?"

"He told me to stay here," Ari mumbles through her tears. "He said Jax would know how to get us out." She pulls at my jacket, burying her face in it. "Alpha struck the Luna, Kade. She fell." Ari sniffles a few times while I take a deep, calming breath. "She is so beautiful."

"There's a mighty wolf inside that tiny beauty," I say, rocking the chair. "She had the chance to escape but sent me away. She made me save her daughter." I chuckle and look down at Ari. "Get this. Bastian's an Alpha. He's her daughter's mate. The kid is huge now."

"Good," Ari says, sighing. "He deserves a better life."

"Thank you for being nice to him," I whisper as she rubs the soft fuzz under my lower lip. "Rooster asked me to watch over you and make sure Bass treated you well, but you didn't have to be good to him. Thank you for not making his life worse."

"I didn't do that for you," Ari mumbles. "I'm not blind. I saw the scars." She snatches her hand away from my face. "He wouldn't let me doctor the new wounds. He said it wasn't allowed. We will never know pain as Bass does."

Sighing, I rest my head back and relax into our rocking. After looking closely at Bastian's scars, I know she's right. It would've been easy for him to flip a switch and turn into the evil he suffered through daily, but he didn't. The kid's temper flared often, but he never raised his hand to Ari.

I glance down to see my friend's mate is asleep. Rooster has done his best since he was allowed to have her, but she's still underweight. Tynan always kept a tight rein on the pack, ensuring they survived, but couldn't thrive enough to overthrow him.

Ari is beautiful in her own right but frail and insignificant compared to Gaine. Clearly, the Luna has done an impressive job of caring for her wolves. If I really want to make amends for what I did to Ari, I need to get her to the Lunar Pack. They will keep her safe without causing her any more pain.

I need to get them all to that woman.

Gently rising to my feet, I hold Ari close and carry her to the bed. It's cold, but I've heated her to such a degree that she snuggles into the pillow and stays asleep as I cover her with a few blankets. I've never cared about anyone crying, so I hadn't noticed how exhausting it was until I held Gaine during her moments of weakness.

Once I've quietly exited Castor's, I break into a run and dart toward Jax's house. The thin layer of snow crunches under my boots, but I don't care about staying quiet. The dark windows mean most of the pack is asleep, and Tynan is too afraid of the dark to venture out after sundown.

I wrinkle my nose when the stench of human blood hits me as I climb the porch stairs. Crashing through the front door, I nearly fall over Rooster's legs.

"Kade," he gushes, relieved. "Man, help me!"

Rooster leans over Jax, holding wounds as blood seeps through his fingers. One of the witch's kitchen chairs is toppled over beside them with rope tangled around various parts.

"What happened?" I ask, kneeling beside them. I wrap my hand around Jax's bicep to slow the bleeding from his right arm and turn his head toward me. His breaths are shallow, and his eyes are losing their light. "Do you have any tea?"

"Cabinet," Jax whispers hoarsely. "Red jewel."

"Jax, tea," I spout. "Do you have any of the tea made?"

Jax weakly shakes his head. "Hang the jewel on Luna," he says before the last breath leaves his lungs.

"FUCK!" Rooster shouts, slamming his fist into the floorboard.

"How are we gonna get out of here now? Why did you lock us in here, you stupid witch?" He flings Jax's arm across his chest before grumbling, "We're all gonna die."

I sit back and cross my legs in front of me. "What happened here?"

Rooster stands and throws the chair across the room. He explains about the Luna and how they tried to leave. Castor's house was the closest to the trail they wanted to use, so he took Ari there to stash her and found our friend dead. He told Ari to hide and came to seek help from Jax.

"He was tied to that chair," Rooster says, collapsing to his knees. "There was so much blood. I tried to stop it."

"So, this is fairly fresh?" I ask, confused. I lean forward and stick my fingers in a few pools of blood, not finding any of them firming from age.

"Yeah," Rooster says, sighing. "Probably just missed whoever it was."

"But he's afraid of the dark," I mumble to myself. "Why is he suddenly feeling so brave?" I jump to my feet and reach for Rooster's hand. "Come on, brother," I say, helping him to his feet. "It's not safe. I left Ari asleep at Castor's. Go on and get her."

Rooster grabs the back of my neck and puts his forehead to mine. "Be careful, Kade," he whispers. "You've been gone a long time, and there's been a shift in the balance around here." My eyes move toward Jax's cabinet when Rooster pushes me away. "You'll find the Luna tied to the tree in the field. He left her there just before sundown. I'm ashamed to say we were too scared to help her."

Smiling, I pat his chest. "It's alright, brother. I wouldn't want you to end up like him," I say, looking down at Jax. "I don't know her plan, but she's right where she wants to be." I shake my head and chuckle. "I'm still gonna try to talk her out of whatever she's doing. You just worry about Ari for now."

Rooster nods and leaves me to rummage through Jax's cabinet.

In the dark, my vision changes to black and white, preventing me from seeing red. Jewels are on every shelf in every bowl, dish, and plate. I slam my hand against the frame angrily, and a gem hanging on a thin wire lands by my feet.

I snatch it off the floor and carry it outside to study it in the meager light of the nearly new moon. Seeing the tiniest hint of red, I shove it in my pocket and sprint toward the only open field left on the compound. Miles used to have it planted with corn or wheat every year. Tynan burned it to the ground whenever anyone tried to grow anything.

Stopping at the tree line, I stand beside some wolves and take in the scene. The Luna is tied to the one tree that stands at nearly the center of the field. She's wearing a thin white dress that catches in the breeze and fluffs around her. Her warm breath leaves plumes of steam, making her appear nearly angelic. She's been tied to face west. I'm sure Tynan meant that as symbolic since she's facing her pack.

I glance beside me at a few wolves huddled together. "Can I borrow that blanket, Aldon?" I ask the man holding a dark blanket around his sister. He nervously hands it to me as if expecting me to kill him if he doesn't. "Thanks, man. Take them home," I add, nodding toward the others with him. "She's an amazing woman but can't bring you back to life if you freeze to death."

We nod to each other as we depart in opposite directions. I start with a wide circle, carefully studying everyone around the edge of the field, looking for Tynan. Not seeing any sign of him, I focus all my attention on the Luna. She's leaning against the ropes with her head lowered.

"Hey, Luna," I murmur, holding the blanket toward her. "You ready to come with me yet?"

She sputters and trembles as I tuck the blanket around her

shoulders and step as close as I can without crushing her. "The kids," she manages to get out. "Are the kids safe?"

"They made it back to your Alpha," I whisper, heating my body for her. "I'm sure they'd like you to join them."

The Luna presses her face to my chest, sighing in relief. "I can't do that, Kade," she says. "These wolves need to be free of that man."

My growl flares. "How is your death going to free anyone?" I snap. "You Lunar wolves are crazy."

"Let me explain so that you will help me protect my family," the Luna whispers, rubbing her face into my skin. "Killing a wolf is against pack law. If any wolf were to kill Tynan, it would be punishable by exile."

I lean down, putting my lips against her forehead. "Luna, he's not even a full wolf."

She sighs knowingly. "From what he's rambled, he's a quarter wolf," she tells me. "Enough that we can't kill him, but not enough for me to help." She leans her forehead against my chin, hiding her eyes. "Killing a Luna breaks a First Law. These are the laws of the first wolves and are enforced by the Guardians. Killing a Luna only has one penalty: Death."

I rub my hands over her arms in thought as she shivers. *These damn women.* I have no idea what to do for the first time in my life. My beautiful, perfect mate wants this woman to survive, and her whole plan was to let Tynan kill her. *How could I possibly say no to the Luna?*

"Can't I talk you out of this?" I ask, hoping she'll give me permission to save her. "What if I just untie you and throw you over my shoulder?"

The Luna smiles at me as she leans against the ropes to put her cheek to mine. "You secured the future for my wolves," she whispers. "You can be one of us now, and we'd be happy to have you."

"At least let me untie you," I beg, losing all hope of displaying the strength that's carried me through my life so far.

"Kade, which one of these wolves should pay for that?"

Realizing she's considered everyone but herself, I step into her and align our bodies. I close my eyes and inhale deeply, pulling in her floral scent. "Well, at least they stopped throwing cloves on you. That shit burned my eyes."

"Was that the horrible-smelling stuff?" the Luna asks, breathing a weak laugh.

"Yeah, it was to mask your scent so your Alpha couldn't track you," I murmur, sighing. "This has been hard on him. He loves you."

The Luna sniffles and takes a shaky breath. "I know he does," she whispers. "I love him very much." She leans back and glances behind her at the brightening sky. "Kade, try talking to Chase. You were both raised under Miles. He could help you find a new use for your talents."

Shaking my head, I wrap my arms around her as best as possible. "Luna, please stop trying to take care of everyone else. Just come with me."

"I gave you a fresh start, Kade. Take it," she pleads, looking into my eyes. "Love Gaine with everything you have, just as I have Tarq. Have an epic love."

I don't know how to handle the emotions these women keep forcing on me. I remember crying as a child when my father died. I was too dead inside by the time my mother passed. I mash my lips together as the Luna holds my eyes captive, feeling my chin tremble.

"You women are making me soft," I grumble, leaning to kiss her forehead. While she's distracted by my rush of emotions, I slip the thin wire holding the pendant around her neck and twist it securely. "I love you, Luna."

"I love you too, Kade," she whispers. "Thank you for saving my family."

I've never met a force as strong as the Lunar Pack. Their words and emotions pack a punch that rivals each of the blows I received from their Alpha. Their love is so fierce it could conquer the world. Yet all they want is peace and safety.

Not finding any words in my current state, I bow and pull the blanket off the Luna as I back away from her. I only take a few steps before she feels the pendant and looks down at it. Knowing I'd only disappoint her with my lack of information about the dead witch's jewel, I dart for the edge of the field.

I break through a group gathered at the edge of the trees and drop the blanket. I have no idea what to do, but I aim straight for Castor's house to check on the only friends I have left in this world. I pass several pack members traveling to the field for a chance to see the Luna, probably hoping for a miracle.

Castor's house is still dark as I run up the porch steps. I charge through the front room and tap on the bedroom door before opening it. Rooster sits on the bed with Ari curled against his chest. He looks up and sighs at the defeat on my face.

I sit beside Ari, causing her to open her red eyes and look at me. "I don't have any answers," I whisper, brushing my fingers over her forehead. "I can't save her. This was her plan all along."

"I could never leave without saying goodbye," Ari mumbles sadly. "All the pain her family must be feeling."

The long hours I sat with Tarq flash through my mind. I couldn't hear him but didn't need to. His pain was obvious. The little Luna wore her brave face for us all day long but still woke up screaming for her mother every night. The Luna saved Bastian from this nightmare, and he ran nearly all the way to Gaine's with me, thinking I would help him save her.

"I have to shift," I announce, standing up. "I was welcomed into the Lunar Pack. I have to shift to complete the change, and then I can talk to their Alpha." I shrug my jacket off my shoulders. "She's the Luna, but he has a right to say goodbye."

When I tear the rest of my shirt and drop it to the floor, Rooster jumps toward me. "What the hell is that?" he asks, catching my shoulder and studying my chest.

I cringe. "It's a judgment scar," I tell my friend. "The Luna said my wolf would be altered. We're all about to find out what that means." I kick my boots off and unbutton my pants before remembering a critical part of Jax's magic. "Guys, Jax's spells are bound by blood. Whoever's blood is binding this barrier spell will need to die to lift it."

"I tested it before coming here," Rooster says, frowning. "He didn't use his own blood. It's still there."

"Nah, he wouldn't," I answer thoughtfully. "It's there for a reason. To keep someone out, you have to keep someone in." I push my pants down. "I assume he was trying to keep someone away from here."

"Who?" Rooster asks.

I just roll my eyes and shrug before triggering my shift. I suppose I could blame the strangeness of this transformation on the fact that I haven't done it in a while, but I know it's because of what the Luna's mark did to me. My fur comes out of my pores like tiny blades stabbing me from within. I grit my teeth and groan through the pain until my muzzle forms.

When my vision clears, Rooster is on his knees before me with his hand over his mouth. Ari's tear-filled eyes shimmer as she stares at me. She extends her hand, and I place my chin on it, letting her feel my fur.

"How beautiful you are, Kade," Ari whispers.

A sudden rush of air hits me like a charging bull. With a burst, I'm thrown through the wall of Castor's bedroom and hurled around his yard. Trees whip past me before I'm tossed onto the ground. I roll a few times before landing with a flop on my side.

As I climb to my feet, I look down at my legs and see what caused Rooster and Ari to stare. I lift my paw and study my silver fur shining in the new day's light. It reflects everything around me, just as the mark had. Gone is the sleek black coat that had earned me the name Midnight. I will never hide the shame of my past. I truly will wear this mark for all to see.

"Kade?" Rooster yells, running toward me. "Are you alright? What was that?" He suddenly stops as if crashing into a wall and falls backward. "Fuck. There's that damn barrier."

I step toward where he'd stopped and nudge my nose at it. Sure enough, I bump into an invisible wall. *It was meant to keep the Lunar Pack out. Jax did this to help the Luna with her plan.*

"You can't get back in?" Rooster asks, crawling toward the barrier. "Kade, man, you are shiny as shit." He shakes his head and sits beside me. "It looks good on you, though. I've always known that there was more to you than what you let on. Now's your chance to find a better life. Don't worry about us. We're survivors."

"I'll get you out of there, brother," I promise, pressing my nose to the barrier beside him. *"I'm not done here."*

Rooster presses his fist against the barrier where my nose is. "I love you too, brother."

I watch as he walks back to the house where Ari is standing, wrapped in a blanket from Castor's bed. Once they are together, I test my new Lunar Pack communications, calling directly to the wolf I need to get here as fast as possible.

"Tarq?" I call out, sitting in the shade of the trees to keep my coat out of the light. I listen in as the guards call out general orders. It seems they are closing ranks around the little Luna, and she isn't doing well. *"Bass?"*

"What do you want, Kade?" Bastian snaps. *"We're a little busy over here."*

"I need to talk to Tarq," I answer. *"Where is he?"*

"*You abandoned us,*" Tarq growls loudly, broadcasting his anger to the entire pack. "*You promised you'd help, but the first chance you got, you left us. You had no intention of saving our Luna. You lied your way onto our boat, and I will kill you if you show your face here again.*"

Sighing, I roll my eyes and flop to the ground. I don't blame Tarq for his hate. I was an asshole. I meant what I said on the boat. I had every intention of helping them even though I knew that wasn't what the Luna wanted. But as we drew closer to Gaine, I didn't care anymore. I only wanted what was mine.

"*I found her,*" I mumble to only Tarq. "*I shouldn't have left as I did, but I found her. We can't get to her. There's a ward. She's being held at the compound.*"

"*Call it out!*" Tarq shouts abruptly.

I lift my head and quickly run through everything he could be telling me to do until I run out of options. "*What the hell does that mean?*" I ask my new pack.

Several of them laugh, but Bastian finally answers me. "*He wants you to howl so he can lock in on your position,*" he tells me. "*You're pretty far away, so you better make it loud. He'll tell you when he's close.*"

17

It took Tarq hours to answer my calls. Rooster and Ari rejoined me at the barrier when they noticed I hadn't left. I assumed my howling drew them to me, but after a few calls, Ari asked if I could hear her. She narrowed her eyes in confusion when I nodded, and it dawned on us that my body wasn't the only thing blocked by the ward. It would seem Jax was quite thorough in locking out the Lunar Pack.

"You can stop," Tarq snarls when he finally responds. *"I can smell her."*

I nod to Rooster and Ari before darting west. Now that he's picked up the Luna's scent, he will take the most direct route. I lean my shoulder against the ward and run along it. From what I can tell, it seems centered on Tynan's basement hell house.

I follow it close to the field, where I attract unwanted attention for a short time before climbing a ridge. I duck inside the trees and slide into a bush to avoid colliding with the large white mare the Luna was riding in the flower fields. Tarq doesn't stop, slamming head-first into the ward.

"DARYA!" he screams, climbing back to his feet. *"How do I get in there?"* He releases a ferocious snarl before turning to me. *"Why aren't you helping?"* He rears up to scrape his claws on the invisible wall.

"There's no getting past it, Tarq," I say sadly. *"They're locked in, and we're stuck out here."* I try to lay my head over his shoulder when he drops off the wall, but he turns away to pace along the barrier. *"She refused my help and sent me away, but I thought you should say goodbye. She said she loves you very much."*

Anthony slides from the white mare's saddle and holds his hand out to feel the ward's wall. "DARYA!" he shouts. His voice echoes around the field, but Tarq and I hang our heads as not one person turns in our direction.

"There really is no way, is there?" Tarq mumbles, sitting beside me.

"It literally threw me through a house when I shifted into the pack," I answer. *"I don't have many friends, but two of them are stuck in there with the bodies of two others."*

My eyes follow Tynan in the field with the Luna. He paces frantically before her, flinging his arms and shouting incoherently. When he marches over to her, he yanks the pendant from her neck and tosses it on the ground.

"Don't do this, My Love," Tarq begs his Luna. *"I'm not me with-out you."*

I remember a few times when Miles grew too tired to direct his communication. He would be giving orders to his guards, but all of our pack could hear him. He told me I could help when that happened by singing to the pack to force them to tune him out.

"Please don't leave me, Dar," Tarq continues. *"Let me in so I can save you. I can't do this without you."*

Sitting up quickly, I watch the Luna turn her head toward us. *That's what the pendant was—a distraction.* There's the tiniest hint of blood coming from the Luna's neck where the wire had hung. Jax always said there were loopholes in magic.

I frown when I push my nose forward, still bumping into the ward. *"Ninety-nine bottles of beer on the wall,"* I start singing, know-ing Tarq has to be communicating with the Luna. She would have no other reason to search for us unless she heard him. *"Ninety-nine bottles of beer. Take one down..."*

As others catch on and join me, Tarq steps forward, unfazed by my horrible singing. The Luna gasps a few times, visibly shaken by the experience. It's only another minute before she catches Tynan's attention, and he stomps toward her, screaming. Even when the unhinged man's blade stabs into her neck, the Luna never looks away from her Alpha.

Tarq jumps against the ward and howls louder than I have ever heard. We watch in horror as blood pours from her neck until her life slips away, and she falls limply against the ropes. The heartbroken Alpha stares at his Luna and whispers that he loves her one more time.

I step toward Tarq, but there's a flash of light, and suddenly, he's not in front of me anymore. I jump as Anthony crashes to the ground behind me and latches onto the Alpha's neck. I spin around, confused and unsure how they moved so quickly to my other side. Neither pays attention to me but continues staring toward the field.

Following their gaze, I find five wolves in the field circling Tynan. When I recognize Miles as one of them, I step forward, running into the barrier. His muzzle is already coated with blood when he leaps into the air and rips Tynan's neck from his shoulders. He bows in our direction before joining the other wolves as they run from the field and vanish before they reach the trees.

"What the fuck just happened?" I ask, more confused than ever.

Tarq nudges where the barrier had been, finding it gone, and sprints down the ridge. I remain frozen as he slides to a stop, shifts, and pulls the blade from the Luna's neck. He slices through the ropes that still bind her and catches her body as she falls from the tree. Anthony jumps on his mare and slaps her with the reins until she's reached Tarq's side.

Although others try to approach, Anthony won't let them near.

He stands guard for days over Tarq as he rocks and cradles the Luna's lifeless body. No one bothers me as I watch the Alpha mourn his mate, the woman he would cross hell for.

On the third morning, I trigger my shift and numbly walk along the field until I can cut into the woods, heading straight for my house. I don't remember walking down the hall, but I'm suddenly standing in my bedroom, staring at my bed. I had laid under these blankets for days, pining for my mate. I thought that pain would kill me.

I pull clothes from my hutch and slip into the pants, barely feeling the motions. Without the Lunar Pack's voices in my head, I can finally hear my thoughts. They are all of Gaine. She sent me away, professing that she'd celebrate my return. *I failed her. No one will be celebrating for a long time.*

When I turn back to the bed, Gaine lies among the blankets. She smiles sweetly and lifts her leg to slide her fingertips over its soft, tanned skin. She twists to gently trail her foot over my chest. I look down and reach for it, grasping only air and seeing the mark my mate's recently deceased Luna left on me.

I snatch a lamp from my dresser and throw it at the headboard. The broken glass sprays across the room, and the oil runs down the boards, soaking into my pillows. Gaine is still there. The long, smooth muscles in her arms and legs beg me to take a taste. Her skin glows in the light coming from the French doors.

I pull a shirt over my head and dig through the hutch, looking for the one useless thing Miles gave me. Clothes fling from the overstocked shelves until my fingers find an old lighter's cold metal casing. Slowly turning it, I recall Miles telling me it would probably only ever light once.

That's all I need.

I flick the wheel against the flint a few times to loosen it before pressing down on the lever for the last strike. The dancing flame is mesmerizing, but my view of Gaine has changed when I look up. Blood pours from the knife jammed deep into her neck. Her cloudy eyes stare lifelessly at the ceiling.

I toss the lighter on the bed as I turn away, not watching it hit the oil and engulf my imaginary mate in its flames. I know I'm walking, but my body seems to float down the hallway until I close my front door and lean against it. Sighing, I hang my head and slide my fingers through my hair.

I've never known the pain that I watched for the past three days. I'm not sure I have anyone loyal enough to stand guard over me for however long I would need, as Anthony did for Tarq. Neither has slept, but they aren't giving up. Tarq can't let his Luna go, and Anthony won't let anyone close enough to force him to.

I push away from the door and step off the porch as smoke begins seeping through an open window. With most of the pack still mourning in the field, it's a quiet walk to Castor's. I slip through the woods undetected until I pass the hay shed and attract the mare's attention. She sneezes at me as something else catches my eye.

Stepping around her fence, I walk toward a large, flat stone sticking out of the ground. The mound of dirt before it is fresh, and Castor's name is etched into the marker. I crouch beside the stone and place my hand on the loose earth. I had heard that the Luna's body would be burned, but wolves are returned to the ground upon our death. Castor will be among our ancestors, while the Luna will continue to watch over us from beyond.

"This was my fault, old friend," I whisper, sighing as I turn my eyes toward the sky. "I'm a selfish asshole and get everyone killed. It's just what I do." The horse nickers quietly, pulling me out of my head. "Except for you," I add. "You must be immune to my curse."

"We're not all dead," Rooster calls out from the opposite direction. I turn to find him approaching with Ari tucked under his arm.

"Brother, I've survived you for a long time. Ari is still alive because of your quick thinking."

They stop before me, and Ari holds my jacket out. "You should go to her," Ari says softly. "There's a lot of pain in that field. I bet she's feeling some of it." She leaves Rooster to step into my arms. "It's time for us all to heal, Kade."

I hold Ari to my chest and reach for Rooster's hand. "What are you two going to do?"

"I'm gonna take her to the Lunar Pack and finish what her parents started," Rooster answers. "We'll pledge ourselves to the young Luna. And then I think we'll head west—start over."

Ari leans back and smiles, sliding her hand over my right arm. "That looks good on you, Kade," she tells me. "Don't forget to send us an invite to the wedding, okay?"

"You just take care of yourselves," I respond before kissing her cheek. "Name a kid after me or something."

Rooster laughs as he ushers Ari back toward the trail that leads to the bar. "Nah. You're one of a kind, brother."

I pull on my jacket as they disappear in the brush and turn back to the paddock. The mare stares at me as if I've been keeping her waiting. "Alright, then," I grumble. "Let's get you home."

* * *

A few days later, I find myself standing near Gaine's house in a cluster of trees. Although she's been fed and watered, the mare is clearly irritated that I've kept her from where she calls home. I made her walk the whole way back, unsure of what I would say to my beautiful mate once we got here.

It's late afternoon when voices in the yard catch my attention. The gray-haired woman, Edith, follows Gaine's sister from the house, holding a coat. The young girl is sobbing as she yells at the older woman, so I can't understand what she's saying.

I don't recognize the man that follows them. "Edith, we don't have time for this," he states firmly. "Darya's funeral is tomorrow. Let her take her meds and help me with Gaine."

"She doesn't want to leave, Nate," Edith huffs.

"Then make her," the man barks.

Edith stops and stares at him, abandoning her pursuit of Gaine's sister. "I will not make any of you do anything," she snaps. "We are all in a lot of pain right now, and I know we all miss Darya fiercely, but you cannot keep lashing out. She wants to wait for him."

"He caused all of this!" the man she called Nate screams, punching a fence post. "He's brought us nothing but misery!"

Edith carefully places her hand on his shoulder. "You know that's not true," she says so low that I can barely hear her. "Darya blew through this land like a tornado. When she made a decision, there was no stopping her. She was dying, Nate, and she wanted her death to mean something. Let us smile at the time we spent with her because leaving us was her decision."

"Hey, I know who you are," Gaine's little sister says from behind me, making me jump. "You're the boy who isn't a boy."

I scowl, irritated by how easily she snuck up on me. "I haven't been a boy for a long time, kid," I grumble.

"You're who Gaine has been sneaking off with," she states, smiling slyly. "The one who makes her blush when I ask about you."

Sighing, I flick my eyes back toward the yard. Edith is quietly comforting Nate as he fixes the post he broke. "Things have been hard lately, huh?" I ask, turning to study the young girl. "Why aren't you sad?"

"Because you're here," she answers. Her smile hasn't faded a bit.

My face pulls to display all of my confusion. "Me?"

The girl gasps when I snatch her wrist before she can touch my chest. "You're the answer," she says quietly, flicking her eyes between mine. "You'll see it too one day."

Shaking my head, I lift an eyebrow. Gaine had said that her sister is the Luna's Historian. She called her "troubled," but I would describe her closer to "disturbed." I'm mostly confused by how she's talking. She speaks as though she's from the past but foretelling the future.

"How old are you, kid?" I ask, releasing her wrist.

"I don't know," she answers, studying me.

"How do you not know your age?" I spout. "What number was on your last cake?"

She shakes her head. "I don't have those," she tells me. "History is timeless. You can't count the years when the story remains the same."

"Um, okay," I mumble slowly, trying to back away from her but landing against a tree. "Shouldn't you be getting home?"

"I am home," she whispers, placing her hand over the Luna's mark on my chest. "Ah, there it is. Gaine told me you had one. Can you feel her?"

"Gaine?"

"The Luna, silly," the girl says, smiling. "She fused a piece of her soul to yours." She moves her hand to line her fingers up with the print and exhales deeply. "Your destiny was always tied to the Luna."

I slip from between her and the tree. "That's enough, kid," I snap, holding my hand out to stop her from following me. "I think you should be running along now."

"What is your name, Shield?" she asks, tilting her head.

My father and Miles often talked about the old ways and frequently spoke of the titles and higher positions held within the Luna's court. The title "Shield" was held by the Luna's most trusted guard. She relied on this wolf for all critical issues, defenses, and battles.

"Tarq's uncle was the last Shield recorded in the books," the girl tells me. "But they were all like you—cold, heartless, and unfeeling until the Luna tamed them."

She steps toward me as I process her words. When she reaches for my chest again, I latch onto her throat. Her smile only fuels my rage.

"I am nothing like them and will not be tamed," I snarl before pushing her away.

"People will only die around you until you swear yourself to the Luna," she says hoarsely. "Everyone you care about—no one will survive your destiny. I don't like death."

I haven't eaten in days, but I still lean over and throw up whatever my stomach is hanging onto. I hate that her twisted words make sense. I can't swear myself to Ayls. My father said the Shield bonded themselves to the Luna. My growl builds as air heaves through my lungs uncontrollably.

I look toward the cottage and grab my chest as I spot Gaine in the yard. *I couldn't stand to see her every day, knowing I could never have her... That I took away her chance for a bonded love...*

When Gaine turns in our direction, I begin to panic. My breaths become short and shallow, and my hands shake.

"Kade?" she calls out from the yard.

I step back, hoping to find cover in the trees.

"Is that your name?" the young girl asks. "We're over here, Gaine!"

I swallow hard as Gaine breaks into a run, racing in our direction. While the young girl smiles and moves toward her sister, I back up until I reach the mare. My fingers fumble with her reins, pulling them free from the limb I'd tied her to. I can't make out what Gaine says to her sister, but I jump onto the mare's back, stopping her from reaching me.

"Kade?" she calls out from only a few feet away. As Gaine approaches, I back the mare away from her. "What are you doing?"

I don't know the answer to that. I no longer know what I'm doing, where I'm going, or who I am. I just keep pulling back on the mare's reins until she starts rearing up in protest.

"Where are you going, Kade?" Gaine asks, frowning. "I need you. The Luna, Kade." She pauses as tears begin streaming down her face. "She didn't make it. Please don't leave me."

Gaine reaches out, but the mare rears again, causing her to step back. The horse slings her head, and my breath catches when she no longer blocks my view. Gaine's still crying and reaching for me, but there's a knife in her neck. Blood pours from the wound, soaking into her shirt as it cascades down her chest.

I spin the mare around and kick at her ribs until she's running full-out. Gaine screams my name, echoing deeply within my mind. For months, I wanted nothing more than to hear that woman say my name. Now, I'm sure that I will only bring her pain. It's my destiny.

* * *

I pushed the mare hard for days. I hadn't planned on a destination, only distance. Surrounded by the pack and close to Gaine with her sister spouting off tales of my horrible destiny, I couldn't think straight. It's been over a week since I last ate, so remaining upright is my new challenge.

The mare had a good rest in Castor's hay shed but is now stumbling as she struggles to keep her legs under her. She steps around a familiar hollow log and pushes through some brush to reveal the catfish pond I'd taken Gaine to. The horse stops with a groan and buckles her knees, finally surrendering to her exhaustion.

I roll to the ground, facing the pond. "How did you know to come here?" I ask her. "This is where our horse left us. Are you planning to go home?"

The mare only rolls onto her side, stretching her legs and neck out. I know how she feels. I don't have the energy to shift, so hunting is out of the question. *If I wanted to prove just how much of an asshole I am, I could kill the mare for food.* I shift my gaze to the horse. Her eyes are closed, and her lip twitches as she dreams. *Nah. She's as good a friend as any. I'll let her survive until my destiny kills her.*

* * *

I wake as a warm rag drags over my face. I try to jump up, but my arm is the only part that moves, and not by much. As my vision clears, Agatha smiles gently in the low lantern light. My mouth is swollen, so I choke when I try to talk.

"Easy, Midnight," the old woman says soothingly. "You trusted me to help Beauty. It's your turn now." She holds a cup to my lips, feeding me some warm water. "We've had a hard winter, so I haven't washed the blankets. I thought you might want to use the one you wrapped Beauty in."

I'm too weak to turn where she's reaching, but Gaine's scent hits me like the General's train when she pulls the blue blanket over me. I had forgotten how wonderful she smells with all that has happened in the past week. Agatha lays the blanket over my chest and beside my cheek. My hum starts as I rub my face against it.

"When you're feeling better, I'd love to know how this happened," the old lady says, touching my judgment scar. "But I'm happy to see this." Agatha slides her fingers over part of my pack marking.

* * *

I walk arm in arm with Agatha to the horses' paddock a few weeks later. She's always been pleasant company, and her calming presence has been a blessing. She talked me through my visions and didn't seem to judge me as I mourned Gaine and the love we could've had. I blame whatever the Luna left behind for any emotions that crippled me.

"Hey, my girl," I whisper, releasing Agatha to reach for the mare. "I think it's time for you to go home."

"You should join her," Agatha suggests, leaning over the railing. "This is not your path, Kade."

Sighing, I rub the mare's neck before turning back to Agatha. "I want something else. I don't want what fate chose for me," I say. "I wanted Gaine, but she's too close to that path. So, I have to let her go."

"Explain this to me again," the old woman huffs. "You said that you have to bond to the Luna. Why?"

"I'm her Shield," I mumble, joining her on the railing. "I fix things that have gone wrong—rescue those who need it. Basically, I'm to be at the Luna's beck and call."

Agatha's brow furrows. "But why do you have to bond to her?"

"That's just what's done," I grumble.

We've been talking about this for a while. Agatha knows quite a bit about wolves and how a pack works but doesn't know much about the Luna. She seems fascinated by the idea of a woman ruling over a pack the size of the Lunar wolves.

"It's easy for them," I had told her. "They come near you, and you just want to do what they ask. They are so sweet and gentle. You can't help but feel their love."

In truth, I miss that feeling. Agatha provided a safe place to fall when I lost myself, but my destiny seems to be pulling me because I miss that overwhelming sense of peace that came with being near the Luna. Even the little Luna had her own presence, which I now crave.

"What are you going to do?" Agatha asks, cupping my cheek.

I close my eyes and lean onto her hand. The comfort she provides reminds me of my mother the first weeks after Miles died. "The kid said my destiny was tied to the Luna," I murmur. "She said my refusal to take my place would cause everyone around me to die. That's been my experience my whole life. It never bothered me until recently."

The old woman smiles. "I'm still here," she states, raising her eyebrow. "So, that's not completely true."

"Oh, Agatha," I say, sighing. "Give it time." I rub the rest of the dirt off the mare and give her one final pat before opening the gate. "Go on, my friend. I'm sure they miss you."

Like last time, the mare tosses her head and jogs a short distance away before turning back toward me. When she bows her head, I touch my brow and nod as if tipping a hat to her. The horse spins away from us and dashes north, heading back to Gaine one more time.

Agatha rubs her hand over my arm. "You said the Luna has a companion," she says, changing the subject. "Tell me about them."

We spent the next few weeks cleaning up her little farm and discussing pack politics and dynamics. Agatha finally helped me see that these Lunas are different from those of the past by pointing out that Chase had not bonded to the Luna. I specifically remember Miles and my father mentioning the Luna bonding with her companion. From what I gathered when meeting Ayls' companion on the barge, she also abstained from that tradition.

Unfortunately, realizing I could have my mate only pointed out that I'd just end up like Tarq in the field if I lost her. Visions of Gaine with the knife in her neck came flooding back in, and there was no stopping them. Now, I wake up every night sweating and screaming her name.

18

The weather is turning cold as the days shorten, but I can't feel it through my silver fur. I worked with Agatha at her farm all summer while she continued to analyze the ways of the new Lunas. Unfortunately, I couldn't get rid of the nightmares. Seeing Gaine die every night took so much out of me that I stopped sleeping unless I had to. I would never survive my beautiful mate's death.

Agatha was nice enough, and I enjoyed the calm she brought to my soul when she was around. The morning she didn't show up for our daily field inspection, I decided to check on her. The old woman had died in her sleep, making her another victim of my destiny.

I wandered around a bit, but the Luna's pull was too great, so I snuck onto pack land last night and followed her scent. I've never been a fan of peaches, but her scent has a beautiful effect on me. It calms my nerves and allows my muscles to relax. My mind takes over as I flop onto her porch, though, and the nightmares push through my exhaustion.

I watch Gaine stumble toward me with the handle of a blade sticking out of her neck. I'm unsure how she can scream my name, but she does. I feel my legs moving against the wooden deck as I run at full speed toward her. She falls among the flowers in the field, disappearing from my view.

When I stop and lift my head, a hand gently slides from my shoulder to behind my ear. I snarl and try to roll over to face the intruder but lack the strength.

"Easy, Kade," the little Luna says gently. *"I've got you. We'll get through this together."*

Having her near me creates some sort of relief but does not stop my dreams. The little Luna's meals are brought to her, and she requests different broths, trying to entice me to eat. When it starts raining on the second morning, she asks her father to help carry me inside, out of the cold. I'd just woken from a nightmare in which Gaine sliced her own arms and legs open, so when they lifted me, I threw up bile all over the little Luna.

The Alpha lays me on a bed near the kitchen and whispers about my weight to someone. I haven't eaten in weeks. I know I've lost an unhealthy amount of muscle and don't have much left. I've watched Gaine die hundreds of times now. I'm ready for the end.

* * *

I wake when a spoon is slipped under my lip. Chicken broth runs over my tongue, hitting the back of my throat and making me swallow. I slide my head along the chest that it's draped over, and the little Luna smiles at me.

"Just let me die," I groan, rolling my eyes.

"I can't do that, Kade," she whispers. "You're my wolf. I will see you through whatever is eating you." She holds the spoon out, but I ignore it. "You saw something pretty terrible. My father still struggles every day with that loss, but he's letting me help him. Won't you give me a chance to help you?"

"Everyone around me dies," I warn her. *"I can't watch that anymore. She's in my dreams and dies every time I close my eyes."*

"Who?" the little Luna asks, lifting my lip and forcing another spoonful of broth over my tongue. "My mother?"

"Gaine," I answer. *"Although I'm probably to blame for your mother too."*

"No," she whispers. "My mother was the strongest woman I have ever known. She told Daddy and Chase many times that she wouldn't leave this world until she was ready." The little Luna rubs my chin and lifts my nose to her lips. "You couldn't have controlled that any more than the weather. That was her decision."

"I don't get it," I grumble, settling back against her chest. *"How old are you? Like, twelve?"*

She clicks her tongue at me. "I'm 15, Kade, but that isn't all that important. I'm the Luna, and I won't let you punish yourself." She slips more broth into my mouth, but I swallow it willingly this time. "Tell me about your dreams."

I don't want to fill this poor kid's head with my nightmares and torment, but I need to get them out. I tell her about seeing Gaine die in my house. I skip ahead to when I woke in Agatha's barn but only make it through a few dreams before the little Luna notices the large time gap.

"Kade, Gaine is fine," she whispers. "Why didn't you go to her?"

"She didn't tell you?"

"Tell me what?" the Luna asks, confused.

I sigh and slide my head off her chest. *"I was there,"* I admit. *"Her sister found me. She's creepy as hell but told me I'm your Shield. I'm destined to serve you."*

The little Luna pulls her fingers through my fur for a while before speaking again. "My mother didn't believe in doing things as they had in the past, Kade," she finally says. "I've heard the term, but I want you to have a beautiful life with Gaine."

"I can't watch her die," I say, closing my eyes.

"Why did you start calling me Ayls?"

I move enough to see her smiling at me. *"What?"*

"On the boat, you started calling me Ayls," she says. "No one else has ever shortened my name. Why did you?"

Sighing, I nuzzle back into the pillow beside her and close my eyes. *"Annalisa is a mouthful,"* I answer. *"It's regal... maybe even noble. It's the name of someone who would look down upon her subjects from an ivory tower. You're more than that. We feel how much you love us."*

"I might not be regal, but I am the Luna," she murmurs.

"You are more than a Luna," I tell her. *"Your mother showed me compassion without even knowing me. You helped everyone on the boat while feeling the same pain. You're not a monarch. You are honored, loved, and probably obeyed, but you are our family, and we love you."*

"Thank you," the little Luna whispers, rolling to wrap her arms around my neck. "I love you too, Kade. Sleep. We'll figure your destiny out tomorrow."

* * *

It took me a few weeks to build up enough strength to shift. The little Luna stayed in bed with me as I recovered, studying books on diets and nutritional values. She requested that her guards search local towns and bring her back volumes about all canine varieties and scientific books about our anatomy. An older wolf named Neala stopped by often to inspect my muscles and joints with her.

We've taken to strolling around the lake near her house daily while the snow stays at bay. Bastian or her father always escort us, but they remain quiet as we discuss some differences between the Lunar and Blood Packs. Ayls was patient when I crept back into my head upon learning that Miles would not be returning after what he did in the field.

"My mother always came home at the first sign of snow," the little Luna whispers, looking over the lake. "She said she could smell it."

"It's cold and clean," I respond, following her gaze. "Like fresh linen that froze on the line overnight." I look down and smile as she clings to my waist. "You can't smell it?"

"No, I can," she admits, sighing. "I don't like the cold."

I chuckle and wrap my arms around her. "I figured," I say, tucking her under my arm. Turning my attention to Bastian, I watch him stare longingly at the water. "Your Alpha used to love swimming when he was little. His parents would try to take him to the pond right at dusk every night."

Ayls reaches her hand out for Bastian's jaw. "Why so late?"

"Tynan imposed a curfew," I explain. "All the other kids went home at sunset, and Bass had the pond to himself."

"He told me the other kids were scared of him," she remarks, looking down at her Alpha. "I liked watching him play with my father. Sometimes I miss it."

I lean over to kiss the top of her head. "Sweetheart, you got me to eat," I say, rubbing her arm. "I still watch that gorgeous woman die every time I fall asleep, but you have me fighting to find an end. You'll get them through this too."

Ayls groans and looks up at me. "Yeah, speaking of that," she says, cringing. "I'm having River brought down to the lake." When I try to back away in protest, she places her hands on my chest. "It's time to get some answers, Kade."

"No, Ayls," I start, shaking my head. "I got answers, remember? I didn't like them." I knew she would do this eventually but still held the ridiculous hope she'd forget. River is Gaine's sister, the little Luna's damaged Historian. The last time I listened to her ramblings, I lost my mind and let fear take over.

"This time will be different," she says reassuringly. "You have Edith and me to help decipher what she says."

"No offense, but you haven't been able to stop the nightmares she caused the first time," I grumble. "How are you going to fix whatever new torture she inflicts?"

Ayls smiles as she cups my cheek before kneeling to Bastian. He nods and rubs his whiskers over her cheek. "I've asked my Alpha to give you some privacy," she murmurs, watching Bastian disappear into the trees before rising to her feet. "I think it's time to discuss these dreams, Kade."

"I don't want to," I state firmly, tucking her back under my arm. I step forward, but Ayls holds me back and pulls me to face her. "Sweetheart, I don't want to relive my nightmares. Gaine is beautiful, perfect, and wonderful. I don't want to talk about knives in her neck, her body covered in blood, or her screaming my name as she dies too far away for me to save."

The little Luna pulls my neck to rest my forehead against hers. "It's that bad?" she whispers.

"It's worse," I answer, sighing and closing my eyes. "So much worse."

Ayls might be nearly ten years younger than me, but she brings an air of wisdom I'm not accustomed to. She is my Luna, and I will do anything to protect her. I feel that in my heart. I'm just not ready to burden her with my troubles or to give in to this demon that haunts my dreams.

Gaine is my weakness. I want her to live more than I want to bond with her. She dies in every dream I have, but my mind also put a knife in her throat the last time I saw her.

"I love you, Kade," Ayls whispers, rubbing her fingers along my jaw. She's learned that it's a sensation that calms me. My mother used to rub my jaw when she sang me to sleep after my father died. "I won't let anything happen to her."

Taking a sharp breath, I pull away from her. "Honey, you can't promise that," I say, tucking her hair behind her ear. "I appreciate you trying, though."

"I can't feel you," the little Luna states firmly, choosing a more direct method with me. She presses her hand to my chest. "I haven't felt a single emotion from you. I understand you're opposed to speaking with River about your position within the pack, but I need answers."

"You don't need to feel what I'm feeling," I assure her. "It's not very comfortable."

Ayls giggles but doesn't offer any other response. I've been with her for over a month and have grown accustomed to her silence. She spends much of her time thinking and listening to her wolves. Our time on her porch swing is a favorite of mine. Ayls never talks when we're on the swing, but her presence screams how much she loves us—*if that makes any sense.*

"Let's go back to the house," she whispers, pulling at the tips of my hair. "You've only just built this muscle back up. I don't want you burning it trying to keep me warm."

* * *

After a few days of hoping she'll forget about wanting to talk to Gaine's crazy sister, Ayls announces that we are meeting her at Edith's house. I've avoided the witch since learning that Jax was her brother. I'm unsure what happened to his body after I left his house, but I've seen what his sister is capable of and would rather not be the one to tell her how he died.

"I've talked to your friends," Ayls tells me as we walk along a trail through the woods with our arms linked. "They have been asking about you, but I wanted to make sure you'd be alright with me telling them how you're doing."

"I don't have any friends," I grumble.

"I'm your friend," the little Luna replies. "And I doubt Rooster or Ari would appreciate you dismissing them so."

Rolling my eyes, I look down to see Ayls smiling at me. "How are they?"

She hums quietly before answering. "They are well," she tells me.

"They've settled on the west side of the river. Rooster said you'd laugh at him for trying to farm."

I nod and chuckle. "He's right."

"And Ari is pregnant," Ayls adds, leaning her head on my shoulder.

"Ari has a gentle heart," I say, smiling. "She'll be a good mother."

"How do you know?" the little Luna asks.

I look down at her curiously. "I imagine she would protect her child with the same fierceness as her parents," I explain. "We learn from the elders around us, and Ari always had a caring way about her... even when she hated someone." My eyes trail further down to Bastian, wondering how much he'd shared about their past.

"Mom was never around," Ayls whispers sadly. "She taught me a lot those last six months, but I'm not sure I know how to be a mother."

Slipping my arm from hers, I wrap it around her shoulders. "Sweetheart," I start, laughing despite her sorrow. "You're a mother to all of your wolves." When she looks up, I wipe a tear from under her eye. "I don't know of many people that would have laid on a cold porch for two days, holding a wolf as damaged as me."

Ayls nuzzles into my shoulder and pulls Bastian's chin to look into his eyes. "I love all of my wolves," she professes. "You are so deeply embedded in my heart that I will do anything for you."

"And we will do anything for our Luna," I add. "Including speaking to some crazy chick about stuff we don't want to know." I shake her a bit to lighten the mood. "That is what a family does for their mother. You already know how to care for a child. We're all your children."

"That just sounds weird," Ayls replies, laughing.

"I know it does, but trust me. You're gonna be great when it's time," I tell her, grinning.

"Thanks, Kade," she whispers. "Sometimes I need to be reminded I'm more than a Luna."

She turns us onto a side trail, and a small cottage appears in the trees. Although we spend a great deal of time walking the grounds, we've primarily stuck close to the lake. We've run into Anthony several times but have never been to his house. He sits on his front porch, rocking his chair as we approach.

"Here we go. Are you ready?" Ayls asks.

Sighing, I cringe. "I don't really have a choice," I answer. "I didn't want to do this from the start, but you want me to be here, and I would never say no to you."

The little Luna smiles and kisses my cheek before turning to the ex-Commander. Anthony is tall with olive skin. He's an ominous character, spending most of his time with narrow, judgmental eyes and a lifted brow.

Without a word, he stands, reaching for Ayls and cupping her cheek. "You remind me more of your mother each day," he murmurs, kissing her forehead. "I haven't seen your father in a few days. How is he doing?"

Ayls presses her hand to his chest. "The same," she answers. "He could use some company. You know where he is."

"I think I know something that might help him," Anthony says, nodding. "Edith has been researching grief and treatments. She would never magically make him move on, but she's found a few alternative methods. You might ask about some for your shiny one."

"My name is Kade," I sneer, my growl rumbling to life for the first time since Ayls startled me on the porch.

"I don't care," Anthony answers, lifting his eyebrow. He nods to Ayls and steps off the porch to disappear into the woods.

"I really don't like him," I grumble.

Ayls opens the cabin's door. "He'll grow on you," she tells me. "Come on. Edith and River are waiting."

While Bastian turns to stand watch on the porch, Ayls ushers me through the door. The witch sits in an armchair with a thick book in her lap, but Gaine's sister jumps up when I enter the room. She bounces toward me with childish excitement.

"Easy, River," Ayls says in a less than gentle tone. "Let's give Kade his space."

"But you're not," River pouts. "Has he accepted his post?"

The little Luna releases my arm and latches onto River, dragging her back to the couch she came from. "That's why I asked you to come down here," she says, nodding at the cushion to tell the girl to sit. "Can you explain to me what exactly you think Kade's post is?"

River smiles and keeps her gaze locked on me as I sit closer to the fire to face them from across the room. "He is special, isn't he?" the young girl asks, switching back to her whimsical tone. "Do you feel the pull? It makes me want to love him."

"What?" I spout. "Ayls, I don't know about this." I shake my head and lean back against some pillows.

Edith closes her book. "River, sweetheart," she gently says. "Your Luna is here to learn about the position you are talking about. You need to explain it to her. She can't hear what's in your head."

"Oh, right," River says as if snapped out of a daze. "I'm sorry, Luna. What did you want to know?"

"Why don't you start from the beginning?" Ayls suggests.

River frowns with a sigh. "Shields were tools for the Luna," the girl starts, closing her eyes. "Deadly. Lots of death."

I cringe and rub my forehead.

"He's a cupid of sorts," River continues, oblivious to my discomfort. "He draws everyone in." She opens her eyes and fixes them on me. "That's when he kills you." She reaches for Edith's hand. "I don't want to look back there anymore."

"Can you try a different time?" Edith urges. "Maybe there's a time of peace where you can see a Luna and her Shield."

The girl shakes her head, looking as if she's about to cry.

"River," Ayls whispers, taking the girl's hand. "I need you to do this. But if that isn't enough, can you try for Gaine? Kade loves her very much and would like to keep her safe." She brushes the back of her fingers over River's cheek, and the girl takes a deep breath, noticeably relaxing. "One more time? For Gaine?"

With a sweet smile, River nods and closes her eyes. "They claim their Shield," she whispers, shaking her head again. "I don't want to watch them either. Why would they do that?" She opens her eyes and stares at Ayls, wanting an answer.

Pursing her lips, the little Luna narrows her eyes. "I'm not sure," she admits. "The Lunas of the past seemed as active in bed as they were in battles. My mother didn't want to leave me with that type of legacy to follow, and I'm not interested in it either."

"As much as I appreciate that, Ayls, how will we protect Gaine from the other side of my curse?" I grumble. Ayls said this would be better because she and Edith would be here to help me make sense of this insane girl's ramblings. Clearly, she was mistaken.

"I will protect all of my wolves, Kade," Ayls murmurs, leaving her focus on the girl. "River, can you look upon those moments one more time for me? Focus on the Shield's chest. Find a time when he has removed his shirt."

River's eyes snap open. "The mark!" she shouts.

Ayls moves to put herself in the girl's eyeline. "So, they had it too?"

"Yes," River spouts. "The blood bond was to calm them. You can't get past the mark. He'll lose control if you don't claim him."

I stand abruptly and throw a pillow across the room. "Yeah, that's about to happen," I growl, turning to lean against the mantle and stare into the fire.

I don't recognize the rage building within me. I've never cared about anyone in the way I feel for Gaine. I trusted Ayls would find a way to make this work, but now it would seem that if she doesn't claim me, I'll probably be the one who kills my mate. I grit my teeth as my growl builds out of control and slam my fist into the mirror hanging over the fireplace.

"Kade!" Edith shouts.

Ayls is behind me in a flash. "Why don't you sit outside with Bastian, Kade?" she suggests, sliding her hand up my back. "He's a good ear to bend."

I spin around and latch onto her cheeks. "Just claim me," I beg. Some kind of desperation has taken hold of me, and I can't control it. "Please." I pull her lips to mine and hate that I feel nothing. I love this young girl. She is my Luna. I will honor her until the day I die. But I want Gaine. My lips miss hers, and I want nothing more than to feel her skin under my hands.

To her credit, Ayls stays still and allows me my moment of weakness. When I lean my forehead against hers and release her lips, she slides her thumbs over my face, catching tears I wish weren't there. I open my eyes to find her smiling gently at me and want to kick myself for doubting her.

"I want you to have the epic love my mother always spoke of," Ayls whispers. "I will find a way to help you that doesn't take that chance away." She reaches up my shirt and presses her hand to her mother's print. "This is blocking us, so we need to find a way around it. I'm not giving up yet. Will you keep trying with me?"

Taking a deep breath, I roll my eyes and pull Ayls into my arms. Her peach scent overwhelms me as I lay my cheek on her head. Its gentle, calming effect stops my limbs from shaking and evens my breathing.

"There you are," the little Luna says quietly. "I am only as strong as my wolves, and you are among the mightiest. Together, we can beat the past."

Grinning, I step back and gently take her cheeks this time. "I do love you," I whisper. "I'm trying to trust you."

"I know you are," Ayls replies. "Go on for now, though. Let the ladies handle this."

A year ago, I'd never let anyone dismiss me. This teenager has turned my world upside down, and I find myself kissing her cheek before slipping out of her grip and quickly exiting the house. I lean against the door, closing my eyes against the blinding sun. Bastian's claws tapping on the porch remind me I'm not alone.

I open my eyes to find him sitting before me. "So, listen," I start, grinning. "I kinda kissed your Luna."

Bastian stands, lifting his lips in a snarl.

"It's not like that, kid," I grumble. "Gaine's sister makes me crazy." I sweep my arm to indicate the steps. "Why don't we sit down and talk? If Ayls can't find a way around my cursed destiny, I might just let you kill me."

19

Distant thunder rumbles as the wind whips my hair across my face. When I step from the woods, lightning cuts through the night sky, turning the storm-ravaged field into a stage for my latest dream. My mate stands in the middle, white as a ghost, except for the blood streaming from her eyes, nose, and mouth.

"Gaine!" I scream.

The tall grass seems to push me back with every step as I fight to reach her. Rain stings my skin like needles, and the thunder drowns out whatever Gaine says when her mouth opens. I'm closer to her tonight than I've ever been. She reaches out to me, showing the long gashes that run the length of her arms.

"I love you, Kade," Gaine whispers, making my chest swell. "Why did he kill me? Why didn't you love me enough to stop him?"

I jump awake, thrashing and pulling at the blanket wrapped around me. Swinging out of the bed as soon as I'm free, I clutch my chest and look around to get my bearings. I'm in the wing beside the kitchen. Annalisa is propped on her knees in the middle of the bed, making soft shushing noises. She knows I can't make sense of her words right after I've had a nightmare.

Tonight's dream was different. Gaine always calls for me. Most of the time, it sounds like the day I left her. Her screams would hit my heart, making my chest ache. But tonight, she spoke to me. A man had hurt her, and I was too weak or stupid to stop it.

"Just give him a minute, Bass," Ayls says quietly.

My eyes dart around the room and find Bastian standing by the corner of the bed. His head hangs low, and his shoulders are braced for an attack. I've accidentally hit the little Luna a few times this past week, and the kid is at his limit with me.

"Someone hurt her, and I didn't stop it," I whisper. "I let someone kill her."

"Come here, Kade," Ayls says gently. She reaches for my hand and pulls me back onto the bed. I hadn't noticed the sweat covering my skin until she let her fingers slide up my arm. "Just lie back and close your eyes for me."

I fold my arms over my face. "Ayls," I grumble. "I don't want to see that again."

Ayls breathes a quiet laugh. "I don't want you to go to sleep, Kade," she whispers. "I want you to use your imagination and talk to me."

"I don't have one of those," I mumble, trying to roll away from her.

"Your imagination is creating these dreams," Ayls says sharply. "You are being haunted by a woman who is very much still alive, Kade. Your nightmares are getting worse, so it's time to try something else."

I let her lift my arms from my face and study her with narrowed eyes. "I doubt you'd receive punishment if I gave you permission to kill me," I tell her.

"I'm going to agree to disagree with you on that," the little Luna says, smiling. "Let's lay these down and relax." She guides my arms to lie on the bed along my body. "Close your eyes, Kade."

My eyes dart between hers before I resign with a sigh and let them close. "Alright, what now, Luna?"

"You said Gaine showed up in the basin," Ayls starts. "Can you tell me about when you first met her?"

"Sometimes it seems like yesterday," I murmur. "Other days, I feel like I've known her my whole life."

I quietly tell her about stalking Gaine through the woods at the basin's edge. She stifles a giggle when I grumble through the part about water seeping into my boots. I frown, remembering that I'd tried to force myself on Gaine. I would kill any man who yanked my beautiful mate from her horse.

"I was an asshole," I whisper. "I told Gaine she belonged to me." I lick my lips, tasting her strawberry soap for the first time in months. "The truth is that I need her. She's a piece of me, or the glue that holds me together."

"We all make mistakes, Kade," Ayls whispers, moving around on the bed beside me. She smiles when I open my eyes. "Keep them closed, please." Ayls has such a beautiful sense of peace that I can only grin as I follow her orders. "Things obviously changed between you two. Do you know when? Can I hear about that?"

Releasing a deep sigh, I recall our moments after that first meeting. No one has ever been able to sneak up on me. I never thought I'd enjoy having an equal, but Gaine made every encounter exhilarating. My fingers tremble as I remember how she felt under their tips.

"She thought I was drowning in a lake," I finally tell Ayls. "I felt sorry for myself and let the water pull me down. She tried to drag me back to the surface but hadn't eaten in a few days and was too weak to climb out of the water. I sat against a tree, cradling her."

"That was very sweet of you," Ayls murmurs, closer to my ear. Her fingers push across my brow and over my eyelids to be sure they stay closed.

"That night, she laid her head on my shoulder for the first time," I continue. "She was talking about her family and how they came to live at the lake, but I wasn't listening. She had rolled and placed her hand on my chest. I couldn't focus on anything but her breath and fingers tickling my skin."

"Tell me about it," Ayls whispers.

The bed feels more like a cloud as I focus on Gaine's fingers. "She probably didn't realize what she was doing," I say, my lips pulling into a grin. "Her fingers were like tiny pieces of velvet touching my soul."

Air rushes from my lungs when a hand slides gently over my ribs. I know it's Ayls', but the imagination I swore I didn't have takes over. My hum rumbles to life as foreign as it is unexpected. Ayls traces the muscle over my ribs on the opposite side.

"I never wanted her to stop," I whisper. "Her touch reached things that can't be felt. Even my memories were happier." Air softly blows over my shoulder. I turn to rub my face over Gaine's hair, but a hand catches my cheek. "She was still in my arms when we woke in the morning. Her little snore is the most adorable thing I have ever heard."

I open my eyes when water drops onto my chest. Ayls is sitting cross-legged, leaning over me. Her face is blotchy and soaked with tears. Despite her obvious distress, she smiles sweetly at me.

"You aren't alone anymore," she whispers through heavy breaths. "Let me carry some of that pain."

Overwhelmed by something I can't describe, I cup her cheeks and pull her to my lips. We sniffle and smile against each other as I feel the tight pain that had settled in my chest release through her touch. "You are perfect," I whisper. "I will always protect you."

Ayls pulls away from me and sits up. "That's good because I'm about to knock Bass out," she replies, giggling. "Come here, my Alpha. There's a lot in there. I need to give some of this to you."

I slide my arms under my head and watch Ayls push her fingers against Bastian's fur. Her eyes close, and she leans onto his muzzle when he rubs his whiskers over her cheek. I can't help laughing when he begins humming. Mine has been gently rumbling since Ayls started it, but Bastian's is so loud I can't hear it anymore.

"Shit, he's loud," I spout, coughing as I try to contain my laughter.

Ayls glares at me before returning to her Alpha and kissing the tip of his nose. "Never you mind that, Love," she whispers. "You are mine and beautiful in every way."

Bastian licks her cheek and falls onto his side. His tongue hangs from his mouth as he flops his paw at her a few times.

"What did you do to him?" I ask, lifting my brow.

"Technically, you did it," Ayls says. She falls back onto my shoulder and nuzzles under my jaw. "What I take from you, I give to him. How do you feel?"

Narrowing my eyes at the ceiling, I consider myself for the first time since I heard about my destiny. The ache in my chest is gone. I don't feel blood poisoned by dread racing through my veins. Even the air seems to have lost the static charge that drove my senses mad and caused my temper to flare.

I look down at the little Luna curled on my chest and kiss her head. "Calm," I whisper.

"Do you trust me?" she asks.

"I do now," I answer.

* * *

Working with Ayls makes the days more manageable, and our conversations slowly turn toward my future and how I feel about the packs merging. Having grown up within the Lunar pack, most of the little Luna's wolves still see her as a child and continue to shelter her from the chaos of the Blood Pack. She seems more curious than surprised by my stories.

"Edith has found something that I think might help you both," Ayls says as she turns Tarq and me away from the pond one afternoon. She taps the strap of a bag she'd flung over her shoulder before we left the house. "I brought some clothes for you, Daddy. You'll need to shift."

Tarq yanks his jaw from her hand and sits. I'm familiar with how he adjusts his paws. He's refusing to take another step toward wherever his daughter is taking us.

Ayls sighs and pats my hand before unhooking our arms. "Can you give us a minute?" she asks, handing me the bag. "Go on ahead, and you'll find Edith. She's going to help us with today's project."

I shake my head, remembering the last time Edith helped us. "Baby girl, I am not going anywhere near them without you," I state.

Smiling, Ayls cups my cheek. "Sweet wolf," she starts, rubbing her thumb over my cheekbone. "I would never ask too much of you. It is only Edith and Anthony. I've sent River home."

Ayls kisses my cheek and turns back to her father, dismissing me before I can object again. I stay long enough to watch her kneel to Tarq and press her forehead to his. Although she's spent most of her time with me over the past few months, the moment another wolf needs her, she doesn't hesitate to drop everything to help them.

I don't know why she's dedicated so much time to me, but I am grateful. I wake in a cold sweat every morning, fighting blankets and nearly knocking the little Luna out. But I trust that one day, she'll help me heal enough that I'll be able to sleep peacefully beside Gaine each night without having to watch her die.

I smile at the memory of holding my beautiful mate wrapped in blankets on the pile of hay in Agatha's barn. I'm ripped from my thoughts when I leave the woods. A sharp breeze lashes through the clearing, stealing my breath and stinging my eyes.

Before me appears an altar donning gifts of flowers, stuffed animals, folded paper chains, and drawings of hearts. The stones have been shaped to fit together, holding a metal grate in the center. Edith and Anthony are crouched with their backs to me as they sift through some gifts. There's only one thing this altar could be.

"Get out of there!" I shout, lunging at them. "Those are the Luna's. Don't touch her stuff."

"Calm down, mate," Anthony says, putting himself between me and Edith. "We were just looking. We have some talented wolves in the pack." He points to the gifts, but I can't turn away from them.

"Those are hers!" I spout, dropping Ayls' bag at my feet.

Edith takes a deep breath and slowly reaches behind them to pick up a large sack. "Kade, I think this will really help you," she says softly. "I've gathered some pencils and paints. Would you like to try drawing?"

"Who the hell cares about drawing?" I scoff at the witch. I kneel before the altar and inspect the gifts as if I would have any idea if they had disturbed them. The thought of someone touching anything that belongs to the Luna has my soul burning. She died for these people. She died for me. No one should ever be so disrespectful that they would lay a finger on something gifted to her.

A hand slides over my shoulder, pulling my mind away from the gifts. I jump up and spin around, my fist aiming for the nearest target.

"Easy, Kade," Tarq says, catching my punch in his hand. "Let Annalisa help you with this."

Smiling sweetly, the little Luna steps around her father. "I've got him, Daddy," she whispers. "I shouldn't have sent you ahead. I'm sorry. This altar is where we burned my mother's body when they brought her down from the mountain. Would you like me to read some of what our pack wrote to her?"

My chest is so tight that I can barely breathe. My clenched fists are jammed down by my sides, and I can't speak with my jaw locked shut. I don't want her to touch anything behind me. It doesn't matter who she is or if that woman was her mother.

"Come sit down," Ayls says gently. "Daddy has joined us for his own therapy." She guides me away from the altar to give her father some room. We sit on the light dusting of snow, and she uses my jaw to direct my gaze to her face. "Close your eyes."

I lean my forehead against hers and sigh with my eyes closed. Ayls is an excellent shot with her bow and arrow, but she doesn't need to carry them for me to let my guard down around her. She is fierce in every way and would never let another touch me in her presence.

"Remember the festival?" she whispers. "Can you hear Gaine's excitement?"

I jerk against her, trying to pull away, but she stays calm and holds my neck. When Ayls begins humming, I lose myself to the memory. I hadn't told her about dancing with Gaine, but we talked about the kites and the small band. She was especially interested in the angelic kites by the firelight and the music played. That's when she realized that her humming triggered a calming memory.

Taking slow breaths, I relax into Gaine's body. She stays pressed against me, following my movements. In my memory, Gaine's hum is the sweetest part of the song. Her head nestles under my chin, and her cheek rubs my chest. I can feel her hand sliding over my arm.

Ayls brushes my cheek with the back of her fingers and causes me to release a noisy sigh as she pulls the anger that caused my tension. Although it takes her a while to drain me enough that I'm functional without trying to kill anyone, the others gathered around the altar leave us alone. When she pulls away, we smile at each other.

"There you are," Ayls says. "Are you ready to try again?"

I wipe the tears from her cheeks and take a deep breath. "Yeah," I answer. "Just warn me next time you bring me to the grave of a woman I watched your father cradle for days in a field."

Ayls narrows her eyes. "I'm not sure I realized you were there the whole time."

"I was in the trees," I admit. "It wouldn't have been right for me to intrude."

"Mourning the dead is natural, Kade," Ayls says, shifting off her heels and sitting in the snow. "These gifts are from wolves who need to heal from that loss. It's part of their process." She sweeps her hand toward the items along the altar. "I wonder if you might be willing to draw something for her. Rooster told me you liked to use burned wood to draw on the hearth."

"That was a long time ago, Ayls," I mumble. "I'm not a kid anymore."

"True," she responds. "But you are lashing out like one."

I roll my eyes and lift an eyebrow. "Nice."

Ayls giggles and pats my knee before leaving to collect some items from Edith. After quickly stopping to check on her father, she rejoins me. "Daddy has agreed to participate in this therapy," she says quietly. Reaching into a small bag, she produces two charcoal pencils and a small stretched canvas. "It's just an idea, Kade. Please try for me."

Tarq had gotten dressed while I was calming down and is now kneeling before the altar, tapping it with something. I adjust Ayls' empty bag so she can sit on it instead of the snow. Her father only looked away from his task when she touched him. Otherwise, he isn't paying us any attention.

I watch Edith back away from the clearing to disappear within the trees, but Anthony sits on a log and leans on his rifle. He's stood over us a few times while Ayls and I walked the grounds. I don't blame him for not trusting me. *I'm broken.*

"Kade?" Ayls snaps me out of my head.

"What am I supposed to draw?" I grumble, sighing.

I hate when she gives me her sweet smile because it makes me feel horrible for being cross with her. Ayls catches the hair that falls into my eyes with her fingers and rubs her thumb over my cheek. "What do you see when you close your eyes?"

"No," I snap. I know what the little Luna wants, but I'm not interested. She's been asking about my dreams, wanting me to describe them. Putting my dreams into words requires me to relive them. I don't want to face my nightmares any more than I have to, but I also don't want Ayls to experience them.

"Why don't we get comfortable?" she says in a soothing tone she uses when trying to distract me. "You've told me about a few times when you enjoyed moments of holding Gaine. Has she ever held you?"

Frowning, I narrow my eyes in thought. They move from focusing on Ayls to studying her father as he ignores us to work on the stone. Most of the stories I've shared were from after I spent time with her as a wolf, letting her settle into my company. My arms needed to be around her when she let me close enough. I'm not sure if she ever wanted to hold me.

"When I kidnapped her," I finally say. "She rode behind me on the Thoroughbred I borrowed. He was fast, so she needed to hold me tightly to stay on."

Ayls breathes a quiet laugh, making me blush for the first time in my life. "You've never seen her ride bareback, have you?" she asks, grinning broadly. "She didn't need to hold onto you. You might want to call it what it was instead of a kidnapping. It's more like the time you and Gaine ran away together."

My mind races too quickly for words, going over the lightning-fast ride we were on as we ran away from her cottage. Gaine took her time reaching into my coat, and I thought my body had melted into her, but she pulled me back to her chest. Her hands were flat, her fingers spread out, touching as much of me as she could without moving. She wasn't looking over my shoulder until we slowed.

"Her cheek was against my back," I whisper, closing my eyes to see the trees whip past us in a blur. "I swear I felt her breath through my coat."

Ayls noisily moves around so she doesn't startle me when she positions herself the way I describe Gaine holding me. Her hands slide into my coat, and her fingers spread to glide over my ribs. Ayls leans her cheek against my back, and I relax into her embrace.

"Keep your eyes closed," Ayls whispers just before a charcoal pencil is slipped into my hand. "Just draw, Kade. Draw what you're feeling. Release some of that emotion through your pencil and give your fear a face."

The little Luna has my mind settled into a deep sense of relaxation, and the pencil seems to be moving on its own. I don't know what is transferring onto the canvas and don't really care. Gaine was beautiful when I finally helped her down from the Thoroughbred's back. I was so distracted by her that I didn't realize she wasn't out of breath like me. I missed a lot of things the first go-round with that woman.

Ayls lets me spend the afternoon reliving my first ride with Gaine. I recall the magic of the first time she touched my wolf. Gaine called me beautiful. Someone so amazing should never call anything beautiful. I could never compare to the perfection of my mate.

A few weeks ago, I mentioned that Gaine's color was white. When Ayls asked why I thought that was, I didn't hesitate to tell her it was because Gaine was so pure. It was strange to learn something new from a person so young, but the little Luna told me what the color actually represents. The aura around our mate is called the "color of our heart" and is designed to reflect what we most desire.

To be honest, I just want Gaine. But Ayls thinks I desire something wholesome and clean. Gaine loved me regardless of my past and how I first treated her. She was as pure as the little Luna's mother. She was strong enough to forgive me, and I threw it all away.

I sit up and open my eyes, but Ayls pulls the canvas from me before I can see it. "I need to try to talk to her," I say, turning to face the little Luna. "There's only so much forgiveness a woman can give, and I think that tank's empty."

Ayls frowns and takes my cheeks. "You're not ready for that, Kade," she whispers apologetically. "You need to take the time to heal. It wouldn't be fair to Gaine if you ran away from her again."

She's right, but I still scowl. I struggle through nearly everything if Ayls doesn't act out what Gaine does in my memory. I haven't figured out how to release my emotions to her without being triggered by the past.

We might have found a way for me to take my position without having to go through a blood bond with the Luna, but we haven't figured out how to stop my nightmares. Seeing Gaine die repeatedly has taken its toll on all of us. Right now, Bastian is back at the house sleeping because he stays awake all night to protect his Luna from me.

"What did I draw?" I ask, remembering the exercise she had me trying. "Where'd it go?"

"It's in my bag, where it's staying," Ayls answers. "It's not meant for eyes. It's only a tool to help you release what is trapped in your mind and causing your fears."

"I don't feel fear," I grumble. "I'm pissed." I throw the pencil toward the altar, instantly regretting it. "I'm a damn mess."

Tarq turns away from his project to glare at me. "I'll agree with that."

Ayls giggles. "Daddy, are you almost done? It's getting late." She rubs my back and stands to approach her father. "That looks beautiful. Mom would love it."

"It's just her name," Tarq grumbles. "She deserves a poem or maybe a song."

Crouching beside her father, Ayls wraps her arms around him and leans on his shoulder. "She has the strongest Alpha in the world honoring her. That's all she would ever want."

Ayls is more subtle in helping her father than with Bastian. She told me she only gives Tarq small amounts of emotion at a time. He's more sensitive to her help and doesn't like to receive it when it's not been requested.

When Tarq sits back on his heels to hug his daughter, he exposes what he'd been working on. I knew Ayls' mother's name was Darya, but I've never been able to call her anything other than Luna. Seeing it artistically carved into the largest stone of her altar feels like a finale to my heart.

I slip Ayls' bag in front of me and try to peek at the drawing I did. I'd taught her a few knots, and she's been using her new skill.

"I'll take that, thank you," Ayls announces, grabbing the securely knotted pack from my lap. "I meant what I said."

20

I stretch my legs to keep up with Ayls as she gallops the large white mare up the mountain. She'd convinced me to shift a few times over the past few months, but today, it was necessary. The little Luna had asked the Alphas to stay behind while we went into the mountains to enjoy the spring day. We all agreed that she should not be traveling without a wolf.

The mare heaves air noisily, running up the trail laden with heavy packs. Ayls has been quiet for the few hours we've been at this. I'm used to her silence when we sit on the porch swing as she listens to her guards' reports. This doesn't feel the same, and I have to say something when the mare begins stumbling under her.

"Ayls?" I start gently. *"You alright?"*

She sits up abruptly and pulls her reins, causing the mare to nearly sit down in her attempt to stop quickly. When she looks down, her eyes are red and swollen.

"Talk to me, kiddo," I urge. *"You carry our pain all the time. Let me lighten your load."*

The horse steps onto a road and turns left without any direction from Ayls. I jog to her side, trying to see what's ahead. We round a corner to enter the front yard of a grand two-story log cabin. Some of the surrounding fencing has been knocked down, and the baskets on the porch are all filled with dead stalks from the past.

"What is this?" I ask as Ayls stops the mare.

The little Luna swings from her saddle and stands stiffly beside the horse. "My parents' cabin," she whispers. Tears silently stream from her eyes as she takes in the abandoned scene.

I move slowly to stand by Ayls' side and rub my muzzle over her hip as I'd seen Bastian do to comfort her. She instinctively reaches for my jaw, curling her fingers to give me a shelf. I step forward to pull her along, but the little Luna doesn't move.

Twisting my jaw out of her grip, I trigger my shift. Ayls helped me realize that Gaine had watched me shift in a sweet, caring way because she couldn't wait to see my human form. But the little Luna doesn't take her eyes off the cabin and appears not to have noticed my transformation.

"Hey, sweetheart," I whisper, softly rubbing her arm. "Are you okay? Do you want to turn back?"

Ayls takes a sharp breath and wipes her nose. "Here," she says, turning to one of her packs. "I brought your clothes." When she lifts the flap of her bag, she exposes the tops of several stretched canvases. "I think this is something we both need."

I lift my eyebrow curiously but remain silent as she hands me my clothing one item at a time. Ayls drops the flap when she's finished and scratches the mare's neck while staring at the house.

"My grandfather built this cabin," she says quietly. "He gave it to my parents when he died. My mother brought my father here to spend time alone. Their bond was so strong."

"Your grandfather said she still watches over you," I murmur, trying to provide comfort without disturbing her.

Her grandfather, Dax, was Miles' brother. His Luna had access to some magic and gave them the ability to visit with the living each full moon evening. Now that Miles is truly gone, Dax is the only

Alpha who visits. Ayls has tried to explain it to me a few times, but it's all rather confusing. I gave up trying to understand and just accept that I'll be called a dumbass and shoved every time her grandfather visits for the rest of my life.

"I wanted to show you your drawings, Kade," Ayls says, stepping forward. "I thought we'd do it here so you could have privacy."

I hook our arms as we walk. "I don't think I understand, kiddo," I respond, shaking my head.

"What do you think about when you draw with your eyes closed?" Ayls asks.

I recall the times we've tried the art therapy Edith suggested over the past few months. "I don't know," I finally answer. "Gaine mostly, I guess. I picture the memories that I tell you about. Why?"

Ayls peers at me curiously. "Because that's not what you draw."

She stops beside a paddock with a run-in shelter on the far side. Some old hay remains piled in the corner, and water troughs along the fencing stand empty even after the recent snow melt. The horses were well cared for while they stayed here.

"Can you tell me about the day my mother died?" Ayls asks, yanking my attention away from the paddock.

"No," I answer firmly. I'd refused to talk about what I had seen that day. A child doesn't need to hear how their parent died. Even during the time I embraced my asshole attitude and role as Tynan's enforcer, I would never do such a thing. She might be my Luna, but she's still a kid.

Ayls pulls one of the canvases from her bag and hands it to me. My arms shake as my fingers curl around the wooden frame. The past year suddenly makes sense as I stare at the little Luna's mother, tied to a tree with a knife in her neck.

"There's more," Ayls whispers, slipping a second over the first. "They're all like this."

The angles are slightly different, and I'd sketched various

moments of her death scene, but they are all of that horrific day. In some, she's looking at us, but most show her already dead. I'm relieved that I didn't draw Tarq cradling her.

I fold my legs and drop to the ground. "I heard Tarq talking to her," I whisper, tracing my fingers over the Luna's face in a drawing where she was looking at us. "We all did." I wipe my face and take a deep breath. "I started singing to stop the others from listening. I can't sing."

Ayls sits before me and smiles. "I know," she says, sniffling. "I've heard you."

Clicking my tongue, I scoff. "Shut up."

"Daddy said Uncle Miles was there when he said goodbye," Ayls says quietly as she takes my hands. "Did you see him?"

I draw a deep breath and roll my eyes up before releasing it, hoping to stop my emotions. "Everything happened so fast," I tell her, trying to slow the memory down. "Tynan stabbed your mother in the neck." I sift through the drawings and pull out the most accurate ones. "Your father jumped against the ward barrier and howled. Oh, Ayls, I've never heard its equal. But then I blinked, and five wolves appeared in the field, circling Tynan."

"The Guardians," Ayls whispers. She slides her fingers over her mother's face.

"I thought I recognized Miles but didn't know for sure until you told me about him not being able to come back anymore," I respond. "I promise, Ayls, he was a good guy. He taught me everything I know."

"The stories are mixed, but I'm not worried about Miles right now," the little Luna tells me. She brushes my hair out of my eyes and smiles through her tears. "You are thinking about Gaine and drawing my mother."

I settle into her touch and feel some of my tension release.

"Watching your mother die was horrible," I whisper. "But the days that followed were worse."

"Anthony stood over my father while he held her," Ayls says, moving into my line of sight. "He said only a few wolves tried to approach them."

I breathe a small laugh. "Those two were... I don't know how to describe it," I say, shaking my head. "They were a fierce presence that would crush the soul of anyone near." I cup her cheeks and pull her forehead to my lips. "Tarq was crying and rocking your mother's body, and yet somehow, we knew we would die if we went anywhere near him."

"He is the strongest man I know," Ayls whispers. "He even bests Bastian when they spar."

"His heartache was on display for everyone to see, and I've never felt pain like that," I say, releasing her cheeks. "He was broken from the moment she left this world. I wouldn't have survived."

Ayls produces a small smile as she gathers up my drawings. She piles them in her lap and rubs her hand over the one on top. "Kade, your dreams are of Gaine dying," the little Luna reminds me as if I'd forgotten what wakes me every night. "But when you think of her, you are drawing my mother. We're dealing with fear."

"Ayls, I fear you might be wrong," I grumble. "I'm not afraid of anything."

"Oh, sweet wolf," she sighs. "You are afraid of a great many things. But today, we will talk about how you fear having to feel the loss of your mate as my father has."

I jerk my head back and narrow my eyes. "How could your father's loss cause my nightmares?"

"You are so strong, Kade," Ayls says, smiling. "I've never seen anyone better than you with a blade, and you've greatly improved my ability with a bow, but you are still a wolf. Your love for Gaine is a powerful force of nature that no other living creature could ever understand. You watched my father lose the woman he loved with the same fierceness as your love for Gaine.

"I imagine most wolves left the field after a short time to return home or maybe come to me at the lake. But you stayed." She searches my eyes for understanding. "You watched more than your fair share of that pain and left before he gathered himself."

"If loving someone that much means I have to experience her loss, I don't want to do it," I mumble, reliving my time at the edge of the field.

"But what about the years together?" Ayls asks. "Isn't that worth it? My parents had 15 years together. They were so happy and in love. They grossed me out. My father was forever trying to sneak my mother away to get her alone." She giggles quietly and grins. "She smiled every time Daddy walked into the room. I wanted so badly to experience a love like that."

"Bastian loves you very much." I take a few of the canvases from her. "This woman," I add, pointing to her mother, "loved you all with such an intensity that I can't imagine the ferocity of her love for her Alpha."

"Kade, your love for Gaine allows you to open up to me," Ayls says, covering her mother with her hand. "You are madly in love with the woman you took on a whirlwind adventure. That's not going away. I bet loving her while she's in your arms would be much more fun."

"How am I supposed to hold her when all I see is her bleeding to death?" I scoff.

Ayls nods with a sigh. "That's why we're here." She stands and holds her hand out to me. "Come on. Edith has been working on a little gift for you. I think you're gonna like this."

Taking her hand, I allow her to help me off the ground. We work together on the mare's packs, piling them in the middle of a wagon trail. Once the mare is locked in the paddocks, Ayls slings the one sack that isn't overly stuffed with framed canvases over her shoulder.

"Come with me," she says, smiling. The little Luna holds her arm out for me to escort her and leads me onto the porch when I take it. "Miles washed my mother's hair on this deck the morning of her wedding," she tells me. "She sat in this chair and let him pamper her while he talked to Edith and my grandmother."

"I don't think I'm much of a hairdresser if that's your plan," I reply, lifting my eyebrow.

Ayls laughs. "I'm not the pampered type anyway," she says, shaking her head. She places the sack on the chair and pulls out glass jars filled with different-colored liquids. "Edith and Anthony have been gathering materials to make these paints for you." She places a horse-hair paintbrush in my hand. "This time, I'd like you to try drawing with your eyes open, and I thought the paints might make it a bit more exciting."

I've never hidden that my mind is not a fun place to be. Admittedly, I thought my drawings would be nonsense and scribbles. At best, they would be monsters. I never imagined they would so accurately depict anything real, never mind Ayls' beautiful mother's death.

"I've never painted anything," I murmur, studying the brush she'd handed me. The hairs are white with dark specks. "Is this your mare's hair?"

"Does that really matter?" Ayls asks, laughing. "Grease was happy to donate to your therapy." She pulls out a small stand and sits it on the table beside the chair to hold the canvas she produces next. "I've heard many of your stories about the Blood Pack, Gaine, and even some of your adventures. I thought you might like to hear some of my tales."

Indeed, the little Luna now has my attention. Ayls has loved me as more than just her wolf. We're family. I do most of the talking and ask daily if she thinks I'm ready to leave, even though I know the answer is still no. We've been fixing me for many months now. The idea of not having to relive a part of my life I'd prefer to forget is a refreshing change.

I watch curiously as the little Luna moves the chair so that she won't be able to see the canvas and settles into it. She curls her legs neatly to the side and rubs her arms briskly, shivering. I pull off the oversized denim shirt Edith made for me and tuck it over her lap like a blanket.

"I would love to hear a story," I whisper, kissing her forehead.

Ayls pulls a thin, sanded board from her pack and hands it to me. "For mixing your colors," she says, smiling. "Our world isn't black and white. It's time to add color to your vision."

The young Luna turned 16 a few weeks ago but has an ageless presence. She once told me that she's supposed to rule with the wisdom of all the Lunas before her but always feels scared and unprepared when a decision needs to be made. Even when she speaks of things that make her feel uncertain, her words still hold the strength of her title and what it means to us as her wolves.

"My mother brought Bastian here after she rescued him," Ayls begins, looking toward the mare's paddock. "It's hard to imagine my Alpha afraid of anything, but he wouldn't leave her side for the first week. He told me he spent hours grooming Grease while my mother told him stories about our pack and the immortal Alphas."

As she details Bastian's recovery, I look through the small jars she'd set out. I watched Agatha mix a few herbs into the poultice she made for Gaine and change its color. I pour a little of each onto the sanded board and use the back of the brush to mix some of them.

"I brought you a variety," Ayls says.

When I look up, she smiles and holds out a few more brushes. "I have no idea what I'm doing," I admit with the first genuine laugh since she found me on her porch. "This should be interesting."

"Did you know my mother thought werewolves were fairy stories when she met my grandfather?" Ayls asks. "If she can learn to be the Luna of wolves after believing you were nothing but a scary children's story, then you can learn to paint what is on your mind."

I smile as she winks at me. "How did I ever survive a day without you?" I ask, raising an eyebrow.

Ayls shakes her head and settles back into her story about Bass. She's telling me about the boat ride down the river as I mix the different colors to create the perfect brown. When I finally raise the brush to start working, a sharp breeze blows across the deck, making the little Luna shiver and pull her jacket tighter.

"Why don't we go inside, Ayls?" I ask. "One of those Alphas will end me if you get sick."

She turns to look at the door for a moment but then settles back into her chair. "I haven't been in there since..." her voice trails off. Sighing, Ayls narrows her eyes in thought. "This was their place, you know? I'm not ready."

"Okay, sweetheart," I say reassuringly. I watch her stare toward the mare's paddock until a tear rolls from her eye. "How come Bass doesn't shift?"

Ayls inhales deeply as I pull her out of her thoughts. "It was a vow he made to my mother," she answers. "He's not allowed to shift around me until we're older. I really did like holding him on the train, though."

Her shy smile makes me laugh. "Gaine feels like silk slipping over my fingers," I say, winking. "I completely understand." I slide the brush over the canvas and watch the colors mix. Some blend while others remain separate, creating streaks. "I thought you would feel a different type of pull as kids."

"Kade, I'm 16," she scoffs. "I'm not some little kid. But as the Luna, my story is different. When Bass and I bond, we'll stop aging.

Mom struggled with the men of this world treating her like a child at 24. I would never be taken seriously at 16."

"You could just kill them all," I grumble, frowning at my painting. "I taught you how."

"I don't want to fight," Ayls says sadly. "Every battle feels like a loss as we bury our fallen. There has to be something better. Mom always thought we could find peace."

Sighing, I put my brush down and kneel before her. "Kiddo, peace killed your mother," I whisper, looking up into her eyes. "If you walk her path, your destination will be the same."

Ayls smiles softly before leaning forward to gently kiss my forehead. "You'll understand when you have Gaine and a few little wolves running around," she whispers. "If you spend all your time defending them, you'll miss the life you could have holding them."

Clicking my tongue, I scowl at the little Luna. It's hard to argue with her. After all the time I'd spent running up and down the country trying to keep Gaine safe, I feel Ayls' words deep in my soul. I missed my gorgeous mate every moment I was gone and hated being away from her, even if it was all for her safety.

"I'm not a human, nor am I a wolf," Ayls continues. "I can't understand why humans hate and fear us. We accept everyone, no matter who or what they are. When one of our people calls for help, the entire pack and the few humans within our fold jump into action. I love you all. I'll find a way to give you a peaceful life."

"It must be beautiful inside your mind," I say, shaking my head. With a sigh, I use her knees to push myself back to my feet. "I hope you get to see your dreams come true, little Luna." I turn back to my painting and smile at Gaine. "I heard Anthony say your companion is coming back tomorrow. That must be exciting."

Ayls releases a soft hum. "I have missed him," she whispers. "There were several militia regiments close to your old compound.

It took them a while to push them back so those wolves could keep their homes."

I narrow my eyes thoughtfully. "I wouldn't think any would want to," I say.

"Some of them showed Brock what's left of your house," Ayls adds. She's studying my face when I look up. "Can we talk about that?"

"No," I answer.

I'm unsure why she asks, and my answer is pointless. She's going to drag the story out of me, and I'll be completely helpless to stop her. A few more gentle urges from the little Luna, and I'm spilling my guts.

Ayls remains silent as my chest swells while I detail Gaine's gorgeous, tanned body beautifully stretched over my bed. I close my eyes and remember her begging me to touch her. Gaine's foot caressed my chest, and I wanted to taste every toe. I lick my lips, wishing they carried her flavor just once more.

I take a deep breath and open my eyes. "She touched me," I whisper. "I reached for her, but she wasn't there." I stare at my painting briefly before dipping a fresh brush in the red paint. "That's when the knife appeared. She was bleeding out on my bed."

Placing the brush on the left side of Gaine's neck, I begin sliding it across the canvas. When there is enough red, I add brown and black to give it the deep oxygen-carrying crimson that flows from the body. Even in death, Gaine is the image of perfection.

Ayls touches my shoulder, making me jump. "She really is beautiful," the little Luna whispers, sliding her arms around my waist. "We'll figure this out, Kade. I promise."

"What's the use?" I growl.

I throw the paintbrush and snatch the canvas from its stand. Turning abruptly, I knock Ayls to her knees and smash the painting over the railing. I know I should pick her up, but I'm so damn mad

I might break her. The palms of my hands press into my temples as I slide my fingers into my hair and stomp away from her.

"Kade?" the little Luna says quietly.

"Ayls, I'm tired," I spout. My growl builds, frustrating me even more. "Every time we step forward, something drags us backward. I'm not getting better. If anything, it's getting worse." I kick the railing, busting a few of the boards.

"Kade?" Ayls whispers from directly behind me.

I spin around as my anger settles in deep and takes hold of me. I pull my fist back, knowing I'm about to do something I will regret for the rest of my life, but Ayls jumps forward and grabs my cheeks. I stumble backward in surprise when her lips lock onto mine. My fingers dig into her hair, intending to pull her off me, but I never find the strength.

Ayls remains still, holding her lips to mine while my mind settles. As my Luna, she's figured out the best way to contain my anger is to shock me. I doubt she could've surprised me more any other way. She slips her fingers over my cheeks and jaw, settling my growl into a hum.

I move from Ayls' lips to kiss her cheek. "I love you, sweetheart," I whisper.

"I know you do, Kade," she responds. "That's why I haven't given up on you yet." She winks and takes my hand, dragging me back to the destroyed canvas. "I have an idea. Come on. Help me."

I follow her curiously as she leads me to the packs and canvases we had left beside the paddock. Without a word, Ayls begins removing the remaining drawings and piling them all in a pyramid style. She collects a few sticks and dry leaves, jamming them into the openings.

Just as I decide there is no way she'd destroy these drawings, Ayls hands me a flint. "I believe you always have a blade," she says, lifting her eyebrow. Her eyes trail down my body and rest on my left boot.

"Do I have any secrets from you?" I scoff, digging out the short blade.

"Why would you need to hide things from me?" Ayls asks innocently. "I'm pretty sure I'm your best friend, Kade."

"You're probably right," I say, laughing.

Ayls hands me a few leaves and twists some twigs together. We sit beside the pile of canvases, and I strike my blade across the flint several times until the leaves catch, igniting the twigs. I lift the twisted bundle and hold it out to Ayls.

The little Luna shakes her head. "When you burned your house, you were trying to destroy a dream or image," she says, studying my face. "It wasn't real. Your nightmares aren't real, but these are." Ayls sweeps her hand over the drawings. "We can touch and feel them. They are not your imagination. It's time to burn the past and move into your future, Kade."

I lick my lips and release a shaky breath as I hold the burning twigs out to the canvases. We stand and back away as they rapidly turn into a blazing bonfire. Ayls leans on me, and I pull her against my chest, cradling her head. Together, we watch the memory of her mother's murder rise into the air, carried in the smoke and ash.

"Goodbye, Mom," Ayls whispers. "I'll see you again, but it's time to let you go."

21

I wake to the sweet scent of fresh blooms riding on the summer breeze months later. Although the wing beside the kitchen stays cool in the shade all day, Ayls likes to sleep with the windows open. She enjoys hearing the kids practice their calls at night, and her excitement is contagious when they hit the correct pitch.

I roll to my right side and nod to Bastian. Ayls is probably sweating, but she sleeps tucked into her Alpha's gut every night now that my nightmares have stopped. Bastian lifts his front leg to check on her, allowing me to brush her hair from her face. I put my fist out for him to bump with his nose before he lays back down.

"I'm glad you found her," I whisper. "You deserve her."

Bastian licks his lips and sighs.

"We should take her to the lake today," I continue. "Have some fun before I leave."

Bastian's ears prick forward at the idea of the lake.

"Yeah," I say, answering his unspoken question. "I'll throw her in for you."

"I don't like it when you two plot against me," Ayls mumbles. Bastian raises his leg to allow her to roll over. "Good morning, Love." The little Luna kisses the tip of Bastian's nose before turning her attention to me. "How did you sleep, Kade?"

"Like a baby," I whisper, smiling as I tuck some hair behind her ear. "I'm going to miss waking up to you."

Sighing, Ayls reaches for my hand. "You need to go slow, silver wolf," she warns. "Your leaving hurt Gaine quite a bit."

"How could she resist all this?" I ask while gesturing toward my body and wagging my eyebrow.

Ayls tugs a belt loop on the jeans I've borrowed from Tarq. "Daddy says he's tired of you stealing his clothes," Ayls reports. "You need to learn to wash your own laundry."

I laugh heartily before catching her confused look and straightening my face. "I've had a lot of help over the years," I say, cringing. I doubt I should explain the weekdays and their many talents to a 16-year-old or the Luna, especially when they're the same person.

"I suppose things will be different for you now," Ayls says. She smiles and swipes her fingers over my cheek. "There is kindness in your heart, but you must learn to be gentle with Gaine. Her emotions are strong, and she refuses to come to the lake for my help."

"I told you not to tell her I was here," I scoff.

"Kade, you are the only wolf that benefits from my surprises," Ayls retorts. "I would lose Gaine's trust if I did that to her."

"Fine," I grumble. "Come here." I reach for her face and pull her lips to mine. This has become a game for us since she used the surprise kiss tactic on me at the cabin in the mountains. Bastian growls every time, making me chuckle. I push the young Alpha's shoulder. "Come on, kid. I'll make breakfast. Your Luna needs a bath. After you cook her all night, her sweat smells like warm peach pie. We might have to eat her if she doesn't clean up."

Ayls scoffs and pushes me away, but Bastian stands on the bed and begins licking her neck and face. "Bass, stop," she yells. "You don't have to agree with him!"

* * *

After a large breakfast, Bastian and I escort Ayls down to the lake for what she probably thought would be a peaceful afternoon. Instead, I drop my bag filled with painting supplies and yank off my shirt while Bass distracts her. Ayls screams as I latch onto her waist and take off toward the water. Bass runs ahead and finds the deeper spot, allowing me to throw his Luna safely into its depths.

As I dive in after her, some of Ayls' guards emerge from the trees to keep her in view. We're never truly alone, but Bass and Ayls don't seem to notice. When I find her hiding from Bass, Ayls wraps her arms around my shoulders, and I pull her back to the surface.

"I hate you," she says, spitting out a mouthful of water.

"No, you don't," I spout, slinging her around to my back and pulling us to shore. "Come on. Let's dry you off," I say, setting her on her feet. "I have something for you."

Ayls studies me curiously as I wrap my arms around her. After the long months I've spent here with them, having the little Luna in my arms feels almost as natural as holding Gaine. I rest my chin on her head, and her hand slides over my chest until it lines up with her mother's print.

"She'd be proud of you," I whisper, rubbing her back as I heat my body to dry us off.

"My mother and father taught me everything I know," Ayls starts quietly. "I still learn new things daily, but she is why I will always fight for my wolves."

Bastian approaches from behind Ayls and rubs his wet muzzle over her hip.

"Bass, I'm trying to dry her off," I grumble.

Ayls laughs, reaching for Bastian's jaw. "Bass wants you to know he's happy you're leaving."

I join in her laughter. "Me too, bud," I say, leaning back to cup Ayls cheek. "Me too." Smiling, I kiss the little Luna's forehead and step away. "Come on," I urge, reaching for her hand. "Bass should see this too."

I pull Ayls up to where I'd dropped my bag and sit in the grass with her and her Alpha. The little Luna smiles at Bass as she leans against his shoulder. He nuzzles her cheek, distracting her so she doesn't see the gifts I remove from the sack.

"You might have said goodbye to your mother, but we wanted you to have a part of her with you at all times," I start quietly. I open my hands to reveal a crystal pendant Edith had made. She encased it in wire, and Anthony fashioned a sturdy chain to hold it around the little Luna's neck.

Ayls gasps, leaning forward for a better look at the pink crystal. "What is that?"

"Edith filled this with some of your mother's ashes," I murmur. "So, you'll always have her close to your heart too."

Covering her mouth, Ayls turns to let me fasten the chain around her neck. She clutches the crystal to her chest with one hand and presses the other to my mark. "Now we'll both carry her around."

I lift her hand from my chest and kiss her knuckles. "I saw your mother a few times before the train," I tell her. "But I wanted to help you remember her before she was sick. Edith has been helping me."

"So that's why you were going down to their house," Ayls says, smiling.

"This is why," I respond, pulling out the painting I'd been working on. It took a few weeks to perfect this large portrait of the little Luna's mother. "Edith told me she was especially fond of a black horse you trained for her, so I painted the Luna hugging him. I hope that was true because I can't take him out."

Ayls sniffles as her face distorts, trying to hide her emotions. "Bones," she whispers. "His name was Bones." She gently slides her fingers along her mother's hair. "She was so beautiful. You captured her perfectly."

"I don't remember her face without a smile," I admit. "It breathed so much life into the air around her. That's the image I wanted you to see whenever you doubt yourself." I catch Ayls as she lunges forward into my arms. "You are doing a great job helping everyone move on."

The little Luna releases a shaky breath. She stays in my arms but leans onto Bastian's muzzle when he puts his chin on her shoulder. They both stare at the painting of our previous Luna that I had poured over for many days. We all grin back at her contagious smile.

"You were the strength I needed to put my pieces back together," I whisper, reminding the kids how strong they are. "I shared how powerful my desire to force myself on Gaine was. I can only imagine the pull you must have on Bastian. His restraint shows his ability as an Alpha. You both will do amazing things for our future as a pack."

Ayls giggles, reaching for my cheek. "Bass says he still doesn't like you, but I love you very much, Kade," she says before kissing me and making Bass growl. "Let's stay out here tonight. We'll sleep under the stars for your last night with us."

* * *

The flower fields sway in the strong winds of an approaching storm. The rumble of thunder is getting closer, but I hold Ayls' large white mare still, staring ahead at the tiny dot of Gaine's cottage. I'd asked the little Luna not to announce that I was on my way. I told her I wanted to surprise Gaine, but the truth is that I didn't want to warn her.

The mare jumps as lightning rips through the air, striking a tree at the edge of the basin below. The crash of thunder is nearly deafening. Not only does this day seem to be playing out like my nightmares, but the storm is clearly telling me to leave.

The breeze turns cold as it shifts direction. I step down from the mare and skirt the rock wall, using it to protect us until we can drop into the trees on the other side. With the gentle sloping of the field, there should be a gully within the patch of trees that would allow us to remain lower and safe until the storm passes.

I roll my eyes at a thick wall of rain that appears from the direction of the cottage. Pulling on the mare, I urge her to hurry along so we can make it to the trees before we get soaked. The horse has a different plan and yanks her reins out of my hand, spinning away from me.

Ayls had told me she was trained to return home like Gaine's mare. I assume that's where she's going as she darts toward the cliff trail we'd used to get up here. The roar of the rain coming closer commands my attention, and I resume my journey at a dead run.

I reach the trees a few minutes before the rain, but it doesn't help. The downpour contains fat waterdrops that quickly make it through the thin veil of leaves. The gully has even fewer trees, and soon, my clothes are soaked and plastered to my skin.

The wind whips around me, and the thunder never stops rumbling. I nearly miss the sound of a tree falling several feet behind me. Cursing under my breath, I crouch against a large rock in the ditch at the bottom of the gully.

Everything about today feels like a warning, but I can't turn back even when it begins to hail. It's been over a year since I last saw Gaine, and I need to fix that. My mind healed with each passing day, and my body called for her. I've wanted nothing but to experience her existence again for weeks.

I close my eyes and let my mind wander. I recall the long days I stood in the woods behind Gaine's cottage, waiting for her. When I knew she was inside, tucked safe and warm in her bed, I cursed the ward that kept me from her. I imagined pulling the blankets down to expose her beautiful body, sliding my fingers over her soft skin, and lying with her to feel her heat up in response to my attention.

I open my eyes, and my chest swells at the thought. Regardless of how much I want Gaine, she's mad as hell at me. She's so angry that she has refused several of the little Luna's invites.

Tarq was furious, but Ayls explained the situation by blaming me. Although the standing Alpha spent a few nights in the wing off the kitchen with us when he needed Ayls' help, his feelings about me have never changed. His judgment is typically silent, but we all heard what he thought of me that day.

I haven't respected an Alpha since Miles, so when he stood over me screaming his feelings and growling so loudly that I almost couldn't hear his words, it took all my strength to remain calm. My muscles fired, causing a mix of emotions to flood through me. I still felt the anger kick in, and my instinct to lash out was there, but an unfamiliar desire to bow and back away was also present.

Tarq's orders at the end of his rant were clear. "Fix this shit with your mate, or your time in my daughter's pack is over," he had yelled. I doubt Ayls would banish me, but Gaine's behavior would not go unpunished for long, and as I am the cause, it's my job to correct it.

I look up when the rain lightens, realizing the storm is finally moving away. *It's time to follow orders.* I stand and push off the rock. The ditch is collecting some of the runoff, so I find a deer trail leading back to the top of the ridge and follow it for a while. The trees provide cover and allow me to remain somewhat hidden on my way to the cottage.

Now that I'm this close, my mind races with different things I should say. Unsure of exactly why Gaine won't see me, I'm having trouble finding the right words. She doesn't need to say anything. I abandoned her. She's perfect. All I want to hear her say is my name.

"KADE!" my beautiful, perfect, and amazing mate screams angrily at the top of her lungs.

I would've preferred for her to whisper my name in my ear as I held her body close to mine, but I'll take what I can get right now. I look beyond the tree line to see her charging across the flower fields on the bay mare. I smile at her bare feet as she easily sits astride the galloping mare bareback and aims her strung arrow at me.

Gaine sits back, making the mare slide to a stop. "Leave," she snarls at me. "You're not welcome here."

Sighing, I furrow my brow. "Gaine," I start with no plan for what should come after it.

"Shut up!" she screams. "I don't want to hear you."

I step forward and reach for the mare's reins.

Gaine lets loose her arrow, piercing the dirt directly in front of my boot. "I don't want to see you," she growls.

Gaine is the most expressive person I have ever met. Her emotions project through her every move and reflect in her voice. My beautiful mate is a wolf through and through. Her teeth may not be sharp in her human form, but her showing them means the same.

"Just talk to me, Gaine," I plead.

Gaine turns the mare to the side, taking her reins out of my reach. "I don't want you," she growls slowly. Each word stabs me as she enunciates them while barely opening her mouth. "Leave!" She kicks the mare, sending her charging back toward the cottage. Her hooves kick large chunks of dirt at me until they are far enough away.

"Well, that could've gone better," I grumble, crouching to pull her arrow from the dirt. I test its tip, finding it nearly as sharp as my blades. Obviously, she meant business when she came out here. I didn't stand a chance.

I duck back into the trees and keep walking until I reach the bottom of the gully. Gaine is mad, but my smile can't be swayed. Ayls was right about her skill on horseback. Not once did she look off-balance or uncomfortable on the mare's bare back. She signaled the horse to do things with the slightest of movements.

I shake my head, recalling the little Luna's advice before I left her house. Ayls reminded me that I needed to shift before Gaine began to feel comfortable around me. She urged me to make this journey and plead for forgiveness as a wolf, but I laughed. I stupidly expected Gaine to run into my arms as she had when I returned from failing her in the South.

I roll my eyes, pulling my soaked jacket from my shoulders. *At least she didn't shoot me.* I slowly remove the rest of my clothing and carefully push my blades into the bark of a rotted tree. With one last look around, I crouch and trigger my shift.

Distracting myself while my muscles shorten and my bones contort to my wolf, I try to figure out my next move. *She wouldn't be so angry if she'd only listen to what I've been through.*

Once my muzzle forms, the pack's voices begin to filter in. Ayls' guards are the only wolves calling out broadcasts and are easy to push to the back, thankfully. I listen for anyone mentioning Gaine or the elders, but there's nothing.

"Ayls?" I call out.

"Hey there, shiny one," she responds quickly. *"How's it going?"*

"Could be better," I admit, jogging toward Gaine's cottage along the ditch. *"She wasn't too happy to see me."*

"Can you blame her?" Ayls asks.

Sighing, I step onto a log and stop. *"What do I do?"*

"You told me that Gaine wouldn't talk to you when you first left the ranch," Ayls says, pointing out again that Gaine didn't trust me until I shifted into my wolf. *"I've noticed that no one lays hands on each other. You shake hands, hug, and slap each other's backs, but you aren't comfortable letting anyone touch your wolf. Why is that?"*

I consider her question for a minute, trying to rationalize our need to shy away from a hand. *"I have no idea, Ayls,"* I finally admit. *"It's an instinct. I've let her touch me, though. She said I was beautiful."* I lift my paw and watch it reflect the foliage around me. *"That opinion will probably be different now."*

"*Oh, you're still gorgeous, Kade,*" Ayls whispers.

"*You have to say that,*" I grumble. "*You're the Luna.*"

"*No,*" she responds, letting me hear her giggle. "*I don't. You are perfect just the way you are. But Gaine didn't love you because you are beautiful. You fought an instinct she knew was there and allowed her to touch you. In your silence, you heard her.*"

"*Her voice is the harmony in my theme music,*" I accidentally tell Ayls.

She hums a small laugh. "*Kade, I think Gaine has something to say. You'd do well to take the time to listen to her and allow her to feel heard.*"

I lie down, resting my chin on my front paws. "*I don't like it when you're right,*" I grumble.

"*She's a wolf, a woman, and an elder, Kade. Everything about your mate is strong and willful,*" Ayls says quietly. "*You told me that her strength drives your senses crazy.*"

My hum kicks on as I remember watching Gaine's wolf jog effortlessly beside me. "*It's distracting.*"

"*Then stop trying to squash that strength,*" Ayls snaps. "*Let her be powerful, Kade. You won't win this war.*"

"*Yeah, alright,*" I grumble, rolling my eyes. "*I'll let you know how it goes.*"

I turn my eyes to the clearing sky. It's late afternoon. It will be dark by the time I reach the edge of the ward around the cottage. Gaine and I have only been together privately, but I'm sure my groveling needs to be public.

Standing, I jog up the ridge and emerge at the edge of the trees. I planned to follow the ditch to remain hidden for as long as possible, but Ayls has a point. I took Gaine's power away when I left her. I promised I'd come back, and I didn't. Out of everyone in my life, I've lied to her the most and let her down in every way. It's time to beg for forgiveness.

I have no idea how to do this.

* * *

After lying in the field in front of the cottage for two days, I'm actually excited to see Gaine's little sister walking in my direction through the early morning fog. My mouth waters when I catch the scent of the raw steak she's carrying on one of two plates. I'd love some eggs and bacon from the other, but beggars can't be choosers.

"You're not going to freak out on me again, are you?" the girl asks, stopping at the edge of the ward.

I sit up and shake my head.

River gives me a thoughtful expression. "Just in case, I think I'll stay on this side." She sits before me and pushes the slab of beef across the barrier.

I lie back down and slide my tongue over the meat, trying to decide where to bite first. The thick cut is large enough to hang off the edge of the plate. Holding it down firmly with my paw, I tear a sizable chunk off the side with a strip of fat.

"You hurt her," River says quietly, pausing before jamming a forkful of eggs into her mouth. "She cried for weeks."

Sighing, I swallow the meat and look up at the young girl. She holds a canteen to her mouth and pulls a few swallows. My tongue slides over my lips. To show the depth of my apology, I have stayed in my spot without food or water. I'm more thirsty than hungry.

"My father wants to kill you," River states plainly. "The Luna said she'd banish all of us if he touches you." She narrows her eyes in thought. "I don't think that's such a bad thing. My sister wouldn't cry herself to sleep every night, and I wouldn't have to see all the horrible things we did in the past."

River has a childish way of just talking to herself. I hated what she babbled in Edith's house, but these words sting like sharp blades. Gaine's pain makes my meal want to come back up. I push the remainder of the meat back across the ward.

"She figured you'd be hungry by now," River says, shrugging.

My ears prick at her words. I look behind the girl and see Gaine marching toward us with her bow slung over her shoulder. Sitting up, I extend my chest to look less like my inner puppy, who wants to jump around excitedly. I contain most of my movements except for my front paws, which can't seem to stay still.

"I told you to leave," Gaine growls, snatching the canteen from her sister. She steps across the barrier and grabs my jaw. I stare into her beautiful eyes as she wrenches my mouth open and pours the water onto the back of my tongue. "You don't listen. You never listen. I loved and wanted all of you, even your flaws, and you still left me. I lost my Luna, and you forced me to grieve her alone. I don't want you or the pain you cause. I told you that you would break my world. You never listen."

Gaine drops my jaw and throws the empty canteen toward the cottage. She slides the bow from her shoulder and nocks an arrow, resting it between my eyes. I swallow the last of the water still in my throat and move just enough to feel the tip puncture my hide.

"I said leave!" Gaine yells, showing her teeth. She presses her boot to my shoulder, shoving me.

I roll over my hip, refusing to budge. I have never rolled over for anyone, but I'll try anything to earn Gaine's forgiveness. This woman is everything I have ever wanted, and I broke her. The pain and anger displayed on her face and ringing in her voice were my fault.

"LEAVE!" Gaine screams, letting the arrow loose. It lodges in the dirt by my paws.

I scramble to my feet and back up a few steps. *Just yell at me, Beauty,* I whisper, lowering my eyes. *Get it out. I deserve to hear the pain I caused.*

"GO!" my mate spouts, letting another arrow loose.

I keep my head down, losing contact with Gaine's eyes as she circles me. River must have run off at some point because her voice is distant as she yells for her father. I can hear Gaine's growl, but with the hollering from the house and banging doors, I've lost track of her position.

When I turn to find her, a burst of pain shoots through my hip. I yelp and jump forward, slamming head-first into the barrier, and my body rolls to the ground. I fall onto the hip that started this whole thing. The sensation of my skin tearing causes the beef and water to jump from my stomach.

"Luna," I call out, hoping she'll hear me. *"Shit. I think she shot me."*

22

I never heard Ayls answer my call, but a hum of voices breaks through my daze several times until I become aware I'm in someone's arms. Light pressure is applied to the bridge of my nose before a hand slides over my head. My ear flops as fingers rub the short fur covering it. I take a deep breath and pull in the beautiful scent of strawberry soap.

"I know you're awake," Ayls says sharply. *"You be gentle with her, or you'll answer to me."*

When Gaine sniffles, her chest lifts my head. "I needed you," she whispers, pushing my jaw so my muzzle is tucked under her chin. "You're mine. I still want you."

I sneak a taste of Gaine's skin as she rolls toward me, wrapping her arms around my neck. I don't know what's happened since I'm pretty sure she shot me, but I have missed her arms more than I thought. I expect her to release me when my hum starts, but she just nuzzles her face into my fur, and the next thing I hear is her soft snores.

"Ayls?"

"Yes, Kade," the little Luna responds.

"She did shoot me, right?" I ask, sliding my nose over Gaine's collarbone.

"Yes, Kade," Ayls repeats.

I sigh as I settle into my perfect mate. *"I love her,"* I mumble.

"I know you do," Ayls says. *"She's been talking to you for a few days. She has a lot to say. You won't like some of it, but you will hear her, Kade."*

"Yes, my Luna," I answer before drifting to sleep in the arms I've been dying to feel.

* * *

"What is that?" Gaine asks, waking me abruptly and making me jump.

"It's a drawing salve, Gaine," Edith whispers from behind me. "Annalisa says he's not allowed to shift until you permit him. This will keep the wound open while drawing out anything that could cause an infection."

My mate's growl builds in her nervousness.

"It's alright, Gaine," Ayls adds. "We need to keep the wound open so it will heal from the tea and not leave a scar. We wouldn't want him to be less than perfect."

"Ayls, can you tell her I love her?" I ask, nuzzling into Gaine's neck.

My muzzle is pulled from my mate, and my head is wrenched around until I open my eyes. "No," the little Luna states sternly. "You will listen for as long as your mate needs you to. She will permit you to shift when she is ready to hear your words. Until then, you will remain silent."

I lift my lips and pretend to nip at Ayls, making her shake her head.

"You're lucky you're cute," she grumbles, dropping my jaw.

Gaine rolls onto her back, letting me drape my head over her chest and take in the room. The bed is soft but small, offering barely enough space for us. Edith stands nearby while Ayls works on something at a desk across the room. Various drawings of birds and different angles of extended wings are pinned on the wall.

I take a deep breath and pull in the scent of beef mingled with Gaine's soap. When I lick my lips, Ayls passes the plate she had been working on to Edith. I watch the witch rub something on the raw meat before handing the dish to Gaine.

These women seem to all know what's happening, and none of them have given me a reason not to trust them. Besides, I'm starving. I eagerly accept the meat Gaine offers, barely chewing before I send it to my stomach, hoping for more.

Edith works on my wound while I'm distracted by the meal. After the first few pieces, Gaine allows me to taste her fingers with each new bite. I don't even care that my hum starts, making the witch laugh. My mate needs me to be humble, and I will do anything for her.

"Alright," Edith finally says, gathering her jars. "He should be fine for the night. That packing is in there pretty deep, Kade. No moving around."

"He'll be fine," Ayls says, standing. "We'll be in Edith's room if you need us, Gaine." She stops to bump my nose. "Behave."

I'm unsure what she thinks I'll do, but I roll my eyes and snuggle back into Gaine. I've never been shot before. It hurt like hell when it happened, and the wound still stings every time I breathe. My mate was worth that pain. It would seem I've made it past the wards and into her room.

"Luna told me that you watched her mother die," Gaine whispers once the door to her bedroom closes. "I felt her leave. Annalisa took her place, but her absence was still there."

Gaine falls silent, slipping another chunk of meat into my mouth. She rubs my jaw as I chew, lost in her thoughts. Having not heard anything over the past few days, I don't know how to comfort Gaine, so I remain still and let her take the time she needs before continuing.

"I couldn't go to her funeral," she murmurs. "I was too ashamed because my tears were not for her. I heard the altar is beautiful, though. Have you seen it?" Gaine's fingers rake through the fur on my neck. "Of course you haven't. Why would you? You didn't know her."

I lean back to rub my nose over her jaw. When Gaine looks down at me, her eyes are red from long hours of crying. I gently slide the tip of my tongue over her cheek, tasting the salt of her tears.

"I knew her very well," I say, wanting to comfort her. *"I've been to her altar many times. She's fun to talk to."*

"You left, and I had nothing," Gaine continues, sniffling. "Luna was helping the entire pack with their grief and didn't even have time to feel her own. I couldn't be selfish and go to her with a broken heart."

"I wasn't doing any better," I grumble.

Gaine feeds me the final piece of beef and moves the plate to a small table. She slides down the bed to lie flat and stares at the ceiling. "In my heart, it felt like you died too," my mate whispers. "I hate you. I didn't want you, but you wouldn't let me go. You forced me to love you and then took away my right to mourn my Luna. You're a selfish asshole, and I hate you."

Ayls said I wouldn't like what Gaine had to say, but I'm not sure I was expecting to hear that. I lie frozen across her chest, unsure what to do. I'm used to people hating me—that's nothing new. However, I love this woman enough to try to change how she feels.

I try to roll onto my belly so I can tuck my nose under Gaine's neck, but when I move my hip, a searing pain runs straight to the bone. I whimper and curl around to look at the wound. They shaved the fur around the opening, and it's been packed with white bandages covered in a yellow poultice.

"The tip broke off in the bone," Gaine says, still staring at the ceiling. "We had to dig it out. I'm not sorry I shot you. You deserved it."

Sighing, I lay my head back across her chest. I can't disagree with her. If I were in my right mind, I would've taken her with me. I would've done exactly what Rooster did with Ari and taken her far away from her pain and my destiny.

The light fades from afternoon to evening as we lie in Gaine's room. She quietly details the past year and how my leaving affected her. If she could hear me, I'd be fighting back with my pain and horrible nightmares. I'd throw my fears in her face and describe every terrible way I'd watched her die.

Ayls was right. I need to be quiet and let Gaine voice her feelings. As she talks, I realize she couldn't share this with anyone else. Every wolf knows how strong a bond can be, but no one would've cared that she felt this way toward an outcast like me.

I move enough to slide my nose over her cheek, catching the falling tears. We were feeling the same pain, so it's easy to understand how it had shut out the rest of the world and made her feel so lonely. I knew my path and where I was headed until I met Gaine. Now I'm on a road of endless screw-ups, and according to everything she's said tonight, I've never done the right thing.

* * *

"Let me take him, Gaine," Ayls whispers, waking me in the morning. "You go get some breakfast and stretch. He'll be alright."

I reach my front leg to wrap my paw around Gaine's ribs, but the little Luna lifts me off her. *"Ayls, don't let her go,"* I beg. *"She hates me. She won't come back."*

"Kade, that woman could never hate you," Ayls snaps, shaking her head. She helps Gaine slide out of the bed and sits beside me. "Your father made pancakes this morning, and Edith brought some strawberries back from her ride."

Gaine smiles before leaving us and closing the door.

"She's the opposite of every woman I have ever known," I admit,

settling into Ayls as she rolls toward me. *"I never really thought about it, but I guess being an asshole was what attracted everyone to me."*

"It wasn't your actions or how you treated people, Kade," Ayls murmurs. "You held power. Your pack was afraid of Tynan, but you weren't. I heard you protected the women from him."

"You give me too much credit," I grumble, rolling my eyes. *"Gaine makes me want to be good, but I don't know how. Ayls, I'm running across a frozen lake, hoping the ice won't break."*

"What does that mean, Kade?" Ayls asks, lifting her head to look down at me.

"It's something Miles used to say," I answer, chuckling. *"He said I'd run head first into things without thinking them through, hoping it would all end in my favor."* I roll my eyes closed, remembering his warning every time he got after me about my lack of plans. *"He always said, 'It'll bite you in the ass one day, kid.' He sure was right about that."*

Ayls pulls my front leg over her ribs and rubs my paw thoughtfully. "Miles was strange, but it seems he taught you many things," she says, narrowing her eyes. "If it took you that long to learn a lesson he repeatedly tried to teach you, I hope you find a way to never forget it."

I twist her words around for a moment while enjoying the pad rub. Hanging out with the Luna has had many perks, but I can't deny my love of her pad rubs. I never noticed how sore my paws get after a full day of running until she rubbed them the first time. Now, I want to give Gaine the same experience.

My head pops up as I realize what I need to do. *"Ayls, let my wound heal,"* I tell her.

"What? Why?" she asks, confused. "We can use tea when Gaine is comfortable enough to let you shift. There won't be a scar."

I bump my nose into hers. *"No,"* I tell the little Luna. *"I need to remember that she is a part of my path now. Wearing a scar from when I forgot would make a good reminder."* I wait for Ayls to lose her quizzical expression before continuing. *"I want to take her to your mother's altar. It's time to right a wrong."*

Ayls sighs, slipping her fingers through my fur. "Okay," she whispers. "We'll get you healed. The first trip to the altar is not an easy one. Are you sure you want to do this?"

"I listened, Ayls," I say, laying my head down with a sigh. *"This is what she needs from me."*

"Like you, she didn't know how to handle the flood of emotions," Ayls whispers. "I'm sorry to say that my own grief paralyzed me. I should've noticed you were gone but missed your absence until I found you on the porch. If I had, I might have known how badly Gaine needed me."

"We all made mistakes, Ayls," I tell her. *"I probably made a few more than everyone else."* I lift my head as she starts to giggle. *"No, it's true. I accept that I'm a selfish prick. Chase told me Miles had a phrase for him, too. He'd tell him, 'Own your role.' So, Ayls, I'm owning my role."*

Ayls continues to laugh and moves down the bed to tuck her face into my chest. "Well, you own it beautifully," she says. "What else have you been discussing with Chase?"

I chuckle and rub my jaw over the top of her head. As Luna, Ayls can hear everything we say as wolves, whether we are talking to her or not, but she chooses to give us privacy unless she needs us. Her mother had suggested I speak to Chase, and when we burned my drawings, I felt that listening to her last piece of advice would help me let her go.

"Why did he leave?" I ask, changing the subject.

Sighing, Ayls leans back to look in my eyes. "Chase and my father loved my mother very much," she starts thoughtfully. "As my mother's companion, Chase was nearly my father when Daddy wasn't around. He supported, protected, and guided my mother. He kept her company while she was away.

"They both deeply felt her loss and needed the other's support, but neither was in the position to give it. Chase tried to put aside his grief to help, but it only seemed to make things worse. Ultimately, we both felt it would be best if he left for a while. Brock goes south to check on him once a month for me. I feel better having that second report on his status."

I'd heard about this companion deal a few times over the years. There were many nights that Brock and his mate spent in bed with us in the wing off the kitchen. *"Ayls, you don't... you know... with Brock, right?"*

I love this Luna with most of my heart, but she's still a little girl. Although my past with the weekdays seems so long ago, I remember having a few in bed at once. Thinking about Ayls doing that with these young wolves makes me sick.

The little Luna's giggle pulls me out of my head. "Oh, Kade," Ayls says, clicking her tongue. "I've heard of your wild ways."

"I'm serious, Ayls," I say, bumping our noses. *"That Alpha of yours has been through hell. I'm not sure I could stomach him having to share you with another wolf."*

Smiling, Ayls sighs loudly. "But he does share me, Kade," she says gently. "He shares me with all of our wolves. First and foremost, I am the Luna. I will never abandon a wolf for anyone, including my Alpha. However, my body is his alone. I long only for his touch."

Sometimes, it's hard to remember little Luna is only 16. Other times, I cringe at the thought of a man touching her in the way her Alpha would. She is a perfect blend of spirit and wisdom. *I suppose that's what makes her the Luna.*

"Brock is my best friend, a brother... he's my family," Ayls whispers, tilting her head with a smile. "He holds me when I cry, lifts me when I'm sad, and applauds my victories. He has spent so much time with Bass and me that he behaves and reacts just as Bass does to things, which is extremely comforting."

"Loving you seems to be a full-time job," I tell her. *"You're a lot of work, Ayls."*

"Kade?" the little Luna whines. "I can tell when you change the subject to hide things. What aren't you telling me?"

"It doesn't matter," I grumble, closing my eyes.

Chase was almost always with Miles when I trained with him. Our Alpha seemed to be accomplished in every skill. He focused mainly on blades with me and Rooster but recognized how cunning and sneaky I was. The Alpha taught me to blend into my surroundings, travel silently, and bend people to my will by exploiting their weaknesses.

Knowing all I've been taught and my strengths, Chase has recommended that I scout beyond Ayls' borders and reach. He feels the pack would benefit from more significant civilian connections and partnerships. The older wolf also pointed out that I'm not one for pack life and thinks it would be best to have a job that would take me away from the bulk of our wolves.

When I sigh and open my eyes, Ayls stares at me expectantly. *"Ayls, I can't do it anyway,"* I tell her. *"Gaine is an elder and your Seer. Her place is here with you, and I won't leave her."*

Lifting her eyebrow, Ayls smiles. "Kade, you don't like living within the pack," she says knowingly. "Staying on the ranch with Gaine would slowly kill you. What did he suggest?"

"Diplomatic scouting," I growl. *"Finding more allies and contacts outside of your reach."*

"Did Gaine ever tell you why her family lives away from the lake?" Ayls asks.

"She said they called her names in school," I snap angrily, deepening my growl.

"It wasn't that she was called names," Ayls says, sighing. "Just like I'm the Luna and River is the Historian, they gave Gaine a title she didn't like. But they moved out here because our wolves drove her nuts. They wanted to find their mate and weren't interested in waiting."

"I can understand why," I admit.

"So perhaps you can understand why I would be fine with you taking her away," Ayls whispers. "Gaine loves you. She's happier when you're sweeping her off her feet. River says there was a spring in her step after you took her south."

I chuckle when my hum starts. *"She has a beautiful smile."*

"Just don't let her get shot again," Ayls grumbles, glaring sideways at me.

"She told you about that, huh?" I ask, shoving her with my paw.

"She didn't have to," Ayls says, sitting up. "I translated the many hues of red her face turned when I questioned her about the scar."

The bedroom door opens, and Gaine slips through, holding a plate piled high with pancakes. I perk up at the smell of strawberries. The cakes are covered in cream, and sliced strawberries are placed decoratively on top. I've never been one for fruit, but this woman has a way of making me change.

Ayls reaches out to Gaine. "Even when she hates you, Kade, she's finding ways to show how much she loves you." Ayls stands and kisses my blushing mate's cheek. "We're going to let the wound heal. Your knight in shining armor has requested the ability to right a wrong. Try not to be too hard on him. He's learning a lesson."

Gaine furrows her brow but doesn't question the little Luna as she ducks from the room with one final wink. I return my attention to my mate and lick my lips, eyeing the pancakes. She smiles and shakes her head as she sits on the bed beside me.

"You used to sleep with your nose to my skin," Gaine says, pulling apart the top cake. "We have a strawberry patch in the north field. Edith helps me fuse the scent into our soaps."

"I don't like strawberries," I mumble, sliding my tongue over her hand as she feeds me a pancake. *"I want to put you in my mouth, and*

you taste like them." I close my eyes, and her flavor starts my hum. "*You're just teasing me.*"

Gaine relaxes into the pillows and continues pulling apart the pancakes for me. "I couldn't leave this room for weeks after you left," she murmurs, not looking at me. "I often wondered where the strength I had in the beginning went. I'll admit that every time you returned was exhilarating. Your touch made my soul sing."

I rest my chin on her arm as she pauses. "*I couldn't stay away,*" I say, talking to myself. "*I tried. I'm not strong enough.*"

"My father wants to kill you," Gaine whispers, finally looking into my eyes. "He didn't know why I was crying all those months. He thought I was having issues like my sister and was too afraid to ask the Luna for help. Now that he knows it was over you, he's out for blood."

"*I don't blame him,*" I say. "*I will end the life of anyone who hurts you.*"

"Kade?" Gaine whispers, rubbing her finger over my whiskers.

"*Yeah?*" I answer as if she can hear me.

"I do love you," she says. "I just don't trust you."

"*That's fair,*" I respond, resting my head beside the empty plate. "*I doubt I'll ever be a good person, but you will always be safe with me.*"

"Luna said she found a way around your scar, though," Gaine says, changing the subject. "River says that's never been done. We've been blessed with some very unique Lunas. They have both worked hard to learn from the past and find a brighter future for us. I always thought Darya would find a peaceful solution with the militia."

Sighing, I roll my eyes. "*Their hate is so deep. Their only desire is annihilation.*"

"Anthony used to be a militia officer," Gaine continues. "He hunted our Luna for many years before she became our leader. Something about our way of life changed his mind about us. Edith said it was love, but I think everyone has love in their life. There's no reason why our love would have changed anything."

"It's not love," I say. "It's the acceptance. This is a pack built on solidarity. Everyone is accepted for who they are and embraced with the same love. There's no need to earn it. It's just there."

Gaine grins at me when I look up at her. "You scared me the first time I saw you," she admits. "When the Luna sent us here to live, I finally got a break from all the young wolves asking me to find their mate. It was peaceful, and I started to wonder what it would be like to have you.

"I waited until my sister had one of her awful days and snuck away. Oh, my father was furious. He had every guard who would listen out looking for me. They called to me for hours, but I wanted to meet you, so I ignored them. You were beautiful. Your aura shined like the lake's ripples on a sunny day. Did I ever tell you you're silver? Kind of suits you."

I probably won't like this story, but I still nuzzle my whiskers against Gaine's cheek, making her smile. I'm reminded of our time in Agatha's barn after her injury. I didn't know what to say, so I spent much of the time holding her while she cried or slept. If I knew any of the love that Ayls has taught me, I'd have talked to her like she's doing now.

"I watched you for a few days," Gaine says, losing her smile. "Just like the reports, everyone was afraid of you. When you killed that man for trying to protect his daughter, I knew I wouldn't survive you."

In my mind, I'd always pictured her seeking me out at an earlier time. Perhaps closer to when we were coming of age. But she's talking about Ari's father. Her interpretation was the same as Ari's. No one heard anything I said. I didn't want them to. I tried to tell her father I was keeping them all safe, but he wasn't interested. He wanted Ari away from Bass and Tynan, no matter the cost.

Maybe one day, I'll be able to explain to Gaine what really happened that night. Ari forgave me, so there's a solid chance my mate will too. I close my eyes and lean against her finger as she slides it over the bridge of my nose.

"Ari came to see me before she left with Rooster," Gaine whispers.

I pause my appreciation of her attention to tilt my head curiously.

Gaine smiles, nodding. "She told me what you had done to protect her from your Alpha," she says. "Rooster said you weren't one of the good guys but a good friend." She sniffles and slides her hand over my face. "They made me hate you even more for leaving me. The wolf they described would've stayed and fought for me."

Ignoring the pain in my hip, I pull myself up the bed to slide my head along Gaine's cheek. Her tears fall into my fur as she rolls to wrap her arms around my neck. Her legs fold neatly against my gut, and she lets her emotions out with exhausting sobs.

"Why did you leave me?" Gaine asks between gasps.

Sighing, I nuzzle her as best as I can within her tight grip. *"Because I'm an asshole."*

23

❦

It took a week for my wound to heal enough to make the trip to the Luna's altar. Gaine stayed with me, only leaving me in Ayls' care when she went to bathe. The little Luna silently pulled my excess emotions as I anxiously awaited my mate's return.

On the eve of our trip, Ayls appears before Gaine requests I call for her. "Gaine," she whispers, opening the bedroom door. "Your bath is ready."

When she closes the door without entering, I turn to Gaine curiously. *"What are you up to, woman?"*

Gaine smiles, sliding her hand over my head. "We need to wash the medicine off your hip, Kade," she murmurs. "Would you like to join me?"

My heart skips a beat before adopting a rhythm so fast that her aura's flashing blinds me. My hum starts as I think about holding Gaine's beautiful body against mine in a hot bath surrounded by her strawberry scent. I rub my muzzle softly over her chest before taking a long taste of her neck and sliding my short front teeth over her jaw.

"Kade?" Gaine whispers, her body heating from my affection. "The medicine is all over your fur. I'm not asking you to shift."

I have never whined in my life. My yelp over my injury is

277

embarrassing enough, but the whimper that slides up my throat makes me glad no one else is in the room. My mind quickly rolls through the pros and cons of heeding Ayls' warning as I rub my nose up Gaine's neck and slide my tongue behind her ear.

When I pull at her earlobe, Gaine leans away to give me a stern look. "Luna is giving us an hour," she warns. "After that, my father will be back."

I pull my lips back in a scowl. I won't be able to stop myself again once our skin touches. The guilt that made me pull away when she offered herself to me is gone. Gaine's warmth will drive me crazy to the point where she will be mine, willingly or not. An hour would never give me enough time to enjoy her.

My mind wanders into the memory of her wrapped around my waist. Her hips rolled, wanting me. I was ready. I could feel her warmth as I rubbed against her, trying to be a better form of myself and waiting for her final permission.

"Kade!" my beautiful mate snaps.

I blow through my nostrils. *"Fine,"* I grumble.

"Are you ready to try standing?" Gaine asks, rolling off the bed.

They've been helping me roll over and move about for bathroom breaks. Usually, it was Anthony or Nate, the head of the little Luna's guard, but Gaine's father helped once. His anger pulsed off of him with every hateful glare. I didn't think I'd survive the short walk, but Ayls showed up before anything happened. Luckily, I've regained most of my strength, and he's kept his distance. I doubt Gaine would forgive either of us if we lost control.

I crawl to the edge of the bed and step off the side. Using my front legs, I pull myself until my back legs slide off the mattress—first, the good hip, followed by the injured left hip. Although Gaine has been helping me stretch it, nothing compares to how it feels when I try to use it.

My beautiful mate frowns as she watches me limp after her to the door. "We can postpone whatever you have planned, Kade," she says, holding the door open. "I'm sure we can wait until you're better."

I hobble past her and look up and down the hallway, unsure which way the bathroom would be. *"No,"* I grumble. *"You've been waiting long enough."*

As I step to the left, which is how I've been leaving the house, Gaine closes the bedroom door. "This way, Kade," she says. "Edith had a big tub installed off her bedroom. We couldn't share the normal one."

I turn to follow her deeper into the silent house. Gaine opens the door at the end of the hall to reveal a bed slightly larger than the one I'd shared with Ayls and her family. She closes us in the room and leads me to a sliding door.

The area we step into is bright, with large windows in the ceiling. There's no lantern in sight, but the room is alive with the sunlight from outside and the plants lining the walls. Gaine pulls a few vibrantly colored towels from a shelf and turns to watch me look around the room.

"Edith had Anthony make a ramp for you to lie on so you can relax in the warm water," she tells me. "She mixed a liquid soap for you. She says it will clean the salve off and medicate the wound."

We move together toward a steaming pool in the corner of the room. I step onto a stool and look into a basin large enough to hold five or six people. The milky water inside is so warm that I feel its heat rising through my fur. I lift my left hind leg, trying to stretch far enough to sniff closer to the water.

"It's buttermilk," Gaine says, pulling her arms from her sleeves. "Our ranch also supplies most of the families at the lake with dairy products. At times, we've been lucky to enjoy a surplus of amenities."

She lifts her shirt over her head and drops it to the floor. My mate giggles at me as I slip from the stool, mesmerized by her beauty. Her tanned skin still glows as it did the last time I touched it. I swallow hard, wanting a taste of her.

Gaine crosses her arms nervously over her chest and looks away. "I always feel like you're judging me," she admits.

I step gingerly toward her until I can slide my nose over her stomach. *"You are perfect,"* I say, biting my tongue to stop it from leaving my mouth. *"I couldn't judge you because nothing compares."*

Gaine's shorts are loose around her legs, so I take the cuff into my mouth, sneaking a quick taste of her thigh before tugging them off her hips. Although her arms remain across her chest, Gaine steps out of her shorts when I hold them at her ankles. Once they are no longer in my way, I slowly rub my whiskers over her legs, watching her skin react with raised bumps.

My eyes fix on her underwear when she begins humming. Using my tongue, I pull the thin strap over her hip into my mouth and work them down her legs to reveal the rest of her perfection. She hesitates when I try to remove them but lifts her feet when I lick her ankles.

As Gaine's body heats up, her scent becomes overwhelming. Our sense of smell is always powerful, but as wolves, it's just as dominant as our hearing. Sweat beads across her skin, but the drop slowly inching down her inner thigh came from the folds between her legs.

I lick my lips, recalling how badly I wanted to taste her over a year ago. We are wolves, but tasting her in this form would be considered disrespectful. Her thigh, however, is fair game, and I've never wanted to taste anything as badly as the fluid that escaped her hidden parts. I can't look away as I step to the side for a better angle.

"Kade, don't," Gaine whispers.

I snap my head up and snarl. *"Why not?"* I growl but then quickly step back.

Gaine's cheeks are flushed, and her hands rub her arms as she looks away. The woman who had torn off her clothes and begged for our bond is gone. She was desperate to feel something other than the pain and heartache of her missing Luna. Now, my mate is only trying to find a way to trust me again.

I hang my head and take another step back. *"I'm sorry,"* I mumble, hoping my actions say what she can't hear. *"Every time you step toward me, I give you a reason to retreat."* I try to sit, but the skin over my hip pinches when I fold my back leg.

"I don't think I've been very fair to you, Kade," Gaine says, stepping toward me. "We never seem to be ready for each other at the same time." She kneels before me, making me uncomfortably look at the floor between us. "The way you desire me ignites a fever within that I've never experienced before. I fear how it makes me want to lose control."

"I completely understand," I say, looking into her eyes.

"I'm not going anywhere," Gaine whispers. "When I trust you with my heart, I will give you my body." She stands and adjusts the stool from when I slipped off it. "Until then, I'd like to take a bath with you. Will you please join me?" Gaine extends her hand to me.

Ayls was my constant companion at the lake. We spent many days talking about the pack and different wolves. She would help me understand their roles and how they all fit together to run smoothly without her having to interfere.

But at night, Bastian and I would talk about our mates and their roles within the pack. He reminded me that Gaine didn't choose her job. It was forced upon her through her bloodline, just like Ayls. He told me if I ever wanted to show my mate respect, I needed to allow her to give me permission.

Being the asshole that I am, I fought him with every excuse I could think up. But in the end, he won every argument. Gaine has very little control over her life. She's an elder and the pack's Seer. The mate of any wolf she touches appears in her mind whether she tries to look for them or not. She can't just tune them out or tell them no.

I step forward, staring into my beautiful mate's loving eyes. Her touch on my chin is warm and gentle, and I know Bastian is right. I may still be an asshole, but I'm going to be a humble one and allow Gaine to make this decision without interference. She deserves to feel control over something in her life.

Gaine smiles as she guides me toward the stool and patiently waits while I step onto it with my front paws. "I want you to try to use your left leg, Kade," she murmurs soothingly. "I'm going to brace your right side and lift that paw so you won't need to stretch so far."

Hesitating, I turn to look at my wound. The fur around it is gummed up and black from the salve Edith packed into the opening, ensuring it healed from the inside out. Now that the wound has closed, I can put it underwater, but it's not any easier to move.

"I've got you, Kade," Gaine says, smiling. "Trust me. You'll feel better after a soak."

I curl around to where she is crouched by my right hind leg and gently lick her cheek before facing my task. Taking a sharp breath, I start with my right front leg and pull my chest toward the tub's edge. My left hind leg naturally begins to follow, but I can't stop the whimper that rushes out once the pinching starts.

"It's just your fur," Gaine whispers. "It won't pull once we clean it."

Ayls might have the strongest mind of anyone I have ever met, but my mate's physical strength easily rivals the Alphas'. She pushes her fingers under my right hind paw, lacing them together and lifting my back end to alleviate the pain my injured leg was creating. She makes simple shushing noises as I continue to move forward until I slide into the water.

Gaine slips into the tub and guides me to the ramp along the far side. It only has a slight slope but allows me to lie down with my hind leg draped over its side. Gaine relaxes next to me on some type of lounging bench. I can't see through the milky white water, so when she rests her head back with a sigh, my imagination has fun teasing me with beautiful thoughts.

"Just let your fur soak for a minute," Gaine whispers, leaving her eyes closed. "The hot water will do your muscles some good, too."

She's not wrong. The heat feels wonderful on the muscles that worked hard to get me here. The water also relieves some pressure on my other limbs, allowing them to relax.

"Sometimes I forget what silence sounds like," Gaine murmurs, still resting with her eyes closed. "I'm never alone. My father is only here for as long as we need him." She opens her eyes and turns to me. "I think he's afraid to leave because he forces himself into every moment, making it all about him."

As she talks, I get the feeling that Ayls gave us this time alone more so Gaine could be away from her family. I recall the night I accidentally found her with her family on her sister's birthday and how they had interrupted us. I close my eyes and relax into the memory of her running freely through the field with my proximity ward, playing where her family and pack couldn't bother her.

"Kade?"

"*Yeah?*" I ask, opening my eyes.

Gaine grins as she watches me. "You look peaceful."

"*I was remembering a beautiful moment,*" I say. Using my claws, I pull myself up the ramp enough to lick Gaine's cheek. "*I want to see you enjoy yourself again.*"

"I can always tell when you're talking," my beautiful mate tells me. "Your eyes give it away."

I close my eyes. "*Now you won't know.*"

"You just better be saying sweet things," Gaine grumbles.

"*Hmm,*" I hum, opening my eyes to scan the parts of her body sticking out of the buttermilk bath. "*I bet everything I want to taste will be very sweet.*"

Gaine sits up and kisses the tip of my nose. "Let's get your hip washed before we run out of time," she says, moving down her bench. "Hold on tight." She pulls something under the water before straining to raise the lower end of the ramp. I dig my claws in to stay still as she raises my hips out of the water. "It's already started to loosen. This shouldn't take long."

I was so focused on the fact that I would be in a tub with my naked mate that I hadn't thought about how she would be cleaning my hip. It would seem that I will forever be compromising my dignity for the sake of this woman. I rest my chin on the side of the tub with a huff as Gaine laughs at the sight of me with my ass in the air, waiting for her to clean it.

Once upon a time, I was feared. People just did what I said because not obeying me would have catastrophic consequences. I could say anything I wanted, and no one dared to test me. Then I met Gaine. I no longer want to be that wolf, but a little dignity would be great.

"You do have a nice ass, Kade," Gaine remarks, making me look back at her with my head tilted. "I'm being serious. Whoever made your pants must've loved staring at it."

"At least I still have that," I grumble, returning my chin to its perch.

"Your scar should be small," Gaine continues. "Luna told Edith to do her best to keep you pretty."

I roll my eyes. I was delighted when I woke in Gaine's arms in her room. It was comforting to have Ayls close by to help me understand what was happening, and Edith was even kind in her daily care of my wound. After being here for a few weeks, though, all this female company has become a bit much.

"Here we go," Gaine says, tugging the tip of my tail. She pulls the same lever and slowly lowers my ass back into the water. "We have a little bit of time left to relax. Do you want me to tell you a story?"

Gaine lies back on her cradle bench and turns to me with a

gentle smile. Remembering her words from earlier, I shake my head. I lean over to rest my muzzle over her eyes so she'll close them, and my hum starts when her fingers trace my jaw. I'd rather she have silence, but hopefully, she doesn't mind a quiet hum.

"I love you, Kade," Gaine whispers.

"I love you too, sweet woman."

* * *

Our time alone in the large tub was short-lived, but afterward, Gaine began telling me about her everyday life instead of only talking about how I made her feel. After a few hours of stories, it was easy to see why Gaine seemed so guarded and overwhelmed. It would appear that her life isn't as free and happy as most wolves in the pack. Due to what her parents did and her destiny, much more has been expected of her, and she was stripped of all decision-making ability.

We left for the altar long before sunrise with Ayls and Bastian. The air was calm enough that I'm sure I heard Gaine sigh in relief when we stepped around the wall at the beginning of the cliff trail. This would be the first time the cottage wasn't within sight, helping her to feel the distance from her overbearing father and familial duties.

"Ayls?" I say, looking up at the little Luna as she stops her horse at the bottom of the cliff trail.

"Yes, Kade?"

"I want to take her out of here," I tell her. Regardless of her position within the pack, I would never allow my mate to continue feeling this pressure that causes her to be unhappy.

Ayls crosses her forearms over her saddle horn as she looks down at me. *"I don't think she's ready for that, Kade,"* she answers, narrowing her eyes in thought. *"You still make her quite nervous."*

I know Ayls is right. The little Luna can feel my mate's current emotions, but I have been listening to her and have heard what she desires. After spending so much time with Gaine and hearing her stories, I know that distance from her life is what she needs.

"Maybe we could take a short trip, like when I took her to the kite festival," I suggest.

"Let me think about it," Ayls replies. *"You've come a long way with her, Kade. I'd hate to see you lose that momentum by pushing her too far too fast."*

"I know a lot more about her now," I grumble.

"She shot you last time I let you make the decisions," Ayls warns, lifting her eyebrow.

"Okay," I say, hanging my head. *"That's fair."*

"Speaking of which, you're limping," the little Luna points out needlessly. *"Why don't you go up front with Bastian and pick a comfortable speed?"*

Appreciating the suggestion, I place my front paws on a tall stump and reach my nose to my mate. Gaine smiles and leans down to let me rub my whiskers over her cheek.

"Where are you going?" she asks.

I nod in Bastian's direction.

Gaine looks ahead and frowns. "You'll stay close, though, right?"

I can't stop my hum from starting. I stretch to press my nose to her cheek, making her giggle. *"I will always be with you,"* I vow.

Ayls winks at me when I turn back to bow to her before joining her young Alpha out front. We walk into the trees, leading the horses onto a trail that will skirt the basin for a while before cutting through the west end. I focus on the hoofbeats. Hearing the difference between each horse's stride, it's easy to be sure Gaine is still following closely.

"Kade!" Bastian snaps, ramming his shoulder into mine. *"What the hell? I've been talking to you this whole time."*

"*Yeah, sorry, kid,*" I answer, chuckling. "*Preoccupied. You know how it goes.*"

"*Whatever,*" Bastian says, shaking his head. "*You're limping. You wanna run it up?*"

"*Probably should,*" I agree. "*Maybe Gaine won't notice.*"

"*You can't hide shit from those women,*" the young wolf says, laughing at me. "*Set the pace.*"

When a hind leg is injured, we can run at a pace close to a horse's canter to give the limb some relief. This makes the other three legs work harder, but it's better than working on the injured one. Bastian and I are the same height, but his stride has always been longer. He works hard to stay by my side as I dart forward along the trail.

"*I'm not gonna lie,*" the kid starts, rechecking his speed to drop beside my shoulder. "*I didn't think it would take Gaine this long to shoot you.*"

I nearly trip as I roll my eyes and look over at him. "*Everything is so much harder with her. Everyone loves me, and I can't get Gaine to give into my charm.*" Bastian is 17. He's played many roles within his years but has no idea what I'm going through. "*How do you stop yourself?*"

Bastian chuckles. "*I don't know,*" he answers honestly. "*The day I met Annalisa, or Ayls as you've got us all calling her, I nearly didn't. I ran up to her, intending to take her right there.*" He scoffs and shakes his head. "*Her whole family was there, and I was gonna take her with everyone watching. I didn't care.*"

"*What stopped you?*" I ask as we emerge from the woods and begin running across the barren basin.

"*First, her father,*" Bastian says. "*Then her mother. But in the end, it was Ayls. She was so gentle with me. Her voice was a melody I wanted to hear for the rest of my life. The part of me that wanted to force myself on her was the insecure wolf who knew no one could ever want him. But then she said I was gorgeous, and that all went away. From that moment,*"

I have known nothing but the love she's given me, and I will always honor her with mine."

"You didn't turn out so bad," I remark.

"No thanks to you," Bastian scoffs.

"Yeah, I know," I grumble, looking back to check on the horses. *"Thanks for not holding it against me."*

Bastian picks up his pace, forcing me to stretch out to keep up. *"Oh, I still hold that whole thing against you,"* he admits. *"I just love my Luna enough to hide my hatred for you when she's around."*

Laughing, I lead us back into the woods near the altar. *"I appreciate that then."*

24

It's midday when Bastian stops inside the trees surrounding the Luna's altar. I'm so focused on the proximity of Gaine's horse that I plow right into his hip. My mate is truly one of the most distracting creatures I have ever encountered, but I'm thankful that Bastian and Ayls know exactly what I'm going through.

"What's up?" I ask, standing to shake the debris from my coat. *"Why'd we stop?"*

Bastian looks up at the little Luna as she approaches, still atop her mare. *"She wants you to try bringing Gaine the rest of the way alone."*

I follow his gaze and narrow my eyes curiously at Ayls. *"Is that so?"*

"This is as far as I go," Ayls announces, stopping her horse and allowing Gaine to ride up beside her. "We will leave you in your shiny mate's capable paws for the rest of this journey. You don't have much further to go."

Gaine's eyes worriedly dart between me and the little Luna. She forces a small smile and accepts Ayls' outstretched hand.

"This was always something Kade wanted to do for you," the little Luna tells Gaine. "Bass and I only accompanied you in case you ran into trouble since your mate is still recovering. Give him the chance to show you how much he's been paying attention."

Ayls tips her chin in my direction as I step between their horses' shoulders. Without standing on anything to boost my height, my head is about the level of Gaine's ankle. I stretch to rub my muzzle over her leg and step back to place my chin on the toe of her boot. Gaine sighs as I give her my most pleading expression.

"How can you deny someone so pitiful?" Ayls asks, giggling.

Admittedly, I'm not excited about being called pitiful, but Ayls' words make my mate smile. Gaine's eyes stay fixed upon me. "He's been listening to me?"

Ayls smiles sweetly, squeezing Gaine's hand. "We'll stay close if you need us," she whispers. "I don't think you will."

With one last squeeze, Ayls releases Gaine's hand and backs her horse away from us. Bastian nods to me as he passes before leading the white mare away. I look up to find my beautiful mate nervously watching their departure.

I allow Gaine a few moments before proceeding up the trail. Her tall bay mare steps forward as I move sideways toward the clearing. Vividly remembering my first trip to the altar, I feel that I should prepare for anything when Gaine sees it for the first time.

The foliage thickens just before it gives way to the clearing. I push head-first through the brush and turn to slow the horse as she emerges. Gaine's gasp echoes through the still air. She slaps one hand over her mouth while the other grasps the saddle horn. Moving slowly, I lead the mare toward the altar.

"Kade," Gaine says between heaving breaths. "I... You... Oh, Luna." We make it halfway across the clearing before she slides from her saddle, standing frozen beside the horse. "It's so beautiful," Gaine whispers through her fingers.

There were a few times on our walks when Ayls held my jaw, and I'd seen her do it countless times with the Alphas. She calls it "traveling in hand." I don't know about that, but I was able to direct her steps and pull her forward. Sliding my head under Gaine's hand,

I rest my jaw on her curled fingers and gently tug her closer to the altar.

"*Hey, Luna,*" I say to the formation of stones. "*I brought you a wolf who was too embarrassed to say goodbye to you. You see, I was a dick. I left her and broke her world, just like she said I would. So, because of the pain I caused, she missed the ceremony and has been too ashamed to come see you.*"

Gaine kneels before the pile of flowers, cards, drawings, and other gifts. "I miss you, Luna," she whispers, sniffling.

My chest hurts as a few tears drop from her jaw. "*I'm trying to right a wrong,*" I continue my conversation with the Luna. "*Don't be too hard on her. These things are usually my fault. Your daughter, though, you taught her well. We'll do great things under her watch.*"

I tuck in close to Gaine, giving her my shoulder to lie against. She whispers through her tears so quietly that I'm only able to understand a word every once in a while, but it's enough to know she isn't talking to me. I roll to my side and give my mate a paw to hold when she begins telling the Luna where she was when she disappeared and how she fell in love with the enemy.

The shadows grow long as the afternoon slowly turns into evening, and Gaine's crying settles into an occasional sniffle. She leans forward to study some of the gifts in the failing light. Tears pool in Gaine's eyes as she reads each card and note within her reach, but she smiles at their words.

Although the large altar contains gifts on all sides, my mate doesn't leave me. When she's read all the cards and given each gift within her reach some attention, she lays her head on my shoulder. Gaine's eyes droop as the last rays of the sun fade.

* * *

"NO! Kade!" Gaine screams, waking me suddenly.

Instantly realizing she's not against me, I jump to my feet and spin around. When I see her, she's kicking her legs and fighting to escape someone. I lunge at them, knocking her attacker away. Gaine falls to her knees, and the man steps back, putting his arms out to stop me. My growl is deafening as I leap into the air and crash against his chest.

"*Kade, stop,*" Ayls orders.

Her words make me pause, standing over the man. He heaves raspy breaths under the weight of my front paws as I allow my eyes to focus on his face.

"*Nate's just helping me bring you somewhere safer,*" Ayls says quietly.

I lift off her head of security, and Gaine latches onto my neck, sobbing loudly.

"I'm sorry," Ayls says, rubbing Gaine's shoulder. "It's not safe to spend the night here. We have a guards' cabin nearby that you can stay at tonight. We didn't mean to scare you. I thought you'd stay asleep for the journey."

Ayls gently pulls Gaine's face from my fur, allowing me to check her for injuries and reassuringly nuzzle her cheek. My mate doesn't need me. She's the strongest woman I know. My chest swells, and I proudly raise my head as I realize that she wants me with her. She wasn't trying to get away from Nate. She was trying to get back to me.

"*I love you too, sweet woman,*" I whisper, tucking my nose into her neck. "*I will always be here.*"

"Gaine, I can help you, but I think you two need to work through your feelings together," Ayls whispers, slowly guiding my mate to her feet. "We have a wagon. Come on. This way."

Although Gaine allows Ayls to guide her, she tightly grips the fur over my shoulders. Grease's light cart is parked on the trail inside the trees. Gaine crouches to hook her arm around my left hind leg and helps me jump into the back before joining me.

"The cabin is quite nice but small," Ayls tells us as Nate hops into the driver's seat. "The guards will be in the bunkhouse if you need anything."

When the cart begins moving, I realize Ayls hasn't joined us. *"Hey, kiddo,"* I say, watching her grow smaller. *"You can't be out here alone."*

"Ah, but Kade, I am never alone," Ayls replies. Several wolves, including Bastian, step out of the woods surrounding her. The little Luna bows her head in our direction and turns, holding her hands out for her guards to slide their heads under. *"Enjoy your time alone with your mate, shiny one."*

I shake my head and turn back to nuzzle into Gaine. This has been an emotional day, and my beautiful mate is exhausted. My heart wants to sing with joy over her desire to be with me, and my legs want to jump and run, but her hold on my neck tells me she needs something else. Using my teeth, I pull a blanket from under Nate's bench and cover Gaine's shoulders.

The ride to the cabin is short, and we soon stop beside a porch covered in honeysuckle vines. The tiny flowers have a sweet aroma that fills the still air, nearly overpowering Gaine's soap. Nate leaves to unlock the door and light a few lanterns. He quickly rejoins us and leans over the side of the cart, lifting his eyebrow at Gaine.

Puffing out my chest, I tuck my chin. *"Alright, sweetheart,"* I say, wishing she could hear me for the millionth time. *"We gotta get out of the cart."*

"I started the kindling, Gaine," Nate says softly. "You'll need to feed the fire soon, or it'll go out." The older guard furrows his brow at me and frowns. "I don't think Luna would forgive me if I left you two out here."

He's probably right. I take a deep breath and puff out my chest as far as possible. When I can't push Gaine further away, I tuck my nose where she's burrowed into my fur and heave a deep breath onto her face.

Gaine's growl rumbles to life. "What?" she snaps.

"We're here," Nate replies for me. "You need to tend to the fire, or it'll go out."

Gaine takes a deep breath and cuts off her growl as she looks around. "Why are we at the guard shack?" she asks.

"Luna said to bring you here," Nate says, lifting the blanket from her shoulders. "I just do what I'm told. You know, being a guard and all." He winks at me as he helps Gaine from the cart. "You need some help, gimpy?"

I lift my lips at him before jumping to the ground. Gaine holds my fur as I guide her over the porch and through the doorway into the cabin. She called it a shack, but it's cozy.

As Gaine feeds the fire, I turn to scan the room. The fireplace is grand, with cut stones and bricks decorating the entire area. The mantle is elm, with a running herd of horses carved across it. The bed along the far wall is smaller than those at the lake but larger than Gaine's, and its mahogany headboard looks custom-made.

I step toward it when Gaine rises to her feet. She sighs and joins me by sitting near the pillows. "Tarq made this for Luna," Gaine whispers, sliding her fingers over the wood. "It's stained and hard to make out in the dark with the shadows." She waits for me to step on the bed and runs her hand over it again. "It says, 'For you, I vow to breathe.' It was the last line of the Luna's wedding vows."

I rub my muzzle over her cheek to catch a tear. *She told me to have an epic love like theirs,* I say. *They loved each other very much.*

Gaine sighs and rolls onto her back with her arm out for me. "Thank you for today," she whispers as I lay my jaw on her shoulder. "Thank you for listening." Gaine slips her fingers through my fur and stares at the ceiling as she had done back in her room. "You asked to come here, didn't you?"

I lift my head, narrowing my eyes. *Yeah,* I say thoughtfully. *I guess I kinda did.* Chuckling, I shake my head. Ayls may not have wanted me to take her away from the lake, but she's given us time together away from Gaine's familial pressures to relax by bringing us here. *I'll have to remember to thank her.*

Sighing, I nuzzle back into Gaine and push my paws under the pillow. She rolls toward me, starting my hum as her arms close around my neck. Throughout most of the past week, I've tried to remember how I felt when I was with the weekdays. I've concluded that I didn't feel anything. I just numbly existed through my days until I met Gaine.

Now that Ayls has cured my nightmares, I sleep peacefully in her arms. I could live in a world where the only sound was her breathing softly into my fur, but her words excite me in ways I could never describe. Even when she's telling me how much pain I've caused, her voice is a song.

Gaine yawns and rubs her face against the fur over my throat. "Don't ever leave me again," she whispers before falling asleep.

I rest my head over hers on the pillow. *"Never."*

* * *

My favorite time with Gaine so far is when we wake. After not having many hands on my wolf, I'm unsure if her touch is special, but she instantly starts my hum when she rakes her fingers through my fur. This morning, I'm surprised by hers mixing with mine.

When I move to give her more room, Gaine takes a deep breath. "Kade?"

Her tone is soft, but I still tense up, sure I've done something wrong.

"Shift," Gaine whispers.

My head snaps back so fast that I pull out of her arms. I've dreamed of her saying that word so often that this has to be one of those moments. *I haven't done anything right. There is no reason for her to want me. All I've done is heal from when she shot me and right one of my many wrongs. There's no way—*

"Shift, Kade," my beautiful mate whispers again, calmly looking into my eyes. "I'm asking you to shift."

When I imagined this moment a million times over the past few weeks, I hesitated and was cautious to be sure this was what Gaine wanted. However, the moment's reality is slightly different as I jump away from her and trigger my shift. My growl builds as the length of time annoys me. It's grown to a full snarl by the time I'm done.

Gaine reaches out for me, smiling sweetly. "Come here, beautiful man," she says softly. "You don't need to rush. I'm not going anywhere."

With one touch, she settles my snarl to a hum, and I bite my lower lip as I crawl back into her arms. Gaine's lips brush over mine, asking for attention. I pull my fingers through her hair and hold her against me. Her lips part, allowing me in for a taste.

While I'm lost in her kisses, Gaine unbuttons her shirt and holds it open to press her skin to mine. My nerves jump at her, causing me to gasp and give her a chance to pull from my grip. I whine as Gaine rolls from the bed and holds her hand out to stop me from following.

With every muscle tense, I actively work to remain on the bed as Gaine slips her fingers into her shirt to push it off her left shoulder. I lick my lips and swallow hard when she does the same on the other side, letting the fabric fall to the floor. Gaine's chest heaves perfectly with every breath. Her fingers pull the bow tied at her waistband.

I can't recall telling my body to leave the bed, but my chest is suddenly against my mate's. My hands slide around Gaine's waist and up her back, pressing my skin to hers and feeling the excitement she creates within the nerves. I slip my fingers under her waistband and lift the shorts from her hips. As they fall to the floor, Gaine's tongue laps over my neck, and her lips pull at my earlobe.

My hands follow the shorts, and my fingers dig into her thighs, lifting her to my hips. Gaine wraps around me and lays her head on my shoulder. Every instinct tells me to take her. Just drop her on me and claim her. But my mate's embrace is one of love. Not just any old affection—the undying devotion of the woman I've waited my whole life for.

I close my eyes and pull in a deep breath, taking a moment to enjoy how she feels. My fingers relax so I can slide my hands over Gaine's legs. Her body heats as her soft moans rise in volume.

When Gaine's lips tenderly rub against my neck, I move back to the bed and gently lay her down. I've never had anyone look at me as she does when I pull away. If every man had a woman look at him this way, he would never have an evil thought. He would only aim to make her happy until the day of his death.

Gaine releases my hips to slide her foot down my leg, igniting those nerves for the first time. Her toes lightly trail back up my leg and command my attention. I reach back to catch her leg and close my eyes as her movement tips her hips to me.

When I thought of this moment while injured in Gaine's arms, I feared I wouldn't be able to control myself. This played out very differently in my mind and made me afraid I'd chase Gaine away forever. However, her touch, eyes, and scent have me calmly accepting her advances and waiting for her final permission.

My limbs shake, wanting nothing more than to release my weight. I part my lips when Gaine lifts herself to lick them.

"Kade," she whispers into my mouth. "I am yours."

Above all else, I am a wolf, and my body begins moving on its own. Lowering the rest of my weight onto Gaine, I slide over her wet folds and plunge myself into her depths. My stomach clenches, forcing me to push deeper and reach her end. Gaine's nails dig into my skin, and her teeth latch onto my shoulder as her body clamps down on me.

We lie there, forcefully stuck together but never wanting to be anywhere else, while our bodies claim each other. Miles had told me bonding was something I couldn't control, but I never dreamed claiming a mate would be a physical thing our bodies would do.

I open my eyes to see Gaine more clearly than ever now that her aura is gone. The tightness in my chest releases, allowing short bursts of air to move through my lungs. Her beauty knows no equal. "You didn't need the white aura to appear perfect," I whisper, watching her eyes mist. "You will know my love every day of your life."

Gaine rocks her hips and releases the grip her body has on me. I whimper as she holds me still and pushes herself into the bed to pull me completely out before allowing me back in. We growl loudly at the sensation of each nerve firing when they meet inside her body. The tension my need creates causes my muscles to shake as her nerves call to mine.

Sliding my arm under Gaine's neck, I roll with her to lie under her body. I've never allowed a woman to ride me. Giving anyone that kind of power would be absurd. But Gaine is not just any woman and has had her power stripped by her family and her obligations to the pack.

When she tries to sit up and pull away, I reach for her cheek and guide her lips to mine. "We only get one first-time, perfect woman," I whisper. "I will have you many times throughout our lifetime, several of which will be before the sun goes down today. But this time... this first time... is yours."

Gaine smiles and slides her legs along mine to lie down on me. Her fingers caress my cheek as she lowers to press her lips to mine and taste my tongue. I've always loved her soft snore, but her moans are now my favorite noise. My hand glides over her body and pulls her ass, triggering her hips.

Women need slower movements to allow the nerves within their bodies time to enjoy the sensation we create by rubbing over them.

Gaine lifts and lowers her hips impossibly slow, sending my body into a frenzy I'm not sure I can control. As one set of her nerves fire, the next reaches out for me, making me want to jam her down into my lap and satisfy their need.

I release Gaine and reach my arms to the side to grab the blankets on the bed. Closing my eyes, I focus on her tongue as it massages mine. My hands ball into tight fists when her moans steadily collapse into a deep exhale. My breaths match her hips' movements, trying to rock myself deeper within her.

When Gaine's arm buckles, she slides her hand under my shoulder to steady herself as her legs tremble. Releasing the blankets, I wrap my arms around her and hold her still. Gaine's deepest nerves aren't ready for me, but the pull I feel from the rest probably overwhelms her. I wait for her breathing to settle before sliding my teeth over her jaw and reigniting her needs.

Gaine widens her hips as she begins moving again. Her moans force me to pull her from the comfortable spot she'd settled in beside my neck. I hold her face and kiss her deeply as I roll my hips. Getting close to the deepest nerves triggers them to reach for me, and my body takes over again.

I rock up into Gaine and hold her still as I hit her end. Her muscles clamp down on me just as they had when we bonded, but I'm still able to move this time. Gaine may be trying to silence her calls with a pillow, but I don't care. I have never enjoyed a woman like my mate. The exploding sensation of my release has me screaming about its beauty to anyone within five miles.

Only the fading of Gaine's moans could convince my body to stop. My hips slow until all that's left is the gentle pulsing within her depths. Gaine had stayed against my lips until I hit her end, and then she'd retreated to my neck. She remains tucked against my skin, hidden from view.

Taking a deep breath, I pull my fingers through her hair. "They really undersold this whole bonding thing," I say, leaning my cheek against her.

Gaine's giggle makes me smile. "I figured it had to be pretty special with everyone trying so hard to find their mate," she whispers over her hum. "Kade?"

"Hmm?" I hum quietly, still focused on how wonderful she feels.

"Thank you for listening to me," Gaine responds.

Licking my lips, I roll us onto our sides. "Gaine, my beautiful woman, you've already thanked me for that," I remind her. "You don't need to keep thanking me for something you shouldn't have to ask for. I will always hear you. I search for your voice in the silence. There will never be another day when I won't answer your call."

"If you were this sweet when we met, things may have gone much differently," Gaine says, rubbing her lips against mine.

"Yeah, you women make us soft," I grumble. "When we met, I killed anyone in my way. Now, I'm gonna die protecting you. On the plus side, at least I get to enjoy your body until that happens."

Gaine wrinkles her nose, pulling back from me. "You're gonna ruin the moment a lot, aren't you?" she scoffs.

"Nah," I reply, grinning. "I'll just make them more fun." I close my arm around her and pull her knee over my hip. "Now, come here. You're done resting."

I roll her back over the top of me, placing her body in the middle of the bed. I bite down on her chest, setting our nerves off again and causing her back to arch against my attack. Pausing, I look over my mate and watch her tanned skin shimmering with beads of sweat. I lick my lips and smile as I realize she is mine to taste for the rest of our lives.

25

A soft tapping on the door triggers my growl. Not finding a blade under my pillow, I throw it and jump out of bed. My hands ball into fists as another knock sounds, but something moves among the sheets, reminding me that my life is different now.

The smooth waves of brown hair reveal a beautiful woman with stunning green eyes. "Kade," she whispers. "We should see who that is. We've been in here for nearly a week."

My chest expands with a deep breath as I smile at Gaine. I have wanted her for so long that I knew I would need days to enjoy her. My exhaustion finally sent me to sleep last night. Gaine should be relieved at the chance to rest, but her soft smile says otherwise.

"It's just food, guys," Nate calls from the other side of the door. "The guards report that you haven't left since I dropped you off. We don't keep food in there."

Leaning forward, I crawl back onto the bed. Gaine cups my cheeks to pull me in for a kiss but then trails her fingers along my chest. I continue my advance, straddling her legs and pulling the sheet down to expose more of her delicious skin.

"I need proof of life, or the next visitor won't knock," Nate says through the door. "Those are my orders."

Gaine giggles as my lips slide down her abs. "Kade," she hisses. "Go get the door."

I nibble at her belly button before moving to her hip. The sheet gives way to display her legs. Gaine's tan skin always seems to glow, and its silky feel begs to be touched and caressed. I have tasted most of her beautiful body but became distracted by my needs before I could sample the one area I've been desperate to taste.

Gently lifting her knee, I hook Gaine's leg over my shoulder. I watch her eyes while I slide my lips over her inner thigh. Gaine's chest heaves as I move closer to her folds. I lick my lips and accidentally touch the soft skin around them, making her jump.

We've equally enjoyed the past few days, but I pause, wondering if this is different. I narrow my eyes and recall some of my conversations over the past few months. I'd discussed mates and relationships with many wolves, but only one took me seriously.

Chase had told me that my mate would be everything I needed to complete my life. He was right about that but also told me my mate would desire more from me. Chase said that my body would not be enough. I had to figure out what she needed and be that.

I flick my eyes back toward Gaine and blow gently over her folds, asking for permission this time. I smile as her hips roll closer to me. I continue to blow air over her skin until I reach it, making her aware of my intentions. Gaine jumps again as I close my lips over her parts, but this time it's toward me.

My hum starts as I drink in her beautiful flavor. Gaine's leg clenches over my shoulder, and her hip lifts to give me full access. I close my eyes and lap my tongue between the folds of skin she's kept from me. The excellence that graces my taste buds can only be described as perfect. I get lost in the flavor until Gaine moans through her enjoyment loud enough to qualify as proof of life for the older guard standing outside the door.

* * *

After another week, Ayls sent word that she would be coming to visit us. I scowled, but Gaine found it funny that the little Luna added a requirement of clothes. We lie in the field across the wagon road, waiting for her. Gaine passes the time by finding images in the clouds, and I smile with my eyes closed, listening to her voice's melody.

"What do you suppose the Luna wants to talk to us about?" Gaine asks, sliding her hand over my chest.

Pulling her fingers to my lips, I take a deep breath and sigh happily. "She probably just wants to make sure I haven't eaten you," I answer, smiling. "I have been compromising her Seer's time lately."

"Kade?" Gaine says softly.

I lift my eyebrows but leave my eyes closed. "Hmm?"

"Marry me," she says.

"What?" I spout, furrowing my brow. "Nah, I didn't agree to that."

Gaine clicks her tongue. "You don't want to get married?"

With a huff, I open my eyes and turn to face her. "Woman, I already got what I wanted," I tell her, shrugging. "Why would I wanna buy the cow?"

My gorgeous mate wrinkles her nose and stumbles over noises, but no words come out. I smile and tuck her hair behind her ear. When she realizes I'm just joking, Gaine scoffs and slaps my chest.

I reach up for her and roll to my side, holding her against me. "I will give you whatever you want, beautiful woman," I whisper, kissing her forehead. "But you know it's not up to me. We'll need the little Luna's blessing."

"You weren't looking at the clouds," Gaine mumbles.

"What?" I ask, leaning back to look at her face. Gaine's probably spent too long with her sister. I wish I understood what she was talking about all the time, but my mate's mind works differently.

"Your eyes were closed," she explains. "You couldn't see the clouds."

Licking my lips, I breathe out a sigh. "But what I see when I close my eyes is beautiful too," I tell her. "Would you like me to describe it to you?"

Gaine smiles and tips her chin to kiss my lips. "Yes," she whispers before snuggling against my chest.

"I see your jaw tighten just before you smile when I catch you off guard," I start, looking up at the clouds she was watching. "I see your thigh flex when you lift your leg to hook it over my hip. Your hands create perfection when they reach out for me, and I watch your chest heave air until I've wrapped you in my arms and surrounded you with my love."

Gaine groans as I hold her tightly and looks into my eyes when I release her. "So the silver wolf has a silver tongue, huh?"

Breathing a laugh, I kiss the tip of her nose. "My favorite sight is one I refuse to imagine," I tell her. "I love the way you look at me." I cup her chin and pull her back to my lips.

"I'll admit, that has certainly changed," Ayls says from behind me.

I wrap Gaine in my arms protectively. "Shit, Ayls," I growl. "I didn't teach you stealth so you could sneak up on me."

Ayls clicks her tongue and sits beside me. "I don't have anyone else to sneak up on," she points out. Ayls leans over me to tuck Gaine's hair behind her ear. "Besides, I wanted to see this for myself." She smiles broadly at my blushing mate. "Happy looks good on you, sweet wolf."

"Yeah, I wanted to talk to you about that," I say, sighing.

A few days ago, I mentioned wanting to soak in the large tub at the cottage again and didn't like the change I noticed in Gaine. Ayls denied me permission to take her away from the lake, but chaining her back to the ranch is no longer an option. I refuse to watch the pressure of her duties crush her anymore.

"Not right now, Kade," Ayls responds, winking. She digs in her pocket and produces the two proximity wards, making my mate stiffen against me. "Edith found these in your room, Gaine."

"They were mine," I say, rubbing Gaine's back. "I had them made so I wouldn't have to listen to Tynan. She was holding them for me."

Ayls narrows her eyes. "Don't lie to me, Kade," the little Luna says, frowning. "I have no doubt why they were made, but her guards report that she was shifting last year, and no one could find her."

"Ayls," I start in a whisper.

Our Luna shakes her head. "This is not how to get me to grant your request," she warns, lifting an eyebrow. "Edith informed me of their use. Although I have ordered their destruction, I thought you might enjoy one more run." Ayls smiles and winks at Gaine when she lifts her head, surprised. "Just for old time's sake."

"You know I could just take her and run," I say, holding my arm out for Ayls. "Wouldn't be the first time."

Ayls lies down beside me but rests her chin on her hand over my chest. "Because you love Gaine, I know you'll do right by her," she whispers, tracing her fingers over my forehead. "Did you know that I've never seen Gaine's wolf?" Ayls turns to brush her fingers along my mate's face. "I'm told she's beautiful."

"She is," I agree.

Gaine sniffles but is smiling when I look down at her. "I love you, Luna," she says, taking Ayls' hand. "I'm sorry."

"Aw, I love you too, Gaine," Ayls responds warmly. "I know you've struggled. Please enjoy some time away with this wolf who will love you with an insane amount of passion. And when you return, we will find a way to give you peace."

Turning my eyes toward the clouds, I squeeze both women. "I'm gonna need your help with something, Ayls," I mumble. "This beautiful woman wants a wedding. I feel inclined to give her one."

Gaine's hum starts when I kiss her forehead. "You think we can make that happen?"

Ayls bolts upright to beam down at us. "Of course we can," she gushes. "Nothing would make me happier than blessing your union." She cringes and rolls her eyes. "But it seems I'm needed elsewhere to handle a situation right now. Why don't we do it when you come back?"

"Luna, I can't go back to how things were," Gaine says. She sits up and grabs Ayls' hand. "Please, I can't keep hiding and being an excuse for my father."

I slide from between the women as Ayls pulls Gaine into a hug. The little Luna furrows her brow in thought while I rub Gaine's back. From my time at the lake, I know Ayls has been allowing her witch to watch over Gaine's family and hasn't been active in their lives. I had hoped to remove Gaine from her situation without telling Ayls that she made a mistake.

Wincing, I clear my throat. "From what I understand, Byron's been requiring Gaine to watch over her sister most of the time," I whisper. "He's also passed on most of the ranch duties, so I'm honestly not sure he's needed at this point."

Ayls sighs, holding my hand against Gaine's back. "The situation at the ranch has been brought to my attention," she assures us. "It is being handled as we speak." Ayls leans back and holds Gaine by the cheeks. "Your father faces an uncertain future. He was told he could only stay as long as his children needed him. I believe that time has passed."

"I do love him, Luna. I promise I do," Gaine whispers. "But I'm ready to start my life."

"I agree," Ayls says, smiling gently. "And there's no better way than with a wedding."

Gaine falls forward into Ayls' arms again. I cup the little Luna's cheek and mouth a thank you as she winks at me.

"When would you like us back?" I ask. "I know it's far, but I'd like to take her across the river to visit an old friend."

"That sounds like a wonderful plan," Ayls answers. "You will need to be back in a week. That should give you a few days with them. A man named Clay can help you cross the river just north of where your friends live. And when you come back, Kade, I will need your decision."

I narrow my eyes curiously as I watch Ayls pull away from Gaine and stand. "Decision about what?"

"Your position," Ayls says sternly. "We have found a way to allow your freedom, but you are still my Shield. I will need your pledge."

"Yeah, alright," I grumble.

Ayls shakes her head. "The wards are attached to leather," she says, holding them out to me. "If you run into trouble, they will easily break to allow you to call for help." She pulls them out of my reach and raises her eyebrow. "Do not make me regret this."

Gaine giggles as I snatch the wards from Ayls. "You know him too well," she says, looping her arms around my waist. "We'll be back in a week, Luna. Thank you for this."

As Ayls leaves us, I slide my arm around Gaine and push her until she's in front of me. I cup her cheek with a smile and rub our lips together. "I think you know me much better than she ever will," I whisper.

Grinning, Gaine nips at my lips. "Come on," she says excitedly. "Let's go for a run."

* * *

My favorite sight might be how Gaine looks at me, but watching her run beside me without a care is a very close second. Her wolf is just as beautiful as I remember. The red tips of her brown coat sway and ripple with every stride, calling my attention and allowing her to laugh when I trip over debris on the trail.

"Well, stop being so stunning," I grumble, shaking the dirt out of my coat after falling the fourth time.

Gaine giggles. *"I love you too, Kade,"* she says, pulling my lip with her tongue. *"Clay's house is just up ahead."*

While resting last night, Gaine told me about Clay. He was a human who worked on the barge we rode north on for many years before Ayls' mother gifted him the house by the river. Although I like to hear the stories of Darya and how she changed being a wolf into something honorable, I'm constantly distracted by how different everything feels with Gaine.

Before I met my mate, I was strong, fearless, and feared. I had a plan for everything, and no one got in my way. Most wolves knew my name, but none spoke it, frightened they would catch my attention. I stood tall and looked down upon the world as if I ruled it. I thought that was what it meant to be a man.

I was wrong.

Last night, Gaine curled her neck to tuck her muzzle under my chest for the first time since we bonded. We were nestled under the roots of a downed tree and could not have been any safer, but I felt more like a man as I lay with her than ever before. My neck covered her eyes and ears, allowing her to sleep peacefully while I protected her from threats.

I didn't need sleep because I was fueled by the pride of having a beautiful mate who loved and trusted me. When she woke and lifted her head, my chest wanted to burst. She didn't even look around before licking my lip in a good morning kiss because she knew I had kept her safe all night.

After wasting 26 years, I spent another trying to fix my head and become worthy of this stunning wolf beside me. My eyes are drawn to her shoulders as she jogs slightly ahead of me. They have a lift that portrays a confidence I don't often see.

I'm reaching over to nuzzle her when I pull in the scent of

a human. *"We're close,"* I say, shaking my head and sneezing. *"He's putting too much spice on his meat."*

Gaine giggles. *"Have you eaten Anthony's venison shoulders? He is such a good cook."* She licks her lips, making me jealous. *"Kade?"*

I tear my eyes away from her muzzle to see she's staring at me. *"Hmm?"*

"You may have turned silver, but you're just as distracted as my handsome Midnight," Gaine says, shaking her head.

"That's because my Beauty has not changed," I murmur, pulling her lip with my tongue.

We push past some thick brush and emerge into a thin grove of trees beside the river. A small dock sticks out over the water in front of a quaint cabin. Gaine stays by my hip as I lead her through the trees and onto a thin front porch. We pause for a moment to hear someone move about the cabin.

"Let's see if he's expecting us," I suggest when a guitar begins playing inside. I scratch the door and step back, curling my body protectively around Gaine. *"I've never knocked on a door of someone I didn't know."*

"Really?" Gaine challenges. *"Did you just plow through their doors?"*

"Well..." I start thoughtfully. I hadn't gone into detail about my life before meeting Gaine. She hated me enough just hearing the stories that she had. I wasn't interested in adding any details that may have been omitted. *"I mean... this isn't about me, woman."*

"And it's all in the past," she adds, rubbing her jaw over my shoulders.

"Mmm, I love you," I hum.

We both jump when the door opens suddenly. The older man eyes us curiously for a moment before chuckling. "You really are silver," the man says, raising his eyebrows. "Ain't that some shit?"

I curl tighter around Gaine, and my growl rumbles out of control when he steps forward.

"It's alright," the man says, kneeling before me. "I'm Clay. Your Luna sent word that you'd be stopping by. You're Kade, right? So that means this lovely thing must be Gaine."

I snap at his hand when he reaches toward her jaw. *"Back up, Gaine,"* I say, moving sideways to push her off the porch.

The man puts his hands up and rocks back onto his heels. "Is that not allowed?" he asks. "I don't get many visitors, and the Luna's guards normally stay out in the woods." He watches me guide Gaine from the porch. "I didn't mean to offend y'all."

Clay's thick southern accent came on strong as he apologized. I lower my head a few times, which is meant to indicate that I accept his apology but am not interested in him coming closer. As a human, he believes I'm nodding an affirmation.

"Alright, well, I'm sorry," Clay says, standing. "I wasn't sure if you'd want to shift, so I have clothes inside for you." He walks through the front door and holds it open for us. "I'll show you where they are and give you some privacy. I know you don't like spice much, but there's a loaf of cheese bread about to come out the oven."

Gaine licks her lips behind me. *"Oh, that brings back memories,"* she says.

"I let you eat," I grumble, turning my head just enough to look at her from the corner of my eye. *"You didn't starve. There was food all over the place."*

"No, Kade," she responds. *"The food was all over me."*

"And you enjoyed it when I ate it off you," I add.

Gaine giggles. *"Yeah, I kinda did. But the cheese bread you fed me will forever remind me how having your teeth and tongue all over my body felt."*

"Well, you are delicious," I hum whimsically as she nuzzles my ear.

"Did you guys want to shift?" Clay asks, reminding us that he's there.

Sighing, I pull at Gaine's lip with my tongue. *"We better not,"* I tell her. *"We need to leave in the morning, and I can't promise I'll be done with you by then."*

"Look at you being all restrained," Gaine gushes, giggling. She turns her attention to Clay and shakes her head in response.

"Alright," he says, moving further into the house. "That bread's just about done. Not sure what your plans are, but the Luna's man said you would be crossing the river. The water's a bit deep here, but if you go north a piece, you'll see a red marker on a tree. That's where the sandbars shallow it out."

We step through the door and stop beside the old man's fireplace. The fire is crackling with fresh wood, but I still hear Gaine's stomach growl as she sits beside me.

"I have some thick blankets," Clay says, reaching into a basket. "Hope you don't mind. I'm too old to be offering up my bed."

Chuckling, I move to stand between him and Gaine and take a corner of one of his blankets. I pull it toward Gaine's feet and nuzzle her head as she lays on it. When her stomach rumbles again, I poke it and look up at Clay.

"Hmm, that's what that was, huh?" he remarks, nodding. "I have salted fish and a few elk hips in the meat shed. Which would you like?"

Gaine's stomach rumbles for a third time, and I poke her hip.

"Good choice," Clay responds, kneeling to lay out a heavy woven blanket. "I'll go grab one while you make yourselves comfortable. It's never easy being on the road." He sits back on his heels and stops as he reaches for the small table beside him. "She really is beautiful, isn't she? I can't recall seeing any other wolf with red tips."

"See?" I say, licking Gaine's ear. *"Everyone appreciates your beauty."*

As Clay leaves us, I keep my eyes on Gaine. I have seen her anger and watched her confidently handle horses and weapons. Her power and ferocity are awe-inspiring. But she's never accepted my compliments and doesn't seem to know how beautiful she is. I love the way she tucks her chin when she's embarrassed.

"I love you," I whisper, overcome with the need to profess my feelings. My hum starts as I rub my muzzle along the side of hers.

This beautiful woman has been an equal partner in the past week. She knows her body very well and confidently handles mine to ensure she always gets what she needs from me. It made it easy to learn what she liked, and I enjoyed watching her take what she wanted. Although everything about her is perfect, she doesn't seem to know it.

When Clay returns, he drops a large elk hindquarter on the floor beside us. "It was recently skinned, but I didn't have a chance to cut it from the bone," he tells us. "That bread should be cool now, too."

Clay seems friendly enough, so I ignore him and move the meat closer to Gaine. Nudging my nose toward it, I urge her to take the first bite, and Gaine pulls at the thickest part in the center. She pushes it with her paw as her teeth rip a small section out.

"Got you a hungry woman, huh?" Clay remarks, reappearing with the bread.

I don't particularly like how he keeps talking to me about Gaine instead of speaking directly to her, but I can't disagree with anything he's said. *"Do you want me to make him stop?"* I ask her.

Gaine hums and licks my lip. *"Humans have issues with women in power,"* Gaine says, still rubbing her nose over my cheek. *"Our humans, Clay included, grew up in that world. Although they respect us and honor our Luna, they have issues letting go of the old habits if they aren't around us all the time. It actually keeps them safe out here."*

"I suppose," I agree thoughtfully. *"Allows them to blend in better. I've never noticed it before."*

"You're a man, Kade," Gaine reminds me. *"Whether they knew you were a wolf or not, you are still a man, and humans respect you more than a meager woman."*

"*You are no meager woman,*" I grumble. "*This world needs a better education.*"

Clay throws another log on the fire and nods to us. "There's more wood there if you need it," he says, stopping in the doorway to a bedroom. "If I don't see you in the morning, good luck. There have been issues across the river lately. Keep your head down."

I stare thoughtfully at the old man, but Gaine nods in understanding. "*Ayls' mother died trying to bring peace to our pack,*" I say, turning to Gaine. "*Watching her die broke me. I don't think I'd survive losing Ayls.*"

"*Why do you call her that?*" Gaine asks before taking a bite of the cheese bread.

I watch her slowly enjoy her food before taking a deep breath. "*I spent a long time at the lake before I came back to you,*" I start, looking at the fire. "*It took her weeks to convince me to eat on my own. She spent the entire time in bed with me, holding my wolf and comforting me every time I watched you die.*

"*Annalisa is a long regal name meant for a queen who stands in her ivory tower and looks down upon her people—a queen who wouldn't have even asked about her broken wolf. Ayls is the name of a Luna who would stop her life to fix the soul of someone who wears a mark of shame. She would care for the happiness of a wolf who didn't deserve it.*" I pause to look into Gaine's eyes. "*That is why I call her Ayls.*"

"*She is a wonderful Luna,*" Gaine says.

"*Yes, she is,*" I agree before turning my attention to the elk meat. "*We have a long way to go tomorrow. Why don't we eat and get some rest? Our wonderful Luna only gave us a week.*"

26

The sun shines brightly through the kitchen window when a low howl wakes me. Since Gaine is still asleep with her muzzle tucked against my chest, I leave my head down so I won't wake her. I can't stop my hum when I hear her quiet snore. Yawning, I roll my head and close my eyes to go back to sleep.

"Kade?"

My eyes snap open again. *That's right. Someone woke me up.*

"Kade? Can you hear me?" Bass asks. *"I knew those stupid pendants would bite us in the ass."*

"I'm here," I say now that I know where to direct my words. I look around the room to see Clay's bedroom door is still closed, but the shadow moving across the crack under it means he's awake.

"Come on," Bass says. *"We have orders."*

I jump to my feet, forgetting about my sleeping mate. *"What happened?"* I snap. *"Is Ayls okay?"*

"She's fine," Bass answers. *"Come on. Get out of bed."*

There's a scratch at the door, and Clay emerges from his bedroom.

"Who's at the door?" the old man asks, staring at me as if expecting an answer.

I nudge my nose in its direction to tell him to open it. Gaine had rolled onto her side when I stood up and is now calmly watching me with her paw on my shoulder. She whines through a yawn and licks her lips. My hum starts again as I tuck under her jaw to tug on the fur covering her throat.

"Good morning, Beauty," I whisper, sliding my nose to her ear. I nibble at the rounded tip as Clay opens the door and Bass appears. *"The kid needs our help."*

Gaine jumps to her feet, crashing into my muzzle. *"Oh, Bass,"* she says, sounding embarrassed. *"I'm sorry. I didn't know it was you."*

"It's fine, Gaine," the young Alpha responds. *"You should stay here. We believe there's been a spot of trouble, and Ayls said to bring Kade."*

"See? It's a good name, right?" I say, laughing.

Bass sighs and simply stares at me.

"Yeah, alright," I grumble. *"But Gaine is coming with me. I can't leave her behind whenever things get difficult."* Gaine lifts her head proudly as I turn to nuzzle her cheek. *"Besides, I like watching her in action."*

"I'll be alright, Bass," Gaine says, pushing me away. *"I've trained just like everyone else."*

"But you're the Seer," Bass starts.

"Who will refuse to see a damn thing if I am separated from my mate for another second," Gaine states firmly.

I love watching my beautiful mate stand her ground. She's not a defiant wolf and has honored our Luna and the Alphas in every way. She felt shame for using the proximity ward because she hid them from everyone and knew the Luna would disapprove. Ayls said she'd never defied them outright until she refused to come to the lake while I was there.

Gaine would never reject an order or openly defy a rule set forth by the Luna or her Alpha, but she looks gorgeous when she stands her ground and states her intentions. My mate is a powerful woman, and I will kill any man who tries to take that away from her. I can't help getting lost in the beauty of her strength.

"*Um, okay,*" Bass says slowly. "*That wasn't meant to be a suggestion, but we don't have time to discuss this, so I guess you're coming.*"

We walk past Clay, who'd remained silent in the doorway, and stop on the porch. "*Come on,*" Bass says. "*To the north. We need to cross the river.*"

"*What's up?*" I ask, following him with Gaine at my hip.

"*There's been reports of humans by Rooster's ranch, and no one has heard from him in days,*" Bass starts. "*Ari is due soon.*"

I don't need any other information. Leading the others across the clearing, I aim straight for the river so we don't miss the first chance to cross. I love Ayls, and I'm eternally devoted to Gaine, but Rooster is the only friend I have left. I wanted to thank them in person for everything they did to help me win Gaine over.

"*Kade, slow down,*" Bass says, sprinting to keep up. "*They're probably fine. Since the baby is coming soon, Ari can't shift, and I'm sure Rooster would want to be able to help when it's time. We can't just rush in there.*"

"*You can't,*" I snap. "*I can.*" I nudge Gaine's muzzle and pick up speed. "*Stick to my hip. Don't fall behind.*"

* * *

The smell of blood hits my nose nearly two days later like a poisonous flare. Bastian charges out in front of me with massive strides and slams into my shoulder when I try to veer around him. I jump back to my feet, snarling, but Gaine stands beside the young Alpha to block my path.

"*Get out of my way,*" I growl slowly, enunciating each word to ensure they're understood.

"*Kade, listen,*" Bass starts.

"*No,*" I snap. "*That's my friend, and I smell wolves' blood.*"

Gaine steps forward and slides her muzzle over mine. I hate that she triggers my hum. "*I love you, Kade,*" she says, making me roll my eyes. *"He's not telling you to listen to him. Let's just be quiet and listen for a moment. I'm sure I heard voices."*

Taking a deep breath, I focus on the sounds around us. A few crows call in the distance, and the breeze moves through the leaves nearby, but we're mostly surrounded by silence. I shake my head and turn in the direction Bastian faces. It takes a moment to find what he's focused on. I can't make out the words, but there are a few voices and laughter, followed by a woman screaming.

"We need a plan," Gaine says. *"You're not going without me."*

I close my eyes and sigh. I know she's right, and Bastian's probably thinking something along the same lines. My head isn't clear, and I'll get them hurt if they follow me. *"You sure I can't convince you two to stay here?"* I ask, already knowing the answer.

"I hate you," Bastian starts, making Gaine tilt her head at him. *"But you are Ayls' Shield. You have to learn to work as a team with the wolves she sends to assist you. Who better to start with than the strongest wolf you know and the wolf you will do anything to protect?"*

"Are you allowed to hate a wolf?" Gaine asks, confused.

Bastian rolls his eyes. *"It would seem we have more important things going on right now, Gaine."*

Chuckling, I nuzzle my mate's cheek. *"Hmm,"* I hum, rolling my head to lick her lip. *"I love you."*

"Two of a kind," Bastian grumbles, turning toward the voices. *"Let's go slow and make a plan once we know what we're dealing with."*

Letting Bastian lead the way, I hang back to jog beside Gaine. My mind isn't clear, but the scream we heard came from Ari, and I have feelings about that. Even though I don't understand them, I know they are there. I rub my whiskers over Gaine's cheek to comfort her amidst the shouting coming from the direction we're heading.

Bastian stops suddenly at the edge of a clearing, and I crash into him. The yelling becomes insistent, but I still can't understand what they're saying. Using Bastian's hip, I crowd Gaine so she'll stay behind us as we peek through the brush.

"*I think that's Rooster over there by the barn door,*" Bass says, tilting his head. "*Jesus. Ari's huge.*"

I follow his gaze to see the extremely pregnant woman holding her stomach with one hand and Rooster's long sword with the other. She does her best to keep it pointed toward the four men surrounding her but doubles over in pain.

"*River told me we were here before him,*" Gaine says, oblivious to what we are watching.

I pull my head back through the bushes and narrow my eyes, confused. "*What?*"

"*Jesus,*" Gaine says, distracted. "*My sister said he didn't like us.*"

"*Can you blame him?*" Bass asks. "*We were barbaric, brutal, and hateful. Hell, I hate who we used to be.*"

I stick my head back through the bushes. "*Maybe that's why humans hate us so much,*" I suggest. "*They don't believe we could change.*"

"*Nah,*" Bass answers. "*They hate anything different. Even Anthony said he dealt with it because of the color of his skin.*" He waits for me to stop assessing Ari's situation and pull my head out of the brush before continuing. "*Any ideas?*"

I roll my eyes. "*Other than charging in there and getting everyone killed?*" I ask. "*No.*" I rest my chin over Gaine's neck. "*I haven't seen Rooster move.*"

"*I haven't either, but there has to be a reason why that man is pointing a rifle at him,*" Bass responds.

"*True,*" I say thoughtfully.

Ari yells in pain, making Gaine step toward the brush. I latch onto her neck scruff, trying to stop her, but she pulls away from me.

"*What's wrong with you two?!*" Gaine shouts, darting through the bushes. "*She's in labor!*"

Bastian drops his head with a huff. "*Shit.*"

"Gaine!" I shout, jumping after her. *"Stop!"*

Gaine's snarl builds as Bastian and I bound after her. The young Alpha cuts to our left, trying to approach from the other side of Rooster. Gaine has a beautiful jog, but due to not shifting for so long, her wolf has a shorter stride when she runs, and I catch up quickly.

Bastian continues calling out his position as I look for somewhere to stash Gaine. I lay my shoulder against hers and shove her toward a small cluster of trees with an ugly palm bush under them. Gaine snaps at me but allows me to redirect her before we're seen.

"Kade, we need to help her!" she angrily shouts, crawling under the palm so she can still see Ari.

I listen to Bastian for a moment, following the positions he calls until his voice cuts off. *"Gaine,"* I say, hoping she'll turn back to me. When she doesn't, I gently rub my chin over her hip. *"Beauty, Ari's already hurt. Look closely."*

Gaine lifts her head to get a better look at the pregnant woman. *"Oh, Kade,"* she says softly.

From further away, I saw the blood on Ari's shirt but couldn't tell if it was hers. Now that we are closer, we can see that it is running from her side and down her leg. Ari's arm has weakened from the blood loss, and the long sword is pointing more toward the ground. She's saying something to the men between heaving breaths, but we can't make out her words.

"None of those men will survive the day," I promise Gaine. *"But if we're not careful, neither will the wolves. I need you to pull this pendant so I can hear Bastian."*

As Gaine backs up, a gun goes off, followed by Ari screaming. I look up to see the man standing over Rooster move away from him and turn his rifle at Ari. Bastian appears on their far side, running at full speed.

Without waiting for Gaine to pull the pendant, I jump forward.

"On my hip, woman," I snap at Gaine, knowing she won't stay in the bush.

Moving as one unit, we close in on the humans as they shove the weakened Ari against the barn. Bastian calls out his position with each stride, letting me focus on Gaine. My mate's lack of experience is evident as her snarl builds out of control.

One of the men turns toward us, hearing Gaine over Ari's cries. "Shit! There's more of them!" he shouts to the others.

Bastian jumps at the man closest to him and latches onto his shoulder. His body rolls, taking the human with him. The man screams as his bones break. He falls into Ari, knocking her over.

The short man who'd shot Rooster is my target. With one final push from my hind legs, I roll down onto my shoulder and wrap my jaws around his leg below the knee. I relish the harmony of his joint disconnecting and the thud of his body, accompanied by his screaming.

I return to my feet and step on the human's chest to snarl in his face.

"Kade!" Gaine's frantic shout pulls me away from my kill.

I glance around to find her latched onto a man's forearm. He's swinging a blade wildly with his free hand. I lunge at her attacker, shoving him away. He raises his knife, but I catch that arm in my mouth and pull against him, shredding his muscle. The man falls onto his back and screams until I bite down on his throat.

Once Gaine's attacker is done, I turn back to my prey. The short man's eyes widen as he watches me approach. I step on his chest with both front paws, making it impossible for him to breathe.

"That man you shot was my friend," I tell this human who would never hear me. *"He was a good wolf. He loved that woman you hurt. You will never know a love like that. You won't know tomorrow."*

I've never taken joy in the fear a man displays before he dies. But this death is different. It was earned. I slowly lean down and open my mouth to show the man the teeth that will end him. My fangs slide over his neck until I'm far enough around his throat. The back teeth rip painfully at his skin before my fangs puncture his artery. His blood spills over the ground, painting it with human hatred.

"Kade," Gaine says softly. She rubs her nose over my ear as the man's head flops lifelessly to the side. *"We were too late."*

The sounds surrounding us begin to filter through my rage. Leaves lift into a spiral nearby as a gust of wind sweeps them off the ground. A crow calls out from the small cluster of trees where we hid. Bastian yells in frustration, and the long blade clangs against the barn's wall.

The sword falls to the ground as I look at the scene before me. *"Oh, Ari,"* I whisper when my gaze falls on the woman's lifeless body. My vision blurs, and my chest uncomfortably swells while I absorb the limp infant dangling from her arms.

"I think she did it herself," Bastian murmurs, approaching her slowly. He crouches beside Ari's body and removes the knife jammed in her thigh. "She was a good person and a caring wolf. She deserved better than this."

"They both did," I add, turning toward Rooster. Scanning his body, I see why he wasn't helping Ari. The men had broken his arms and legs. Judging by the lack of blood around the wound, the bullet wasn't necessary.

"Ari's wound was in her abdomen," Gaine tells me. *"That's what killed the baby."*

"I don't want to be what they hate anymore, Gaine," I whisper. *"We're better than the past. How do we make them see that?"*

Gaine joins me beside Rooster's body. *"We follow our Luna,"* she answers. *"She is the color in our rainbow. With her guidance, we will find our place in this world."*

"Take this thing off me," I say softly, my eyes still locked on my friend's body. When Gaine doesn't move, I snap, *"Now! This pendant!*

Get it off!" I sit down and frantically scratch at my neck until Gaine finds the necklace and pulls it with her teeth, breaking the leather.

The panicked voices of Ayls' closest guards instantly flood in, wanting a report. Ayls taught me how to filter out the broad calls from her guards, but they're overwhelming.

"*SHUT UP!*" I scream at them.

Gaine jumps, letting me know I'd yelled at our entire pack. "*Easy, Kade,*" she says soothingly. Her whiskers rub over my muzzle. "*The damage is done. We've ended the threat. It's okay to feel their loss.*"

"*Ayls?*" I call out, accepting Gaine's affection. We hook our necks and rest our chins behind each other's shoulders. "*I'm ready. You said Gaine's safe. She'll be safe, right?*"

"*Every day,*" Ayls promises softly. "*She will always be with you.*"

Pushing her with my jaw, I hold Gaine against my chest and think about the future I want to have with her. There's only one thing left to do. "*I accept you,*" I whisper to Ayls. "*I am yours to use as you wish.*"

"*A Shield was a wolf bound to the Luna,*" Ayls says. "*He would die in his Luna's place, jump in front of danger, and take the brunt of an attack. You are more than that. You are my wolf. There will no longer be a Shield. You may roam as long as you return when I call.*"

Closing my eyes, I relax into Gaine. My chin digs into her opposite shoulder, pulling her into a tighter hug. "*We will always come back to you,*" I vow. I open my eyes and find the pendant tangled directly under my nose in the grass. "*How do I destroy these things?*"

"*Hmm,*" Ayls hums so that I can see her gentle smile. "*Your teeth, my shiny one. Only a wolf's teeth can break the gem holding the ward.*"

"*I'm going to handle business here,*" I tell the little Luna, backing up and pulling Gaine's ward from her neck. "*Then we'll come home.*"

"*Do you still want to have the ceremony?*" Ayls asks.

Gaine's head rises, but her ears move nervously.

"*I don't want to give this woman a chance to get away from me,*" I tell

Ayls, staring into Gaine's eyes. *"I will love her with all I have and give her everything she wants, starting with a wedding."*

"Alright," Ayls responds as Gaine rubs her muzzle over mine. *"Take all the time you need, Kade. Give our wolves a proper burial and bring my Alpha home."*

"I love you, Ayls," I whisper. "We both do."

"I know, Kade," is all she says.

Nodding to Gaine, I trigger my shift and close my eyes to use this time to think. I relive the horrific event that just unfolded in front of us. I doubt I can understand what happened, but I have to try.

When we arrived, the short man stood over Rooster with his rifle pointed at him. No one else moved around them, which meant his limbs were already broken. He must have been internally bleeding because there was no blood around him. Bass said he hadn't seen him move either, so he very well could've been dead the whole time.

I noticed the blood on Ari's shirt during my first scan. The other three men stood just outside the long blade's reach, taunting her. When she yelled, it was more of a moan in pain, probably caused by her labor.

I wince as my muzzle molds back into my face and sit before Gaine once it's done. "They were waiting for the baby," I whisper, sliding my hand under her jaw. "I think Rooster was dead the whole time. They were waiting to be sure Ari saw her dead baby before they killed her."

Gaine moves closer to slide her head over my shoulder and down my back.

"She would've been a great mother," Bastian says, holding Ari's body.

I wrap my arms around Gaine's neck and look up at the young Alpha. "Did I cause this?"

Bastian sighs, rolling his eyes. "Not everything is about you, Kade," he grumbles. "Humans have hated us for much longer than you've been around. Did you hear about the collars they're making now?"

I sigh, knowing I don't want to hear about this. "No."

"They made them to fit around a human's neck," Bass says, propping Ari's body against the barn wall. "They slap it on a wolf, and if they're one of ours, they have to shift to keep breathing." He crouches before the young mother and adjusts her arms to cradle her baby. "You would've loved being a mother. I'm so sorry, Ari."

"What if it's just a wolf?" I ask, shaking my head. "What then?"

Bass shrugs. "I suppose they just die," he answers.

I hold one of the gem wards out to Gaine and carefully place it between her teeth. "Did you ever think about leaving?" I ask Bass as Gaine breaks the first ward. "Just gather the whole pack and go somewhere else?"

"Where?" Bass asks, stopping to watch us break the second ward.

"I don't know," I grumble. "Another planet."

Bastian stares at me for a moment before looking down at the dead bodies. "It's funny. When the world was full of electricity, cars, and some kind of web thing, our kind easily hid among them. They had no idea we were real." The young Alpha grabs one of the men's arms and pulls the corpse away from Ari. "They thought we were fairy tales."

"Well, they're about to wish we were just nightmares," I hiss, climbing to my feet. "I'm going to take Gaine around back. Rooster was always modest. He'll have a clothesline behind the house."

Gaine rubs her head against my hip as I lead her between the house and the barn. As soon as we are out of Bastian's sight, she stops and triggers her shift. I'd prefer she waited until I checked the area or at least had clothes for her, but I can't deny that I need to feel her arms right now. I quickly look around the corners of the buildings and check on Bastian before feeling the touch I've yearned for.

"I'm so sorry, Midnight," Gaine whispers, grabbing me from

behind. Her hands slide across my skin as her arms wrap around my waist. "I liked Ari. She was sweet."

I turn and hold her to my chest. "Her life was hard," I say, closing my eyes to focus on Gaine's touch. "I caused a lot of her pain, but for some reason, she forgave me. She was special like that."

"She told me everything you did was to protect her for Rooster," Gaine whispers between sniffles. "They both loved you very much. We'll find a way to honor them."

I've never been emotional, so this flood of feelings is difficult to process. I hang onto Gaine and let my mind wrap around the loss of my last friend. Having spent time with Ari, Gaine is experiencing the sorrow of losing a friendly wolf and packmate. I am here for her, but I can't deny I need her comfort more than ever.

"Let's find some clothes and shovels," I whisper. "We'll start with a proper burial." Leaning back, I cup Gaine's cheeks and kiss her forehead. "Bastian was close to Ari in the past. We shouldn't leave him alone too long."

As predicted, we find clothes hanging behind the house. I don't like the pit in my stomach when I slide Rooster's jeans over my hips, so I decline the shirt Gaine holds out. Ari's short, flowy dress looks adorable on my beautiful mate but also reminds us of the mother and child who will never meet.

Gaine carries an extra pair of pants for Bastian while I pull different tools from a small shed. It's long, hot work, but we dig a deep grave large enough for the family to rest together.

Bastian lowers the bodies to me, and Gaine helps me place them in each other's arms. I can't even find the energy to be ashamed of my tears as we gently wrap the tiny baby boy in one of Rooster's T-shirts and settle him between his parents. I wait until Bastian helps Gaine out of the grave before I crouch beside the family.

I wipe the tears from my cheeks and touch my damp fingers to their foreheads. "I can't take this one away," I whisper. "I don't know how we'll honor your memory, but we'll find a way."

Taking a deep breath, I stand and stretch my back. Bastian reaches down for my hand, pulling me from the grave. We each take a shovel and begin filling the hole slowly.

"We give you this family to lift them into your promised land," Bastian murmurs. "These wolves will guard your riches, love your children, and care for your vegetation. They were loved, and we thank you for giving us that time with them."

27

We return to Gaine's cottage late on a moonless night. We didn't care to bury the humans that killed our friends, so we piled their bodies on the porch before firing the house. Following wolf tradition, if there is no family to leave a dwelling to, it is burned to the ground for someone else to start anew. None of us felt like traveling after the burial, so we stayed together and watched the flames for nearly a full day before shifting.

Our journey was silent, and the collective sigh we released upon seeing the cottage was more about letting go than reaching our destination. While Bastian wanders into the barn, Gaine pushes me toward the field where I had laid, waiting for her to forgive me.

"I watched you through the window," Gaine says softly. She stops beside the small patch of dirt I had laid on. *"I wished you would leave but also hoped you wouldn't."*

Gaine lies at the edge of the dirt, creating a bowl around where my body had been. I slowly step into the empty spot and wiggle into the void. She rubs her chin over my muzzle before licking my ears.

"You're the most beautiful man I've ever seen," Gaine whispers. *"I love you."*

I pull her lip with my tongue and settle my head beside hers.

"I love you too, Beauty," I respond as she begins to snore softly. *"You have no equal."*

Since we bonded, Gaine hasn't spent one night as a wolf where she didn't tuck her muzzle under my chest until tonight. As we lie together, it would seem this is how she wanted to sleep when I re-appeared, hoping for her forgiveness. I rub my nose under her jaw and trigger her hum. Settling in, I smile at the symphony created by her snore and hum mixing.

Before we left the river, Ayls told me she had arranged for Gaine's father's departure. Byron had attempted to stop our union, which was the little Luna's final straw. I fought her, but Ayls ordered me to allow her to tell Gaine herself. I think he is part of the reason we're sleeping outside tonight. I doubt Gaine is ready to face him.

My mind races all night, not allowing me to sleep. Our union is tomorrow. I spent the three days of travel trying to find anything that would qualify as acceptable vows, but nothing came to me. I have screwed so much up since meeting this woman, and I was hoping that pattern would end soon.

"You awake?" Ayls calls out after a few hours.

Sighing, I give up finding anything that will tell my beautiful mate how much I love her. *"Yeah."*

"You ready for today?"

"No," I answer honestly. *"Tell me what to say."*

The little Luna giggles. *"She would know it wasn't your words,"* she says. *"Gaine asked for this union, Kade. She knows you and all your baggage. Why are you trying to give her something that isn't authentic?"*

I lift my lip in a scowl. She's right, but I don't have to like it. *"She deserves someone better,"* I tell her. *"She deserves a wolf who would never run from her."*

"Let's try something else," Ayls suggests. *"What do you love about her?"*

"Everything," I answer instantly.

"Do you love how she runs blindly into danger?"

I tilt my head in thought. *"Well, I love watching her do it."*

"That sounds more like Kade," Ayls says, letting me hear her smile. *"What do you think she loves about you?"*

"What's not to love?" I ask, chuckling. *"I'm perfect, sexy, smart, and loved by all. Who wouldn't want me?"*

"So, it sounds like you could stand before our pack and say anything, and it would be amazing," Ayls says. She gives me a moment to think about her words before continuing. *"Stop trying to be someone else, Kade. She doesn't want anyone else. She wants you."*

Breathing out a small laugh, I nuzzle Gaine. *"Thanks, Ayls."*

"You're welcome," she answers. *"You only have a few hours until sunrise. Get some rest."*

* * *

I leave my eyes closed against the sun's blinding light when Gaine wakes me by licking my ear. *"I never want to know a morning where I'd be forced to wake without you,"* I murmur, sliding the top of my head under her throat.

"Then you should probably shift and clean up," Gaine responds. *"I want you spotless when I meet you at the altar this evening."*

"I will always wait for you," I profess, licking her jaw.

"You have mud on your legs," Gaine says, looking cross.

"It's just ground glitter," I tell her, hooking my front leg over her shoulders. *"I can share some with you before our union. We could shift and put on a show. You gotta be on the bottom, though. I don't want anyone else looking at you."* My hum starts as I close my eyes and lick her lip lovingly.

"Kade?" Gaine says sternly.

"Yes, Beauty?" I respond, still licking her lip.

"If you ever want to see my skin again, you will give me my union," she growls.

"Mm-hmm," I hum, pretending not to pay attention.

"I hate you," Gaine grumbles.

I snap my head back, breathing out a chuckle. *"No, you don't,"* I reply. *"You tried that, remember? It didn't stick."*

Gaine rolls to her feet and pokes my face with her nose. *"I tried to stay away. I admit you made that pretty difficult,"* she says. *"But you look so good trying to catch me."* My beautiful mate takes a few steps sideways before I realize what she's doing.

"No, no, no," I start. *"Ayls will kill us if we disappear on our wedding day."*

Laughing, Gaine takes off across the field. I'm tired after only sleeping for a couple of hours, and my muscles are weak from not eating for the past few days, but nothing will stop me from chasing my beautiful mate. I jump up and dig my claws into the dirt, pulling at it to lengthen my stride.

Gaine leads me through a few fields before ducking into a line of trees in a ditch. I lift my head to get my bearings. I'd been so distracted by her happy laughter as she bound joyfully across the fields that I hadn't noticed she'd brought me back to where I found her when she snuck away from her guards.

"I came back here almost every day after you left," Gaine says, stepping out where I can see her. "When I lean against this tree, I feel your hands on my skin."

I lie in the grass, allowing it to engulf me so I can watch her through the stalks. Gaine presses her back against the tree where I'd held her. I watch with growing hunger as her hands slide across her stomach. One travels up between her breasts and wraps around her neck. My chest heaves when she pushes her chin up with her thumb and licks her lips.

"Your desire drives my senses crazy," Gaine whispers through soft moans. "I tortured myself by remembering your breath on my skin and the pressure of your fingers digging into my thighs."

Gaine's hands roam along her body. They brush over her hips

and press against her skin. Bending her leg, Gaine rests her foot on the tree and gently rubs the back of her fingers over the inside of her thigh.

"I remember your hips holding mine," Gaine groans. "How excited I was when you put me in position. I wanted you in every way that scared me. I was always yours."

My muscles tremble in my attempt to stay still when a breeze carries her scent in my direction. I lick my lips as my eyes settle on the fluid slowly creeping down her thigh. Giving up, I release a shaky breath and trigger my shift.

Gaine continues to slide her fingers over her skin with her eyes closed, and I curse the insanely long time it takes me to shift. My fingers dig into the dirt, wanting to feel her heat instead of the cold soil. I can't control my growl when my muzzle sinks back to form my face.

As soon as my vision clears, I crawl on my hands and knees to the woman I will destroy everything on Earth to protect. I slide my hand across her foot and lap my tongue over her ankle, making Gaine sigh noisily. My lips brush her calf, and I blow gently over the back of her knee after licking the sensitive skin.

My breath catches as I move up her thigh and find my target. I moan when my chest releases the trapped air as I clean the skin of her perfect flavor. Staying on my knees, I settle before Gaine. Her intense gaze captures my eyes while her foot sliding over my arm holds my attention. I brush my fingers over her inner thigh, asking for permission to taste her folds.

Gaine's hand cups my cheek, and her fingers pull my jaw, lifting me to her lips. "Give me what I want," she whispers, breathing heavily. Her fingers slip through my hair, pushing it out of my face. "Then you can have your taste."

Giving myself over to Gaine is easily the most erotic thing I have ever done. She takes care of my needs but enjoys the power I give her when it comes to her body. She hooks her legs over my hips and slides me into her. My eyes roll, and air rushes from my lungs as I pin her to the tree.

Gaine remains still as our nerves fire painfully, demanding more than we are ready for. When our muscles relax, she whispers, "You know what to do."

I'm thankful Ayls is planning a sunset wedding as I spend hours in the tree grove, giving Gaine's body everything it wants from me. Her beautifully soft moans fill the field's silence, warning anyone who comes near that they are not welcome. I love hearing her call my name when she desperately needs her deepest nerves satisfied.

When she's had enough and lies back in the grass smiling, I enjoy some extra time tasting more of her skin. Gaine hums happily and pulls her fingers through my hair. It's not long before I'm lying in her arms, enjoying the simplicity that comes with our bond.

"Luna's gonna kill us," Gaine whispers, giggling.

"Nah," I say, sighing. "Just tell her I tied you up."

Gaine clicks her tongue and tugs my hair. "She'd never believe that."

"I would," I answer, nipping at her chest.

"Well, we can't all be evil like you, Midnight," Gaine says. "But we should get going. We need to be readied, and Luna said she wanted to speak with me before the ceremony."

I cringe while she can't see my face. Gaine's father understandably hates me after I took his daughter away for weeks without permission and then caused her months of pain when I left. After everything Gaine told me, I'm not his biggest fan, but Byron is still her family. Although Ayls assured me I wasn't the reason for his ordered departure, I still feel responsible, and I'm worried Gaine will think the same.

"Are you happy?" I ask, changing the subject before I defy Ayls' orders.

Gaine pulls my hair so I'll look up at her from her chest. "I smile every day because you are with me," she says, grinning. "You make me very happy, Kade."

"Then I suppose we better continue that trend," I tell her, climbing to my feet. Stretching my back, I look around to see we're still alone. "Come on, Beauty," I say, leaning over to scoop her into my arms. "I need a lot longer than you to get pretty."

Gaine giggles and rests her head against my shoulder as I carry her back to the cottage. Loving my beautiful mate is easy. She doesn't have to try or do anything special to bring me joy. The simple act of sliding her finger over my jaw to rub its soft fuzz is enough to tell me she loves me with the same fiery passion.

We arrive at the house too soon, and I place Gaine on her feet at the door. "Ayls is probably inside waiting for you," I whisper against her cheek. "I won't be far if you need me."

Gaine smiles sweetly and kisses the tip of my nose. "Just be waiting at the altar, Midnight," she says. "That is all I will ever need from you."

I pull her tightly into my arms and press my hands down her body to hold her against me. "I will need a little more than that," I admit before capturing her lips.

My beautiful mate smiles into my kisses and pushes against my chest until I release her. "Go," she whispers, slipping through the door and closing it before I can follow.

Sighing, I turn to look over my surroundings. The yard is quiet, with only a few cardinals singing in the apple trees nearby. Gaine wants a spotless mate at the altar, but I'm unsure how to make that happen if I'm not allowed in the house.

Luckily, Tarq emerges from the barn wearing a well-fitted suit. "Come on, jackass," the grumpy Alpha shouts. "My daughter is very excited about blessing your union, and you are not allowed to make her frown. Get your grubby ass in here."

* * *

In the Blood Pack, couples just called themselves married. There was no ceremony or union. Most were not mates and nothing more than two wolves that could tolerate each other. Those who were lucky actually cared for one another.

"Kade, get over here," Ayls hisses from an archway covered in grapevines. "Where have you been?"

The sun has dipped low on the horizon, and our little Luna anxiously paces before Anthony. Grinning, I stop her and cup her cheek. "Do you know how many men it took to clean me?" I ask. "It was an uncomfortable number of men. That's how many."

Ayls smiles broadly. "But you are gorgeous," she whispers. "Are you ready for this?"

"Because of you, sweetheart, I am ready for anything," I proclaim. I pull Ayls into my arms and let her settle against my chest.

The little Luna would typically slip into my shirt and press her hand to her mother's print, but tonight is not ordinary. I'm dressed in a stiff button-up white shirt and black jeans. Ayls seems to know my black jacket was her grandfather's as she slips her fingers over the fabric.

"I have spoken with Gaine and Byron," Ayls whispers, eyeing the growing number of wolves gathering for the ceremony. "Your mate is torn about my decision. Be gentle, but help her through her feelings."

"There's no changing his mind?" I ask.

"Kade, so much was happening, and wolves were disappearing," Ayls says, reaching for my cheeks. "One died."

I cringe. "Yeah, I know."

Ayls narrows her eyes but continues without pressing me for information. "You took his little girl away without saying a word," she murmurs, checking my expression for understanding. "We both know he'd never have allowed it, but Byron feared the worst after weeks without contact."

Sighing, I pull her jaw and kiss her lips. "You taught me how important family is," I whisper, listening to the gathered wolves murmur about my forwardness with the Luna. "I don't want to be the reason she loses hers."

"Then be her family," Ayls says softly. The young Luna holds my cheek to hers and brushes her fingers through my hair a few times. "I think they're ready, my shiny wolf."

I pull back and follow her gaze to find the most beautiful woman standing at the corner of the cottage. The sunset's orange rays shimmer through the trees while a torch's firelight flickers across her face. She looks nervous as her eyes dart in my direction. The smoky blue dress is shorter in the front than the back, and her tanned legs shine in the fading light.

I grab Ayls' arm before she can move away. "She's mine, right?" I ask, losing my mind completely. "Please tell me that's mine."

Ayls giggles and pries my fingers from her arm. "Kade," she whispers. "Settle down, and she will come to you."

Gaine's eyes never leave mine as Tarq escorts her through the sizable gathering of wolves that came to witness our union. Braids hold her hair back, and flowers cover every pin, creating a crown. Gaine's chest swells as Tarq murmurs to her. The closer she gets to me, the harder it is to stay still.

When they reach the small step leading up to the archway, Tarq stops and holds Gaine back. My body tenses, and I move to snatch my mate from him. My shirt tightens as the back of it is grabbed.

"I won't be helping you tonight," Ayls hisses. "This is Gaine's night, Kade. It is your job to make it perfect for her."

Ayls pulls me back into position and releases my shirt. She rubs her thumb over my lower back a few times before removing her hand from under the coat, trusting me to stay put.

Anthony steps beside me, facing Gaine, and clears his throat, starting my growl. "We are all gathered here to witness the union of Kade, the Luna's..." his voice trails off in a confused tone. I narrow my eyes at his delay as Ayls leans to whisper into his ear. "The Luna's fixer?"

Our guests laugh and murmur while Ayls snickers, and I shake my head.

"Whatever," Anthony grumbles. "His union with Gaine, Seer of the Lunar Pack. Does the Elder bless this union?"

"I do," River says quietly from behind Gaine and Tarq. I hadn't even noticed she was there. Byron's sour expression as he escorts River makes me thankful that he's standing behind Gaine so she doesn't have to see it.

"Does the Luna bless this union?" Anthony asks.

"I do," Ayls whispers. I can hear her smile without having to turn to see it.

"Who is here to escort this wolf?" Anthony asks.

"What the fuck?" I spout. "Did you suddenly go blind? Hurry this shit up!"

The gathered wolves laugh while Byron's growl rumbles to life behind Gaine. Ayls rubs my back, making me turn my baffled expression on her. Smiling, she puts her finger to her lips before pointing toward my mate. Gaine is smiling broadly while shaking her head.

I lean to kiss Ayls' cheek. "She really does know me well, doesn't she?"

"She didn't think you'd stay up here for her walk down the aisle," Ayls whispers.

"Are you done?" Anthony asks, as close to growling as a human can get.

I wink at him and turn all of my attention to Gaine. My perfect mate smiles sweetly at me. I never cared about getting married. I didn't think it was necessary even after I met Gaine. I don't need a union to tell me where I want to be.

However, as I look upon this woman who tenderly holds my heart, I desperately want to be bound in this union with her. Everyone here and who comes across our names at any point in the future will know of the great love we share. My world will never be as empty as it once was.

"Kade!" Anthony barks, making me jump. "This is such a shit show. Your vows, Mister Shiny."

My eyes refocus on Gaine as she stands before Anthony, having been released by Tarq to join me. I step forward and latch onto her cheeks, pulling her lips to mine. I'm sure this is not what I'm supposed to be doing, but I love that Gaine smiles into my kisses.

"Give them a minute, Anthony," Ayls whispers from behind me. "Daddy, stop laughing."

I've never seen Tarq laugh. I lean away from Gaine to watch the inherently angry Alpha covering his mouth and looking away from us. "I doubt I'm supposed to be kissing you right now," I whisper to Gaine, rubbing my lips over hers.

"I don't care," she responds, pushing her tongue into my mouth.

Groaning, I answer her need with my own. Since we bonded, balancing what I have to do and what I want to do has been difficult. *She does not make it any easier.*

I gather my senses and push Gaine back, glaring at her. "Somewhere inside this stunning shell is the woman who asked me for this union," I grumble. "I'm gonna need you to let her come out for a little while. I'll play with you later."

Gaine smiles broadly and bites her tongue. "I love you," she whispers, rubbing her nose against mine.

With a deep breath, I turn to Anthony. "Alright, mate, we're back," I tell him, smiling. "What are we doing?"

Anthony glares at me, his face as red as the sunset. "Your vows," he spouts.

"Yeah, my vows," I say slowly, turning back to Gaine. "Woman, you ruined my life." I cup my beautiful mate's cheeks to stop her from looking at the wolves around us as they erupt with laughter. "I was happy being an asshole, all alone in my bubble of hatred and sarcasm. Then you showed up, being all righteous and sweet, and blew up my world.

"I've never needed anyone until you. I need your words to soothe my soul, your touch to ease my heart, and your body to blow my mind. You will never know a day when I won't be by your side. I will protect you from anything wishing you harm and give you all that you desire as long as you let me enjoy every inch of you until the day of my death."

Gaine giggles and shakes her head slightly as I wipe the tears from her cheeks with my thumbs. "Are you about done?" she asks over the roaring laughter of the wolves surrounding us.

"No," I respond, lifting an eyebrow. "I will never be done with you. You were mine from the moment I saw you, but I have always been yours. I was broken and incomplete until I found you. I have no idea why these fools are all laughing because they know exactly what I'm talking about. I will make you smile every day for the rest of your life because you, Gaine, are perfect, and I love you."

"I am so glad Darya's not here," Anthony grumbles as Gaine sighs through her tears and rubs her soaked cheeks over mine. "I really don't want to do this... Gaine, please don't make me regret asking you for your vows."

Gaine takes a minute to compose herself and catch her breath. We may have spent much of the past two years apart, but my feelings for my beautiful mate have never been a mystery. Gaine didn't need me to express them in words. *But I think I got pretty damn close.*

"I wanted to hate you," Gaine whispers, still sniffling. "You had no idea what it meant..." Her voice trails off as she shakes her head.

Pulling Gaine to my chest, I tuck her away from the crowd and let her have a moment. Ayls brushes her fingers over my shoulder to touch my mate's forehead. Their hands meet under my coat, and I feel Gaine pull Ayls closer.

"This is your night," Ayls whispers to my mate. "Take as much time as you need."

Gaine pulls back from me and grabs my cheeks. "I don't need any more time," she says sweetly, staring into my eyes. "We've wasted far too many years apart, which was my fault. I will right my wrong by loving you with every fiber of my being for the rest of our lives. There will not be another moment where you will doubt my feelings for you.

"My paws will run for you, my claws will maim for you, and my teeth will kill for you. I will fight for the future we deserve by your side and end each day in your arms. You are mine, Midnight, and I will forever be your Beauty."

The crowd of wolves around us may not know what Gaine means when she uses the names given to us by a human who showed us kindness, but they cheer when I lift her to my hips and latch onto her lips. Nothing could've stopped us.

Although we've been using the names, it wasn't until this moment that I realized she was referencing the first time she'd kissed me. A human wouldn't understand how meaningful it is for a wolf to pull at another's lip, but I loved her first kiss. It was the moment she gave me hope and made me want to be something other than the asshole I'd always been.

"Oh, for fuck's sake," Anthony grumbles. "Y'all are married. I'm going home."

28

Gaine talked a lot while I was in her arms, healing from her arrow's wound. If she wasn't explaining to me how badly I hurt her, she was telling Ayls about every moment she spent with me in secret. My beautiful mate gasps as I walk with her cradled in my arms around the back of the cottage. A small table sits at the edge of the woods, where the stream flows into the yard.

"What did you do?" Gaine whispers.

Smiling, I watch Ayls pull a chair out for me. "This was her," I answer quietly. "If it were up to me, you'd already be naked on a bed."

Gaine giggles and kisses my neck.

"I stood just inside these trees for longer than I care to admit, wanting to feel you again," I whisper, sitting on the chair Ayls offered. "What was that ward against anyway?"

"I had to come up with something that would stop you but allow others through," Gaine says, cringing. "I knew there was one thing that would always keep you out no matter what you did."

"She asked for a ward that would keep unbonded male wolves out," Ayls answers, lifting her eyebrow at Gaine. "I remember when she asked for it." The little Luna rubs her fingers over my cheek.

"We had no idea it was meant specifically for you, but she broke the barrier pendants before I made it up here when you were shot."

"Hmm," I hum, rubbing my lips over Gaine's face. "So you couldn't stand to leave me wounded in the field, huh?"

Gaine nips at me before licking my lower lip. "You deserved my arrow," she whispers against my mouth. "But I wanted you with me more than I wanted you to leave."

"To be fair, she asked for a ward to keep you in when I got here," Ayls says, giggling.

"Yeah," I say, licking my teeth. "That sounds about right."

As my equal, Gaine doesn't spend much time letting me cradle her in my arms, so I tend to take advantage of it any time she does. I sit back in the chair and tuck her under my chin while looking over the wolves who are enjoying the feast laid out. I only know a few of them, but I have a reputation that makes everyone want to lay eyes on me.

A hateful glare catches my attention. Byron is near the cottage with his back against the one tree allowed to live in the clearing. I only know of the resentment he harbors for me and the unhappiness he's caused Gaine, so I've never wanted to speak to him.

"Hey, Beauty," I whisper, tucking into Gaine. "Why don't you stay here with Ayls? There's something I need to take care of." I kiss her forehead and help her sit up in my lap. "I'll send some food. Maybe there's pumpkin pie."

I love that Gaine's face flushes bright red. "Kade," she hisses, slapping my shoulder.

"What?" I ask innocently. "I still haven't been able to watch you enjoy it in your human form. I bet it's just as exciting."

After kissing her deeply, I lift Gaine to place her on my chair and bow to Ayls. Byron hasn't moved from his spot under the tree. He holds his arms tightly across his chest, and the closer I get, the narrower his eyes become. I may match Byron in height and size, but I can tell I'd never beat him in a fistfight.

When I step before the fallen elder, he puts his hand out. "I'm supposed to welcome you," he sneers when I accept his hand. "I can't welcome the butcher of the Blood Pack into my family."

Lifting my eyebrow, I drop his hand. "Byron, we all have a past," I snap. I close my eyes and take a deep, calming breath. Byron's look of hatred hasn't changed when I open them. "Once upon a time, you loved a woman so deeply that you defied not only the Luna but a magical law for her. I know it cost you dearly, but that love made you want to do anything for her."

"Don't speak of my wife," Byron growls. "You will never know a love like that."

"You're right," I agree, shocking the fallen elder. "We each have our own experience. I love your daughter in a way that makes us happy. I will do anything for Gaine, but she won't ask me to defy our leader. We love and honor the Luna in a way you never will."

I step closer to Byron, grabbing his hand as if in friendship but matching the intensity of his growl. He tenses while I rest my cheek on his in the customary way a son would his father.

"You don't have to accept me, but I'm here to stay," I murmur into his ear. "That woman is my mate and my wife. You have heard my reputation. You know what I am capable of. She will never know pain. Every day she is with me, she will be cared for in a way you never could. Gaine is mine now. You don't have to be happy about it, but you will pretend for her because that's what she deserves."

The little Luna's familiar hand slides up my neck, and I step back from Byron. "Your guests are waiting to congratulate you, sweet wolf," Ayls says, tucking my hair behind my ear. "Byron, I believe it's nearly time for you to leave. Your daughter should have a dance before that happens."

"Yes, Luna," Byron says quietly. He bows his head before slipping away.

"How do you always know when to do that?" I ask Ayls.

"Do what, Kade?"

"I don't know," I answer. "Be there at the right time, I guess."

When I open my arms, Ayls steps into them and settles against my chest. After watching how her wolves reacted to my affection toward her, I understand why she enjoys my comfort so much. Our little Luna lost her mother and inherited thousands of wolves at a very young age. They love and respect her but require too much of their Luna to give her any support.

"I love you," I whisper, tucking her under my chin just as I do with Gaine.

"I know, Kade," Ayls responds. "I love you too." She leans back and cups my cheeks. "Thank you for trying with him. He's been angry for a long time, and I can't help him."

I take a deep breath and look over the crowd to find Byron hugging River. "Do you know where he's going?" I ask, narrowing my eyes thoughtfully.

"I do," Ayls answers. She rubs her fingers over my jaw until I look down. "You don't need to worry about that. I have arranged a surprise for your bride after the feast. Would you mind escorting her to the western field once the meal concludes?"

I lift my eyebrow and grin. "What have you done?"

Ayls taps her wrinkled nose. "Loved you enough to remind your bride why she fell in love with you," she answers before kissing my cheek and leaving me to watch her mingle with her wolves.

I lean against Byron's tree and look over our guests. I scan the clusters of smiling wolves, looking for my beautiful mate. Most are here just trying to glimpse the elusive killer that found his way into their Seer's heart, but none of them approach me. I prefer solitude over crowds, so I don't mind.

"The father of the bride has requested a song," Nate announces from somewhere in the clearing.

The strumming of guitar strings silences the crowd, and my mate steps from a cluster of guests, looking as beautiful as the day I met her. Byron leaves River to take Gaine's hand and leads her to the center of the clearing. I can see the tears pooling in her eyes as he kisses her cheek.

Nate begins to sing a song I remember my mother singing to me when I was a little boy. It's in a different language, so I don't know what it means, but if it's a song Byron requested for this dance, it must be about a parent and their child. Gaine's eyes dart around the crowd. I can tell she's looking for me, but my presence would only interfere.

Byron twirls his daughter and guides her through the grass. Gaine smiles broadly as he speaks softly to her. Her eyes shine, and she laughs happily a few times. Her father might hate me, but he's doing as I requested, and Gaine will believe Byron is blessing our union when he says goodbye.

"What did you say to him?" Tarq asks, pulling me out of my head and making me jump. He holds out a plate of food and nods in Byron's direction.

"I just helped him see things my way," I answer, taking the plate. "It won't matter tomorrow anyway."

"True," Tarq says, narrowing his eyes at the fallen elder. "Annalisa said you were leaving. When's that happening?"

I chew a chunk of chicken leg slowly before answering. "When she's comfortable," I answer, nodding toward Gaine and watching Byron hand my beautiful mate off to another wolf. "She's happiest away from the pack, but leaving your daughter creates a fear she tries to hide." I turn to the grumpy Alpha. "When are you leaving?"

Tarq sighs and looks out over the crowd to watch his daughter. "When she's ready," he responds.

"Your daughter is pretty special, Tarq," I say, picking through the meat on the plate. "I promise she'll be safe."

The Alpha snorts and snatches the plate from my hands. "I know she will," he snaps. "I'll be here to make sure she is."

I had hoped we would finally stand on equal ground. Instead, I find myself watching Tarq stomp away with the olive branch he didn't mean to extend. I frown and turn back to the dwindling crowd of wolves. Many of those remaining are dancing to a soft melody from Nate's guitar.

When my gaze finds Gaine, she's staring at me. Her expression is one of calm understanding as she watches me take in the crowd, happily celebrating our union. The folds of her dress flow freely around her legs with each step she takes in my direction. My chest cramps painfully until I exhale when she reaches me.

"You look happy," Gaine whispers, rubbing her fingers over my lips.

I hadn't realized I was grinning, but there's no denying it now that she's turning it into a broad smile. "I am," I say, kissing her fingertips. "I will never know another emotion as long as you are with me."

Gaine giggles and wraps her arms around my waist. "I wish that were true." When I tuck into her, Gaine's hum graces my ears like a beautiful song. "I don't know how you did it, but thank you for making my father's departure so smooth."

"You looked like you enjoyed your time with him," I murmur, smiling. "That's all I asked of him."

"Kade, I love you," Gaine starts, pulling away from me with a knowing look.

"Well, that's good," I say, cutting her off. "I'd hate to be married to a woman who hates me."

She lifts her eyebrow. "I also know you very well."

My eyes flick up to scan the crowd. They narrow as I try to think of anything to steer the subject away from my threat to Byron. One day, I might find a way to truly be worthy of her purity, but for now, I'd rather not discuss how I threatened her father if he didn't make her happy before he left.

Just before Gaine cups my cheeks to make me look into her eyes, I see Ayls signaling it's time to take my bride to the western field. I look down and smile, kissing Gaine sweetly. "Come with me," I whisper against her lips.

Gaine protests briefly but soon shakes her head with a smile and follows me away from our guests. "We can't just leave everyone," Gaine says, giggling.

I break into a jog, pulling her along. "Yes, we can."

The field is empty when we arrive except for a wood pile in the center. My breath catches when a few wolves emerge from within the tall grass. I hook my arm around Gaine, shoving her behind me. I may not have a blade, but my snarl fires up as if it could cut them at any moment.

"Easy, Kade," one of them calls out. "I told the Luna it wasn't a good idea to surprise you."

I narrow my eyes and find the face of the wolf who'd given me the blanket I covered Ayls' mother with the night before she was killed. I step forward slowly, keeping Gaine behind me. "What are you doing, Aldon?"

"It'll be ready in a minute," he answers. "There's a blanket just in those trees there."

I look where he points and instantly smile, knowing what Ayls has done. "Come here, Beauty," I murmur, scooping Gaine into my arms. "I think I smell popped corn."

Gaine raises her eyebrow and smiles. "What are we doing out here alone in the dark?"

"I have no idea, but Ayls has one last gift for us," I tell her, grinning. "I don't care as long as it makes you smile."

Kneeling, I lay her on the blanket and steal a kiss before I lose her to the bonfire and kites being readied in the field. Gaine's hands tenderly hold my face, pulling me into a deeper kiss while her leg slips over my hip. I roll down onto the blanket beside her and rub my lips over her face, gently halting her affection.

"We didn't get to eat much of this last time we had some," I whisper, producing the bowl hidden under a towel. I hold a piece of popped corn over Gaine and lick my lips when she opens her mouth for it. "I assume I'll wake from this dream at some point, but I hope I get to have you a few more times before I do."

Gaine giggles at me, shaking her head. "If this is a dream, we're both having it, and I never want to wake," she whispers. Her hands are like silk as they slide over my face and push my hair back.

I can only stare at Gaine as the wolves light the fire in the field. My sight switches from the black and white night vision to the warm glow of tan skin from the fire's light. Tucking my arm under my head, I look over her soft features and loving eyes.

"You get more beautiful every time I look at you," I whisper.

Gaine's lips curl into her gentle smile. "I dreamed of you as a little girl," she whispers. Her hand covers her cheek to hide that she's blushing, but I pull it away and kiss her fingers. "Your silver eyes haunted my dreams for years."

"They're blue," I grumble, nipping her fingers as she giggles. "I don't remember my dreams, but I wish you had haunted me." I slip my fingers over the folds of her dress and pull at the hem. "You could've worn this, and I would've hunted you down long ago."

"My mother was skilled with the needle," Gaine says, still watching my eyes. "This was hers. Edith helped to alter it."

I roll onto my back and look up at the moonless sky. "That witch's brother was a good guy," I say thoughtfully. "He tried to do the right thing whenever he could. She seems like one of the good ones."

"That's the Luna's doing," Gaine says, moving to look down at me. "She was a beacon in the darkness. Her daughter is proving to have all of her strength and more. Thank you for finding your place in her world."

Smiling, I pull her down for a kiss. "I don't think she'd have it any other way."

Movement in the field catches my attention, and Gaine gasps when she follows my gaze. "How did she know?" she whispers, sitting up and covering her mouth. "I never told anyone."

I sit behind Gaine as I had for the festival and pull her to my chest. "Ayls never misses anything," I murmur, sliding my arms around her waist. "I was down at the lake for months with her. This was the story I told her when she asked why I loved you."

We quietly watch the white kites float in the air warmed by the bonfire. They aren't as decorative or spectacular as the ones at the festival but still hold all the magic from that night. Gaine giggles when a few become tangled and fall as if fighting to the death.

After a while, one of the wolves sits by the fire and plays a tune on his fiddle. I'd heard someone playing it several times on the compound but never knew who it was. As I stand and reach my hand out for Gaine, I'm glad it survived Tynan's reign.

"Why was the festival the reason you loved me?" Gaine asks as I gently twirl her around the trees.

"Your smile," I whisper. "You brightened my world that day when you saw the first kite take to the sky. I've never been that excited about anything, and I wanted to see you do that every day for the rest of my life. I love the way you smile."

When Gaine looks up, her eyes are pooled with tears as she graces me with the smile that ended the life I used to lead. "I'm so glad you're mine," she whispers.

29

Seven Years Later

A late spring frost causes the grass to crunch under my paws as I jog through the ranks of the small team I've been training. I've never cared to work with other wolves, but our lovely Luna wanted to give me a purpose in our new territory. Settling in the Rockies has been good for the pack, and with my beautiful mate due any day, I don't travel often anymore.

"*Kade,*" Myla calls out. "*You gotta see this.*"

Scowling, I run along the ridge they're scouting until I reach the wolf running point. "*What?*" I grumble, sitting beside her.

"*Look,*" she says, nudging her nose over the edge.

I follow her gaze and stare at a group of bears traveling together at the bottom of the gorge. There are six in all—four are brown, and two are older with gray coats. Mothers would escort their cubs, but these are all mature. I lie down to watch them undetected with Myla.

"*Have you ever seen them move together like that?*" the young wolf asks, tilting her head.

"No," I answer. "There were stories about mountains of bears, though. The unicorn said she made it up, but maybe that wasn't quite true."

"You think they're friends of hers?" Myla asks.

"I don't know," I say, narrowing my eyes. "Maybe we should ask her."

Myla rolls onto her side and giggles. "She'd never tell you," she says, pushing me with her paw. "I've never seen someone hate another like Aisling hates you."

"That's because you haven't been around Gaine's father much," I say, pushing her back. "I only hope he gets over that shit for the kids."

"She looks so uncomfortable, Kade," Myla reminds me.

Gaine is carrying twins. Byron worked with River for months to look back through the past but never found another wolf who birthed more than one baby at a time. I normally don't come out with my team, but Gaine told me if I didn't get out of her hair, she would send my children back to wherever they came from.

I never wanted to be a father, but Ayls told me I had to because there needed to be a next generation of elders. That news came too late as Gaine's fate caught up to us on our journey west. I have stayed with her almost continuously since I learned she was expecting. After what we witnessed beside the river only a few years ago, I was not going to give anyone a chance to hurt my family without a fight.

"What are they doing?"

"Hmm?" I hum, turning to the young wolf. "What?"

"The bears," Myla snaps, staring over the ledge. "Kade, you're worthless to us when you're this distracted. Why don't you go home?"

"She kicked me out," I growl. I rest my chin on my crossed paws and close my eyes. "Why does anyone ever choose to have kids? This has been a terrifying nightmare."

"I'm a kid, Kade," Myla says, pushing my shoulder.

"No, you're not," I respond. "You're just half my age."

"*Seriously, Kade,*" Myla says, sounding confused. "*What the hell are they doing?*"

"*Who?*"

"*The bears!*" Myla shouts in my head. "*Look at them!*"

"*I don't care,*" I say, opening my eyes to roll them at her. "*I only came out here because Ayls said her guards tracked a bear out this way. I'm not sending my team after six bears. That's murder. I don't do that anymore.*"

The young wolf stares at me, probably trying to figure out if I'm being serious. Myla didn't meet me until a few months ago. She's only heard stories of the past and often asks me if any of it is true.

My reputation might have altered, but I'm still one of the most respected wolves in the pack. Myla was the first wolf placed under my charge. Her very young mate, Timothy, was the second, but their ranks multiplied since my need to stay home with Gaine repeatedly affected my duties.

"*Have you heard from Timmy?*" I ask, rolling onto my side with a sigh. "*He's been quieter than usual.*"

"*No, not for a while,*" Myla answers.

"*How long's it been?*"

"*I don't know, Kade,*" the young wolf grumbles. "*We were walking through pines last time he checked in.*"

"*There's nothing but pines up here, Myla,*" I growl. "*Which pines? Where?*"

"*How the hell would I know?*" she snaps. "*They all look alike to me.*"

I was nervous about leaving Timothy to stand watch over Gaine when she shoved me out of the cabin this morning, but I can't stop from chuckling at my young charge. Myla has been a force to be reckoned with since I met her. She turns more into me every day. I shake my head and look in the direction the bears are heading.

"*What the hell are they doing?*" I ask, watching them move in a formation. "*Are they hunting together?*"

"*Kade?*" Ayls calls out in her most gentle voice. "*Sweetheart, are you busy?*"

I back away from the ridge and stand. "*Never,*" I answer. "*Are you okay?*"

"*Yes, sweet wolf,*" she answers in a sugary tone that would hurt a wolf's teeth. "*I'm just wondering if you could start making your way back here soon.*"

"*Ayls?*" I growl. I nearly lost the little Luna this past winter. After experiencing the loss of one Luna, I'm uncomfortably obsessed with her safety, and her guards spend a few days each month training with me.

"*Timothy asked for me,*" Ayls starts.

"*Myla, get the team together,*" I bark.

"*Be calm, sweet wolf,*" the young Luna says gently. "*You have a team of young wolves out there with you. We will care for your wife until you make it back.*"

"*NOW!*" I shout at Myla as she stands dumbfounded before me. I turn on my haunches and dart back down the trail we'd followed up the ridge. "*On me! All of you!*"

"*What about the bears?*" Myla asks.

I glance back to see she's running right at my hip. My young charge questions everything we do, but my favorite thing about Myla is that she always follows orders. I know she will always have my back.

"*Leave them,*" I order. "*Timmy's requested the Luna. There's something wrong with my family.*"

"*The bears acted like a family, don't you think?*" she asks, distracted.

I swerve to avoid a thorn bush. "*Run by Aisling's this afternoon,*" I tell her. "*That damn unicorn knows something.*"

Tracking these bears, we'd traveled miles from the little cabin I call home now. My team sticks with me as I push them over the thawing hills. Mud collects on our paws, gradually slowing our progress to a jog.

"Kade, we gotta get this clay off," Myla needlessly tells me.

These hills are filled with red clay soil, which is equal parts sticky and slippery. Once it begins building up on our fur, it only worsens until we wash it off.

I don't care. The most beautiful wolf in the world is about to do something no other wolf has done. No one knows if she will survive this, and I will not recover if I lose her.

"Do whatever you want," I snarl, digging my claws into the nasty mud to pull myself along faster.

Myla lets me hear her order the rest of my team to stop at a small watering hole to clean their paws, but she stays at my hip. The journey is slower than I'd like, and it takes a few more hours to reach my cabin.

I slide on the caked mud across the little porch and crash into my front door. Gaine screams from inside, increasing my desperation. Since we rushed to build our house on time, it lacks windows. I jump against the door while Myla tries to break down the wall beside it.

A baby cries, and we stop for a moment to stare at each other. Taking advantage of our pause, someone opens the front door, and I lunge through it. I fling mud all over the room, bounding past the small tables and the rocking chair where I've cradled my beautiful mate every night for the past few weeks.

"Kade!" Edith shouts. "You're getting mud everywhere!"

The baby cries again.

I try to reach Gaine without putting my feet on the bed, but my nose only reaches the mound of pillows they've piled under her shoulders. I know my growl is building, but I can't help it. When Gaine screams again, I jump around to the other side of the bed, nearly knocking Edith over.

"Easy, sweet wolf," Ayls says only to me, reaching for my jaw as I approach. I shove her leg with my head, trying to reach Gaine. The little Luna snatches my muzzle and forces me to look into her eyes. *"Gaine is very scared. She's never even seen a birth. Will you please calm down?"*

Behind me, a baby coos quietly, catching my attention momentarily before Gaine screams again. I jump onto the bed and crawl beside my beautiful wife. *"Don't leave me,"* I beg her, rolling my head to lay my muzzle across her chest and wipe my nose along her jaw. *"I need you. You are perfect and beautiful. You're so strong. You are the only wolf in the world who could do this."*

"He wants you to know how strong you are," Ayls whispers, petting Gaine's head.

"It's a boy, Kade," Gaine says, breathing heavily. "We have a boy. He has your eyes." My mate latches onto my neck and squeezes with a force that nearly severs my head from my shoulders as she screams.

"Ayls," I choke my thoughts out. *"Tell her I'm sorry. Tell her I'll teach him not to be like me. Holy shit, tell her I'll never talk to him."*

Gaine limply falls onto her pillows, pinning me down with her weight. I forcefully pull back as Ayls lifts my mate's arm. Her eyes are closed, and her breathing is shallow.

"Gaine?" I move closer, poking her cheek. *"Beauty?"*

Crying erupts from the foot of the bed. I turn to see Edith holding a second baby covered in goop. Torn, I'm not sure what to do. My beautiful mate is the one I need right now, but she would want me to check the baby.

"It's a girl," Edith whispers. She rubs a clean rag over the baby's face as her husband ties the blue cord trailing from its belly. "It's too late for your firstborn, but would you like to cut her cord?"

I look back at Gaine. She's not moving anymore except for the slight rising of her chest.

"She's only resting, Kade," Ayls whispers. "Giving birth is very hard, and she did it twice. Cut the cord and then shift while Edith cleans your little girl. We'll help Gaine finish up once you're done."

I bump my nose against Ayls' cheek and nuzzle my sleeping mate. *"I'll be right back,"* I whisper to her. *"Don't go anywhere."*

Ayls giggles at me and kisses my whiskers before I slip past to visit with my daughter. Through and through, I am always a wolf. I lick her neck and chest to help clean her off. Edith smiles as Anthony cuts the string he'd used to tie the cord off. The witch holds my squirming baby out, showing her to me.

"Hi, little one," I say as my hum starts. Her tiny fist bumps into my muzzle, and I rub my whiskers over it. *"I don't think this will hurt, but I'm sorry if it does."*

I rub the front of my muzzle over her chest before studying the cord I need to cut.

"Close to the tie is good, Kade," Edith whispers. "It will fall off in a few days. She can't feel it."

I open my mouth to let the witch place the cord between my teeth. Gaine whispers my name when I bite down, making me pull away.

"Easy, Kade," Edith says, checking the baby's belly. "I think you better shift."

"I agree," Ayls says, lifting her eyebrow.

Sighing, I look around at the room full of people. Two are caring for the first baby. Edith and Anthony are swooning over my daughter, and Ayls gently wipes a rag over Gaine's forehead. I back up and bump my hip into Myla. *Her loyalty knows no bounds.*

I sit down and trigger my shift. Ayls giggles about my lack of modesty, but I don't care. I want Gaine to hear my words so they'll all be watching me shift today. As my hands form, Ayls grabs them and guides me toward my mate. I squeeze Gaine's fingers and rub her arm while my muzzle sinks in to form my human face, blinding me.

"Hi, Beauty," I say as soon as my vision clears. I brush my muddy hand over Gaine's forehead and kiss her lips. "I'm right here. You're almost done, sweetheart. Ayls says you just have to finish up."

"Are they okay?" Gaine whispers without opening her eyes.

"They are perfect," I say, smiling through my tears. "They are just as strong as their mother. We have a little girl, too. I bit her."

"Kade," Gaine breathes out with a sigh. "Don't bite our children."

Laughing, I kiss her cheeks.

"Can you give me one more push, Gaine?" Edith asks. "Then you can hold your little ones. I bet they'd like some food."

I stay against Gaine's face, rubbing my lips over her skin and whispering about my love for her. My nervousness settles when she kisses my cheek and moves to look into my eyes.

"There we go," Edith says. "All done. You did wonderful, Mama. Let's get your little wolves."

Ayls retrieves a bowl so I can wash my hands and urges me to lie with Gaine. Anthony throws a blanket over us, grumbling about being tired of seeing naked men, and Edith lays our daughter over Gaine's chest.

Our son appears next and is placed gently in my arms. He looks up at me with his nearly silver eyes, and I'm overcome by emotions I've never felt before. I lift him to my lips, kissing his forehead. Gaine moves our daughter so they can be near each other.

"Have you thought of any names?" Ayls asks, sitting on the foot of the bed.

I never wanted a family. I never wanted to care about anyone. I was an asshole. People feared me, and I liked it that way. These women changed my world and created a life for me where I love them with all the heart I didn't think I had. Losing them is un-imaginable.

These two tiny wolves have expanded my existence and opened a new chapter of my life. In a world that never seems to stop trying to kill us, no harm will ever come to them. They will never know pain. They will experience a life of love and honor because I can do that for them.

I kiss Gaine before turning to Ayls. "Their names are Rooster and Ari."

LM Lissette is known best for her ability to connect readers to her characters. After living all over the US, she has settled into a quiet country life in Missouri with her daughter and writes about the sweet love she hopes still exists. Her fabulous sense of humor, sarcasm, and wild imagination emerge in her writing. Prepare to immerse yourself into her world of fantasy, love, and unbreakable family bonds.